Circumstances

By

Robert John Sand

Circumstances

Dedicated To:

Harry Macgregor O'Shea

TITLES BY ROBERT JOHN SAND

THE ACTS TRILOGY:

Act Of Revenge

Act Of Fate

Act Of Vengeance

RICK TAYLOR MYSTERY SERIES:

No Clue

The Austin Murders

Deceit

Bones

Kiowa

Chameleon

Junior

Crow Basin

Borders

NOVELS:

BlackOut

Thunder In The Sky

Dangerous Moves

Brain Dead

Broken Faces

Circumstances

Circumstances

Chapter 1

Detective Brent Williams was sitting in his small cubicle, completing the paperwork on an especially nasty assault case that he had just closed, when Lieutenant Art Thomas walked in and handed him a registered letter.

"This arrived at the front desk late yesterday and someone signed for it. I heard that the Postman wanted to see you in person, but the desk sergeant told him that you were out on a case doing undercover work. Anyway, the guy finally relented and let it go."

"Must be from my fan club," Williams joked. "Or maybe some gorgeous blond saw me pass by and now she wants to buy me dinner?"

"Nope, it's from some law firm. You in any kind of trouble?" he asked with a smile.

"Not that I'm aware of," he replied, "but then its still morning and you never know what the day will bring."

The Lieutenant handed him the letter, patted him on the shoulder, turned and walked away. Williams had become one of his better detectives, and he just plain liked the guy. Honest, reliable, great personality, a quiet sort with more than his share of common sense, he'd come to look at him as definitely being officer material and had mentioned it to his Captain numerous times. He'd taken it as his personal responsibility to see that Williams signed up for the promotion exams the next time they were given.

Williams looked at the return address on the envelope and felt it with his fingers. Not only was it printed in fancy letters on fine stationery, but the darn thing was embossed too. He read the name, *"Sheffield, Andrews, Preston and Blatt PC, Denver, Colorado"*, but didn't recognize the name or connect it to any of his current cases. While he was curious, he had papers and photos on the assault case spread out everywhere and he slipped the envelope into his inside jacket pocket, intending to look at it later. From his experience, letters from lawyers never meant good news, so it could wait. He returned to his assault case just as the word raced through the building that there was a uniformed officer down and gunfire on the southeast side. He yanked open a drawer, swept everything on his desktop into it, slammed and locked it, and ran for the stairs. Within minutes, he was in his unmarked car, accompanied by several other detectives on their way to the crime scene.

By the time they arrived, the wounded uniform officer had already been transported by ambulance to Memorial Hospital's Emergency Room with non-life threatening injuries, and the K-9 dog had quickly tracked the perp to a nearby business. With the building now surrounded by the "SWAT" Team or now it was called the "TEU", police negotiators were currently doing their thing using a telephone connection. The case had officially been assigned to another detective, and seeing that there wasn't anything they could do to help, they returned to their offices after making a detour to Milt's Coffee Shop on Platte Avenue. By the time they reached their office, Detective Williams had already forgotten about the registered letter as he plunged into finishing the paperwork that he'd begun earlier this morning. By eight o'clock that evening, he had finalized everything, and placed it on his Lieutenant's desk.

His exciting off duty life that evening consisted of him returning to his small rented apartment on south Tejon Street and popping a TV dinner in the microwave, while he opened a can of beer and turned on his only luxury, a new flat screen television. Five minutes later, he was devouring the mediocre food and washing it down with the beer. Just another night in the neighborhood, he laughed to himself, as he settled into his favorite chair and opened the newspaper. Hours later, he would be in the same position, but his eyes would be closed and he'd be sound asleep.

Detective Brent Williams was 32 years old, stood 6' tall and weighed approximately 175 pounds. His blue eyes sparkled, and his smile was comforting to most people. He just looked like a nice friendly sort of guy, the kind that you'd like to invite over for a drink, or asked to join you at a ball game. However, his short GI haircut immediately identified him as either being military or a cop. Brent was divorced, his wife having moved on to bigger and better things after they'd moved out to Colorado Springs from Chicago. He'd been in his last semester of law school at the time, but had been so infatuated with her, that he quit school after she'd been offered a job transfer and accepted it. His five brothers and sisters and even his parents had tried their best to discourage him, but he'd been oblivious to any common sense and had meekly followed along. However, while she had a good job, he found it difficult to locate one and had been reduced to taking anything that he could find. Eventually they'd parted and he'd been devastated and lost. Too humiliated to return to Chicago and admit his mistake, he'd taken up the bottle to solve his problems. While he had never become an alcoholic, he knew he'd been close. So close that he had joined an AA group that met in a church basement over on Bijou Street. It was there that he met a ranking police officer who became his mentor and pointed him in the direction of police work. The next time applications for employment were being accepted he applied and had entered the Police Academy.

In the beginning, he'd been just like a lot of other people living from paycheck to paycheck. Slowly he began to get his act together, found a small affordable apartment in an older area, purchased a 12-year-old car from an estate sale, and bought his clothing from either a consignment store or thrift shop. Brent found that police work was his passion and he gave it everything that he had, slowly rising through the ranks and finally winning a spot as a bona fide detective. Along the way, he recognized that his social life was nonexistent, but he'd already had his disastrous marriage and divorce and he certainly didn't want to go through that again. Occasionally when he finally became financially stable and had a few dollars tucked away in the bank, he'd date, but the women he was coming across in his line of business, really didn't fit in with his hopes and dreams. Fellow officers and their wives hated to see anyone free and single, and constantly tried to arrange dates for him, but rarely did they result in anything more than a one-night stand.

His job had become his life and he realized that, but he personally believed that not only did it involve solving crimes, but treating the victims in a respectable and polite manner. Most of his co-workers questioned his approach and some of his efforts, but after a while, they all realized that it was just the way he operated. However his Lieutenant was probably the most impressed, and whenever an especially sensitive case came up, he'd do his best to see that Detective Williams was assigned.

It was the following morning during his standard breakfast of cereal, milk and slightly burnt toast, that he'd remembered the registered letter and had retrieved it from his jacket pocket. While eating, he used the table knife to open it, and then shook out the single sheet of paper. If nothing else, the stationery was impressive, and with the back of his hand, he flattened out the page and began to read it. Past the fancy embossed letterhead, he saw the date, followed by his name.

"Dear Mr. Williams," it began, and he wondered for a moment if the next words would say something like he was being sued, or his ex- wife had found yet another way to attack him, although he hadn't seen nor heard from her in years.

"I regret to inform you of the passing of Georgiana Augustine Harrington. I am the attorney of record for her estate, which has recently been released by the Probate Court. The distribution of her assets will be made on," and the letter went on for another paragraph stating that the attorney was hereby notifying all of the people named in her last will and testament of the time and place. It was short, to the point, and final. The woman had died and maybe she had left something to you, and maybe she hadn't, but if you wanted to find out, you had to

be there when the cookies were handed out.

Brent sat thinking about the older woman he'd met some time ago called Gus. She'd been assaulted after leaving the Fine Arts Center on north Cascade Avenue. He'd been working in uniform that evening, an after hours part time job to make a few extra dollars. Some perp had rushed out of the bushes as she walked to her car and grabbed her purse knocking her to the ground. Unfortunately, despite her advanced age, she'd held on and the perp had kicked her repeatedly, as she screamed for help. It was a Mexican stand off, with him beating on her and while she screamed bloody murder. Of the three officers working that evening, Brent had been the first to respond to her cries. His shortcut to the attack took him through some foliage so that the perp never saw him coming. He had swung his heavy 4-cell flashlight about the same time he'd ordered the perp to give up. The man collapsed to the ground and finally the old lady quit screaming, got up and proceeded to use her last ounce of strength to kick the hell out of him, eventually fracturing her ankle. Brent had watched with a smile and caught the lady when she finally passed out. By now, the other uniforms had called for help and as a patrol car rolled up, and then another, Brent had handcuffed the perp, and turned him over to the driver of the first car. Then he did a surprising and unorthodox thing and picked up the old woman, who was covered in blood, carried her to the second patrol car and climbed in the back seat, asking the driver to get to the Hospital as quickly as possible.

The Emergency Room technicians at Penrose Hospital just to the north, had been alerted about the incoming injured woman, but they hadn't been prepared for her to be delivered by a police car running under red lights and siren, nor a bloody old woman being carried in by a young police officer now himself covered in blood. No one knew if he'd been hurt too, but the experienced ER team quickly took over. While she was treated, he walked to the restroom and did his best to clean up, then walked back outside and waved to the officer in the car, who called it in and returned to patrol. Back in the ER, some administrator had recognized the name of the woman and made some phone calls. Soon a few suits appeared and Brent, despite his appearance was ignored and pushed to the side. Finally he learned from a nurse that the woman had been taken up to an operating room to have her ankle repaired, and he had to smile to himself since he was probably the only one that knew what had happened to it. With nothing more that he could do, he left the ER and walked back down to the Fine Arts Center, about a mile and a half to the south. By this time, the parking lot was empty and the lights had been turned off. Brent found his old car, and drove on home, totally exhausted.

The following day was his day off, his time to sleep in and catch up, but the telephone began recording messages shortly after daylight. He'd long ago disconnected the phone's ringer so when a call came in, it immediately went to the answering machine. Sometimes he'd have the monitoring speaker on and occasionally he'd leave it turned off and rely on the flashing red light to alert him. This morning it was the flashing light that caught his attention. There were eight messages, five from his boss, one from the local newspaper and two from television stations, and all asked him to return their call as soon as possible. He called his boss, Sergeant Moss first.

"Where the hell have you been Williams?" the man asked, and not very politely.

"Sleeping, it's my day off Sarge. Check the schedule," he replied sounding about the same.

"I don't know what went down last night, but the Lieutenant and his Captain both want to see you ASAP at the Police Operations Center. I need you to come in now," and the line went dead.

Brent showered and shaved, ate breakfast, glanced at the TV, then drove over to the Colorado Springs Police Operations Center and presented himself to the desk sergeant. In minutes, he was upstairs explaining to a room full of brass exactly what had gone down last night and what he had done. He covered it so thoroughly that not one question was asked until the end.

"Did you recognize or know who the old woman was?" asked a Deputy Chief.

"No sir, I have no idea who she is. She just needed help and I did it," he replied.

"Why did you use one of our patrol cars to transport her?" asked another.

"Because it was there and she didn't look good. I was afraid that with her advanced age, she might have a heart attack and then we'd get blamed for it. So I just loaded her in and we took off for Penrose Main. It didn't seem like it was any big thing."

"Well the old woman's name is Georgiana Augustine Harrington, that's Mrs. Harrington, the wife of Frank Harrington III, now deceased. If you remember, he was a leading trial attorney around here for many years and a back room politician. Anyway, she woke up this morning and wanted to meet you in person. Would you know why?"

"No sir, she was unconscious when I picked

her up and when all of the suits began arriving at the Hospital last night, I just thought that it would be better to disappear, so I walked back, got my car and went on home."

"So you've never met her, nor did you know who she was?" asked the Deputy Chief.

"Not a clue. She needed help and that's our job as I remember it," he replied somewhat sarcastically.

"Ok," said the Chief standing up. "I've heard enough. Someone needs to take Officer Williams up to Penrose Main. Let's get our PR people involved because we can use the good press."

Brent read the attorney's letter for the second time. That was the first time he'd met the old woman who only allowed her best friends to call her Gus. He'd become one, and since that day in the Hospital, they had talked on the telephone at least once a month, sometimes more. She had a large family, nearly all of whom only wanted her to die off and leave them some money. During their long conversations, he learned a lot about them while she learned a lot about Brent and his past and present life. She had warned him about becoming a workaholic as her late husband had been and he had listened, but somehow it had fallen on deaf ears. Occasionally he'd see her name in the newspaper, usually tied into some charity event or as he thought of it as some high society fundraiser. But after that first day at Penrose Main, they had never again met in person.

Now Brent was wondering as he smiled to himself, if Gus wanted him to attend the reading of the will in order to keep her family and relatives from killing each other. She had a strange sense of humor, probably after watching all of her family jockey for position for so long. Several times, they had discussed her disinheriting someone, or even the entire group. Brent had no idea how much money she had and she had never mentioned it either. He just assumed that she was fairly well off since she lived somewhere over near the Broadmoor Hotel, a world famous five star resort. Apparently, she had been there for many years. She had mentioned having a cleaning lady, a cook and a gardener who doubled as a handyman. But as time passed, she had told him that she rarely entertained at her home anymore and that the cleaning lady and the cook had become the same person. Despite all of the time that they had spent talking on the telephone, it now appeared that most of it was in talking about him and his job. In a strange way, he guessed that he'd miss her calls despite how nutty that sounded. A bored old lady and a young lonely cop listening to each other's beefs and complaints. It even sounded strange to him and he decided to never mention it to anyone.

Brent called his parents in Chicago on anniversaries, birthdays or holidays. Occasionally he'd call or receive one from his brothers and sisters, but they were a thousand miles away and had interesting lives of their own. It was just that they didn't have much in common anymore. He wasn't married, didn't have any kids, never took vacations and basically lived in a tiny inexpensive apartment like a hermit. But now he'd have to attend a reading of Gus's will, and if it went as he imagined it would, there may even be a book in it, that is if he listened carefully and took notes.

Chapter 2

Detective Brent Williams had never missed a single day of work since he'd been sworn into the Colorado Springs Police Department. He had never taken a single sick day nor a personal day off. Vacation days accumulated until his superiors ordered him to use them or lose them, but Brent had never cared. So today, when he'd entered his Lieutenant's office and asked for a personal day off, the man had looked up in surprise.

"Are you ok?" asked the Lieutenant.

"Yeah, no problem. Remember that registered letter that I got?" he asked and the Lieutenant just nodded his head.

"Well I was asked to attend the reading of a last will and testament of an old friend. It's being handled by a big time Denver law firm and I'll probably spend most of the day driving up and back and listening to them. Thought that I would ask you how to handle it. Maybe a personal day isn't right, maybe it should be a vacation day?"

"No that'll work. You just go and I'll handle it on this end," he replied and Brent thanked him and walked out to his personal car. While it didn't look like much especially parked next to all of the fancy new models owned by fellow officers, it was paid for and the insurance was cheap. He stopped for gas and then drove down the northbound entrance ramp onto Interstate 25. An hour and a half later, he had parked the car in a downtown Denver parking lot, placed his money in the box and walked to the address on the lawyer's stationery. While it was cold outside, the sky was a beautiful shade of blue and the sun was out in all of its glory.

Brent had presented himself to the receptionist, who had placed a call and now a beautiful young woman in a really tight short dress was escorting him to a conference room. He thought that maybe he should return to law school, finish up his last semester and apply for a job here. She opened the door and escorted him to the only remaining seat, one off to the side in the back of the large room. As Brent looked around, he counted nearly 25 people. He immediately wondered just how much money Gus had. He also wondered why he was here? They weren't related or connected business wise, and apparently, all of these people were. But he noticed that no one was talking to the person next to them or to someone across the room. It just seemed hostile.

The lawyer began the meeting, read the beginning of the will, explained everything in the greatest of detail and then began with Gus's bequests. Right up front, contrary to how most wills were written, he began to read off the charitable gifts. Twelve charities received bequests of millions of dollars, more than Brent could keep track of. They were handed their checks and the sexy young woman in the short dress escorted them out of the room. It surprisingly took nearly an hour to accomplish. Then a bequest to the gardener and cook who Brent noticed for the first time were an oriental couple. He wasn't sure whether they were Japanese, or maybe from the Philippines, but then it really didn't matter. He did notice that they were in their mid fifties and fairly well dressed and mannered. They too, were escorted out. The reading went on and on, until only Brent, a man and a woman were left. He wondered exactly who they were? Perhaps a son and maybe a daughter? He couldn't really go by resemblance since he'd only seen Gus once in daylight and that was in a hospital room.

"Now we're down to nearly the end," the lawyer smiled. "Mr. Williams," he said looking directly at Brent. "You have been left the main residence of Mrs. Harrington III, and all of its contents, also a small trust fund to provide for the upkeep, maintenance, taxes, utilities, and the continued employment of the current maid/cook and gardener/handyman, for as long as you wish. Also, Mrs. Harrington III has added a provision that you must return and complete law school in order to obtain this inheritance. However, you have eighteen months to accomplish this and you will have the use of the residence while you're doing it. Just let me know when you've finished, and I'll have the necessary transfer papers finalized."

"You're kidding, aren't you?" said a stunned Brent Williams.

"No sir," he replied. "Is there a problem?"

"I guess not," he answered, just as the sexy young woman appeared and escorted him out.

It was three days later when Brent had finally managed to corner his Lieutenant. While he knew practically everyone in the Department, he wasn't close friends with any of them. Not that he couldn't have been, but most had families, hobbies, and things that they liked to do during their off hours and Brent didn't share any of those interests. Some of the younger officers liked to party and while he'd been invited along, he wasn't much of a drinker anymore because he knew his limitations. So he had looked around for someone and had decided that his Lieutenant would be the one he approached.

"So what can I do for you this morning Detective?" the man asked.

"I need your help, if you have the time?" he replied.

Knowing that he'd never asked for anything since he'd been in the department, and from the look on his face, he thought for a moment before answering.

"Something big?" he asked.

"It is for me," he replied. "Maybe a couple of hours of your time, at most."

"Ok, you've got it," he answered, picking up the phone and telling the secretary that he'd be out of the building for a while.

Brent was driving west on Lake Avenue towards the Broadmoor Hotel as he occasionally looked at a map he'd printed from a computer program last night. He made some turns, finally found the street and the correct address. He hadn't been here before. It was a huge estate on a corner lot about a block from the Hotel, and a tall black wrought iron fence surrounded it. He pulled into the driveway, drove up to the gate and pushed the button on the post. Almost instantly, a voice answered and he identified himself. His Lieutenant, who he'd been making small talk with, sat open mouthed as the gate swung open and Brent drove in.

"You know these people?" he asked.

"Just hold that thought for a few minutes, ok?" Brent replied as he drove the old car around the circular drive past the oversized four-car garage and up to the front door. Despite the frigid cold weather, the fountain in the center was gushing streams of

20

water into the air, but ironically, it wasn't freezing when it landed. The two men got out and walked up to the massive double front doors just as an oriental woman opened them.

"Ah, welcome home Mr. Williams," she said with a smile just as her husband rushed up, bowed and said "welcome."

"Thank you," replied Bret, as if he did this sort of thing every day.

"Will you be moving in today?" the man asked as politely as possible.

"No, this is just a short visit, but thank you for asking. Is everything all right?" Brent asked with one of his infamous smiles.

"Yes sir," they both answered at the same time. "But sir, Mrs. Harrington left a letter for you on your desk. We saw how long it took her to write it and didn't want you to overlook it. If you'll follow me to the drawing room, I'll bring you some coffee or tea."

Brent and the Lieutenant just followed the woman like two sheep into the drawing room and sat down.

"Now?" asked the Lieutenant.

"Do you remember way back when I first joined the Department and I was working some special after hours duty at the Fine Arts Center? Well an old lady got mugged that night and I helped her out. Broke a few Department rules, but the old gal turned out to be some widow with a lot of money and connections. I only met her face-to-face once after that night and that was arranged by the Chief. We got a lot of good press out of it and so no one ever pushed my infraction of the rules. Then months later, I got this phone call one night and it was her thanking me again for helping her. We talked and it

21

became an outlet for a bored old lady and a lonely young cop. Over the next few years, we'd talk maybe once a month or more, then I didn't hear from her and finally the registered letter arrived. Now I hadn't heard from her in well over a month or more and when I called, no one answered. I didn't know if she'd died or had just gotten tired of listening to me. Then the letter arrived announcing the distribution of her estate. Yes, I got the house, but until a few minutes ago, I hadn't ever been here, nor did I know where she lived. So, now it's mine in name only."

"What do you mean, name only?" he asked.

"It came with a condition. I get to use it for the next 18 months without charge, including the help. I'm one semester away from my law degree, the result of being stupid enough to follow the girl of my dreams westward when she probably just wanted to get away from our marriage. The condition is, that I finish school within the next 18 months and then this is all mine, free and clear."

"Wow, I'm speechless," he replied.

"Me too, that's why I asked you to come along. I know a lot of people, but I don't know how any of the guys I work with would handle this. Jealousy is a nasty word and let there be no doubt about them being jealous. I mean just look at where I live now down on south Tejon, it's a dump, but it works for me because after I lost everything I finally learned to live with very little. I'm not really cheap, but I like to have a couple of bucks in the bank to fall back on if I need it. Anyway, now you know the situation, and I hope that you'll have some suggestions on how to handle it?" Brent said. The man just rubbed his chin as he thought.

"Ok, I have a plan. Now hear me out," he

22

replied. "First off you need to apply to a law school and the closest one that I know of is up in Denver. I believe that this will necessitate a personal visit, so call ahead and make an appointment. Next is your apartment and I think that you should hold on to it until you see how the law school thing works out. Odds are you'll get accepted, but then you never know until the ink is dry. This house, I'd keep quiet about it for a while. Visit, stay overnight, but keep the apartment as your home base. Now for step two. The Department has a little known policy of granting time off to attend a special school. I can begin the paperwork tomorrow to buy time for you to finish up your degree."

"How much time?"

"Six months is normal, twelve months is a maybe? But the question is this, if you take a leave of absence it's unpaid, and can you support yourself for six months?"

"I'll have to sit down after talking to the school and figure it out."

"Next point is that we already have several department members with law degrees, which is a plus for us. Now if you do get your degree, what are you planning on doing with it? Private practice, maybe? Or can I put down that you'll be remaining with the Department?"

"Hell Lieutenant, I don't know how to answer that question," he replied just as the coffee arrived in delicate china cups and saucers.

"Just like Milt's Coffee Shop," laughed Brent.

For the next hour they toured the first and second floors of the house, which was really a mansion with more rooms than either man had ever seen. Luxurious furnishings beyond belief, antique furniture costing a years salary for each piece, imported Turkish rugs, the place just reeked of old money and status. Brent's first impression on entering the kitchen was that it was spotless and really, really big, more like a commercial kitchen in some fancy new restaurant. Finally they finished, thanked the caretakers as he'd come to think of them and returned to the Lieutenant's office.

"Boy, this place sure looks like crap," laughed the Lieutenant very quietly.

"Kind of like a starter-upper," laughed Brent.

"So tomorrow you call the school from home and let's see where this goes, what kind of a reception you'll get. I'll cover for you here and I'll get the paperwork started on our end. Now don't be too discouraged if the Denver thing doesn't work out because there are a lot of law schools around the country and no one ever said that you had to attend the one in Denver."

That night Brent returned to his small rented apartment, tossed a frozen pizza in the microwave and sat down at the tiny kitchen table with his calculator and bankbook. Until he finally fell asleep much later, he would add up the figures, do his projections and make some adjustments and then do them again. It wasn't until much later that he remembered the envelope that Gus had left him on her desk and that he had put in his jacket. He began to read it just before falling asleep in his favorite chair. In the morning he awoke with it in his hand, his fingers cramped from holding it. A single page thanking him for being her friend and spending all of that time on the telephone without ever asking for anything other than her friendship and opinion. Simple, yet elegant.

"Williams," barked the loud voice of the

Lieutenant over the many sounds emanating from the cubicles. "Come into my office."

Brent had walked in closing the door behind him, as was normal procedure.

"So what's the story? Are we in?" he asked.

"My call just started the ball rolling. They're going to contact my old school in Chicago and request a transcript of credits. It's been a while, so I'll need to take a refresher course or two, and another one strictly on Colorado law, but the graduating requirements seem to be about the same. The main problem is money. If they accept me, between tuition cost and books, it will more than wipe me out. The apartment has to go, and the commuting expenses won't be cheap. I'll have to find some part time work to keep food on the table," he laughed.

"I thought that might be a deal breaker, so I contacted a guy over at the Police Protective Association and he steered me to another guy at Ent Credit Union. They are very receptive to making you a student loan, and not tie it into the Federal Loan Program. To you, it'll just be an unsecured signature loan at favorable rates. They'll extend it out to five or ten year's amortization, your choice. So what do you think?"

"Sounds great to me, but first I have to take a trip up to the school and talk to some people," he smiled. "Suppose that I could take a vacation day?"

The next day he drove up to the school in Denver, talked to all of the right people and for the very first time in his life the God's smiled on him and he was accepted. The startling part was that the new semester would begin within two weeks.

As he looked back now six months later, he was amazed that he had actually been able to pull it off. He had notified his landlord that he'd be leaving for school at the end of the month, cleaned out his apartment in record time, storing his few personal possessions in the garage at the mansion and moved north. His Lieutenant had handled all of the Department's paperwork and had called an old friend still on the job for the Denver Police Department and had found a cheap room to rent within easy walking distance of the school. As long as he was so deeply involved and the information was so fresh in his mind, he decided to take a refresher course for the Bar exam and subsequently thereafter through a quirk of fate, he took the exam and passed it. While he might not have been the best student at the law school, he was far from being the worst.

During his last night in Denver before returning to Colorado Springs, he sat down and reviewed his finances. He was 25K in the hole despite him living like a street person for the past six months. His biggest concern was that before taking the Bar exam he could have returned to the Police Department and his old job, but now due to some internal changes in policy, after passing the Bar, he wasn't certain whether or not he'd be offered the job. His friend the Lieutenant was looking into it. However on the plus side he'd been offered several jobs with Denver law firms, mainly because of his practical law enforcement experience and his class standing. He was now ten days away from the end of his 6-month leave of absence, broke and with no idea whether or not he'd be reinstated.

What no one knew was that the house he'd been willed, came with several additional clauses, one of which stipulated that he couldn't sell it for 20 years, a figure that he guessed Gus had pulled out of the air. So, now after notifying the law firm of *"Sheffield, Andrews, Preston & Blatt PC,"* that he'd completed the original terms of Gus' will by finishing law school, he owned the house and all of its contents or at least he would as soon as the necessary papers were filed. Ironically, at 33 years old, he now owned a huge palace free and clear but didn't have a job or any money in his pocket. He wondered if maybe he could borrow some money from the oriental people that managed the big old mansion, then laughed about it.

Chapter 3

Harrington House sat on a large corner property of nearly two acres, one block from the world famous Broadmoor Hotel. The two-story structure and its attached four-car garage were surrounded by a tall black wrought iron fence. The grounds were professionally landscaped and perfectly maintained by the full time gardener and handyman. The circular driveway was paved with hand laid cobblestones, each perfectly set and of the exact same size and color. The fountain in the center of the circle sprayed water 24/7 regardless of the weather since the entire unit and the catch basin were electrically heated.

The massive teak front doors had been imported from the Philippines and the marble floors from Italy. It was like a league of nations with over 18 different countries contributing materials for the interior of the structure. Above the oversize garage were the large servant's quarters and next to them was a "House" office and several guest rooms with private baths. According to the El Paso County Assessor's Office the building above ground consisted of 11,700 square feet of living space. That didn't include the full basement used primarily for storage, utilities, a wine cellar, gym, and a laundry. Nor did it include the additional space over the garage.

The furniture all appeared to be antique, extremely expensive items purchased through specialty brokers, each with a specific destination in the house. Original artwork hung on the walls and each had special lighting provided for it in the tall ceilings. Natural gas fed fireplaces abounded throughout the home, as did bathrooms and closets. The professional kitchen was large enough to feed a small army and the formal dining room was set up for 20 people. One of the more interesting features was the security system installed several years ago after Mrs. Harrington III had been attacked. Panic buttons were strategically located, surveillance cameras covered both the inside and outside, infrared motion detectors, glass breakage monitors and every opening, window and door hardwired into the system. The fence around the perimeter was wired and sensors placed in the ground next to them. In addition, the entire home was hardwired with a smoke alarm system and ceiling sprinklers were cleverly hidden in each room and hallway.

The home had belonged to one of the rich and famous and it definitely looked it. No expense had been spared to make it one of the most outstanding homes in the area. It was an asset to the neighborhood, and if the truth was known, many of the neighbors worried about its future once Mrs. Harrington III had passed on. Rumors ran rampant about either her son or daughter moving in, something that concerned everyone because based on their past actions, they were considered to be less than desirable. So as time passed and nothing changed, the stories and rumors grew even more.

The oriental caretakers were rarely seen, probably due to the cold winter weather, but at night the neighbors could see the lights going on and off throughout the building. Once a week a truck would arrive and deliver groceries and dry goods, parking in the street and using a dolly to bring them up to the first garage. Daily, the mail would arrive and the postman would unlock the large mailbox welded into the fence, insert the mail and relock it. Later the handyman would reverse the procedure on the other side. Otherwise, the home seemed quiet and abandoned. It had become the topic of evening conversations since when Mrs. Harrington III had been alive or at least shortly before the end years, the home had been a center of activity.

Originally built in the late 1920's, it had that old world charm and mystery about it. Since then it had been renovated and upgraded four times, the latest being only three years ago. During that time Mrs. Harrington III had moved over to a suite at the Broadmoor Hotel, a block away. The work had taken nearly eight months and during that time the neighbors rarely saw her and when they did, she was usually instructing a contractor in exactly what she wanted.

Now this museum-mansion was owned by some mysterious person who no one had met and who hadn't even moved in yet, although he'd owned it for nearly six months. Rumors abounded about the man and his wealth, since the home had last been appraised at 4.5 million dollars not long ago. Then someone added that the man was single, had lost his entire family in some disaster, and he was young too. Neighbors began looking through their immediate families picking out suitable matches, but so far no one had seen him.

*

With nine days to go until the Department notified him whether or not he'd be reinstated, Brent had moved into the mansion, which he now affectionately referred to as "Harrington House," under the cover of darkness. It wasn't planned that way; it was just that he didn't get there until after dark. He'd been buzzed in and his old car now sat in the middle of the cavernous garage looking lonely, lost and definitely out of place.

Brent was sitting in the kitchen much to the amazement of the oriental woman maid, drinking coffee and making small talk. He could see that she was uncomfortable with the situation, but wasn't certain why, so he'd asked her to please call her husband so that he could clear the air.

"Please sit down," he asked, once the man arrived.

They sat quietly and looked at him as if he was about to fire them.

"Look, I'm sorry about what happened to Gus and I'm really out of place in this house. I don't even know your names or how to properly pronounce them. Honest, I'm not that comfortable being here, but right now I'm broke, don't know if I'll get my job back and I have nowhere else to go. I have nine more days until the decision will be made, so maybe we can work out something that we'll all be comfortable with. On top of everything else, Gus set it up so that I had to go back to law school and that took all of my money and left me deeply in hock to the Credit Union. And, I couldn't sell this place if I wanted to, at least not for another twenty years."

"Our names are Alice and Henry Yasukuni," spoke up the woman pointing towards her husband who just nodded and smiled. "We're second generation California Americans and we prefer to speak English. Twenty years ago jobs were hard to find and having oriental house servants was fashionable, so when we found out that Mrs. Harrington III wanted oriental, we gave her

31

oriental."

Knowing Gus, Brent thought that was one of the funniest things that he'd ever heard and burst out laughing.

"I'm sorry, but that is a funny story. So for twenty years you've been acting?"

"Exactly," she replied with a smile.

"Well my name is Brent Williams and up until Gus's will was read, I was a detective for the local police department."

"What do you want us to call you?" she asked.

"How about Brent, for a start," he smiled one of his most engaging smiles and she nodded, yes.

"I've only walked through the house once and that was a quick tour, but this place is huge. My whole apartment could fit in one room and have space left over. Like the formal dining room which is set up for 20 people. If you don't mind, I'll just eat here in the kitchen. And with the work I do, sometimes I have difficulty in sleeping. Guess I can't get the images or ghosts out of my mind, so I watch television and fall asleep in the chair. But I work at home too and I'll need either a desk or I can work off the kitchen table, its no big thing."

"When Mr. Harrington was alive," spoke up Henry, "he had his office set up in the room just inside the front door on the left. When he died, Mrs. Harrington had his law books and furnishings removed and her antiques moved in. Maybe you could move in there?"

"I don't have a desk to move or law books to put on the shelves," Brent laughed.

"Yes you do," Henry said. "They're all being stored downstairs. I'll start bringing them up in the morning. Everything is there including the big desk, the side chairs, the couch and a ton of law books. Alice and I can clean out the room and move that in."

"I'd like to help," Brent said. "It's not like I have anything better to do."

So the next morning the three people began to clean out all of Gus's cherished knick-knacks and furniture, properly boxed it and loaded it into the elevator, which Brent hadn't known existed. By noon, the room was empty and they had begun to carry up all of the deceased Mr. Harrington's furniture and law books. By dinnertime, the office was a mess, but at least everything was there. Brent began to fill the shelves and organize it.

"I'm sorry, folks. About this time I should be ordering in some pizza or something, but I'm flat out broke. Would there be anything to eat in the kitchen," he asked looking at Alice.

"I'll make dinner," she replied, getting up and leaving the room.

It was during dinner eaten in the kitchen that Henry had glanced at his wife and spoke up.

"We could lend you some money if you need it," he smiled.

"Thank you both, but I can't do that. Without a job I couldn't pay you back and that wouldn't be right. Besides friends don't lend money to friends if they want to remain friends. You folks have been here for twenty years and I don't want to do anything to make you move on. This is your home as well as its mine. We'll just have to get to know each other before it settles down. When I'm working on a case, I'm usually not home for long periods at a time. And while I actually passed the Bar exam," he smiled as if in triumph, "I don't have any clients or a law practice, so those law books on the shelves might get a little dusty, but they do look good."

It took nearly three days to get the room straightened out and properly organized. Henry had appeared with a carpet steam cleaner and cleaned the expensive Turkish carpet as Alice wiped everything down and cleaned the front windows and the fancy double French doors to the room. When they finished, all three of them stood in the hall and admired their work.

"Maybe we should take a picture before I dirty it up," laughed Brent.

"Do you wish me to get the camera?" Alice asked.

It was the last working hour on the last day, when the Lieutenant had finally called.

"I am the bearer of good news Detective Williams," said the caller. "Word has just come down that you have been reinstated to your old job and that you are back on the payroll as of tomorrow, assuming that you show up for work," he laughed. "However the bad news is that during your absence the promotion exams were given and the promotion board met. Obviously since you weren't here, your name is not on the promotion list. On the other hand, since you passed the Bar exam I'd guess that you came out ahead. There's always a next time."

Bright and early the next morning Brent Williams was sitting in the Lieutenant's office waiting for him to appear. Brent would have to sign some papers before he was reinstated and his weapon, badge and identification card were returned to him. Then he'd need to be assigned to a desk, or cubical if one was available and finally a case. He didn't care if the case was one that needed to be cleaned up or the tedious paperwork done on it, it all was police work and he loved every moment of it.

That night he returned home long after dark, a happy man. While he was exhausted, at least he was employed and could now begin paying off his loan from the Credit Union. At $500 a month, he figured he'd have it paid off in 60 months or five years, unless he put in a lot of overtime.

Chapter 4

It had been a most interesting month, Brent thought as he sat in his fancy new office awaiting the arrival of Allen Sheffield, the managing partner of the firm of *"Sheffield, Andrews, Preston and Blatt PC."* He'd been working almost around the clock trying to catch up and keep up with the ever-expanding caseload at the Colorado Springs Police Department. As it had been before Gus's will entered his life, being a police detective meant everything to him. His social life barely existed as his partner's wife and the others gave up on finding him a permanent mate.

As he looked around the office, he remembered that evening when Henry and Alice had mentioned that Gus's husband Frank Harrington III, had once used the room for his law practice. Then they remembered that when Mrs. Harrington had remodeled, she'd had all of her husband's furniture and books moved downstairs into storage. The following day they had begun to reverse what she had done. It took days to sort everything out and even now, Brent wasn't exactly certain that everything was in the right place. But it did look professional, and for a cop like him, it was very impressive.

But what a month it had been, learning about Gus and her life just a little at a time, and her magnificent mansion. He found it hard to believe that he now lived in a building as the owner occupant, and commanded over 11,000 square feet of space not including the basement, the garage or the servants living quarters. He found it even more unbelievable that he had a staff of two human beings catering to his every need. They were servants, but Brent preferred to think of them as being caretakers. But despite his best efforts, they both found it difficult and nearly impossible to call him by his first name. He thought that maybe after a lifetime of serving people like Gus who demanded a master slave relationship, they were just conditioned to it, but still he'd continue to work on it.

He awakened from his daydreaming by the sound of the buzzer at the driveway and he heard Alice, using her best oriental voice answer it. His guest was shown into the office several minutes later and Brent walked around the desk, shook the man's hand and then surprisingly sat down in a chair alongside of him, rather than the power chair behind the desk. Allen Sheffield placed his expensive leather attaché case on the desk and paused.

"This sure brings back old memories Brent. Back then, I spent so much time here that the neighbors all thought that I lived here."

"You and the Harrington's were good friends?" Brent asked.

"I guess you could say that. Actually Frank and I grew up and attended law school together. I tried to get him to join me up in Denver, but by then he'd married Gus and she had other ideas. Over the years I passed through what I called my period of confusion, which consisted of four divorces. Then the three of us became something like the three Musketeers. When I wasn't in the Denver office, I was here. Believe it or not, it was Gus that made us wealthy, not the law practices. She just had an eye for making the right investment at the right time. That changed after Frank died because by then he was a very rich man and my law practice had expanded into the big bucks area. Along the line she had two kids, but they spent most of their time away at school and when they were old enough they moved out on their own. Gus could be a very demanding woman and I guess that carried over somewhat into her personal life. But after Frank passed away, Gus changed a bit. She'd always been the high society type, and slowly she began cutting back. That's about the time she was mugged and you stepped in and saved her."

"I think that story might have been exaggerated a bit," smiled Brent.

"Well whatever happened is mute now, but at the time you were her hero. She told me that she waited for you to call her and ask for something, but you never did. She was convinced by that time that everyone including her kids had their hands out. I think that her first call to you was sort of a feeler, wanting to know what you were really after."

"Her first call came at a time when I needed to talk to someone. I'd gotten involved in an especially nasty case and I'll admit that it was getting to me. If I hadn't been so new to the position I probably would have gone to a shrink. But then she called and we must have talked for several hours. When I hung up it was like I had been reborn as corny as that sounds. Must have been a month or so later and by then my nasty case had been closed out, when I returned her call. After that I guess it just became a regular sort of thing."

"Well whatever she did for you, was returned in spades. You have to understand that we were really close. In fact if Frank hadn't married Gus, I probably would have. So when he died, we became even closer. My wives were long gone by then and so was her husband. We talked daily and sometimes more than once. Then you stepped in and she became obsessed with you. Perhaps the word obsessed is too strong, but you know what I mean. She couldn't believe that you had never finished law school and that you lived like a hermit."

"How did she know that?" asked Brent.

"She hired my firm to find out who you were and we in turn hired a private investigator," Allen answered.

"But once she read the report she stepped in, as was her style and decided to change your life. I think by then she knew that she was dying. But you became the subject of many phone calls and discussions. She wanted to do something to better your life, but she had this underlying fear of betrayal. She finally decided to offer you something, but only if you agreed to do something in return."

"And that was my finishing law school?"

"Exactly." he replied.

"I have to admit Allen, as silly as it may sound because I'm not family or a blood relative, but I really do miss our telephone conversations. You do realize that besides the night she was attacked, that we only met face-to-face once and that was the following day and she was all bandaged. If I had met her on the street, I wouldn't have known who she was."

"After the attack she seemed to go downhill. Her health robbed her of her beauty as the saying goes and she rarely left this house. We talked about you and she really wanted to see you in person, but she didn't want you to see her. Actually towards the end she didn't want to see me either."

"Well she accomplished her goal," Brent smiled attempting to break the tension.

"More than you know Brent and part of that is why I'm here this morning. First, here are all of the legal papers concerning this property. It is owned by a Limited Liability Company named BD LLC. BD stands for big dreams and that was her idea. She didn't want your name attached to it, just in case you chose to remain with the police department. Now the ownership is a LLC company that you solely own and my firm remains the registered agent. That way your name remains out of it."

"I just have to mention that I like the way you've returned Frank's office to something useful. In case you haven't discovered it yet, the last time Gus remodeled she added a small bathroom right behind you. It's hidden and you have to push that piece of molding on the right, on the third bookshelf and the whole wall opens up. Go ahead and push it."

Brent got up, walked behind his desk and pushed on the molding. An entire section of the wall swiveled and the ceiling light came on in the small bathroom. A broad smile covered his face, as he pushed it again and walked back to his chair.

"I don't know how much time you've spent going through this place but there are all kinds of secret hiding places, especially the one up in her bedroom."

"Honestly Allen, I've walked through several times but the master bedroom suite is huge, so I just moved into one of the six smaller bedroom suites. Actually it was the smallest one, but normally I just fall asleep in my chair at night."

"So when you have the time, go up to her bedroom and look for a similar molding button behind her headboard. It should be about a foot or so off the floor on the left hand side. Perhaps I better explain this a little better. After Frank died she became worried about her safety, especially at night, so she had all of the alarm stuff installed and a secret small security room constructed right behind her bedroom. If she heard a noise or an intruder, she could push the molding and disappear. Then she added a big safe because she was afraid that the people at the bank, the ones that handled the private vaults might be watching her. So she moved everything here, but only kept the really nice stuff in the safe thinking that if the robbers got in, they wouldn't leave unless they found something of value. Who knows what else she had stored there, but at this point it all belongs to you anyway."

"My God," exclaimed Brent, "she was really something."

"That is probably an understatement," laughed Allen, "but let me continue here."

"My firm is one of the more prestigious law firms in Denver, but occasionally we do conduct some business down here in Colorado Springs. As the city has grown, the business has increased. We don't touch anything that's of a criminal nature, but pass it off to others more specialized. Now my options are, to either open an office down here, which is really expensive, or have my people drive down here. The bottom line is billable hours and while we have charged for our time from the moment that we leave Denver, our clients have begun to resist paying for drive time. Fortunately we don't do that much here that requires a lot of our time, but it definitely is becoming a problem. So my proposal to you is that we pass off anything of a criminal nature regardless of where it occurs to you, and also to sweeten the pot, any normal requests for our services. As I see it, you've already passed the Bar exam and you definitely have the office for it. I will personally guarantee that if you agree, either I or someone that I trust will help you if you need it. So it's not like I'm just going to turn you loose with a hope and a prayer."

"You forget that I already have a job," said Brent. "And I also have a big loan to pay off which means that I need to keep it."

"Funny, Gus told me that you'd say that when I explained it to her. We both believed that you'd turn out to be a really fine lawyer, if given half a chance. I tried to explain about the setup costs to her, how it takes a little time to get going. So now I'm going to tell you exactly what she answered me. She said that you had a house full of really premium antique furniture that she'd collected over her lifetime or since Frank had come into the bucks. If I remember correctly there's a bunch of it stored downstairs because if anything, Gus liked change and every so often she'd have her house rearranged to suit her mood. Like the old antique desk she had in this very room for several years. I know that she paid over 30K for that thing and I wouldn't have given it houseroom. It was so fragile and dainty that I considered it useless. Guess that she figured that eventually you'd move Franks stuff back in here because she told me to just sell the desk and get it over with. And if that wasn't enough, then to start downstairs and clean up the place. I'm no antique's expert, but I bet that these days you could probably unload that thing for 50K or more. That should help wipe the slate clean," he smiled.

"And if you find that you're still uncertain about that, I'll arrange to pay you a retainer, just to keep you available. Now give this some thought because I know how Gus set this whole thing up with the accountants and the Bank. Oh, and I almost forgot to mention that you'll need to pick out a local bank and set up some accounts including an escrow account for your law practice. Maybe a house account, a personal account, a business account and the escrow for starters."

"Now finally, is your appearance and your car. Gus believed that appearance really counted and so she dressed both Frank and I accordingly. You really need to find a custom tailor, and then something suitable to drive."

"My car looks a little lost in the big garage," Brent laughed.

"Didn't Gus tell you about that?" he smiled and Brent nodded no.

"Well Frank was a bit of a car nut. He liked the old Duzenberg's or at least that style. So he had one that he tinkered around with. But it got a scratch on it from the car parked alongside of it. So Frank parked all four cars, the Duz, his car, Gus's car and their show off evening car, side by side on the driveway and opened all of the doors. He wanted exactly three feet between the edges of the doors when they were wide open. Then he measured the length of the longest car and doubled it. Anyway the next time they remodeled he got his garage and as you said, it is huge. But people deal on perception. If they perceive you through your clothes or vehicle to be poor, then you're treated different than if they perceive you to be successful and wealthy. So my suggestion and I bet Gus would endorse it, is to dump the car you have and get some really nice clothes. You don't have to go overboard, but the stuff you have is late bargain basement, no offense intended."

"Exactly what kind of a car would you suggest?" Brent asked.

"Oh, these days I'd probably go for either a Lexus or a Mercedes. Both are fine cars and don't forget you're going to write it off as a business expense anyway so who cares what it costs. You're young so you might just want to lease one for a year and see how you like it. My secretary Diane, can give you the name of several dealers that furnish our stuff. We do some work for them that's off the books and in turn we get some good deals."

They talked for another hour, mainly reminiscing about their experiences with Gus and finally Allen left, with the understanding that Brent had until the end of December to make up his mind about the future.

So much had been covered that his head was still spinning when Alice and Henry quietly knocked on the outer door to get his attention.

"Please come in and sit down," he said. "What's up?"

"Well Mr. Brent," began Alice. "Every year our two nieces come and spend Christmas with us and we wondered if you would object to that?"

"Not a problem with me," he laughed. "When do they arrive?"

"Usually two or three days before Christmas, and then they leave two days afterwards. They stay in the small guest rooms next to our apartment and they won't interfere with you or make any noise, I promise."

"Did Gus set up a tree at Christmas?" Brent asked.

"Not exactly," replied Henry. "She hired a landscaping service to come in and decorate the house, both inside and outside. Alice and I helped but she had everything professionally done."

"So what do you propose that we do this year?" Brent asked.

"That would be up to you Mr. Brent," replied Alice.

"Honestly folks, it's been a long time since I've had a Christmas tree or even put any presents under one. But this year if you don't mind, I'd like to call that landscaping service and see if they could possibly fit us in. And don't worry about your nieces because we have plenty of empty bedrooms in this house. Actually I'd like to throw a Christmas party but I don't know who to invite, so I guess it's just the three of us and your nieces. Alice, would you and Henry please contact the Landscape Company and just order whatever you'd like and I'll be happy with it."

Chapter 5

It was five days before Christmas and Brent had taken Allen Sheffield's advice and leased a brand new, top of the line, four-door Lexus automobile. It was parked in the huge garage next to his old car, which he sometimes drove back and forth to work every day and the unmarked police car he occasionally brought home. The house both inside and out looked like Santa had arrived and sprinkled magic dust over everything. Now he wore new custom tailored suits, socks that matched and looked as if he was a successful young businessman, but one that carried a badge and a gun.

Gus's old antique desk had netted him 53K, most of which he used to pay off his law school loan at the credit union. The rest went as a down payment on the leased car, his clothing, the Christmas decorations and into his personal bank account. Allen Sheffield had called several times just to keep in touch, not mentioning anything about work or the retainer and Brent had invited him down for Christmas dinner surprising even himself. He had also invited his Lieutenant Art Thomas and his wife, Sally.

It was mid evening on a Saturday night when Brent was flipping through the TV channels attempting to find something to take his mind off work and the decision that he needed to make. He kept going through Allen Sheffield's discussion that day in his office when he finally remembered him mentioning the hidden safe up in Gus's bedroom. He shook his head, wondering what kind of an inquisitive detective he was forgetting something like that. He turned off the television and climbed the stairs. Elevators were nice, but he thought that he was far too young to begin depending on them. He found the molding switch after a short search, pushed it and the wall next to the headboard clicked as the locks unlatched and the light inside came on. He slid the door open and stepped inside. The room was about eight feet by ten feet, had a chair, a table, a phone and against one wall a huge metallic green safe, kind of like the ones you always saw in gun shops, but bigger, heavier looking and more substantial. The electronic dial lit up as soon as he touched it and he remembered Allen telling him from the open window of his Lexus, that first afternoon to try his birth date, because Gus always set any combination locks to birthdays. It took several minutes before he got the hang of it and the heavy steel door opened. Taped to the top shelf and impossible to miss, was an envelope addressed to him.

"My Dear Brent," it began.

"If you're reading this letter, then I'm long gone, you have successfully finished law school and my best friend Allen Sheffield has accepted you. We've been together for more years that I'd care to admit but he and Frank were childhood friends. But that's ancient history now and I'm certain that you aren't interested in an old lady's ramblings. From our many telephone conversations we got to know each other better than anyone would ever believe. You became like a surrogate son and I couldn't help but worry about what would happen to you after I

passed on. I hope that you're not upset with my meddling, but you deserved better than what you had. Now, I just hope that you'll follow Allen's advice because he really isn't the curmudgeon that he sounds like and he has only your best interests in mind. And I sincerely hope that you now have a big luxurious car sitting in Frank's old garage, it would make him so proud."

"Whether you have discovered it or not, you are a full fledged member of the Broadmoor Golf Club, which I always called the Country Club. When Frank died I left his name on the membership list for a while and then when you proved to be legitimate I added yours and dropped his. So the next time that you're over there please have them remove my name. Oh, and the membership is paid up for the next five years, however I don't know when you'll be reading this letter so you might want to check that out. That allows you to use all of their amenities including the golf course, but then I doubt that you play golf, or at least not yet."

In the top drawer of the safe is the very best of my jewelry. I would suggest that you not sell it unless absolutely necessary because it's worth a lot of money and hopefully some day you'll find the right woman and give it to her, maybe just a piece at a time. Franks old Rolex watch, which I got him for his birthday is on the second shelf. I sent it back to the factory to be cleaned and checked, and I would like you to proudly wear it. Ok so maybe it's a little too fancy for your tastes, but that's the same thing that Frank said too. But he wore it with style."

"Now on the third shelf is $100,000 in cash, non sequential bills, of many dominations. I always kept it for a rainy day or in case some unexpected event cause chaos in my household. I want you to

have it and I suggest that you use it for the same purpose. However if something goes very bad, do what you have to with it. I always thought of it as my getaway fund. Over the years I'd add some and spend some so there may not be exactly that figure but it should be close."

"My family albums are on the next shelf and I've included a lot of notes. Maybe sometime in the future you could contact my son and daughter and see if they're interested in keeping it as a family heirloom. I doubt that moment will ever occur, but it's worth a try."

"Frank had accumulated a bunch of odd lot old stocks and bonds and over several years I converted them to bearer bonds and they're on the next shelf along with his fancy pistol that I bought him for Christmas one year. I honestly don't know how much the bonds are worth, but Frank always said that they were negotiable anywhere in the world. Again please keep it for a rainy day."

"Well, I guess that's it my dear boy. I can't begin to tell you how much your telephone calls meant to me during a trying time of my life. Actually I became ill shortly after we met and my activities were slowly being curtailed until I finally became housebound. I actually looked forward to the end because it would release me from my pain and also because I fully believed that with the ending of my life, another would spring forth. I know that you'll do your best to make me proud."

Signed, *"Your loving friend, Gus."*

Brent Williams, the tough police detective sat in the safe room and cried his eyes out. He had given Gus so little and she had rewarded him with riches beyond belief. He wondered why he hadn't made a better effort, like why hadn't he called her more often? But then as Allen had explained, she probably would have believed that he was after something. Finally regaining his composure he slipped the Rolex into his pocket, closed and locked the safe, and slid the sliding wall back into its locked position. He walked back downstairs to his office, placed the watch in his desk drawer and locked it. Then he checked to make certain that the alarm system was turned on and he went to bed.

Two days before Christmas, Alice's two nieces had arrived just before a snowstorm was expected to hit the Colorado Mountains and Front Range. With one in California and the other working as a model in New York, they had met as usual at DIA in Denver and had flown down to the Springs together. As they had done so many times before, when the cab arrived at the gate, they got out, stacked their luggage next to it and pressed the button. Mrs. Harrington III did not allow cabs in her driveway and they knew it. But Alice had buzzed them in and Henry had rushed to greet them and carried everything inside by way of the servant's entrance next to the garage. They had been visiting their Aunt and Uncle once a year either in July or at Christmas time, since they were ten years old and Alice had warned them about not entering the main house and always staying in the servant's quarters and guest rooms. By now the girls were 26 and 28 years old and they knew the rules by heart. Whether Mrs. Harrington was alive or not didn't matter. But they quickly settled in and began to bring everyone up to date on their lives. Tani the oldest one worked for a national modeling agency operating out of New York City and Michi, the youngest worked in the fashion industry in LA. The girls were considered to be exotic beauties, their father being Japanese and their mother Irish. The combination resulted in two tall black hair Eurasian beauties.

Brent had forgotten that Alice's nieces were going to visit but he had picked up the Christmas spirit, something he never had before and was bursting with happiness when he'd returned home that afternoon. Way out of character, he had called the Broadmoor Hotel, and made a reservation for dinner in the exclusive Penrose Room. At first the woman had hesitated, but when Brent had given her his name, she had apparently entered it in their computer and suddenly he was Mr. Williams, not some stranger from the street. He had to smile at that one and looked up to the ceiling thanking Gus one more time. Now all he had to do was let Alice and Henry know, so he'd gone to their apartment over the garage and knocked on the door.

"Alice, Henry, are you in there?" he hollered and Alice immediately opened the door thinking that something was wrong.

"Come on folks, you need to get dressed. I just made reservations for dinner at the Broadmoor. You've got about an hour," he said before turning and beginning to walk away.

"Wait Mr. Brent," Alice replied. "What do you mean reservations?"

"We're going out to dinner," he shrugged. "Tell Henry to wear a tie, too," he smiled.

"But Mr. Brent, that's not proper. Mrs. Harrington would not approve. Besides we have guests," she said.

"I'm not Mrs. Harrington and bring your guests along. It's Christmas and we'll have a party. And don't tell me that you have nothing to wear because this house is still full of Gus's clothes. I'll meet you down in the garage in an hour," and he turned for the second time and disappeared into the main residence.

An hour later he was sitting in the Lexus thinking what a nice car it was and how right Allen had been, when they appeared. Barely noticing the young women who both wore hoods over their hair because of the snow, he loaded the women in the back and Henry in the front. He was humming Christmas carols as he drove one block over to the front of the Hotel and stopped. The snow had let up for the moment and he handed the keys to the valet, who greeted him as "Mr. Williams," and ushered everyone inside. Having never been here before, he asked the front desk for directions and the clerk immediately called for someone to escort "Mr. Williams and his party" to the Penrose Room. Again, Brent had to smile and thank Gus.

Despite Alice's hesitation to order anything off the expensive menu Brent had finally told her to either order or he'd do it for her. Then for the first time as they ordered a round of drinks he noticed the young women and instantly fell in love with both of them. The dinner turned out to be a resounding success and Brent had grabbed Alice's hand and asked her to dance. He urged Henry to do the same and before it was over he'd actually danced with all three women several times. For Brent it was again way out of character, because he hadn't danced since his wedding, years ago. But he'd had a ball and when the check came he merely signed for it, a luxury of being a member of the Club. Back at the mansion, he invited everyone into the living room for a nightcap much to Alice's dismay.

"What's the matter?" he asked seeing the look on her face.

"It is not proper for us to be here, Mr. Brent," she said.

"Why not, it's my house and I invited you?"

"Mrs. Harrington would definitely not approve!"

"Come on Alice, its Christmas time. Lighten up a little. And you have guests too. Lets all enjoy the season."

Alice stayed, but she definitely wasn't happy about it.

The next day was Christmas Eve and Allen Sheffield drove down from Denver a day early because of the snowstorm accompanied by Diane his secretary, a woman about Brent's age.

Since he'd invited the Thomas' for Christmas dinner and since the weather front was ahead of schedule, Brent had called them and suggested that they come over tonight on Christmas Eve and spend the night, and Sally Thomas had immediately agreed. Apparently her husband had already told her about the mansion. But by the time they arrived it was quite late and the snow was beginning to accumulate on the ground.

By morning on Christmas day nearly a foot had fallen and Brent got dressed and went looking for Henry intending to help him shovel the drive and walks. He found him down in the heated garage washing the Lexus.

"Henry, I need a snow shovel. I'll start on the front drive."

"No need to Mr. Brent," Henry replied with a smile. "When Mrs. Harrington remodeled the last time she had all of the driveways and walks fitted with underground heaters. They work automatically and melt the snow as it falls. I actually think that she might have slipped on some ice, but when she had the chance she fixed the problem. But I do have a snow shovel if you really need it?"

"Gus strikes again, huh Henry?" and the older man just smiled.

Brent found Allen sitting in the den reading the newspaper.

"How about a game of pool," Allen asked when Brent walked in.

"Sounds good to me, but do we have a pool table?"

"Yup, in the back of the game room. But its more fun with four so where's Art this morning?" Brent went looking for his boss who was just coming down the stairs.

"We need one more, how about Diane or Sally?" he asked.

"Neither one is up yet," Art answered.

Brent had gone into the kitchen and found Henry, but he declined, and Alice was cooking, Michi was helping and finally the oldest niece said that she played some and would be happy to fill in.

Like the remainder of the house, the recreation-game room was lavish, and the pool table ornate and expensive looking.

"And you didn't even know that you owned a pool table," laughed Allen.

"Nope, actually I didn't," Brent laughed.

"Well then I'll tell you that you own two of them. Way back when, Gus remodeled and Frank's old heavy pool table with the green felt top just didn't fit in with her plans and color scheme. So one night Frank came home from a long day in court and he found this fancy new table with red felt in the place of his old one, and his was now downstairs. Well Frank never faltered and the next day he had some guys building a room for it downstairs and he put a lock on the door to keep Gus away from it. Ask Alice because she used to keep the keys for Frank.

The pool game lasted most of the morning and by then the three men had learned that the beautiful tall Eurasian woman was somewhat of an expert. She explained it by saying that between modeling jobs she had to keep herself occupied and she had chosen pool. But everyone had enjoyed the game. By now the entire house smelled of Alice's dinner and Brent couldn't wait until it was ready. Then about 2 PM, Henry entered the formal living room and announced that dinner was being served. Everyone rushed for a seat, but there wasn't any shortage in the formal dining room that sat twenty people. However Brent immediately saw that the end of the table had been set up for only five. He walked into the kitchen and confronted Alice who had set the kitchen table for four.

"Ok, Alice this is Christmas and this isn't a segregated household anymore. Either you join us in the dining room or we'll join you in the kitchen. What's it going to be?"

Alice reluctantly watched as Brent and her nieces moved everything into the formal dining room. Henry just stood off to the side and smiled. But after the most wonderful dinner that anyone could remember eating and a fantastic desert, Brent stood up and announced that now they had to pay for it and they could either be busboys, washers or dryers. Alice nearly had a heart attack as everyone pitched in to clean up with Henry and Brent being the dishwashers. Of course having three top of the line heavy duty automatic dishwashers under the counter, helped.

It had been a wonderful day and night

however the next morning the Thomas' left after a snow plow cleared Lake Avenue. Allen had checked with the Colorado Department of Transportation and all roads in and out of the Springs were closed, so he and Diane settled in. With most businesses and schools closed, they spent the day getting to know each other. During this time Brent tried to include Alice and Henry, but only succeeded in getting better acquainted with her nieces. Then on the second day, Michi had asked to be taken to the airport, which had just reopened, because she was due back at work tomorrow and Brent had reluctantly agreed to drive her there. Both girls were so darn attractive in an exotic way and such good company when Alice wasn't around, that he hated to see either of them leave.

Brent had chosen to use the unmarked police car simply because it was heavier, belonged to the city and he could park it at the airport in restricted parking zones. He loaded her luggage into the back seat figuring that it would be easier to unload at the airport. She said her good-byes and they drove the one block to Lake Avenue, turned east and settled into the grooves in the snow that the plow had left behind. He intended to follow Lake to where it became South Circle Drive and it up to the Hancock Expressway. Then he'd follow the Expressway to Academy Blvd and go south to Drennan Road, where he'd turn east and go to the airport. It was two o'clock when he passed through the snow packed intersection at Hancock and Drennan Road and everything went blank.

Chapter 6

"Where am I?" he whispered to the person sitting beside his bed. He barely had one eye open, his head hurt and his throat was so dry that it caused him pain just to swallow.

"You're in Penrose Hospital, Brent," he heard Allen's voice say.

"You were in a traffic accident. You were hurt, but you'll be ok. Don't try to talk because they just took the tubes out of your throat and it has to be sore. You had a minor concussion and broke your leg, but you'll be ok."

The last words that Brent heard said "ok" and he went back to sleep.

*

The drunk had left the bar on Academy Boulevard, climbed into his old pickup, determined that he wasn't about to let a foot of snow stop him, and according to witnesses, had roared out of the parking lot eastbound on Hancock, which turned south and crossed over Drennan Road several blocks away. According to the traffic accident investigator, he probably never even saw the white unmarked police car passing through the intersection on the green light. He had plowed into the heavy car hitting it just behind the driver's side door. The impact had blown all of the air bags in the car, but the pickup had been knocked off course to the right, as it pushed through a snow bank and into a fence line. One of the steel t-posts had somehow penetrated the windshield and struck the driver square in the middle of his chest, instantly killing him.

The passenger side door of the police car had popped open, snapping the seatbelt and throwing the young woman into the snow packed street where she rolled and eventually collided with the snow bank on the east side. The driver of the car had struck his head on the top of the door frame and had also managed to shatter his left leg in three places. Once the paramedic's and firefighters arrived and cut the top off the car, they discovered that the driver was alive but unconscious and armed. Then they found his badge and called it in to dispatch. Patrol cars outfitted with tire chains had immediately responded although no one was certain whether this location was in the city or county. Nevertheless, the ambulance transported the survivors to the hospital and notified their next of kin, which in Brent's case was his boss Lieutenant Thomas. He in turn called Alice and she broke the news to Allen Sheffield.

He awakened sometime later and asked for water, but only heard the sound of someone shuffling around, and then the door closed, and opened again seconds later.

"Well son," said the familiar voice, "guess you're going to make it after all. I was just a tad bit worried there for a while. Good to see you back amongst the living. So let me tell you exactly what happened."

Brent listened as Allen slowly walked him through it.

"Michi, what happened to her?" he barely whispered.

"Surprisingly she walked away from it with only a few bruises. The cops said that the heavy snow broke her impact with the side of the road. Oh, she pulled a muscle in her shoulder, but she was ok. I put her on a plane back to California as soon as they turned her loose. But Tani has been here with me babysitting you. She was here when you just woke up, but was afraid that you wouldn't recognize her voice, so she rushed to find me. Oh, and before I forget it, you broke your left leg in three places and they operated on you to put it back together. Something about having to insert a stainless steel pin, but you'll be ok, and I'm certain the doctor's will explain it all to you. Now on a personal note I think that you should take another look at Tani because she's really something. Jumped right in to help me, no questions asked. I overheard her call her modeling agency and back out of her trip to France. Said that she couldn't get out of Colorado due to the storm. At that point the Colorado Springs Airport was open, but DIA in Denver was still closed. Told me that she'd stay around as long as you needed her. Listen to this old man son, she's smart, gorgeous and attracted to you so don't screw it up, ok?"

Allen looked down at Brent, but he'd fallen asleep again.

Two days later the doctors had released him, and Allen accompanied by Tani had gone to pick him up. He looked like hell, but the doctors assured Allen that he'd be ok, given enough time. Allen let everyone know that he wouldn't think twice about suing the whole damn bunch of them if they lied to him. But he'd driven him back to the mansion fighting the heavy melting slush along the way. Henry met him in the garage and helped to get him into the elevator and to his small bedroom towards the back of the house. He was exhausted lying on the bed, his eyes closed, when the most gentle hand he'd ever felt slowly lifted his head and tried to feed him some soup. Her perfume smelled so good after all of the hospital smells, that he just wanted to stay in that position and smell it forever. Then he closed his eyes and fell asleep.

Hours later when he awakened, he thought that he was alone until he saw Tani slumped in a chair with a blanket wrapped around her, sound asleep. Even with her hair messed up and her clothes wrinkled, she looked awesome. He tried to remember what Alice had told him about her nieces, but couldn't remember much. Perhaps she hadn't said that much or maybe he hadn't listened. He stared at her for a long time and wondered who she favored, her mother or father? She didn't exactly look Asian, but then she didn't look Caucasian either. Maybe a blend of the best of both. She was tall and slender, had long black hair, an exotic face with high cheekbones and there wasn't any doubt in his mind that she was a model, and probably a darn good one. But she was also his house guest, and he doubted that Gus would approve of him hitting on a house guest, even though for the first time since his divorce, he really wanted to. Finally she awakened, stretched and yawned. Then she looked over and saw him staring back and she was embarrassed. He saw her blushing and tried to think of the last time he actually saw a woman blush and couldn't remember one.

"Are you ok, Mr. Brent?" she asked in her soft velvety voice.

"No, I think that I died and went to heaven," he smiled. "And please call me Brent. I keep fighting with Alice and Henry about that and I doubt that I'll ever win, but with you I might," he smiled again.

"Do you wish me to get Mr. Sheffield for you?" she asked.

"No thank you. Just sit there and look beautiful for me," he heard himself say and wondered just how strong the painkillers were. Then he dozed off again.

"Ok son, wake up. We have to talk," he heard the loud commanding voice of Allen Sheffield and tried to resist it. He was on a beach with the Eurasian beauty and she was in a bikini and he'd lost his heart. Then he heard Allen again.

"We've lost a whole day here son, and its time to talk."

"Ok," he said trying to get his bruised arms behind him to push up on the pillows. Finally Allen helped and now he was sitting with his back pushed against the headboard and his cast resting on several pillows.

"You've slept through the afternoon, the night and now into the morning. Time to go to work, so listen up."

Now wide awake and feeling pretty good but hungry, he just nodded to Allen.

"What do you think of these business cards?" he asked handling one to Brent. On it in gold leaf besides the address and phone number were the words "Sheffield & Williams PC."

"Figured that you might be out of action for a while, but you can still do the office work, so I decided to join you down here for a bit."

"What about your practice up in Denver?" Brent asked.

"That's why I have partner's son. Actually I'm looking forward to this. As firms grow the leaders get further and further away from where the action is and I was at the top and bored out of my mind. Now I'll go in maybe once a week and otherwise it'll be just you and me. For the firm it will be a satellite office, but we'll get to keep the money down here. For them it will eliminate a headache and they won't have to worry about it since I'll be here. It's a win-win situation for everyone and we already have several cases waiting on us. By the way, how are you and Tani getting along?"

"I think it's great, but what happened to Diane?" he replied ignoring the question about Tani.

"Well she's half my age for one thing, but she had a really abusive marriage and finally walked out of it. Actually my firm helped to put her ex husband in jail for a long time. That's where I met her. She was beaten and broke and we offered her a job. She really is a sweetheart and so we had a long talk and she's going to be joining us. We're going to keep it light and I'll be leasing a condo on the other side of the Hotel, where we'll live. She claims that it's within walking distance from your place, but we'll see."

"So what's the other reason you're doing this, I mean condos around here are expensive?"

"Bottom line is Gus. She showed me that all of the money in the world couldn't bring happiness. Hell I've already had four wives, wouldn't you think that I'd figure this marriage thing out somewhere along the way? But when we're young we want money and unfortunately most don't get much before they're old like me. So what do you do with it? Leave it to some ex wives? Maybe endow a chair or let it go to the government? Nope, not this kid. I'm going to enjoy every dime that I have and hide the rest. So now I have an attractive young divorcee that wants to share a condo with me and I'm all for it, lock stock and barrel."

"Works for me," smiled Brent. "So when do we start?"

"We already have, my boy. The cases are stacking up on your desk as we speak. Oh, and we have some new stuff to play with. Your office now has a high speed plain paper fax unit connected to my office in Denver. And you can now pull up the Internet and the law service websites. They'll do all of the research for us. And I filed a lawsuit against the bar that turned that drunk loose that ran into you. And another one against his estate although I doubt that he had two nickels to his name. And Art Thomas is making out your retirement papers. According to his schedule you were supposed to be on duty at the moment of impact and so you'll qualify for a medical disability retirement or so he figures. He said that he hated to lose you because you were like a son to him, but that he enjoyed having Christmas together and wished you well. So now I'm down to the bottom line and that is the question you didn't answer before. What are your intentions regarding Tani, and be careful how you answer that because I may be representing your housekeeper," he laughed.

"I don't know how to reply Allen, for God's sake I've only know her for what, a week? And most of that time I was under the influence of drugs," he laughed.

"Hell son, I married," he paused, "I think that it was Number 2 after meeting her in Las Vegas. She was a showgirl at the time. We sort of got drunk together and at the time it seemed like a pretty good idea. In fact she turned out to be one of the better ones."

"Well I don't want to screw up anything between Alice and Henry either," Brent said.

"You just aren't keeping up here, son. I already talked to them, as your attorney of record of course, and they're all for it. Surprisingly both said that it was about time that Tani settled down and produced some babies. I won't dwell on the baby part, but apparently this girl is 28 years old and a top fashion model based in New York City. She flies around the world doing fashion shows for various top of the line clothing manufacturers. I guess she started when she turned 18, and its ten years later and she's still right up there on top. Must be pretty good, but confidentially before you get too involved I did ask my firm to pull a background check on her. I forgot about doing that on wife Number 3 and I paid dearly for it. But just for openers, she doesn't swear, she doesn't smoke, rarely drinks and smells good. That pretty much sums up my list of qualifications." Allen sat back and laughed and Brent joined him. He wondered if Allen was really that funny or if it was his painkillers, but only time would tell. Then he heard a quiet knock on the door and Alice walked in carrying a tray of food. She glanced at Allen who suddenly decided that he had to use the bathroom and left.

"Thank you for bringing this up to me," Brent smiled and Alice nodded.

"Ok Alice, go ahead and say it because Allen just spilled the beans. What are you two up to?" he smiled.

"Mr. Sheffield mentioned that you might be interested in my niece Tani."

"What are you going to do, auction her off to the highest bidder?" he joked.

"Well I could talk to her parents about that if

you wanted me too?"

"Alice, I'm kidding. I barely know the woman and she doesn't know me. I've been a cop and who knows if she even likes cops?"

"Well Mr. Brent, I talked to my brother on the telephone yesterday. None of us have ever seen her act like this before. That's why her sister wanted to leave so quickly, because she saw how Tani was attracted to you and didn't want to interfere. She's pretty much been on her own since she was 18. She apparently had the look the modeling agency wanted, sort of like being in the right place at the right time. She's been all over the world many times, but she told her sister last year that she was tired of it and wanted to settle down but couldn't find the right man. I don't know if you're the one, but Henry and I won't get in your way if you decide to try. No hard feelings either way Mr. Brent, because Henry and I like our jobs here at the Harrington House and don't want to lose them."

"Alice you're not going to lose your job, ok." Brent smiled and she felt better, but in affairs of the heart one never knew.

Ironically it was two days later before Brent got the opportunity to speak to Tani alone. Every time that he had tried either Henry, Alice, Allen or Diane would walk in the room, or pass by the open doorway. Finally today he'd been experimenting with his crutches when she'd appeared and he ushered her into his office and closed the door.

"Please sit down," he said pointing towards a side chair, before he collapsed onto the couch.

"Trouble with the crutches?" she smiled.

"Absolutely no coordination with these things," he laughed.

"In case you haven't noticed, there is a

definite conspiracy underway in the Harrington House," and he paused for several moments, "and it involves both you and I."

"I have noticed, now that you mentioned it," she smiled.

"In your infinite wisdom, would you have any suggestions on how to handle it or proceed," Brent smiled.

"It's your house," she laughed, "I'm only a guest, so by rights it's up to you."

"Well I think that it's kind of funny and at the same time it's nice that we have people close by that actually care about us. Allen wants us to run off to Las Vegas and get married. Your folks are considering holding an auction, and Alice just wants you to settle down and have many babies."

"Yes, I've heard about all of those options," she smiled.

"Any one of them interest you?" he asked and then got all embarrassed about being too pushy.

"For a cop or ex cop, you sure get embarrassed easily," she smiled.

"Well the people that I deal with are either dead or pointing a gun at me, so usually I'm a bit more interested in getting out of the way."

"I see your point," she smiled again and he crumbled like burnt toast.

"Unless you want to elope this afternoon," he smiled. "How about if we spend some time together and see if we're compatible?"

"I kind of liked the elope thing, but I can see that you're getting cold feet already," she joked.

"Actually I've been through this once before and it didn't work out very well. No actually, I think that the word devastating better describes it, and I'm not that anxious to repeat my mistakes."

"Well then Mr. Brent," she said as she stood up and bowed in his direction, "I will await further word from you," and she laughed before turning and leaving the room.

Brent thought that at least now he knew that she had a sense of humor.

Over the next six weeks as Allen Sheffield did the grunt work, Brent and Diane handled the office and any contact with the firm of Sheffield, Andrews, Preston and Blatt up in Denver. Always available to help and normally close by was Tani. She chauffeured him to his doctor appointments, to his physical therapy, to meetings with clients when Allen was busy, to the liquor store and once to the Colorado Springs Operations Center or Police Headquarters. If anything, that visit had been the pinnacle of Brent's career in law enforcement as he later described it to Allen when they were alone in his office.

"I wish you could have been there Allen. A uniform on the way out saw us park at the curb and rushed over to help me. As usual I was having a problem with my cane, which I had just graduated to. Those damn crutches nearly killed me so the cane was definitely a step up. Anyway, the guy helps me to get to the door and then he noticed Tani for the first time and he actually froze for a moment. She walked up and finished opening the door and the uniform finally got his act together. So by now the people inside have seen me coming. They called for a patrol car to park behind mine because we had parked in a "No Parking" zone. Now we're inside and the men are quickly moving in our direction wanting to get a better view of Tani before the elevator doors close. Once upstairs on Art's floor it was the same thing all over again. Apparently Art had jumped to conclusions and mentioned to his secretary that Tani and I were getting engaged and people were walking up and congratulating both of us. The guys all had broad smiles and the women all looked jealous. It was really funny and Tani played right along with it although sometimes I wonder if it wasn't just normal for her to be treated that way. But people were asking where she modeled and whatever she answered, they obviously were impressed. But the action moved into Art's office and I turned in my weapon, which belonged to the city, and my badge. They had a bunch of papers I had to sign and they gave me a new identification card and a small retirement badge. Overall, my part of it was quick and easy, but Tani was definitely the center of attention and envy. So now we're back outside walking to the Lexus and the uniforms are still guarding it but by now they've gotten the message and they're standing next to it to get a better view of her. They even opened the doors for both of us but I think that I was just an afterthought. Finally one of the guys asked for her autograph and she accommodated him."

"Brent, I told you to quit fooling around and to get that girl off the market as quickly as possible, didn't I?"

"Yeah, you did and at last count I think you said it 763 times, and that was just this month alone."

"Well don't screw it up son," he replied with a smile, before turning and leaving the room.

Feeling that he had to tell someone else he'd gone looking for Alice and found her alone in the kitchen, peeling potatoes. He went through the story for the second time.

"It's been like that for both of my nieces

68

from the time that they were little girls. Fortunately my brother was a large man, and kind of scary looking too. When he was around no one would come anywhere near the girls. Unfortunately he had to work and couldn't always be around them so they grew up pretty fast. I think that by the time they were ten years old they knew what they were going to do with their lives. Both had put together this master plan and openly talked about it. They'd visit Henry and me every year and we could see how they blossomed out and matured. Actually I guess that early on we envied my brother and his wife but as the girls grew up we were happy that they only visited and didn't live here. In their early twenties they seemed to calm down a little, but they're really exotic looking and men just seem to fall all over themselves whenever they appear. Guess that's why Tani was so successful at modeling. Henry and I have discussed it and we think that she made a lot of money in that business. My brother told us that for years Tani had secretly sent money to her sister every month until she could support herself. The girls are still very close, but I think that I mentioned that to you once before."

Brent just nodded, grabbed a snack and hobbled back to his office.

"Propose yet," laughed Allen as he looked up from Brent's desk.

Chapter 7

"So how's your love life going, big sister," Michi asked.

"Pretty slow so far," Tani joked. "I don't think that I've ever met a man with both ethics and morals before. Everyone seems to want us to get together, including Alice and Allen Sheffield, but so far all we've done is talk and that's either in his office or while we're running some errand."

"Bummer," Michi said.

"You're right about that part," replied Tani. "But he's been operating under a handicap with that broken leg, so I'll cut him some slack," she laughed.

"He seemed like a really nice guy at Christmas and if you hadn't claimed him first, I would have. Honestly, it would be good to see you married and then I wouldn't have to worry so much about having an older spinster sister. It sort of reflects on me when people ask if I have any siblings with children."

"You're lucky that I can't reach through this phone line and grab you," laughed Tani.

"Do you think that he's the one Tani?" she asked suddenly getting serious.

"He certainly could be," Tani replied. "I've spent the last ten years on the high fashion modeling circuit and beating off the wolves. I'm tired of that life and have been for some time but didn't really know how to get out. It's addictive Michi. You get paid tons of money for doing practically nothing.

70

Not all of it is lingerie; most of it is just walking down a runway wearing some designer's new clothing line and having people stare at you. If you have the body for it and can erect a shell around your brain, you have it made. But after every show is a party and the models are always invited to them. Some get pretty wild because the designers that hired you sometimes believe that they bought the use of your body not only on the runway, but afterwards. I've been doing my best to avoid those parties for a long time and my agency has even asked me to loosen up. One way or another, I've decided to quit. If this doesn't work out with Brent pretty soon, then I'll be moving on."

"To where, sis?" Michi asked.

"I've put some money away, and I have a girlfriend down in Grand Cayman Island. At least it's warm down there and I don't look too bad in a bikini," she laughed.

"I heard on the nightly news how Colorado seems to be getting hit by one winter storm after another."

"Trust me Michi, for once the weatherman wasn't lying," replied Tani.

"Well you could always use plan "B" with Brent.

"Don't think that I haven't thought about plan "B," laughed Tani. "But after the accident I didn't want to kill the guy. Me running around naked and jumping his bones might have been more than his heart could handle."

"Well I have to go, but don't give up on plan "B". It's always worked for me, but then I was pretty desperate at the time. Or maybe I was drunk, can't remember which, but it did work at least for a short time. But that's about all I qualify for anymore. I can't remember when I last found a guy I wanted to spend much time with. And with all of the diseases floating around today, I practically demand a full medical report on a guy before I'll sleep with him. Anyway, good luck sis and let me know if you have any castoffs." Michi hung up and Tani sat with the telephone in her hand until she heard the buzzing sound coming from it. She hung up and wondered if it wasn't time for plan "B".

Without any warning Brent had invited her on a date. They'd have dinner at the Penrose Room after watching an early movie in the Hotel's small theater. Allen and Diane had decided to drive up to Denver and check in with his law firm, a weekly occurrence for both of them. Alice and Henry were in their apartment over the garage anxiously awaiting the next installment of their favorite television program.

It had seemed so natural, as they drove up and left the Lexus with the valet who addressed Brent as Mr. Williams. Not knowing the way, they had passed by the front desk asking for directions to the theater. An alert desk clerk had recognized Brent and directed a bellman to escort them to their seats. When the movie ended they found the bank of elevators and stepped inside. In the elevator he had put his arm around her waist and held her close to him. Their reserved table was off to the side away from the band and from it they could see the lake and the lights on in the surrounding buildings. They danced, holding each other tightly even thought it was somewhat awkward with him holding his cane in one hand, but they found a way. Dinner was outstanding as usual and afterwards they wandered through the many exclusive shops, window shopping. Now back at Harrington House they had a nightcap and held each other tightly, as if they had never done that before. Then he led her up the stairs and into his bedroom.

In the morning, they awoke and he was afraid it had all been a dream, a figment of his imagination, but she was still there beside him.

"So where do we go from here?" he asked, holding her tightly.

"It's still your house and your problem," she giggled, something that she couldn't ever remember doing.

"Allen mentioned Las Vegas. Think that it would work?" he asked.

"I'm in," she smiled as she turned over and climbed on top of him.

*

Allen and Diane hadn't returned to the mansion until late Tuesday afternoon and by then Brent and Tani had flown to Las Vegas on the red eye special, had gotten married and caught a early plane back to Colorado Springs. Alice had met them at the front door and from the look on their faces she knew exactly what had happened. After congratulations, she rushed to tell Henry and to call her brother.

"You did what?" asked Allen.

"You heard me, Tani and I got married over the weekend,"

"No prenup?" he asked.

"No time," he laughed.

"That was part of my problem too Brent," Allen confessed. "I never got any of my four wives to sign off on a prenuptial either," he laughed while extending his hand to Brent.

"Well, why not?" Allen finally said. "You're both young, she's beautiful, and you're on your way up. What do you have to lose? Come to think of it," he laughed. "That was the same thing I said the first time I did it."

Over the following six months, activities at Harrington House had settled down. Allen and his secretary-live-in-divorcee Diane, had organized the law practice of Sheffield and Williams and while Allen made the big decisions, he was slowly moving Brent into the number one position. As the weather warmed up and spring arrived, the grass on the golf courses began turning green and Allen had promised Diane that they'd play every course in the area, weather permitting before Memorial Day. So far they were right on schedule.

Brent's leg had healed nicely and now he was walking with only a slight limp. The physical therapy had been the answer and Tani had learned how to do it and each morning would insist that he follow her instructions. Their love life had improved and many times he had thought that he had died and gone to heaven. She had become the ideal wife and with Alice's help was quickly becoming the mistress of the manor.

With his leg returning to normal, Brent was now able to get out of the office and meet with clients, some acquired through word-of-mouth and others as a referral from Sheffield, Andrews, Preston & Blatt in Denver. Occasionally he'd meet one of his old police buddies for lunch and especially Lieutenant, recently promoted to Captain, Art Thomas. Art claimed that he live vicariously through the exploits of his young friend. And every so often the Thomas' would join the others at the mansion for a backyard barbeque, once Allen had told him that the house actually had a large patio area and a fantastic outdoor stainless steel kitchen set up on it.

Overall life for Brent Williams had noticeably improved. He had a beautiful wife that he loved, good friends that he trusted and wonderful people to take care of what he owned. What more could he ask for?

Chapter 8

For Brent, the day began just as many others had for the past six months. Make love, do therapy, shower, dress and eat breakfast, but not necessarily in that order. He'd left his loose schedule open this morning since he had an appointment at the El Paso County's Sheriff's Office at 10 AM. Allen had finally convinced him to get a concealed weapons carry permit to protect himself and Brent had to admit that after years of carrying a gun on his hip, not having one made him seem unbalanced. Allen claimed that in this day and age, it was just common sense to be able to protect yourself if need be. That and recently they'd been doing a small amount of criminal law, on a referral from the Denver office. So Brent had gotten the form, completed it and was due at 10 AM to be fingerprinted and have his picture taken at the building on Costilla Street. Since he had recently retired from the CSPD on a partial medical disability the requirement for a background check by the Colorado Bureau of Investigation (CBI) had been waived. He had appeared on time, completed the processing and on his way out had been handed his new identification card. Allen already had one but rarely carried a weapon preferring to leave it in his attaché case.

As usual whenever he was around any of his old law enforcement buddies, he'd get involved in a conversation, stop for coffee and would spend an hour or more just killing time, which he'd allowed for this morning. They told jokes, discussed old war stories and it wasn't until nearly noon that it had finally ended. He'd been invited to join a couple of the Sheriff's detectives for lunch at a nearby restaurant. He'd accepted although he knew that as a lawyer, they'd probably try and stick him for the lunch. So it wasn't until nearly 1 PM that he returned to the mansion, intending to check in with Allen on what was scheduled for the afternoon. Allen's tee times were never before 2 PM so he knew that he had plenty of time.

As Brent approached the closed front gate, he leaned over and pushed the button on the car's remote and the heavy black wrought iron gate slowly opened. Once inside he pushed the button again and it closed behind him. The gate had become a bit of a joke because most of the time it was left open during the day because of everyone coming and going. However anytime the house would be left empty, or someone was alone then it would be closed and the alarm turned on. He wondered what Gus' schedule had been before she'd become housebound?

Allen Sheffield's white Lexus was parked in front of the main door and Brent, who was destined for the garage hesitated for a moment and then pulled up behind him. Carrying his attaché with the handgun Gus had given Frank for Christmas in his left hand, he inserted the key in the front door and stepped inside, locking it behind him. The huge foyer echoed his footsteps and as he passed by his office on the left, he glanced in looking for Allen or perhaps Diane. He found both and froze. Allen was slumped over the desk, his face buried in the open laptop computer and a pool of dark blood surrounding him. Diane was seated on the leather couch, her arms flung back and dried blood on her chest over her heart. Her eyes were wide open and the look on her face was that of fear. Brent, removed his gun from the attaché case and quietly made his way to the kitchen, where at this hour he'd normally find Alice and Henry. Then he remembered that this morning Alice had an early doctor's appointment and Henry had borrowed Brent's old car to drive her there. Normally they took a bus. As he entered the kitchen, he saw Tani lying face down on the floor in front of the big eight burner gas stove, a pool of dark blood surrounding her head. He immediately backed out of the room, crept quietly down the hall and out the front door. He walked to his Lexus, retrieved the remote for the front gate and pushed the button. As it opened, he passed through, pushed the button again and sat down heavily on the curb as he took out his cell phone and called Art Thomas.

While it seemed like hours, it was only minutes before the first uniform patrol car arrived and Brent quickly explained what he'd found. As the second and third cars arrived they cordoned off the street and strung yellow crime scene tape around the entire house and the street fronting it. Finally Art Thomas arrived with two detectives, the paramedics, and closely behind them were the Crime Scene people. The detectives entered and cleared the house, then the Crime Scene technicians and the Coroner's people, who'd just arrived, entered and began their grizzly work.

Brent had been sitting in Art's car going over and over what he'd seen, and asking why? Why would anyone want to kill Art or Diane and especially Tani? Art talked to one of his detectives, and then drove Brent to his home where Art's wife Sally consoled and babysat him. He spent the night with the Thomas' and at noon the following day he was sitting in Art's office at the Police Operations Center listening to the two tired detectives, Matt Jones and Jimmy Cane explain to their Captain exactly what they had found. Brent, still shell-shocked, just sat and listened.

"This is what we have so far," said Cane who seemed to be the lead detective.

"We've confirmed that Brent left the house at approximately 9:45 AM and arrived for his appointment at the El Paso County Sheriff's Annex over on Costilla Street at a few minutes to 10 AM. He didn't return until just around 1 PM. During that time, the shooter or shooters managed to gain entrance to the property through the front gate, which we assume was left open after Mr. Sheffield and his secretary arrived. According to a neighbor who was walking her dog, that was about 10 AM. Somehow the perps got the front door open. The lab tech's are examining the high security lock to see if it was picked or if they had a key, or maybe it had been left open by mistake. We believe that the target was Mrs. Williams and that they stumbled over Mr. Sheffield and his secretary by accident. At that point they had no choice but to take them out. Then they moved through the house searching for their target and found Mrs. Williams in the kitchen, which is at the far end of the first floor nearest to the garage. Our assumption is that they intended to steal a car for their getaway. Now Mr. Sheffield's Lexus was parked right out front, but in order to find the keys they'd have to go back through the house, reenter the office and search his body which was too time consuming and messy. So they just walked out in the garage and unfortunately encountered Alice and Henry the housekeepers, returning from her early

79

morning doctor appointment. With no choice at this point they took them out too and stole the car. Now this was Brent's old car that he had driven back and forth to work while he was with the CSPD. Anyway it's gone and we're looking for it."

"Have the next of kin been notified?" Captain Thomas asked.

"Next of kin for Mr. Sheffield is Brent here," said Detective Jones. His secretary had no one other than her ex husband who's in prison. I talked to a Mr. Andrews at the law firm in Denver and he said that he'd be in touch with Brent. Now Brent's wife is actually the caretaker's niece and I did manage to find a phone number for Alice's brother out in California and I called him. He, his wife and daughter are flying in tomorrow morning."

"Just for the record Captain, we found absolutely nothing to implicate Brent Williams in any of this. He's made out his statement, we've checked it out and there is no reason for us to pursue him as a suspect any further. Because he used to be one of us, my partner and I wanted there to be no misunderstanding regarding him."

"Do we have any solid leads?" asked Thomas.

"The autopsies will be this afternoon, but we already know that they were all shot with a .22 caliber weapon. That leads us to believe that this was a professional hit and that Brent's wife was the target. Everyone else was just collateral damage. And so far we don't have much to go on."

"Who's handling the press?" Thomas asked.

"Because it involved an ex-cop, our people are handling it."

"When will the house be released?" Thomas asked.

"Our last Crime Scene tech left over an hour ago. He said that he hadn't found much but that as far as he was concerned, that was it for the house. I'll check with his boss and if he doesn't object, you can have it back late this afternoon," said Cane, knowing how unusual that was..

"Ok, just wanted to get a time when the clean up specialists could get in," replied Thomas.

The meeting ended and Brent still sat quietly in the corner, rehashing the events of the past two days.

"It had nothing to do with the others," he finally said. "They were after Tani, but I don't have a clue why. It must have been something in her background. Let me know when I can get back inside. She must have kept a diary, or a booking log or had something to give us a start. Even the name of her modeling agency or coworkers would help out."

"When I get the call, I'll drive you out there."

The call hadn't come until nearly 8 PM that evening and Art Thomas had called the privately owned clean up crew and asked for a favor. By noon the following day the house had been cleaned and restored to its original magnificence, and anything that couldn't be saved had been removed. Large electric fans had run through the early morning hours to eliminate the strong odors of the solvents and chemicals that had been used. The crime scene tape had been removed and a street sweeper had passed by the mansion several times picking up gum wrappers, empty coffee cups and anything else that had been left behind. By noon, it appeared that nothing had ever happened within the high black wrought iron gates.

Art Thomas was worried about his friend and

had discussed it with his wife last night. Brent had kept everything to himself and he could just imagine the rage that was eating him inside. So late this morning he had driven him back to the mansion to pick up his Lexus, then followed him out to the Colorado Spring Airport to pick up his deceased wife's family, who were due in shortly after 1:30 PM. As he followed Brent, he contacted the dispatcher and asked for a uniform car to meet him at the airport. Art had to attend a meeting of the brass regarding this case and he didn't want Brent to be left alone. The man that met them knew Brent from his time on the street in a uniform and liked the guy. They went inside the terminal and waited.

The commercial flight landed on time and Brent and the uniform cop searched the faces of the deplaning passengers looking for some indication of Tani's family. Then in the back of the crowd, he spotted Michi, Tani's younger sister and near look alike and he lost it, collapsing into a seat and breaking down. Tears freely flowed down his face and his body shook as he removed a hankie and attempted to regain his composure. The cop placed his hand on Brent shoulder, but he too was overcome and wiped his eyes with the back of his hand.

Michi saw what had happened and rushed over to console Brent, but through his tears he couldn't see her or her parents, Alice's brother and his wife. Finally the moment passed and he tried to apologize, then he looked up and saw Quasimodo standing in front of him, trying to help him up. Tani's father stood about 6' 5", was bald, had fierce black eyebrows and the meanest looking face Brent had ever seen. He probably weighed in at 250 to 300 pounds and was solid muscle. His eyes looked black, as if they were dead and he could tear your head off in one move and use it as a bowling ball. Quasimodo was the only word that Brent could think of to describe him. Brent apologized again, shook hands and asked them to please follow him down to the incoming baggage counter, where they collected their bags and then followed him out to his car. Brent had arranged for them to stay at a hotel about a mile east of his house, just off Lake Avenue and he drove them there and got them settled in. The uniform cop followed along staying as close as possible to Brent, and he constantly scanned the area, his eyes never stopping their searching. Finally they sat in the Hotel room, called for room service and began to talk. With the cop at the door, Brent told the story, excluding nothing.

Quasimodo was a welder, his Irish wife a school teacher, and his daughter Michi worked in the fashion design business. They lived outside of LA. Michi had been married in her early twenties for only a short time, before she divorced. She had just turned 27, had returned home to live with her parents and was obviously the apple of her father's eye. Tani had left home at 18 and they rarely heard or talked to her as she gained fame in the modeling industry. However the sisters remained close and kept in touch.

They slowly worked their way through the family history, including Alice and Henry. Quasimodo's name was Ta Mishinko and his wife's name was Christy. The top of her head barely reached his broad shoulders, but Brent had immediately liked them which was unusual for an ex-cop. It was about this time that they noticed that Brent was carrying a gun.

"You're armed?" asked Ta.

"Yes sir, I am armed," Brent smiled.

"I thought that you were retired from the police department?" he asked.

"I am, but after what's happened, I'm not stupid," he replied.

"And the police officer at the door?"

"A friend was worried about me," said Brent. He paused for a moment. "I've arranged for the services to be held tomorrow morning, assuming that the Coroner releases the bodies this afternoon. They'll be waked tonight and buried after mass tomorrow. I thought about cremation, but I'd rather have Tani buried in a cemetery, maybe under a tree or on a hill. I have to go pick it out this afternoon. Let's meet for dinner when I get back."

"Where are you staying?" asked Ta.

"Here for the moment. I'm close, but not ready to go home yet. My old boss arranged for the place to be cleaned up and sanitized, but it isn't going to be easy," he said.

"Maybe sell it?" asked Ta.

"Can't for twenty years according to the terms of the inheritance."

Ta nodded his huge head and said, "aaah, I see."

*

Three days had passed and finally Brent, reinforced by the Mishinko's, had returned to the mansion. When he entered the garage, the floor was spotless, showing absolutely no signs of what had happened. The house was the same. While the Mishinko's looked around in awe, he found Allen's keys and moved his Lexus inside the garage, next to his. He walked out front and checked the front gate to make certain that it was locked and secure, then back inside and checked the security alarm panel.

"This is such a large house," said Ta and his

wife just nodded.

"Aunt Alice and Uncle Henry took care of it for Brent," spoke up Michi. "They did the same for Mrs. Harrington III."

Ta walked outside and Brent joined him so that the neighbors would not call the police after seeing him.

"Really nice grounds," he muttered to himself. He bent down and checked out several plants, then moved on to a bush, sort of admiring it.

"Daddy's a closet gardener," said Michi rushing out to catch up. "He and Uncle Henry always liked to talk about gardening on the phone."

Ta looked embarrassed, but Brent guessed that Quasimodo could probably pull the bushes out of the ground with his bare hands and rip the limbs off trees with little effort.

"Such a big house," Ta repeated again as they walked inside.

The next day the Mishinko's returned to California, but Brent had the distinct feeling that Quasimodo wasn't going to let his oldest daughter's death end with her burial.

*

Brent had returned from the airport just as Stewart Andrews, one of Allen's partners had driven up to the gate. He invited him in and they sat talking in the formal living room since Brent wasn't ready to return to his office yet.

"I just wanted to reassure you that with Allen's death, nothing will change in our business relationship with you. In our Denver office Sidney Blatt has chosen to retire, and Hank Preston is taking over the day-to-day operation," he said.

"What about you?" Brent asked.

"Honestly I've always been jealous about

Allen being able to step away from the hustle and bustle of our busy practice and get reborn again down here in the Springs. We have nearly seventy-four attorneys on our payroll and a bunch of paralegals and secretaries. It's a zoo, so I had the opportunity to cut back and I took it. The wife and I are looking for a condo down here and we're planning on doing a little traveling. However, I will be available if you need my help. I'm not trying to horn in on your operation, but if you need my help, just pick up the phone." He handed Brent a business card with his private cell phone number on the back, before he turned and walked out. The automatic sensors for the front gate had been disabled and Brent pushed the button on the remote to open the big gate for him.

Brent suddenly jumped up and ran for the locked security closet, the area where all of the security cameras transmitted their images. He scanned through the tapes but the 24-hour recorders were set to record over anything that was there if they weren't changed every day. He removed them anyway, wondering if some high tech lab could pull anything out of the background. Eventually he'd find that the tapes were useless.

*

"Mishinko residence" said the sexy voice on the telephone.

"Michi its Brent. I found Tani's diary but it's in some kind of code. Do you know how to translate it?" he asked. He'd been searching through the house and had found it in the library by accident. It had been placed on a shelf with a number of similar looking leather bound books. From a distance, it looked just like one of them, except that the title wasn't embossed in gold leaf.

Two weeks had passed since Michi and her folks had returned to California and during that time Brent had been acting as the executor of Allen Sheffield's estate plus that of his girlfriend and his own caretakers and Tani's. Alice and Henry had been simple because all that they really owned besides the clothes on their backs was a small saving and checking account. He'd applied to the Court for permission to close out the accounts and send the proceeds to the next of kin which was the Mishinko's, and was waiting for a court approval. He'd done the same for Allen's friend Diane, but she too only had a small checking and savings account and didn't have much in it.

Allen, who both his partners and Brent knew had money, had done such a good job of hiding it from his four ex-wives, that Brent couldn't find it. He'd searched through tons of records both in the Springs at his condo, his condo up in Denver and his office at Sheffield, Andrews, Preston & Blatt without success. Finding it was important because Brent had paid $9,500 apiece to bury his wife and each of the others and he had to dip into Gus's emergency fund to do it. He couldn't believe how expensive cemetery plots were, especially if you wanted five of them side by side. He'd even called Stewart Andrews on his cell phone, but he didn't have any suggestions other than what Brent had already tried. He was now out nearly 50 grand, and began to wonder if Allen hadn't spent every dime, as he had told him some time ago. In frustration, he walked out to the garage and inspected Allen's Lexus. However, just like his, the vehicle had been leased and all of the papers stuffed into the glove compartment. In the morning, he'd notify the leasing company to come and get it.

While he'd been searching through Tani's personal stuff looking for her diary, he'd found the three pieces of expensive jewelry that he'd given her and returned them to Gus's safe where he'd found them. He also found a pendant that he'd never seen her wear. It was heavy and looked expensive and he wondered where she had gotten it. Tomorrow when Michi arrived, he'd ask her.

Her plane had arrived right on time. Unable to get a direct flight on such short notice, she had flown to Las Vegas and had caught a red eye special directly to the Springs. Brent wondered if it was the same plane that he and Tani had flown on. But this time when he met her he was all composed and businesslike, the perfect uncaring lawyer. At the mansion, he simply asked her to pick out a bedroom she liked and as she went searching, he walked into the kitchen and put on some coffee. It was the most difficult walk that he'd ever taken because he kept seeing Tani lying on the floor face down in a pool of blood. He finally made it through the coffee and asked Michi to join him in the dining room where he had cleared the big table and set up his temporary office.

"Does this make any sense to you?" he said handing her Tani's diary. She carefully examined it for a minute and smiled.

"When we were kids we used to pass notes around in school. We were the only Asians in the school and just to confuse our teachers and so the other kids couldn't read it if they found one, we invented our own language. Honestly this is going to take a while to translate because it was years ago and I forgot all about it. But I'll start right now," she smiled and Brent saw Tani's face staring at him. These girls were sisters and only two years apart.

They looked like twins, but somehow he'd never taken the time to notice. Suddenly the tension was broken by his stomach growling and he broke into a laugh.

"I forgot about lunch, Michi. I'm sorry, but there's nothing in the house. Come on, grab a coat and we'll go find a restaurant."

"No Penrose Room?" she pouted. "I'm disappointed."

"No reservations and no money," he laughed and she had to believe him.

"It's ok with me. I'd prefer a big burger and fries anyway," and she got her wish.

That night after Michi had gone up to bed; Brent sat in the den thinking about Allen. The guy had money, but what had he done with it. If it was in a bank, then he'd have to pay taxes on the interest and the ex-wives could petition the courts and find out how much. What about a safety deposit box, but that left written records of how often you visited and how long you were there. So maybe he'd converted everything to cash, split it up into smaller amounts and had hidden them. Damn, if Gus was alive, she'd know where to look. He thought about earlier conversations with Allen and how much time he'd spent visiting the Harrington's. Now he wondered if maybe some of it was hidden right here in the house. Or how about in his Lexus and he rushed to the garage and began a closer inspection of the luxury automobile. In the trunk behind the spare tire, he found a paper bag with $75,000 stuffed in it. He wondered if he'd find more if he searched the house and grounds, but he immediately marched upstairs, and replaced what he'd borrowed from Gus' emergency fund. The remainder he'd locked in his small office safe, normally used for files and important papers. Tonight he'd sleep peacefully for the first time since Tani's death.

Chapter 9

Three months had passed and Brent was lying in bed holding Michi after a strenuous lovemaking session. While she and Tani might have looked alike, they really were two different people and a lot had changed since June.

Quasimodo and his wife Christy had pulled up stakes and moved to Colorado to replace his sister Alice and her husband Henry as caretakers for the Harrington House. Upon returning to California after Tani's funeral, the company that he worked for as a welder, had unexpectedly been sold to some conglomerate, and they had discontinued his entire division. Brent and Michi had just about given up trying to run his fledging law practice and the Harrington House at the same time. They'd discussed the idea but he was hesitant about interfering in her family. After an unsuccessful local search, she had asked him to make her folks an offer. The trust fund that Gus had established had the money set aside for the operation of the house and Ta needed a job, so why not? The fact that he was sleeping with his daughter concerned him, but Michi told him that she'd handle dear old Mom and Dad. And surprisingly she had, explaining in great detail exactly what Aunt Alice and Uncle Henry had done and how they had done it. While Brent was back to eating in the kitchen again, every so often, he'd look down and walk away and everyone knew why.

While Ta wasn't entirely happy about his

youngest daughter sleeping with his boss, both she and her mother had told him to mind his own business and surprisingly, he had. His wife was happier than he'd seen her in a long time, he loved his gardener-handyman job, and his daughter seemed more bubbly than ever, so what could he say? His car, driven all of the way from California, now resided inside garage number 4. He didn't even have to go outside to get in it. And the chances of being mugged along the way were practically nil. Then he remembered what happened to Henry and Alice and sighed. But for the Mishinko's, life had definitely improved.

The platonic relationship between Brent and Michi had quickly changed once she had spent some time working with him and finally made up her mind, as she had once told Tani, to go for it. That had taken nearly three months and it was only recently, actually a week before her parents arrived that they'd begun sleeping together. By then Brent, despite his sorrow over losing Tani, was hooked, lock, stock and barrel as Allen would have said.

Then at dinner one night in the huge kitchen, Brent had gotten their attention and made an announcement.

"Folks, it has come to my attention that your daughter Michi is living in sin."

Ta looked up from his plate and wondered if this was the end of the line and if Brent had decided to move on to another woman and Michi was now out? He waited for the punch line, considering whether he'd just kill him here or wait until later.

"It's nearly the end of September and winter will be setting in fairly soon. I've fallen in love for the second time and unbelievably in the same family. I want to ask Ta for his daughter's hand in marriage.

Michi and I have talked and if you folks will agree, we'll all fly to Hawaii after the beginning of the year and we'll get married over there." Brent sat back and looked around and then he saw a big grin break out on Quasimodo's face and he knew that he was in.

He was sitting in his office in the same seat that Allen had been sitting in when he'd been killed. He'd convinced himself that one just had to move on and get past all of the bad things. Besides he couldn't sell the place for twenty years and that was a long time to keep feeding his grief and guilt. And he didn't have the money to set up a household and his practice elsewhere and maintain both of them. The local police had located his old car, the one that the killers had stolen from his garage and had escaped in. It was found in an isolated pasture, way east of Fountain, Colorado. The killers had torched it and nothing was left but a rusted out shell. So much for fingerprints or evidence collecting, he thought. And the diary that Michi had been able to translate parts of had been turned over to the two investigating Colorado Springs detectives who had copied the book and sent the copies to their contacts at the New York City Police Department, but they doubted that much time would be spent on it. Even Captain Thomas had personally called and had sent an official request to have them look into it. New York was a big place and Brent had discovered that the modeling agency that represented Tani was a long established, reputable one. Apparently that was somewhat unusual in NYC and in the industry.

Michi turned out to be the bubbly type, with an unbelievable amount of enthusiasm and energy. From the moment the sun rose until it set, she was on the go, organizing, helping and keeping busy.

She'd even been reading books on becoming a paralegal and was now helping Brent in his office. Stewart Andrews was dropping by on a more frequent basis either at Brent's request or the parent firm in Denver. Brent surprisingly found himself working longer and longer hours and that pleased him because it meant that he wasn't that bad a lawyer after all.

As Thanksgiving approached, Brent had invited the Andrew's and the Thomas' to dinner. As an afterthought he'd contacted the two detectives that were still working the murder case part time and invited them and their wives too. As Michi had told him many times, the house was huge and the dining room table held 20 people. But he didn't know anyone else that he could ask.

That night everyone had gone to bed and Brent was still working in his office trying to catch up. It had been a year to remember, he thought. If Allen hadn't convinced him to get a gun permit then he'd probably be dead too. The killers had robbed him of his best friends, his wife and his caretakers. For a guy like him, that was nearly everything except for his house. He wanted revenge in the biggest way, but as an ex-cop he knew that it would be stupid for him to get involved at this point in any way. And now he had Michi and didn't want to lose her. While her sister had been more refined and could probably walk naked through a crowd and not bat an eye because she just had that self-confidence about her, Michi was equally as beautiful but not the extrovert that Tani had been. And while Tani had been happy to just sit and talk or to read a book, Michi was always on the go and exploring, doing new things. As lovers, Michi certainly had the enthusiasm of youth. But despite her exotic

Eurasian looks, she was as American as apple pie and the Fourth of July. He laughed to himself as he remembered overhearing a conversation between her and her parents as she outline exactly what their jobs would entail based on her experience with Aunt Alice and Uncle Henry. When she finally finished he doubted that they had any misconceptions of what was involved. But Brent was pleased, because Christy jumped right in to get the house in order and Ta had immediately begun preparing the flowerbeds for their winter hibernation. And every time Brent took a walk he'd see Ta, pruning, cutting, washing cars, always on the move. He wondered what the neighbors thought when they saw Quasimodo moving in stealth mode around the property?

The Thanksgiving dinner had gone off pretty well in Brent's estimation, considering that of the twelve people consuming the feast, four had seen the dead bodies. Cane and Jones were somewhat surprised to see their Captain and his wife walk in, but everything was kept very light and no prior business was discussed. Quasimodo frightened everyone at first, but Brent guessed he did that no matter where he went. But he did notice that Ta seemed to remain fairly close by him, as if he was expecting some trouble and he made a mental note to mention it to Michi later on. But after good food and lots to drink, they socialized, enjoyed the benefits of the recreation/game room and sat by the natural gas fireplaces. When it finally ended late into the evening, Brent was pleased that all of his guests seemed to have had a good time, and there was even some mention of a repeat at Christmas.

Chapter 10

The early morning meeting was being held in Captain Art Thomas' office, at the Police Operations Center. He'd gotten a call from Brent early yesterday requesting a sit down with he, and his two detectives that were working the Harrington House case. With Brent being a friend, an ex-cop and one of the victims, he'd readily agreed. The two detectives weren't sure why they'd been included since the case seemed to be in limbo. The ball had been passed to the NYPD, and now all that they could do was sit and wait for their response. Until they had more information to go on, they'd be working on other cases.

"Thanks for humoring me and coming this morning," smiled Brent using his most lawyerly smile, which Michi had coached him to use.

"When I had my accident and was under the influence of drugs, my partner Allen Sheffield kept pushing me to make a move on Tani. Somewhere along the line he mentioned that he'd requested a complete background check on her, but at the time I was groggy and high on painkillers, and he was a great kidder. Now Allen had been married and divorced four times and was working up to his fifth by this time. He was a wealthy guy, but he swore that he'd never leave another nickel to any of his ex-wives or get married again without a background check and a prenuptial agreement. I'm his executor, and despite my best efforts, so far I haven't found a dime. However I know that his law firm farmed out any background checks to a private investigating company in Denver. I checked with the remaining three partners and they knew nothing about it, so apparently Allen being the senior partner, personally handled those requests."

"Then early yesterday I was going through some of his completed files prior to storing them down in the basement, and I came across an unopened envelope from a company that sounded familiar. It was the same company that at Gus' request to Allen, had prepared a report on me sometime back. So I opened it, and it turned out to be the missing report on Tani. I think that it may have taken longer to prepare than Allen expected, and by the time it arrived Tani and I were already together, so he just tossed it in the stack of files and forgot about it."

"You need to copy this and read every word of it," smiled Brent as he handed the envelope to Art Thomas. "I think that we may have a tiger by the tail about now."

Thomas had quickly scanned the contents and handed it to Jones, instructing him to go downstairs and make some copies.

"Think that it's true?" Art asked, as they waited for Jones to return.

"I have to believe that the law firm only hired the very best. One mistake or omission and they'd never be hired again. So my gut feeling is that it's got to be close to the truth," replied Brent.

They discussed the report in general terms, then Jones returned and handed Brent the original and copies to the others, keeping one for himself.

"This fits with what we heard last week," said Cane and his Captain just nodded his head in agreement.

"What happened?" asked Brent, thinking that he'd been left out of the loop. He wondered if it was because he was the grieving husband or he'd become a lawyer.

"When we didn't hear anything from the NYPD for a while, I called to see if it was even being worked," said Cane. "I got transferred up the line, until I reached some Captain. He asked for my name, badge and phone number and said he'd call me back. So I figured that was the brush off and that I'd never hear from him again. Then twenty minutes later as I was about to leave, the phone rang and it was him. Guy's name was Captain Harry Grimes and he wanted to check me out before saying anything," said Cane referring to his notebook. "Anyway they got the copy of the case file we sent to them and assigned it. The two detectives found the address of Tani's modeling agency in the phone book and decided to pay them an unannounced visit. Now this wasn't some half-assed, cut rate operation, where the girls wind up as prostitutes or I guess they call them escorts now. This was 100% big time legitimate and had a reputation to match. Definitely a first class operation, even though by industry standards, it was a smaller one. The offices were on an upper floor of some upscale high-rise office building. So when the detectives got there, the place is dark and locked up. But the odor of a decomposing body had begun to seep out into the hallway. With all of the money floating around this building they didn't want to screw it up, so they called it in. As soon as the locksmith popped the lock, it was obvious that one or more dead bodies were inside. Actually turned out to be three, including one man and two well dressed older women," said Cane pausing.

"When I called, the Coroner had just finished the autopsies and the detectives had positive identifications on the bodies. The oldest woman was the sole owner of the agency, the man was her administrative assistant and the third victim a middle aged female, actually ran the place on a day-to-day basis. All three had been tortured and then had their necks broken. But a canvas of the nearby tenants for anyone that might have heard or seen something came up flat. Now the building does have some security and they do use security cameras on the loading dock, the entrance doors and at the main elevator banks on the first floor. But this place is really busy and looking through those tapes would be like looking for a grain of sand in the Sahara desert," said Cane. "But one of the security guys did remember seeing two green Kawasaki motorcycles parked illegally out in front of the building on the sidewalk a few days back. He was going to call it in, but got involved with something else and when he returned he saw two young well dressed oriental youths, walk out the front door and take off on the cycles."

"But Ta was here the entire time," said Brent a bit confused.

"Ok, let me jump ahead here," said Jones. "According to the NYPD detective, they called in the Organized Crime people and the Gang guys, and everything here fits right in with a planned hit by the Japanese Yakuza. Apparently they use the street punks to handle most of their dirty work."

"Aren't they the Japanese mafia?" asked Brent.

"Yup, one and the same, except unlike our mafia, they have hundreds of thousands of members and they have a very complex hierarchy."

"I can't believe that Ta was involved in any way," said Brent. "He may look like Quasimodo, but I just can't see him mixed up in something like this. Besides, aren't those guys covered in tattoos?"

"My understanding," said Cane, "is that they favor full body art. I've actually never seen one in person, but have seen pictures of them."

"Well someone has to confront Ta about this and I guess the best candidate is me," smiled Brent. "Now if you don't hear from me in the next 24 hours, then please check out the flower beds at the house," he joked as he got up and walked out.

Brent stopped at the courthouse on the way home and it wasn't until noon that he returned to Harrington House and found Quasimodo packing mulch around the bases of some young trees in preparation of colder winter weather. His massive arms lifted the 75-pound bales of mulch as if they were weightless. While he was his girlfriend's father, Brent still couldn't see him involved, but he had to ask.

"Ta, we need to talk," said Brent as he pointed towards a fancy concrete bench in the sun, one of many on the large patio, and sat down. He removed the report from his attaché case and handed it to Ta along with the same explanation concerning Allen Sheffield that he'd given to the CSPD. Ta took the report after wiping his hands clean on his pants and carefully opened it. As he read, he grunted as if in agreement and several times, he had nodded. When he finished he handed it back to Brent, folded his arms and nodded again. Brent patiently waited.

"From the look on your face, there is more?" Ta asked.

Brent explained what he'd learned about the deaths in New York.

"Aaah, Taniaka!" he immediately said. "There will be more deaths, just wait and see, Brent."

"What or who is Taniaka?" Brent asked.

"He is my uncle, and he is Japanese Yakuza. Tani was named after him. Let me explain. When I was born in Japan I was pledged to an uncle. My father had been killed, and the custom was for each son to have a male to guide him through life. This applied only to male sons, not females. My family in Japan knew he was connected to the Yakuza, but no one knew how much. Yakuza is somewhat like the Mafia, only much stronger and deadlier. The top man is called the kumicho and when you join, you pledge your life to him. His next in command is the saiko komon, who you could call his senior advisor. Next in line is the so-honbucho or headquarters chief. Following him is the wakagasira or #2 man. He's also the regional boss. Beneath them are more layers of command and sub command, then the troops and gangs and street punks. Uncle Taniaka is a wakagasira for a kumicho in Japan who controls a big chunk of Japan and most of the west coast of the US. At one time he had great plans for me in the Yakuza, but it wasn't my thing. When I was old enough and could get away, I moved to California. My sister Alice was already here, but I can't remember where she was working, but jobs were hard to find. Finally I got a job in a welding shop as an apprentice and shortly thereafter she married Henry and they found a job working together as caretakers. I guess back in those days they were pretty much indentured servants," he smiled. "Uncle Taniaka has never forgiven me for not being Yakuza and following in his footsteps. In Japan it was a sign of great disrespect. Since then we have never met again, but he has always kept an eye on Tani."

"How and why?" asked Brent.

"She was the firstborn child and despite males being the preferred ones, I named her after him as a sort of appeasement. I was trying to make peace in the family, but he never responded. Taniaka can nod his head and a hundred Yakuza will try to kill you. It doesn't matter where in the world you are, because they will find you. The sad part is if they are given the assignment and fail, then they must cut off part of their little finger. So anytime you see a Japanese man, always check on how many fingers he has before you decide to trust him. Tani learned over the years that he was keeping track of her. She'd tell her sister Michi that she'd be doing some show in a foreign country like France, and see some young Yakuza watching her from a distance. He'd be young enough that he wouldn't have any visible identification or markings, but she had learned how to pick them out. When you came along, you immediately joined his list of threats, but since she seemed happy and Alice and Henry were here, he left you alone. You have to understand that Tani left home just after her 18th birthday. It wasn't her home life that drove her away, but her passion to be independent and follow her dreams, which didn't include any of us. Taniaka knew that and had his people follow her. Rarely did she ever contact us, especially in the early years but she always kept in touch with her sister Michi. That's where we got all of our information. However during the past few years Michi said that she inquired more and more about us, our jobs, our lives and our health, like she was really interested. So Michi just told her the truth. Sometimes when she'd call Michi, I'd overhear the conversations. Christy and I didn't know what to do, but since she was in her twenties, she was an adult and could handle her own life. But Christy and I often wondered if Tani had an affair with some young man, if Taniaka would let him live after it ended? I doubt it."

"So you think that Taniaka is outraged that someone from her past killed her?" asked Brent.

"Maybe, but it could also be from another Yakuza family too. They bring drugs and guns into Japan, mostly through Hawaii. Maybe there's a territorial disagreement? Or maybe some rival wants to get even with Taniaka. Kill his niece and you kill a part of him too."

"So exactly how safe is Michi, and you and Christy?" asked Brent.

"If he wanted Christy and I dead, it would have happened a long time ago. And I doubt that he'd ever make a move on Michi. She is the second born, has never met him and is a female. Yakuza have a very strict code of honor that they live by. It dates back to the days of the samurai warriors when they protected the small villages. But when they came to California they formed alliances with the Korean and Vietnamese gangs and even with the Chinese triads. I have heard that they even have contacts in the American Mafia in New York City."

"So as I see it, what happened to Tani probably originated outside of the City of Colorado Springs and maybe even outside of the country," said Brent.

"I think that the deaths of her employers in New York confirm that," smiled Ta. "It's where it goes from here."

"Tani was killed by the bad guys and it

didn't have any connection to either me or this city, right?" asked Brent and Ta just nodded.

"Then on Taniaka's orders, someone went to the people that she worked for and tortured them for information before killing them too, right?" Ta nodded again.

"Now as I see it, Taniaka's killers will move on to Tani's friends, other models and the people that hired her. But now with the people at the agency dead, there's no way to find out who those people might be. Do you think that Michi might know some of them?" Brent asked.

"Anything's possible Brent, but from what I know, most of their conversations were one sided. She'd call Michi and after a minute or two, Michi would begin talking until the conversation finally ended. Whenever she hung up, Christy would always ask if Tani was ok. Michi would answer, but we never learned much of anything else. Come to think of it, we never even knew where she was calling from." Ta bowed his head for a moment as if wondering where he and his wife had gone wrong, but from what Brent now knew, he seriously doubted that they had much to do with it. His dilemma was what to do with the information without getting Ta more involved. Even if he told the CSPD detectives Cane and Jones the entire story, what would they do with it? The cause of the action was outside of Colorado Springs, maybe in Japan? And the latest deaths were in New York City, thousands of miles away. Maybe it was time to bring in the Feds, but right now they were preoccupied with terrorism and immigration. A few Yakuza killings might not get their full attention and Brent knew that as soon as they took over, he and the others would never hear another word about the case.

"What are you going to do now?" Ta asked.

"I'm your lawyer, right?" Brent asked.

"If you want to be. Why, do I need one?" Ta asked, now concerned about whether he'd already said too much.

"Ok Ta, officially I'm your lawyer and as such, everything that we've discussed is lawyer client privileged information. What that means is that I can no longer pass any of it along without your permission. Now if the local police or the NYPD figures this out and contacts you, then you will say absolutely nothing and call me immediately."

"Do you think that they will?" he asked.

"I really don't know Ta, but I don't want you, Christy or Michi getting pulled any further into this thing. Right now the local cops have nothing to go on, but most likely the NYPD isn't going to turn loose of it. If they run into a dead end they might just hand it off to the Feds. And if they begin poking around they're eventually going to follow up on this Yakuza business and that means that at some point they'll want to talk to you and your family. Understand me Ta, I lost Tani, but I'm not going to lose Michi regardless of what it costs me."

Ta just nodded his large head that he fully understood.

Brent slept on it that night, discussed a little of it with Michi, and this morning after holding and making love with her, he went downstairs to breakfast. As usual Ta had eaten earlier and was hard at work somewhere outside. Christy had laid out his morning newspaper next to his plate, and when he read the headlines he froze. "Popular Clothing Designer Plunges to His Death in NYC."

Chapter 11

Captain Art Thomas was sitting in his office deep in thought when Detective Jimmy Cane, the lead man on the Harrington House case knocked on his door and walked in.

"You ok Cap?" he asked as Thomas turned to face him and motioned towards a chair.

"Yeah, I'm ok, but I just got a phone call from Captain Grimes in New York. Said he'd tried to reach you yesterday."

"I was out on another case all day and haven't checked my messages yet this morning. What's going on?" Cane asked.

"Well first off he said that we can add another murder to the case file. Some well-known clothing designer that Tani modeled for took a leap off a rooftop. And his organized crime guys are positive that the first hits at the modeling agency are Yakuza, and most likely this latest one too.

"My God, another dead body. What's that make it now, 9?"

"Yeah, that's my count but the night before last someone broke into the modeling agency's offices and torched the place. That was what, on the 41st floor?" Thomas asked.

"I think that's right, but I'd have to check the case file to be certain. So how'd they get in and out?" Cane asked.

"No problem, just killed the late night

security guard and tore the seals off the door and stole the tapes from the recorders on the way out."

"So now we're up to 10 bodies."

"Looks like it, but the day is young."

"Want me to call the Captain back?" Cane asked.

"Why not, but we don't have much to tell him so far. We lost five people and we already believe that four of them were collateral damage. That leaves Mrs. Williams or Tani as the target. Next the action moves to New York and we lose three more and they turn out to be the people that represented her. And then somebody breaks into their files killing a guard along the way, and then kills one of the people that hired her."

"Man, if I was in the clothing design business right now, I think that I'd take a long vacation," Cane commented.

"So it all goes back to the beginning and that's Tani. Who wanted her dead and why? And who is now cleaning house looking for her killers?"

"What about Brent? He was going to talk to Quasimodo and ask him about the background check that Allen Sheffield ordered?" asked Cane.

"I talked to him on the phone last night. He said that before he had a chance to question Quasimodo, the man asked him to represent him. Now as his lawyer of record, there wasn't anything that he could answer at this time."

"Wow, that's a turnabout," said Cane.

"I'm still trying to figure that one out," replied Thomas. "But he was one of us and I can't believe that he'd withhold anything pertinent regardless of his legal obligations. Especially since it was his wife that was the target."

Cane left the room and once back in his

cubicle, he began sorting through his telephone messages for the previous day. He tossed most of them away, but the few remaining ones he put in order and began returning them. Fifth on his list was Captain Grimes in New York and he reached him on the first attempt, explaining why he hadn't called yesterday.

"I talked to your Captain earlier when I couldn't reach you, sorry about that. But I guess that now our dead list is tied. You got five dead and so do we," said Grimes.

"Hey, that's more than enough for me," Cane joked. "But this Yakuza stuff still amazes me. I mean we're out here in the middle of Colorado and some Japanese killers take out five of our residents? Guess that I'm just having a hard time getting a handle on this," said Cane.

"It's not that much different here. We have millions of people and suddenly we're in the middle of World War II with the Japanese all over again. Just to keep you in the loop, this case has been catching some heat and has been pushed up the line and our Police Commissioner is going to meet with the Japanese Ambassador this afternoon. Maybe he can direct us to the right people in Tokyo. Short of that, it's just sit and wait for the next one."

They ended their conversation, each agreeing to keep the other one updated with anything new, but Cane seriously doubted that he'd be the one doing the calling. In the meantime, he planned on doing as much research on the Internet as his Captain would allow him time for.

*

"Hey Cane, its Harry Grimes. You got time to talk?" asked the voice on the telephone. Two days had passed since their last conversation and as usual Cane's caseload had forced him to return to the problems at hand, rather than the Harrington House case.

"You calling to tell me that you solved the case?" Cane joked.

"Another comedian, just what I was hoping for this morning. Maybe I could get you a spot on Broadway, or maybe close to it?" Grimes laughed. "Listen up my friend, because our PC actually got some action on his request. Seems that several people in Tokyo have disappeared too. All were connected to one of the local Yakuza families. They don't actually call them families, but I can't pronounce the name the guy over there used. Rumor on the street is that two of these families are upset with one another. No one is certain why, but the police are speculating that it has something to do with the drugs and guns that they bring into the country. The guy that is second in command of one family is in seclusion and heavily guarded. The police are just sitting and watching, but their guess is that if they aren't seeing any action at the moment, then it must be taking place somewhere else, like here in the US. The cop also said that this was very unusual for someone so high up in the food chain to be involved."

"Well all is quiet out here, at least for the moment and that's definitely a good sign. But I do appreciate the call since in all honesty we're at a dead end with the Harrington House case. Both Jones and I have picked up several others. But I will add this conversation to the murder book. Thanks again and please keep in touch." The line disconnected and Cane sat back thinking about what he'd heard. How did a war between two crime families in Japan ever reach the shores of the US and wind up in Colorado Springs? And most of all how did a beautiful Eurasian model married to a local ex-cop ever become a target?

Chapter 12

Brent had suddenly awakened from a deep
sleep, looked over at Michi and checked his watch.
It was much too early for her to get up, but he
quietly slipped out of the bed and walked into the
huge bathroom. Twenty minutes later he was sitting
in the kitchen sipping strong coffee from a dainty
china cup, while talking to Christy as she prepared
his breakfast.

"You do know that I could do that myself or
at least help you?" he said.

"You could," she smiled, "but then I
wouldn't have a job, would I?"

"Ok, we're back to that are we?" Brent
laughed.

"Brent, for years Ta and I watched his sister
Alice and her husband Henry and listened to their
stories about living and working here. And then our
own daughters would visit and come home and add
to the legend of the magnificent Harrington House
and the strict old woman who ran it. To us,
regardless of her, it sounded like a dream job. Ta
was working as a welder and I was teaching school.
We both commuted a long distance and by the time
we got home at night we were exhausted. Weekends
were spent doing all of the chores and catching up so
that we could begin the cycle all over again on
Monday. We weren't complaining because at least
we had good jobs, but it cost us dearly in other ways
and I think that it was slowly wearing down both of

us. Of course you know about Ta's employer closing up shop and everyone losing their jobs, but we still would have been able to survive on my salary if we cut back to the bare bones. But California isn't a cheap place to live. Then you asked us to replace Alice and Henry and it was like a gift from the Gods. We both love our jobs and now see why Alice and Henry bragged about it. We live in a mansion, eat extremely well, do whatever's required to keep the place looking new and don't have any pressure. It is really perfect for us. So if you begin doing your own thing in the kitchen, maybe next you'll start washing windows or vacuuming the carpets or doing the laundry and I'll be out of a job," she smiled.

"Christy, you're family. How could you be out of a job?"

"One never knows in affairs of the heart, Brent," she answered.

"Ok, so where's Ta this morning? Sleeping in?" he joked.

"Oh no, he's the first one up every morning and the last one to go to bed at night. Didn't you know that?" she asked.

"I guess I didn't," Brent replied.

"With everything that has gone on here, Ta gets up early every morning, checks the alarm system, and the security tapes for the last 24 hours, changes them and then goes outside and personally checks the grounds. Even if you were up, I doubt that you'd ever see or hear him. I call it his stealth mode. As big as he is, he's like a cat. Only after he's made his rounds and checked outside will he come in for breakfast. And he does nearly the same thing at night. On the lighter side, how would you like to meet him in the dark?" she laughed.

"Between us, he reminds me of the old comic book character Quasimodo," smiled Brent.

"Excellent analogy, but you're right. However in his defense he's one of the kindest, most gentle, caring men that I've ever met. In all of our years together, I've only seen him mad on one occasion and that was because some jerk in a restaurant had insulted me. At that point we'd only been married a short time and I was terrified that he'd get killed. There were five of them and it was obvious that they'd been drinking too much. But Ta quietly escorted me to the car after he'd paid our bill and I think that he intended to just walk away from it, but they came outside after us. Now the restaurant manager or maybe he was the owner, I can't remember which, anyway he called the police. A crowd had gathered and they egged on the drunks. Here was a white woman and a Jap, apparently not a good combination in that neighborhood. But Ta bowed to the waist and then went to work. By the time the cops arrived on the scene, all five were lying unconscious, side-by-side and two more that had jumped in to help out were kneeling on the ground in front of him bleeding profusely. The cops were about to arrest Ta when the restaurant manager spoke up and defended him. We left and never went back to that area. Funny, I haven't thought about that day in years."

"Ta is Japanese, he was born and raised over there and they have their own customs. I quit trying to understand them years ago. It's easier to just let him do his own thing. Like here in the house. He told me that it needed to be cleansed and the spirits pacified, that it had bad, what do you call it, karma? So he's set up a little altar and lit a bunch of candles just as his mother taught him and he moves it from room-to-room. I don't say anything or get in his way. If he's convinced it's the thing to do, then I'm all for it. However he didn't want you to see it for fear that you would think that he was weak. So whenever you leave he picks up where he left off." Christy smiled wondering if she'd already said too much.

"No problem with me," said Brent. "If he thinks that it will work, then I'm all for it. But how far along is he?"

"Nearly finished I think. Said he had only your office and the garage left. Now you are definitely going to think that I'm nuts, but since he cleared the kitchen, I have not burned or overcooked a single thing. And when I come in here first thing in the morning, it feels better, happier maybe? I can't find the right words to explain it, other than to say that maybe Tani's spirit has been appeased and has moved on. Did you know that Mrs. Harrington died in this house too?" she asked.

"No, I just assumed that she died in the hospital. Actually I guess that I never really asked Allen about that. You'd think that I'd have mentioned it?"

"Well both of the Harrington's died here according to Ta. He said that both of their spirits were still here until he did his little Japanese ritual thing. Like I said Brent, he's Japanese and his mother taught him local customs and he's made a believer out of me."

"Whatever works, count me in. Now that we've talked about the job and the clearing of evil spirits I have something of a more local nature to discuss with you. How would you feel about spending Christmas in Hawaii and Michi and I being married there? We could turn it into a vacation for all of us," he said holding up his hand to silence her until he finished. "I've been able to put aside a little money and it would be my treat," he smiled.

"Ta won't go Brent. It's a very nice gesture, but he can't leave the grounds for ninety days according to his ritual. I don't exactly understand it, but it's somehow tied into the moon and what happens in about 3 months. Right now the only time he can leave, is if you are threatened. Then his God will allow him to become your Oyabun, which I guess would be like a surrogate father, and you would be the Kobun, or child. Trust me its easier to just go along with it than try to understand it," she laughed.

"Well I was hoping to get this marriage thing over with. Its not right for Michi and I to be together if we're not married, especially with her own parents living in the house."

"I've been going to church on Sunday's to a little chapel just the other side of the Hotel. I think that it's been there as long as the Hotel has been. I gotten friendly with the priest and I asked him about marrying my daughter. At first he threw up a lot of roadblocks like attending marriage courses, being baptized in his church, going to counseling, just a bunch of things. I agreed that they were probably a great idea for someone in their teens or early twenties, but not you and Michi. After many discussions he relented and agreed to perform the ceremony either in the chapel or here at the Harrington House, your choice. But I'm not going to let you off the hook about a free trip to Hawaii," she laughed again, a very pleasant kind laugh.

"Should I buy the tickets for say, spring?" he asked.

"I'm kidding, Brent, I thought that you knew

that. Ta will not let you go to Hawaii until this thing with his uncle is over with. Hawaii is close to Japan and is the transfer point for drugs and guns that the Yakuza smuggle into Japan. I thought that you knew that too?"

"Ok, so my part of the decision seems to be to decide whether to be married in the chapel or here at home. But if I choose the chapel, then Ta can't attend because he can't leave the property, right?" Brent asked.

"Right," she answered. "Every mother wants to see her daughter married in a huge expensive church wedding complete with a white wedding gown and hundreds of friends and relatives attending. But realistically, we don't have any relatives here, nor do you. And from what you've told me about your relationship with your family, I seriously doubt that any would attend. So that leaves the four of us and maybe a few friends of yours. I seriously doubt that Michi would approve of spending a lot of money for appearances sake since you're already living together, so what's the point of a big wedding if no one but us is there?"

"You've already discussed this with Michi?" he smiled.

"A done deal, Brent. She's just worried about how you'd take it?"

"What about Ta? It's his only daughter."

"He told me that whatever Brent decided would be best for the family and that he'd agree to it. So now it's just about choosing the date," she laughed as the oven bell pinged and she got up and removed a coffee cake from it. She quickly dripped some white sugar frosting on the top and placed it on the table in front of Brent. As long as Christy stayed around, he didn't care if Michi could cook or not.

A week later, just before Christmas, Michi and Brent were married by a priest in a short ceremony held in the formal living room at Harrington House. In attendance were the Mishinko's, attorney Stewart Andrews and his wife, and Colorado Springs Police Captain Art Thomas and his wife. The ceremony lasted less than ten minutes and thereafter Brent switched from wedding music to popular music on the house stereo as Christy finished preparing a huge feast. It was a happy day, but Thomas noticed that Brent's new father-in-law said very little and always seemed to be standing or sitting right next to him, like an alert cat waiting to spring forward. His young friend had certainly changed.

Chapter 13

A week after New Year's, Brent was sitting in a restaurant on the south side of the Springs having lunch with Art Thomas. Despite their differences regarding cases, they were still the best of friends and would maneuver shamelessly to stick each other with the check.

"How's the law practice coming along?" asked Art who still considered himself to be Brent's mentor.

"Honestly Art, if it wasn't for Sheffield, Andrews, Preston and Blatt up in Denver, I'd probably be standing in some soup line about now. Pickings are pretty lean out there and I don't know whether it's just the time of the year, or if we have too many attorney's around here. But fortunately Allen set everything up and even now his old partner Stewart Andrews comes around and keeps in touch. Funny how one thing leads to another. They sent me a client who just wanted a simple will, no big deal. Like everyone else he kept putting it off and then a close friend suddenly passed away and now it was a priority issue. Hank Preston personally called me and asked if I had any time to handle it. Hell that day I had nothing but time, so I called the guy at his office and because his schedule was full, I agreed to make a house call that evening. Bottom line was that it was a simple will and two days later I delivered it to his home, along with my bill. Shortly after I dropped it off, his wife had some friends over to play cards and they got to discussing my house call and billing rate. The very next day I received a call from one of the wife's friends inquiring about a property transfer and some other things. My point is that I went from sitting around doing nothing to being nearly overloaded, all in a few days."

"Then just after Christmas I stopped by the Courthouse to drop off some papers and a young lawyer I met while I was still with the CSPD, stopped me in the hall and asked if I might be looking for a partner. Seems that he and a lot of others are sharing the pie and his slice seems to be getting smaller and smaller. He told me that he saw my Lexus, what I wore and had an idea of where I lived and wanted to join someone who was successful rather than the group that he was with. I thought that it was kind of funny in a way, yet sad too."

"So what did you tell him?" Art asked.

"Just tried to be polite and said that I worked better by myself and that if I ever changed that, he'd be one of the first people that I'd contact. But the guy actually knew what I drove and the neighborhood where I lived. I guess it all goes back to Allen Sheffield telling me that it was all in the perception."

"Hell, I'm impressed," laughed Art, and since you're so successful and have a big car and a huge house, you can buy lunch."

"I think that it's my turn anyway," smiled Brent.

"I know that you won't ask so I'll tell you that nothing is new on the Harrington House case. NYPD apparently notified Interpol, asking to have them check out a list of clothing designers that Tani had worked for. Sounded like they had questioned everyone in New York that was in the industry and came up with a list of shows she modeled in covering the last 24 months. Now the last 6 months or so she was out here with you so basically they went back 18 months before that. As of late yesterday NYPD hadn't heard a word. Captain Grimes told me that he had one of his men going through the foreign newspapers in the New York Public Library looking for unexplained deaths in the clothing industry. I don't know where that will go?" said Thomas.

"I personally believe that it was all about the Yakuza and somebody getting mad at someone else," said Brent. "Tani's death was no more than a message from Group A to Group B. And the deaths in New York were all by group B wanting to catch up with Group A. Where it goes from there who knows, but I seriously doubt that it'll ever return back here or be solved."

"Yeah I kind of had that idea too," said Thomas.

The two old friends had talked for a long time before returning to work. Brent ran an errand on the way home and arrived late that afternoon. Ta was in the garage, lying under his California car fixing something when he pulled in.

"Something break?" Brent asked, kneeling down next to the car so that he could look under it.

"It's just getting old, Brent. Needs more tender loving care than it used to." They talked for another minute and Brent entered the house and walked to his office, plopping behind his big desk. It was all perception Allen had lectured him over and over. It was what people first noticed and here was his handyman-gardener working on a car in the garage not because he enjoyed tinkering with them

120

but because the darn thing probably needed to be replaced. His Lexus was all about business and write-offs. But Ta's car was what Christy and Michi drove on errands or just shopping or even in going to church on Sundays. He took a pad of yellow lined paper from his desk drawer and walked downstairs to the basement. The entire south end of the basement was crowded with Gus' old antique furniture. Each item had been carefully wrapped in moving blankets and as he began to examine the closest one he suddenly remembered Henry telling him that he maintained a complete inventory up in his small office next to the servant's quarters. Brent took the stairs to the second floor two at a time and found the file cabinet and drawer just as Henry had told him. He took all of the file folders and rushed back down to his office. An hour later he had separated them into different piles on his desk. Then he picked out several larger pieces that he just thought looked ugly, and made a phone call back east to the broker he'd sold Gus' desk to. Because she had only purchased collector items, within a few minutes it was all over with, and he locked the remaining stack of folders in his desk drawer. The three pieces would bring in a huge amount of money even after all of the fees were paid to insure, transport and sell them.

Brent sat wondering if he'd done the right thing, or whether Gus' ghost would be haunting him forever. Then he remembered Allen Sheffield telling him that Gus was out of the picture and that it was solely his decision when he'd sold her antique desk. She had trusted him to do what he thought best, and to just get past the guilty feeling and go for it.

As soon as he got the check deposited in the

bank he would purchase a four door, four-wheel drive truck with every available option for Ta. Up until he'd performed his ceremony where he couldn't leave the grounds for a while, he'd been using his own car to get gardening supplies and maintenance materials. A house this big and old, always needed maintenance and a truck would certainly make Ta's job easier. Besides if he placed a logo on the side and had his company, the one that held the title to the house buy it, then it would be a write-off for him.

That left the crappy old car for Michi and Christy to run around in and again it was perception. The more he looked at it safety entered the picture. After what had happened to Tani, he didn't want Michi or her mother stranded by the side of the road because the clunker had broken down again. But women looked at cars and SUVs differently than men did. Maybe he'd just let Michi pick out whatever she'd be happy with?

Chapter 14

Like her sister Tani, Michi Mishinko was a strikingly beautiful young Eurasian woman, who could easily have joined her sister in the modeling business. In fact Tani had even suggested it on numerous occasions. The two sisters separated in age by only two years were almost carbon copies of each other, tall, leggy, long black hair, slim figures, exotic features and overwhelming smiles. But Tani had the personality and attitude to parade around nearly naked on a runway and Michi didn't.

While growing up the two sisters had been extremely close. Being Eurasian at a time and place where that combination wasn't that popular, they had quickly learned to look out for each other. Having a doting father who closely resembled Quasimodo hadn't helped their social life either. But again being different and looking Eurasian probably contributed to their lack of boyfriends. But by the time they entered their teenage years both girls had begun to mature and suddenly the boys their own age were hesitant to ask them out for fear of being refused or embarrassed by them. Rumors circulated about them dating older men and they were considered too mature for young men their own age. Of course it was all a lie and the girls spent many dateless nights wondering what they'd done wrong.

Right from the beginning Tani always had a plan for her future and when she finally turned 18, she told Michi that she'd be leaving soon and going to New York City to pursue a modeling career. She never returned, but as her career grew and she traveled around the world, she always kept in touch with her younger sister who had chosen to become a clothing designer. Since she was struggling in her chosen field, Tani had begun to send her money on a regular basis to help keep her afloat. By that time Michi had moved out on her own renting a small one-room apartment. However it wasn't long before she returned home after moving from one moderately successful job to a growing company that eventually closed up. At that point Michi decided that maybe living with your parents wasn't that bad after all and she plunged back into the fashion design business with a vengeance.

As far back as they could remember each summer at the Fourth of July, or wintertime around the holidays, they would visit their Aunt Alice and Uncle Henry in Colorado Springs. They'd been told to stay in the servant's quarters and to never ever get in Mrs. Harrington's way. The one thing that they really looked forward to during each visit, was when Uncle Henry took them to the Cheyenne Mountain Zoo just up the road and they could see all of the animals and ride on the carousel. Sometime during their visits they'd always play dress-up and pretend that they were the Mistress of the Manor. Who would have guessed?

Michi had been the first one to notice Brent, their Aunt and Uncle's new boss. She'd immediately been drawn to him, but her sister Tani had laid first claim. Michi knew in her heart that if she didn't quickly move on, then she'd somehow screw everything up for her sister. They'd discussed finding guys and settling down for several years and she knew that Tani was about at the end of her modeling career, her choice and not the industry's. She best described it as having been there and done that once too many times. So with no competition whatsoever, Tani had married and settled down, something that she'd dreamt about doing for several years. Then the killings of her and the others. Michi was horrified, but when Brent had asked for her help, she'd discussed it with her parents and then agreed.

Now she was the Mistress of the Manor, a position that she'd never in a million years would have guessed she'd get. She doubted that old strict Mrs. Harrington III could have foreseen it either. But here she was, married to a handsome lawyer who treated her like a queen, and now she was the honest to God, Mistress of the Manor. And her husband had even hired her parents to be his caretakers. So much had happened in so short a time.

Looking back at their youth, if the truth was known, Tani was always the one that dressed to the nines and looked like a queen. Michi had always been the tomboy type, dressing in whatever was handy and comfortably helping her father in the small garden he maintained or washing the family's car. Years may have passed, but Michi hadn't changed a bit. She was proud of what she had become, very conservative and dedicated to her husband and her family. Several times Brent had caught her vacuuming one of the rooms as her mother cooked or did the laundry. He'd tried to tell her, but she just wasn't the type to sit back and let someone else do something that she considered necessary.

With their membership at the Broadmoor Golf Club came a number of other advantages, like the fantastic spa and salon. And the Hotel's small shops were unbelievable in every way. However

Michi had always been concerned about money and what things cost so in the beginning, about the only time she patronized any of the Hotel's businesses was when Brent insisted. From the Hotel's management standpoint having a beautiful young woman using any of their facilities was a definite plus and something that they'd like to photograph and brag about.

About the only thing that had displeased her so far had been the weather. From a lifetime in sunny warm Southern California, she'd entered an icebox with bone chilling cold and deep snow. But Brent had purchased a shiny new 4-wheel drive vehicle for her, and at least if the weather was bad and she had to go out, she'd be ok. He'd even gotten a huge new truck for her father, who still couldn't drive it beyond the front gate, but it wouldn't be much longer before his ceremony time was up and he could hit the streets again. But the huge 4-door truck just looked his size and at lunch one day he'd excitedly explained to Michi how it had every option the manufacturer offered and a few aftermarket items as well. Never in a lifetime would he have been able to afford such a truck. And Brent had even offered to have a plow installed on the front end, but Ta couldn't figure out what he'd plow since the drive and walks were all heated, so he'd thanked him and declined the offer. In fact Ta didn't even have to spread any Ice Melt either. Old Mrs. Harrington sure had known how to live he thought and said a quiet prayer to thank her.

Michi looked forward to the arrival of spring. She liked the flowers, trees with leaves and being able to walk outside and around the grounds without a jacket. The smell of freshness in the air and the privacy the shrubbery provided when it was in full bloom. Knowing how busy her father would be preparing and planting all of the flowerbeds and maintaining the landscaping. For him this was a dream job and she was very pleased that Brent had made him the offer. Even her mother seemed happier than she had in a long time. In reality, most of the rooms were rarely used. Brent used his office, the bedroom, the kitchen and the garage. He occasionally would shoot pool with her, but that was about it. He joked about walling off the rooms he didn't use and at first she thought that he was serious, but then caught on.

Guests were few, mainly his friend from the police department and his wife whom she liked, Stewart Andrews and his wife who she also had grown to like, and a few others. Visitors were many, all clients and entertained in his large office just inside the front door. She sometimes wondered when the client would be an attractive woman, all by herself, but Brent had told her that business was business. Occasionally someone from the law firm in Denver would appear and most recently it had been the same pretty young woman, who Brent identified as the managing partner's granddaughter who had a great figure and favored skintight short dresses. However Brent seemed to handle all of them with ease.

She knew that something was wrong with the newspaper story about the five deaths at Harrington House, but so far neither her husband or father would elaborate on it. What had Tani been involved in? Their phone conversations covered nearly everything, but for the life of her she could never remember being told about anything dangerous that Tani had done. Sure she'd had many suitors and occasionally would stay with one or another, but she always moved on. Could one of them been seeking revenge. She doubted that they'd kill everyone or have the courage to kill only her. It was a mystery that was never far from her mind.

With Tani's death, all of her personal effects and clothing had become Michi's to do with what she wished. Her request to Brent had been for a sewing machine so that she could alter them, not in size, but style. She didn't like everything hanging out or so short that it was difficult to sit down, so being an experienced clothing designer she had begun at one end of the closet and slowly worked her way through it. Each item was stylized exactly for her and by her. Brent was so happy with the way they turned out, that he insisted on visiting the various restaurants and amenities at the Hotel on a more regular basis. Besides it was all perception, and Allen had warned him about forgetting it, and becoming too complaisant.

As their appearances at the Hotel's facilities increased, so did their invitations to social gatherings, many of which turned out to be fundraisers for the host's favorite charity. Knowing what Gus had told him about these affairs, and wannabe social climbers, he'd do a lot of research before accepting one. Ironically the more he turned down, the more he received including invitations to join several businesses' board of directors. It soon became obvious to Brent how the high society social structure of Colorado Springs was set up and he suggested that Michi join one of the more prestigious groups. Again it was all perception.

Brent's law practice was becoming profitable, but a good portion of his business still was derived from the referrals of Sheffield, Andrews, Preston and Blatt in Denver. He'd discussed it with Stewart Andrews, who to a certain extent had replaced Allen Sheffield as both his friend and partner.

"It just makes me nervous Stew," Brent said.

"Its just business Brent, and they've been around for a long time. But while their practice in Denver is growing, the original partners like me, are getting older and want out. So Hank Preston ascended to the Number 1 position and he's happy to avoid having to set up another office down in the Springs. That part is just a question of economics. You get the business and the money and they're pleased that their client is happy and that they didn't have to send someone all of the way down here. Now on the other hand the client is pleased that he has local service and in some cases you even make house calls. Now could you picture making a house call up in Denver? I can't recall ever hearing of one in my firm."

"I guess that as I look around and see a lot of starving or marginal law firms, I don't want to be in that position," said Brent.

"You just have to lighten up a bit. You have it made and you have to learn to sit back and enjoy what you have. Building a bigger and better practice is a great idea, but from where I stand, you really don't need it. You have all of the business down here from my firm and you've also managed to pick up a lot on your own. And Allen was right, it's all in how people perceive you. With this house, your Lexus and how you dress, they automatically think that you're a winner and they want to be represented by a winner, not a loser. As I look around, you're so far ahead of the curve, that I suggest doing a little pro bono work on the side."

"Like what?" Brent asked.

"I don't know, maybe something for one of the charity groups, or maybe talk to a Judge you know and see what he has to offer, or better yet just look around, maybe even talk to Art Thomas.

Chapter 15

"So you're the big time lawyer man that going to save my ass?" laughed the man sitting across the table. He was dressed in an orange jumpsuit and wore flip-flops with white gym socks. His head was cleanly shaven and his muscular arms were covered with jailhouse tattoo's, most of which Brent couldn't decipher.

They were inside the El Paso County Jail and the prisoner was wearing handcuffs attached to the arms of his chair and leg irons. The heavy steel chair was bolted to the concrete floor with Grade 5, 1-inch steel security bolts, the kind that you can't unscrew but have to cut off with a torch. Brent looked around and smiled. He hadn't been inside the County Jail since he'd retired from the police department, but nothing had changed. Everyone wearing orange was innocent and had been set up for the bust. Even a guy who'd been apprehended driving a carload of drugs north on Interstate 25, a direct shipment from friendly old Mexico, claimed that he didn't know where it had come from. It wasn't his. Nor was the man found holding onto a smoking gun, aware that he'd killed another person in a grocery store parking lot all over a parking space. Nope, everyone here was definitely innocent, he was sure of it.

This dumb ass had beat his wife to a bloody pulp in front of witnesses, before he pulled out a gun and fired a shot at her. Their 2-year-old child had been killed because he'd been such a lousy shot and now he was pretending to be Mr. Big in a lockup of some really nasty people.

"You're wrong Carlos, I'm only here to see if you're worth representing. Next I'll talk to your wife and get her spin on it. Maybe I'll represent one of you, but I'm not certain that you're worth saving. I mean what kind of a piss ant shoots his own kid?"

Carlos was seething with anger and tried to get up but the cuffs held him down. One of the guards standing outside the closed door heard him yell out some obscenity and rushed in only to find Brent with a broad smile across his face.

"You're a real loser Carlos," Brent smiled before closing his attaché case and standing up.

The man in orange was ready to explode. Who did this freaken lawyer think he was, and he yelled out "I'll get even with you," as two deputies dragged him down the hallway.

"You don't even know how to shoot," laughed Brent egging him on and hoping that his heart would explode and save the County some money.

He had returned to his office, looked up the number for the County's District Attorney's Office and dialed it. Brent really didn't know anyone there so eventually he got shuffled around to the Volunteer Coordinator. Finding that wasn't the right place, he finally was transferred to some faceless Assistant DA. He identified himself, related his meeting with Carlos Gonzales, said he'd decided not to represent him and that if whoever was assigned to the Gonzales Case, needed any help in prosecuting him, then he was available at no charge. The ADA copied down his name and phone number, thanked him for calling, and hung up. Brent figured that was the end of it and the next morning he called Stewart Andrews to tell him about it and also Art Thomas.

"You haven't heard?" asked Thomas.

"I hate this old routine, but you haven't left me any other choice. Heard what?" asked Brent.

"They kicked Carlos Gonzales loose early this morning. Somebody inside tried to knife him last night and this morning his Public Defender got his case thrown out because none of the arresting officers could remember reading him his rights. They all remember hearing it, but the scene was a mess and no one could testify to actually doing the reading. The Public Defender was taking him over to Memorial Hospital to get him patched up and recommended that Carlos consider filing a lawsuit against the County. I talked to the Sheriff and he said that it was a mess from the start and that he was going to talk to his men again."

"So the guy kills his own kid, beats his wife to a pulp and walks?"

"He's a free man until the District Attorney finds something that he can charge him with. Right now it's just his word against hers and he's willing to admit that he sometimes drinks and abuses her."

"What about the gun? It must have his fingerprints on it."

"They've got the gun and it matches up to the bullet that killed the kid and several more that they dug out of the walls and furniture from past attempts, but his prints aren't on it and there's no trace of powder on his hands."

"So the guy wore gloves, that's nothing original."

"You'd guess, but when the paramedics arrived there was blood all over the tiny room. She was bleeding and the kid's heart was pumping out the rest of it. The paramedics were switching gloves, too many people in the room trying to help and messing it up and Carlos was like a caged rat trying to get away. I've got another call, got to go," and Thomas hung up.

Brent sat for several minutes, his anger nearly boiling over. He dialed the garage, found Ta and asked him to join him. Minutes later Ta walked in and Brent motioned him to a seat and began to explain what had happened and that he should keep a close eye on things for a while, including his daughter and wife. The phone rang for a second time and he answered it.

"It's me again," laughed Thomas. "I just got the real story from the Judge's bailiff. Seems that our bad boy was asked by the Judge if he'd been read his rights and how did he plead? Carlos answers yes, but not by the cops. The Judge then asked who read him his rights and Carlos tells him one of the Paramedic's did. Now I'm just guessing here but I think that maybe the fight to take Carlos down thinned the ranks and with the mess and gore in the room one of the uniforms probably began to read the card, then got taken out or sick and the paramedic picked it up and continued on. That's why everyone heard it, but none of the cops had actually read it. A technically maybe, but one that turned him loose on the street again."

"You're kidding?" smiled Brent.

"Justice at its finest," laughed Thomas. "So now the wife is in the hospital under guard, her son is in the mortuary awaiting an autopsy, and he's free as a bird. I bet this will keep the lights on tonight over at the DA's offices," Thomas joked.

"Yeah, I called over there yesterday and volunteered to help hang the guy, but now that he's out, I can forget about that one. Think that the wife will sign a complaint or testify against him?"

"Would you? She's an illegal alien so the Immigration people will probably pick her up as soon as the hospital turns loose of her. Adios and goodbye."

"That really sucks," replied Brent.

"You bet it does. Got to go my friend, keep in touch and watch your back," and Captain Art Thomas hung up.

"I can't believe it Ta, the very first time I try to do something nice and help out, it blows up right in my face. Now the perp is out on the street ready and willing to terrorize anyone that comes in contact with him and there isn't anything that the police can do to stop it until he kills someone else."

Ta just sat and listened to his son-in-law but his mind was already racing ahead. If Brent had somehow exposed himself or the family to danger, then it was up to Ta to protect them. However, he still had two weeks to go on his ceremony, but until then he'd increase his surveillance of Harrington House both inside and outside. He'd lost one daughter to the Yakuza and he wasn't about to lose anyone else to some crazies.

Unbeknown to Brent and the others, Ta had built a small Shinto Shrine in a service room at the back of the oversized garage. The small rooms had been included during the last remodeling at Henry's request to provide indoor storage space for the garden implements, the various lawn mowers and edger's, fertilizers, seeds, starter plants, wheel barrels, garden tractor, trailer, sweeper, ladders, paints and anything else that was needed to maintain the house and grounds. Frank Harrington had been happy to oblige since by moving it indoors he could eliminate the unsightly metal shed in the back yard and by building rooms he could eliminate most of the dust and dirt that settled on his prized Duzenberg.

Periodically when Ta disappeared and no one could find him, he'd be there doing what his mother had taught him to do, worshiping his Shinto "Gods," called "Kami." While they lived in California Christy knew about it, but found it difficult for a westerner to understand and so while she practiced her religion, he practiced his. Candles burned most of the time and he was making his own by melting down some large ones that he'd found in the basement. Ta had hand made his own Torji gates to mark the entrance to his shrine and a pair of miniature wooden Komainu (guardian dogs) to protected it. A small battery operated fountain was near the entrance, which Ta used for purification of his hands and mouth. Today he entered, performed his small ritual, lit another candle and paid his respects. Then, he left the room, returned to the small security room between the main house and the garage and checked on the status of the front gate, and the monitors for the surveillance cameras. Henry had always maintained a small workbench in the corner room of the garage and Ta found an old Japanese sharpening stone and began to sharpen his knife. Let them come, he thought and they did.

It was just past 1 AM when the low-rider quietly passed by the front gate at a slow speed. At the corner a block north, it turned around in the intersection, paused for several minutes and returned the way it had come. It slowly circled the block twice as its occupants looked for an easy way to get inside the large estate. The eight foot tall black wrought iron fence was climbable but it wouldn't be easy, so the car circled again and finally stopped 100 feet north of the front gate and across the street in front of a neighbor's house. Since the homes on that side sat back from the street and were protected by shrubbery, there wasn't much chance that the car or its occupants would be seen by the neighbors. The two men now high on meth got out, but the ceiling light hadn't turned on. They quietly closed the door, walked to the trunk and removed two large red plastic containers of gasoline. One man crossed the street and tried to keep to the shadows as he approached the front gate and surprisingly found it unlocked. Thinking that it was a trap and that if opened an alarm would sound, he checked for tripwires, pushed it open and ran back across the street to the bushes. Nothing happened, other than the gate slowly and quietly swung back to its original position. He waved to his partner and the two men quickly crossed the street carrying the plastic red gas cans, stepped onto the grounds of Harrington House and slipped into the bushes and evergreens. The first man had been here before, but Carlos didn't know it. As high as they were on meth, they were invincible and nothing could stop them. They sat quietly whispering for some time, planning the best approach. One would make his way to the rear and start a fire and the other one would do the same out front. As the occupants rushed out, Carlos would simply shoot them and hope that he got the bastard lawyer. Then it would be back in the car and escape, and escape now meant all of the way back to Mexico.

They had coordinated their watches and his partner had seven minutes to get in position. As soon as Carlos heard or saw the flames, he'd splash gas on the front of the house and light it, before running back to his hiding place in the shrubbery. The plan was set and his partner disappeared around the corner. Five long minutes passed and Carlos wondered why he couldn't smell the gasoline fumes? What the hell was the guy doing? Maybe he'd wait a few more minutes.

Ta watched the monitors as the low-rider drove up and back on the street in front of the house and then as it rounded the corner and circled the block. He watched the two men enter the estate and he watched as they carried in the red containers of gasoline. Then suddenly the big man turned off the alarm system, backed away from the security room and left the building in stealth mode. In seconds he was outside hidden by the very bushes and evergreens that he'd been carefully taking care of. The first man approached the rear of the house and Ta reached out and in one blow broke his neck. The man collapsed to the ground as Ta easily picked him up and then the container of gasoline and raced around the north corner of the garage. He quietly laid the man on the ground, set the can beside him and moved back around the building and through the shrubs to Carlos.

By the time Carlos heard Ta, he was standing behind him. He tried to speak, but had lost his voice as the large man reached out and touched him on his neck, pressing a nerve. Carlos instantly collapsed to the ground. Ta checked his watch, looked up and down the street and carried both bodies, one dead and the other alive to the low-rider. He positioned them in the front seat, went back and got the gasoline and emptied the gas cans inside the car and tossed them inside. Ta paused looking up and down the deserted street, lit a match, tossed it inside and raced for the mansion. He heard the fumes ignite as he ran and he cleared the gate just as the car exploded. In seconds he was back inside the house, the alarm turned on and the front gate locked. He turned on the video recorders, and added a "power surge interruption" message to the computer. Another minute and he was lying on the couch in the servant's quarters pretending to be asleep. Alongside of him lying on the floor was a book, its pages well worn.

"Ta wake up," yelled Christy. "I heard an explosion."

Ta jumped up, forgetting his shoes and slippers and raced down the hall and into the main building with his wife right behind him. Christy raced up the stairs to find her daughter and Brent as Ta disarmed the house alarm system and then raced to the front door. He could hear the sounds of the approaching fire engines, then the flashing lights bounced off the entrance door and he pointed across the street to Christy who had just come up behind him. A car parked at the curb was burning furiously and as the firemen arrived they struggled to find a working unfrozen fire hydrant for their hoses. Now police cars were arriving followed by an El Paso County Sheriff's deputy and the private service that protected the Hotel and the immediate area. Soon there wasn't any place to park, but by then the flames had been doused and the fire nearly extinguished.

By now Brent had run upstairs, gotten dressed and walked down to the entrance gate as he and Ta watched the excitement, just as all of his neighbors were doing. Ta ran back to the house and the big entrance gate slowly opened. Across the street everyone had gathered to discuss what had happened and the police wandered over to see if anyone had witnessed it, but no one had, especially at this hour of the night, or was it early morning? They filled out their reports, called for a wrecker and it was about that time that it became interesting.

"Hey Sarge, take a look at this," yelled the tow truck operator who had just winched the car onto his flatbed truck. The metal carcass of the vehicle was still smoldering as the cop reluctantly climbed up on the bed and shined his flashlight inside. By now the fire trucks were leaving, as were most of the police vehicles. The sergeant immediately called his dispatcher at the communications center and reported that he thought that the car contained the remains of one or more bodies. The Crime Scene Technicians were immediately dispatched and the crowd of bystanders seemed to grow. Just as the snow began falling, two detectives arrived on the scene and by this time one of the police officers had found a big green tarp and he had covered the remains of the car on the back of the tow truck.

Brent saw the detectives arrive, didn't recognize either of them, so he said good night to his neighbors and walked across the street and back up his drive. As he approached the front door, he heard the sound of the gate locking after it closed. They talked about it between themselves for a few minutes and went back to bed. Ta turned on the house alarm, and then crawled into bed with his wife, before falling fast asleep.

Of course the next morning the event of the previous evening was the topic of conversation around the breakfast table. Everyone had his own version, except Ta who just quietly ate while checking out the Sports Section of the local newspaper. After finishing, Brent walked outside, estimated the depth of the snow at two inches, and looked up and down the street. It was as if nothing had ever happened. A beautiful white blanket covered the entire area including the trees and bushes. It reminded Brent of a picture he'd seen on a Christmas card long ago. A winter wonderland, he laughed to himself as he settled into his office chair preparing to complete a client's last will and testament that he'd begun yesterday.

The ringing of the telephone next to his desk brought him out of his trance and he immediately answered it.

"Sounds like you had a barbeque last night and forgot to invite me," joked Art Thomas.

"Morning Art," said Brent. "When that thing blew up it had everyone in the neighborhood on the move. Christy got Michi and me up thinking that the building was on fire and by then Ta was running down the driveway in his bare feet. I guess we all forgot about the smoke detectors and the fire sprinklers here in the house. We just rolled out and ran."

"Well I just wanted to let you know that we have a tentative ID on the victims," said Thomas.

"Like in more than one?" asked Brent.

"Two, exactly," Thomas replied "and you're never going to guess who they were?"

"Door-to door salesmen or maybe some religious fanatics out to save my soul?" Brent joked.

"Nope, Carlos Gonzales in person and some unknown guy. We'll know more later today, but those were the ID's that were found on them. Their wallets were packed so tightly that the insides didn't completely burn. The tow truck driver actually discovered them and because of the weather the detectives had everything brought back to our garage. The Coroner removed the bodies at that point and our tech's spent the remainder of the night going over it."

"Ok Art, now give me your best guess about what happened, because suddenly I'm starting to get concerned here."

"I figured you might be that's why I called. Now last night one of the uniforms managed to get a City Street sweeper to make several passes up and down your street. About that time the snow was falling pretty hard and the guy figured that any evidence left out there was lost so he took a chance and rounded up the sweeper. Our techs will start going over it next, but we don't know how full it was when it reached your street."

"Ok, so far I have a clean street," Brent joked.

"Well," Thomas paused for a moment. "According to my detectives apparently Carlos and his buddy were out at a bar on east Platte Avenue drinking heavily. In fact the bartender was just about to shut off both of them. Then a third party appeared and the bartender thinks that the guy sold them some meth. I guess in this joint that isn't too unusual. So the bartender gets busy and when he turns around they're both gone, and so was the drug dealer."

"As I understand you, you believe that they got drunk and then took some meth? Then they decided to kill me?" Brent asked.

"Maybe he'd been thinking about it all day. What I heard was that you really seemed to piss him off over at the County Jail. I keep telling you to be nicer to people, but you don't seem to hear me," Thomas chuckled.

"I swear that I'm never ever going to

volunteer to help somebody out ever again. Especially anyone sitting in the County Jail."

"Brent this investigation is just beginning so I'll let you know if anything else develops. I knew that you'd read about it in the papers or hear it on the radio so I just wanted to get you out front of the story. As of right now we don't believe that Carlos had any other people involved, other than the two of them. We are curious about how they managed to blow themselves up. And finally, the autopsies will be performed sometime today. I'll keep in touch," and Thomas ended the conversation.

Mid morning, Stewart Andrews arrived, Christy buzzed him in and he now sat in the kitchen with a hot cup of coffee in his hand. During the past month Brent had asked him to replace Allen Sheffield and Stewart had quickly agreed with the promise that he wouldn't have much to do and was more a partner in name than anything else. That would make Hank Preston the only remaining partner in the Denver office extremely happy, because by rights Stewart was senior to him and could reclaim the throne any time that he wanted. To confuse the competition Stewart had suggested just leaving Allen's name on the practice and adding his, something that Brent hadn't thought about. Sheffield, Andrews & Williams sounded a lot bigger and more impressive that just plain old Andrews and Williams. Brent had agreed and was in the process of changing the State charter.

As they sat discussing the topic of the day, namely one Carlos Gonzales, the UPS delivery arrived at the front gate, followed closely by FedEx. Since UPS usually brought boxes and FedEx legal documents from Denver and elsewhere, Ta would normally open the fourth garage door, take out his 2-

wheel dolly and push it down to the gate. He'd use his key to unlock it and then he'd reverse the procedure and return to the garage where he'd sort through the two deliveries. Priority was always given to Brent's FedEx deliveries. So today he'd sorted through it looking for Brent's name, and then quickly carried it into the kitchen where he found Stewart and Brent in the middle of a discussion. He placed it on the table, turned and left.

Back in the garage he began opening the boxes and when he reached the largest and heaviest one he found that it was addressed to him. He read the label not recognizing the sender, then carefully took out his knife and slowly cut around the top of the box, staying within a half inch of the edge. Carefully he lifted a corner while looking inside for any sign of a trip wire or connection. Finally satisfied that it was a legitimate shipment he opened it and froze. It was packed very tightly with Japanese Shinto Shrine objects, things that one would use to build a shrine in one's home. Material, candles, statues, whatever was needed for a small shrine was packed in the box. He looked for a card or something from the sender, and when he couldn't find one he knew who had purchased it. Very carefully he carried it into his small shrine in the back of the garage and placed it on a table. He'd get back to this tonight, after Christy had gone to sleep.

Stewart had hung around for several hours then left to pick up his wife for a charity fundraiser. Finally Brent was alone in his office when Quasimodo quietly knocked on the door jam and Brent motioned him in getting up from behind his desk and joining him in a side chair. He could see that the big man wanted to say something, but didn't exactly know how to say it.

"You look like someone with something on his mind," joked Brent and Ta just nodded his head.

"Are you happy with it?" Brent asked.

"Very much so," Ta smiled for the first time.

"Good, then lets shake hands on it, ok?"

"How did you know?" he asked.

"Ta, it's a long story and I guess that Michi mentioned something about you cleansing the house. Then Christy and I talked and we both felt that whatever you were doing was working because the house seemed to feel different. Neither of us could actually explain or describe it, but the house felt better than it had in some time. I'm the first to admit that I'm not a very religious guy, but I've come to believe that you are. So I called Hank Preston up in Denver and he connected me to a Japanese client that had been using the services of the firm for many years. I explained what I knew and he agreed to get everything that you would need and send it down here directly to you. Since I was an outsider, and I can't remember what he called it, he felt that you should be the one to open the box."

"Some of it is very expensive," said Ta.

"My guess is that he'll just take it out in trade with the Denver office. If Hank Preston is having a bad day, maybe he'll bill me, but I'll just get even the next time he asks for my help. Over and above everything else, I want you to know that I fully approve of what you're doing and I will not interfere. If you need something else, just tell me."

Ta sat quietly for a moment not knowing what to say, then stood up to his full height, grunted and extended his hand to Brent, who gladly shook it.

Chapter 16

The young man was carefully watching the cross streets as he drove west on Lake Avenue. The weather had finally cleared and while it was still cold, the weatherman promised that spring wouldn't be that far off. The man hoped so, because the heater on his car had gone belly up last week and right now he didn't have the $1,200 to repair it. In his mind the car wasn't worth much more than that and if he had the heater repaired it would double the value of his investment. But no matter how he looked at it, the car was still a clunker. Finally he saw the right street sign and turned north. Half a block down he read the address on the huge wrought iron gate and turned in. He was awestruck with the size and beauty of the home and then he saw the sign "Harrington House" and the button for the maid. He rolled down the window, pushed the button and identified himself. The lock on the gate unlatched and he watched it swing open. With some trepidation, he drove in and around the fountain to the front door. He adjusted his tie and jacket, brushed off his pants and paused for a moment. He jokingly wondered if they offered valet parking and as he turned to get out, his door was blocked by a huge Japanese man who politely inquired who he was.

The man had escorted him to the front door, unlocked it with a key and ushered him inside. He'd taken his coat, patted him down like it was a police station, and led him through the double French doors into a dream office. He pointed to a chair and stood watching him. Phillip Paulson, shifted in his chair still wondering why Brent had called and asked to meet with him. He was probably one of the more successful young attorney's in Colorado Springs and from the looks of his surroundings he was doing a lot better than anyone else. In fact, it seemed like the guy really had some bucks, including a huge manservant that was still standing quietly beside him. Then the oriental guy was gone and standing in his place was Brent Williams, who eagerly shook his hand and surprisingly sat down in the chair next to his and put his feet up on the very large desk. Phillip thought that if he owned a desk like this, he'd probably spend most of his time polishing it.

"I'm glad that you could come," said Brent letting out a sigh.

"This is some place you've got. I'd come just to see what the inside looked like," joked Paulson.

"I actually inherited it," smiled Brent. "Sure is better than living in my car. Came complete with caretakers too." Brent paused.

"You look nervous, Phil," he said just as Christy knocked on the door and brought in some coffee. Phillip noticed the expensive looking coffee set and the dainty looking china cup and saucers.

"Maids too? Man I need to get a better job." he smiled.

"Actually they're my in-laws," smiled Brent. "The original couple that came with the house were killed and I asked these people to replace them. Ironically, they're blood relatives of the original ones. Ta gets a little protective about me, but let me assure you that it's not without cause. Now the reason that I asked you to stop by goes back to the day we met at the Courthouse and you asked me if I needed a partner, and if I did to please contact you first. You said it as sort of a joke. Well I don't need a partner at this point, but I do have a job that I don't have the time to handle. From what we've heard, you're a fine attorney, but the town seems to be overloaded with attorneys right now. So what I'd like to do is have you read through this file, and then if you're interested, let's talk about it. I have something to do in another room here, so make yourself at home and I'll be back in a while," Brent said, handing him the file and walking out.

Phillip Paulson got comfortable and read the contents of the file, then went back and read it again. Finally Brent stuck his head in the door, saw that Phil was through and joined him.

"I just noticed that it's past my lunchtime. Came through the kitchen and Christy wasn't there, so how about if we interrupt our business and go get something to eat cause I'm starved?"

"Sounds good to me," replied Paulson. But Brent had already turned and walked out. Phillip ran to catch up and they passed through a restaurant size kitchen, several smaller rooms and into the cavernous garage. The large Japanese man was standing next to a pearl white Lexus holding the door open and Brent slid in behind the wheel. Phillip got into the passenger seat and took a deep breath. There wasn't anything in the world that smelled as good as a new car with leather seats. But within minutes they had cleared the front gate, driven up the street to the Hotel and Brent was handing the keys to a valet. Being a starving attorney, Phillip didn't patronize places like this, preferring to grab a quick lunch from some fast food restaurant along the way, sometimes using coupons, but he quietly followed Brent into the Broadmoor Hotel's Tavern Room. Phillip noticed that everyone seemed to know Brent and they all addressed him as "Mr. Williams." Unfortunately the restaurant was filled with customers and the man immediately called the Broadmoor Golf Club Grille only to find that they too were filled and had a waiting line in the bar. Finally space was made available in the Golf Club Dining Room. Apparently Mr. Williams had some clout around here and again Phillip was most impressed.

"Sorry about the hassle Phil," Brent said. "I usually call ahead and they find someplace to hide me, but today I forgot that Christy would be out."

"Is Christy your wife?" he asked assuming that she was and wanting to confirm it.

"No, no, Christy is my mother-in-law and my housekeeper-cook. My wife's name is Michi. I've gotten her involved with several charities and today one of them had a luncheon. In fact I think that it was being held here on the other side of the lake."

"You play much golf when the weather's nice?" asked Phillip just to make some conversation.

"I belong to the Golf Club, but I'm not a golfer. Michi told me that I owned a really nice set of golf clubs, but I haven't seen them so my guess is that they're either in storage at the house or maybe I have a locker here at the Golf Club. Perhaps when the weather warms up I'll check it out."

"So you belong to the Broadmoor Golf Club, but you don't play golf?" Phillip smiled.

"Hey, it came with the house. The will didn't give me any options," Brent laughed just as their food arrived.

The two men ate and talked and when the bill

arrived Brent just signed it. The valet either saw them coming or someone had called ahead because by the time that they reached the entrance, the Lexus was waiting. In minutes they were back in the cavernous heated garage and the large Japanese gentlemen was opening Brent's door.

"Thanks for lunch, I appreciated it," said Phillip settling into his original seat in the office.

"You're welcome. I enjoyed the company. Usually Michi will have her mother prepare something and she'll bring it in here, or I'll just catch a bite to eat in the kitchen on my way out," said Brent.

"I couldn't help but notice that you have a sizeable dining room. Don't you use it?"

"Phil this is one huge house. That formal dining room is set up for 20 people. I don't even know 20 people that I'd want to invite to dinner. Since I've owned it I think that it's been used maybe three times and then it wasn't filled. When Gus was alive she was always entertaining and she ran this place like a general. She was the master or mistress of the house and everyone else was either a guest or slave. God bless her, but I can't live that way. Maybe I spent too much time on the street with the CSPD? When I lost my closest friend Allen Sheffield and Diane, then both of my caretakers, and my own wife, I guess my attitude changed a bit." smiled Brent.

"I can see where that might happen," agreed Phillip.

"The killers are still out there, that's one reason that Ta is so protective of me. I am now on my third marriage, extremely happy, have a gun permit, and my own law practice. In my mind it doesn't get much better than that."

"So please get to the part of why I'm here," said Phillip.

"I prefer not to handle any criminal cases. The name of my law firm is Sheffield, Andrews & Williams. Sheffield's dead, Stewart Andrews is mostly retired and that leaves me. Stew is constantly on my case about slowing down and smelling the roses. I think that he's probably right and that's exactly what he's done, but sometimes I just get caught up in something and won't let it go. My first marriage ended in a disastrous divorce. My second wife Tani who was Michi's older sister was murdered. Now that I'm able too, I'd like to cut back on my workload and who knows maybe I'll even find those missing golf clubs and learn how to play," Brent broke out in a broad smile.

"A good deal of my work comes from local referrals, however the better paying jobs are all out of the Denver office of Sheffield, Andrews, Preston and Blatt. Stew likes to think of us as a branch office. I'm told that as of yesterday they had 85 attorney's working for them up there, and down here it just me. Periodically I'll farm something out just to get it off my caseload, but everything originates and ends up here on my desk."

"Now as I understand this," said Phillip, "this is a criminal case that you want me to handle?"

"I do have a few preliminary questions," Brent replied. "Like I know that there are 8 attorneys working out of the building that you're in. Obviously my first question and maybe the deal breaker is how are you connected? Is there a firm in existence? Or do you merely share expenses?"

"In the beginning when we all thought that we were young and invincible we formed a law firm. Actually filed all of the papers, but then it fell apart because everyone believed that they'd be the best leader. Eventually we dissolved the company, paid off the IRS and we now are all independent operators or practitioners," said Phillip.

"I've obviously been watching you for some time. My suggestion is that if you accept this case and handle it properly, you'll need to get your own office and secretary. Put some space between yourself and the others because they will never be much better than what they are today."

"Why don't you just enlarge your own firm and hire me?" asked Phillip.

"I don't want the headaches. I work from home, dress anyway I want, call my own hours and don't have a Human Relations Department. I actually enjoy my job, but Stew is right, there's more work than we can handle. Hank Blatt took over the Denver firm as senior partner, and he's now calling the shots up there. Stew is actually senior to him and could return and take over if he wanted to, but he likes retirement and being my partner. I guess it's all who you know these days. Denver is really big on customer service so I guess if you're a businessman and you're happy and your only kid wants to get married down here, then we're just the people to prepare the prenuptial. Then you'll buy a home, need a will, lease a car, have kids and need an update or sometimes a divorce. Maybe you're injured on the job, run over on the Interstate by a semi or get pissed off at a neighbor's barking dog. Whatever it is, we're there for you. I farm out all of the DUI's because no matter how well it ends it's going to cost the client a bundle and he won't be happy about it. But you'll remember that I told you up front how it might end. Now the businessman decides to expand and we handle acquisitions and mergers too. We farm out most bankruptcies, tax cases and most criminal cases, not because they aren't profitable, simply because they're too time consuming. But for this to work to your advantage, you'll have to take some directions from us too. Like you need to dump the wreck that you drive, and lease something nice. Give the off-the-rack suits to Goodwill and get a tailor. Find a nice office or work out of your home. If you don't have the room, then look around for a better house. If you don't look the part, then you'll just wind up like the other attorney's in your building."

"To be honest about it Brent, I just don't have the money to do that and set up my own office. While it's always been my dream, that costs a bundle too," replied Paulson.

"Being connected to us has some advantages, like we're always online to several legal research firms. Also we have all of the fancy canned legal document preparation programs too. If it has anything to do with the law, then we have it either here or up in Denver. You can see where having the resources really cuts down on the time normally spent in researching, editing, filing, document preparation, proofing and the like. You'll have an entire staff at your fingertips."

"Wow, that's really some setup. Ok, what do I have to do to get on board?" Paulson asked rather humbly.

"Do what we've discussed and handle the preliminaries including meeting with the client on this case. Oh, and if you're interested Stewart can refer you to a suitable bank for a low interest loan. He actually sits on the board of directors and owns an interest in it so it's a done deal," Brent laughed.

Phillip Paulson was sitting behind the

steering wheel of his old car, looking around at the interior and at the building that he rented space in. Both left a lot to be desired. Then one of his fellow attorneys rushed out the back door, waved and took off running for the Courthouse two blocks away. He found a parking space in the alley, pulled in and again looked around. Compared to where he'd just come from, this really sucked and Brent had been 100% correct. If he intended to remain in this profession and not become an ambulance chaser then he definitely needed to change. Tonight when both he and his wife got home, they needed to talk.

At Harrington House, Stewart had wandered in, dropped into one of Brent's side chairs and looked around.

"You look bored Stew?" smiled Brent. "Nothing exciting going on?"

"Actually it's quiet for the moment. I just got off the phone with Hank Preston. You know it's funny. When you're young and fresh out of school you want to build a huge organization. Then as you get older and the practice grows you get pushed up the food chain and away from the everyday action and your passion begins to cool. Hank just signed an agreement with some big privately held high tech company that wants to go public. We've done some work for them over the years and now they want us to put the whole package together. He figures that we'll need to hire at least a dozen people to replace the ones he's going to reassign. Actually it quite a coup for us, because we had a lot of competition. But I just can't seem to get as excited about it as I used to."

"Good, and since you don't have anything to do other than complain about making money, then you can join me tomorrow morning. Art Thomas called earlier and asked me to meet with him at around 9 AM. Said that he had a few things to go over. That is, if you can fit it into your tight schedule?" he laughed.

Chapter 17

Sitting around the conference room table at the Police Operations Center at 9 AM this morning were Captain Art Thomas, his two detectives Cane and Jones, Brent Williams and Stewart Andrews who had come along for the ride. Brent had stopped along the way and purchased six cups of some fancy hot steaming coffee concoction, which he'd handed out to everyone.

"You brought coffee and your attorney?" Thomas joked.

"Figured if I couldn't buy you off with the coffee then he could arrange bail," replied Brent with a smile.

"Brent, I'd like you to walk us through the night of the explosion, if you would?" said Jimmy Cane.

"No problem Jimmy. Around 10 o'clock, Michi and I went upstairs to bed. She'd been out in the caretaker's apartment helping her mother Christy hem a pair of slacks. I'd been working in my office and Ta was repairing one of the dishwashers in the kitchen. Apparently a clamp of some kind had come loose and he was replacing it with a new one. Christy said goodnight to him and went to bed about 10:30 or thereabouts and Ta checked the alarm panel in the security room, saw that all of the lights were "green" and then walked through the house. He does that every morning and every night before he goes to bed. We do have motion detectors, but they are never turned on unless no one will be in the house and that would be rare. So Ta fell asleep on the couch up in his apartment while reading a book. Ok, now at this point Harrington House is secure inside, and outside all of the alarms and spotlights are turned on. Regardless of the season, Mrs. Harrington had huge ground mounted floodlights installed and they are connected to a light sensor unit and automatic switches. I forget how many there are or how many watts are used, but they are commercial units that light up everything."

"Now it's the middle of the night and Christy is awakened by an explosion. Her bedroom is closest to the street and it apparently rocked her out of bed. She jumped up, grabbed a robe and rushed out thinking that something in the garage beneath her on the first floor had exploded. Ta who's a sound sleeper was on the couch still asleep, but she grabbed him and they ran through the house to warn us. I guess maybe I heard the explosion, but I must have been way off in la-la land, because it didn't register until Christy rushed into the room and woke us up. By now Ta was in the security room checking the lights. Because of Gus' paranoia, we have a superb fire alarm system in the house. Hidden sprinklers are everywhere, and then it dawned on Ta that it must be something outside, so he disarmed the house alarm and rushed out the front door in his bare feet. The rest of us were a few minutes behind him and by the time I caught up he was standing at the locked front gate watching the burning car and we both watched as the fire engines began to arrive. I then told Ta to go back inside before he caught a cold and I unlocked the front gate just as he pushed the button in the house. Then I joined the growing number of neighbors gathering across the street."

"Skipping ahead, we stood in the cold and watched until the tow truck arrived and then most of us went on home. I used my key to unlock the gate, relocked it and went back in the house and to bed. Guess that pretty much covers it."

"Didn't Ta's feet freeze in the cold and snow?" asked Jones.

"The entire driveway and all of the walks are heated. The story goes that Mrs. Harrington might have slipped on the ice at one time and when she remodeled the last time she had heating cables or maybe they're pipes installed, I'm not sure. It's really nice because even the garage floor has radiant heating in the concrete and floor drains too. One thing about Gus was that she definitely didn't scrimp on anything."

"So the burned out car wasn't on the flatbed tow truck when you went back inside?" asked Cane.

"I don't think so. About that time it really began to snow and everyone quickly disappeared," answered Brent.

"Let me bring you up to date," said Art Thomas. "The car was a low-rider and it was registered to one Carlos Gonzales. I assume that name strikes a bell with you?" he smiled. "The tow truck driver thought he saw a charred body inside and he called the sergeant over to check it out and eventually due to the weather, the Coroner hauled it to our indoor garage. They removed two charred remains from it. The Medical Examiner positively identified Carlos through both DNA and dental records. He apparently was sitting in the driver's seat at the time of the explosion and fire. Now in regards to the second body, well I'll let Matt explain that one."

"We found wallets from both bodies in the

burned out car. They only survived because they were so tightly pack together. Let's forget about Carlos for a minute. Perp 2 had a wallet and identification and at first we just assumed that it, like Carlos' was legitimate. But the driver's license was from California and when we tried to confirm it, it bounced out of the system. If that was phony then most likely so was everything else. So, we have a crispy critter here and no way to get fingerprints, nor could we get them from the car either since it was a burned out shell. But the techs did manage to get enough off the body to run a DNA. It indicated a strong possibility that the man was oriental or Asian. Now we ran it against the FBI databases and got zip. However when the killings first took place at Harrington House and your wife was killed, that was about a year ago. We were the lead detectives on that one too and we did recover some evidence that we didn't tell anyone about. One item was a cigarette butt found just outside the front gate. We already knew that no one in the house smoked and so we ran a DNA on it anyway hoping for the best, but couldn't match it up to anything. Then bingo we ran our burn guy against our in-house database of DNA samples and we got a hit. Brent, the second guy in the car most likely was one of the killers of Tani and the others."

Brent sat silently for a moment, stunned by what he'd been told.

"There's more too?" he asked.

"The Asian might have been killed before the car blew up? The ME has some concern about his neck being broken and whether it occurred before or after the explosion. We kind of think that maybe he got tossed around inside the low-rider, but who really knows?"

The killer or one of the killers had returned Brent thought. He reached over, pulled the telephone closer and punched in some numbers while turning on the conference room setting. Everyone in the room heard the phone ring once and then Ta answered it.

"Harrington House."

"Ta, it's Brent. I need you to tighten up our security and to keep Michi and Christy inside until I get there."

"Christy's here with me," replied Ta. "But Michi and Mrs. Andrews walked up to the Hotel just after you left. They didn't say exactly where they were going. Do you wish me to find them?"

"No you stay put, ok?"

"Ok, Brent."

Brent dialed another number from memory and everyone in the room listened as the phone at the main desk of the Broadmoor Hotel was answered.

"Good morning to you too. This in Brent Williams and I need to be connected to Hotel Security." They could hear the connection being made.

"Hotel Security, Adams speaking. How can I assist you?" said the distance faceless voice.

"Good morning Mr. Adams, this is Brent Williams. I have a emergency security issue in hand at the moment and I need your help. My wife Michi and her friend Mrs. Andrews, are somewhere on the Hotel's grounds and I need them to be found, protected and taken to Harrington House as quickly as possible. Are you staffed well enough to handle that this morning or will you need the help of the locals?"

"No problem Mr. Williams, I'll personally handle it. Should I be armed?"

"Definitely and be careful. And thanks for the help," and Brent hung up and looked around the table.

"I don't know what the hell is going on, but I sure wish that I did," he said with a sigh.

"We always figured that Tani was the target and the others collateral damage," said Thomas. "Then we passed it off to the NYPD because we ran out of leads and wanted them to follow up on her employers. Suddenly they're dead and the NYPD attributes it to the Yakuza. Next up is the clothing designer who flew off the rooftop and finally the NYPD contacted Interpol. Am I on track here?" asked Thomas.

"Yes," answered both Cane and Jones at the same time.

"So now Brent is convinced to do some pro bono work by both Stewart and myself, and he winds up with a perp in our County Jail and they get crosswise of each other. The perp gets turned loose on a technicality and wants to get even. He and his buddy show up at the house and I'm guessing they're ready to burn it down and shoot whoever comes out and something goes wrong. Now we discover that the buddy was probably involved in the original shootings? That's just about more coincidence than I can handle. So where did Carlos pick up the Asian guy? And since so much time has passed since the first murders, why was the guy still hanging around in Colorado Springs? Was he just watching and waiting for another crack at someone? Because the only one that he missed the first time, was Brent."

The room was deathly quiet, no one knew what to say. Then Brent broke the silence.

"If we're through here gentlemen, I need to

go."

Everyone nodded in agreement, but on his way out, Thomas motioned him aside.

"You still armed?" he asked.

"Yes, but I haven't been carrying, just keeping it in my attaché case, but I'll change that. However, this afternoon or tomorrow morning I plan on visiting the gun shop and buying enough for a small war. Whoever they are and for whatever reason they have me in their sights, I'm not about to go easy!"

Brent and Stewart raced home and by the time the Lexus was safely in the garage, the Broadmoor Hotel Security car was honking its horn at the gate. Finally Ta must have opened it because suddenly it swung open and when the car stopped, two large men got out, looked around and when they saw Brent they opened the back doors for the women to get out. Brent got their names, thanked them, tipped them and got the wives safely inside. He quickly explained what had happened.

"Are they after you?" Michi asked.

"Honey, I really don't know, but we're going to have to be careful until this thing plays out," Brent said.

He and Ta were sitting in the kitchen drinking coffee. Michi and Christy were upstairs, the Andrews had left and they were alone in the room.

"This just gets stranger and stranger," said Brent. "How many more days until your ceremony is over?" he asked.

"Five days," Ta answered.

"I called a guy I know that owns a big gun shop. He's going to meet me there tomorrow morning before they open. I'll fill out all of the forms and he'll send it into the CBI for a background check. By the time it gets approved which is usually a half hour that early in the morning, I'll have purchased a bunch of guns. Anything in particular that you favor?" Brent asked.

"No, I've never been that good with guns. Knives yes, but not guns."

"I'll cover that too, but a couple of double barrel shotguns might be nice. And some assault rifles, a few revolvers and some semiautomatic pistols would be good too. I have no idea what's going on, but we're sure not going to be caught unarmed anymore."

The following morning Brent purchased three Smith & Wesson revolvers, 2 double barrel shotguns, 2 AR-15 assault rifles with scopes, three Kimber .45 caliber semiautomatic pistols, and 3 AK-47's which are the choice of the world's terrorists. In addition he purchased three expensive knives, thousands of rounds of ammunition and a half dozen air pistols for training purposes. While Ta unloaded the car, Brent sat in his office working on the computer doing Internet searches for his favorite manufacturers of holsters, gun cases, shooting glasses and cleaning supplies. If this was going to be a war, then he planned on being prepared.

Later that evening Ta walked into Brent's office and sat down.

"I assume that the knives were for me?" he asked.

"I wasn't sure what to get so I just took one of each style. There also was a set of sharpening stones. Did you see that too?" Brent asked.

"Yes, I already have it on my workbench. Your choices were excellent and I'm going to put a razor edge on them."

"I bought those air pistols for training and I thought that we could set up a small practice range in the back of the garage. It doesn't need to be more than 15 feet long. Anything that we might get involved in is going to be up close and personal. I'm going to ask Michi to take a training course so that she can get a carry permit. Would you and Christy be interested in taking one too?" Brent asked.

"We rarely leave the house and as I said, I'm not too good with guns. But I will ask her tonight. I moved everything into the tiny security room. Is that ok?" Ta asked.

"That will work for tonight but tomorrow I'll load all of them and scatter them around the house. I think that you should keep one of the AK's in your apartment. They have 30 round clips and you can't screw them up. Just point and start pulling the trigger. They may not look like much, but they always work. I used to know a guy that loved them. He'd shoot up a storm and then lay them on the ground in the dirt and sand. When he got home, he'd wash them off with a garden hose and spray a little oil down the barrel and inside. In all of the time that we shot together the AK's never failed. Sometimes you could see the rust on them, but they just kept on going. Try that with one of the AR-15's or 16's and see how far you get," Brent laughed.

Two days later Brent had driven Michi and her mother to an all day gun safety-training course. With nothing else to do, he drove over to the Police Operations Center to see if Art Thomas was busy, or free to go to lunch later on. Jimmy Cane had seen him walk in and waved him over to his cubicle.

"You ok?" Cane asked.

"Yeah, I'm alright Jimmy. Concerned about the family, definitely. Still can't figure out why the guy would be after me?"

"Well I'm glad that you stopped by. Late yesterday we finally got some feedback on the NYPD's request to Interpol. Seems like two more people that your wife modeled for were found dead. One in France and another in Italy."

"So it's not over, is it?" asked Brent.

"Not by a long shot, especially after what happened here."

"I've talked to Ta about it, actually I showed him the private investigator's report that Allen ordered on Tani. The report mentioned the possible connection between one of her family members and the Yakuza. The guy didn't elaborate on it and I don't blame him. If he got too close then he might have been perceived as some kind of a threat and taken out. Ta told me that his uncle was a high ranking Yakuza and that Tani had been named after him as atonement for Ta coming to America and not following in the traditional family business. He's been here in the States a long time and he swears that he's never communicated with the uncle since leaving Japan."

"So that's the connection to the Yakuza?" asked Cane.

"I really don't know because from what I've learned, girls aren't that high up on the totem pole over there. But I guess if you have no one else and someone names their first born daughter after you, maybe you'd come around? Michi doesn't even know who the uncle is, so she's not involved. I'm just tossing some things around here, but do you suppose that someone in another family or gang or whatever they call them, got pissed off at the uncle and decided to send him a message? He's so well guarded that he knows that he can't get to the uncle, but he does have a niece living in the States that's highly visible."

"I guess it's a possibility," said Cane.

"Let's take it a step further. The uncle hears of the death of his namesake, knows who's behind it and starts cleaning house. Now both of these guys are in hiding and the troops are killing each other."

"But the troops are killing civilians, not other Yakuza?" said Cane. "The ones in New York were business people and they were the first to go after your wife."

"So maybe there's more to it than just some guy getting mad?" smiled Brent. "Maybe Tani was somehow involved with whatever it was and when she decided to retire that upset the applecart? She told Michi that she had some money put away, but I was never able to find it. Now somebody is killing off the people Tani worked for. Why? New York was nothing more than an information killing. They wanted info and tortured the people to get it and then killed them. The other three were just clothing designers who hired her to model their line of clothing."

"Ok, now you've got me interested," smiled Cane. "Suppose Tani was killed because of something she did or something that happened to her and the uncle wanted to find out what that was so he sends guys to NY to interrogate the people that she worked for. It got out of hand or they just didn't know anything and they wound up dead. So they got nothing but some files telling them who she modeled for. Now they're going through them and questioning people and when the people don't come up with the right answers they just kill them to cover their tracks."

"I don't know Jimmy, right now it all sounds

like a stretch to me."

Brent paused. "Were you ever able to come up with a travel itinerary for Tani for the last 18 months that she was working?"

"Not really. Oh I have bits and pieces but can't connect anything. You have any ideas?" he asked.

"Well she kept in touch with Michi and maybe she'd be able to fill in a few spaces. Let me have a copy of your notes and I'll ask her tonight. I had hoped that her diary might help out, but even Michi couldn't decipher most of it."

"Well if it isn't the Lone Ranger," laughed Thomas as he passed by the cubicle. "Where's Tonto, oops I mean Quasimodo?"

"He's got guard duty this morning, smart ass," laughed Brent. "Here I take pity on a poor public servant and stop by to cheer him up and buy lunch and what do I get? Harassment and I think that I'll call my lawyer and sue," Brent smiled.

"You are a lawyer, you forget that?" asked Thomas.

"Been too busy buying guns and tanks and almost forgot about what I did for a living."

"Well I like the lunch offer, especially if you're buying and it isn't some cheap greasy spoon. Last time you took me out I had the runs for a week," Thomas laughed.

"You can pick anyplace you want as long as it's not over $2.50," said Brent.

"Well I guess that narrows it down a bit, doesn't it? Let's see, I think that there's a Roach Coach just up the street. Or maybe we could flag down a roving taco wagon?" Art laughed.

"Jimmy, are you up for lunch?" Brent asked.

"Not today, but thanks for the offer. Got to

pick up the wife and drop her off at some afternoon gun safety course. Said that she talked to Michi and found out that she was going. So now she wants to go, but had to spread it out over a couple of afternoon sessions. But you guys go ahead and please don't bring me anything from the Roach Coach," he laughed.

They were sitting in Brent's Lexus when Art suddenly spoke up.

"My car is parked just up the street and I need you to stop alongside of it," said Thomas.

Brent pulled up and stopped, parking parallel to it. Thomas quickly got out, popped the trunk on his car and yelled at Brent to do the same. He carried a cardboard box and something wrapped in a blanket to the Lexus, dumped it inside and closed the trunk lid. Then he walked back and closed his own.

"Wow, a little exercise and now I'm really hungry," laughed Thomas.

"So if a cop flags me down, should I be nervous?" Brent asked.

"Nope, I can handle the locals, but if it's a Fed or State guy then just keep on going."

They were just finishing their lunch at a small restaurant on South Nevada, just north of Lake Avenue. With the early hour the place was nearly empty and they could talk with some privacy.

"So what's in the trunk?" asked Brent.

"Let's see," Thomas paused for a moment. "Seems that there's a couple of untraceable handguns, including a silencer for one of them, a sawed off double barrel shotgun with the numbers ground off and some night vision binoculars, a few scopes, maybe a grenade or two, a few flash bang devices, couple of really nasty looking razor sharp knives, and several pairs of untraceable handcuffs.

Guess that's about all for the moment." he smiled.

"Somebody you want me to kill?" asked Brent with a grin.

"Yeah definitely! Especially if they're anyway connected to this case. Just shoot them and dump the body, guns and all up in the mountains. We've got more guns if you need them, but after what's happened to you, I just figured that you might have use of some items that weren't traceable and these definitely aren't."

"Man-o-man, I just wonder what your garage sales are like?" laughed Brent as he picked up the check.

Chapter 18

"Hey Jimmy, how you doing?" asked the voice of Captain Harry Grimes of the New York Police Department. It was just after 8 AM on a Tuesday morning and the weather in Colorado was definitely improving.

"I'm fine Harry," replied Detective Jimmy Cane as a smile spread across his face. He liked Grimes and since the two of them had talked on the phone at least 15 or 20 times so far, they gotten quite friendly.

"Look kid, I don't have a lot of time right now so let me get to the jest of it. Our Police Commissioner is a spineless political appointee and someone higher up in the food chain suddenly decided that your case needed to be passed off to the Feds. Before any of us could voice our opinions, as if that would ever change his mind, our guys discovered five dead bodies all rotting away in a warehouse on the lower east side. The guys were covered with tattoos and the speculation is that they were Yakuza. They found them last Friday night and tried to keep a lid on it. Then on Saturday one of our detectives in organized crime got a call from a buddy he'd been talking to out in California. The guy told him that they had found nine dead Yakuza, but to keep quiet about it. By now our PC had already passed this off to the Feds so only 2 or 3 of us back here know about the West Coast stuff. I figured that I'd give you the heads up because sooner or later the Feds are going to be knocking on your door."

"Boy you just said a mouthful," laughed Cane.

"Yeah I did, didn't I?" Grimes laughed. "But around this Department the Feds aren't very welcome. Oh we have liaisons between us, but cooperation with them is always a one-way street, so we don't give up very much. And the uniforms in the street hate their guts and sometimes I think that they get real creative just to screw them up."

"Same here, Harry and I appreciate the call."

"Well kid, if it was me, I'd clean out my files to the very basics and hide the rest. I expect that like always, they'll swoop in like little arrogant Gods and seize everything, so make certain that you have copies of anything that you give them. Good luck compadre!"

When Captain Art Thomas passed by Cane's cubicle later that morning he couldn't help but notice how hard both Cane and Jones were working. They had papers spread out everywhere and were running back and forth to the copy machine on the floor below. Rather than interrupt them since they obviously were busy, he just made a mental note to ask about it later. That evening when he left work around 6 PM, he noticed that both Cane and Jones were still hard at work.

"Harrington House," said the voice answering the telephone without identifying himself any further.

"Ta, it's Jimmy Cane. I need to talk to Brent right away."

"Hey Jimmy," Brent answered a moment later. "Must be something important to have you call me after your bedtime."

"Just listen up wise guy. I'm at a payphone and on my way home. Do you know how hard it is to find one of those things these days? Anyway, Grimes called me this morning. They've got five dead Yakuza back there and he heard that out in California they have nine more. His PC passed off the investigation to the Feds and he expected that California would do the same. Matt and I spent the day redoing the Murder Book. Just wanted you to know where this thing's headed."

"Does Art know yet?" Brent asked.

"Nope, and I'm not sure I'll tell him. Better for him to be really pissed off when the suits arrive, which Grimes was certain would happen in the next day or so. I felt that you should know because they'll probably want to talk to you too. Might be smart to keep Stewart Andrews close by for a while. Talk to you later," he said before his quarter ran out and the line went dead.

Brent knew how the Feds operated because he'd dealt with them several times while he was working for the CSPD. They were Gods and everyone else was insignificant pond scum. Local opinions and practices were always grossly inadequate, despite the fact that during the past few years the FBI had managed to lose their automatic rifles, their information packed laptop computers, uncountable court cases due to a lab screw-up and couldn't get their expensive new in-house computer system to work. Talk about being incompetent. He knew what Cane and Jones would do to the Murder Book and he didn't blame them a bit. It would be pared down to the absolute bare essentials and willingly surrendered to the Special Agents due to arrive soon. He would have done the same thing.

"Ta, you know that stuff I brought home

several days ago, the stuff in the trunk of the car. Well it needs to be stored where no one can find it but you and me. Oh, and congratulations," he said extending his hand, which Ta smiled and shook. He had completed his ceremony and for the first time in nearly three months, tomorrow he'd be able to leave the grounds. He couldn't wait to drive the big new truck that Brent had purchased after spending countless hours either sitting in it, washing it or driving in and out of the garage and around the fountain until he was dizzy.

"You need to know that Tani's case and the others are being taken over by the FBI. Besides all of the deaths that you already know about, five dead Yakuza turned up over the weekend in New York and nine more somewhere in California. Jimmy Cane tipped me off that the Feds will probably appear here at Harrington House sometime soon. I just wanted you to know," smiled Brent.

Ta just nodded his head.

On Thursday morning Detectives Cane and Jones were summoned by Captain Thomas' secretary and told to bring the Harrington House Murder Book with them. They appeared in the doorway and saw two men dressed in dark suits, wearing shirts and ties and looking like bored aristocrats, sitting in Thomas' office. Cane ignored the men, made a point of blowing the dust off of the Murder Book and dropped it on the desk.

"This is FBI Special Agent Jake Parr and Special Agent Trevor Kimes," said Thomas but neither of the Feds stood up or offered to shake hands. Both just nodded and Cane could see that Art Thomas was seething and about to explode.

"That everything?" asked Parr.

Cane, obviously the senior man just nodded.

Two could play this game. The Feds stood up, handed Thomas a signed release form, picked up the Murder Book and walked out." It had taken less than ten minutes from the time they arrived until the time they left.

"Calm down Captain," said Cane. "We got it covered," he smiled.

"Arrogant assholes," Thomas kept repeating over and over.

"We were tipped off by Grimes," said Jones with a smile. "Jimmy and I have been cleaning everything up. We made three copies of everything. We only gave them the bare minimum, but I've got one full copy, Jimmy has another and the last one is hidden just in case."

"I let Brent know too," said Cane. "No doubt that the Feds will want to visit the crime scene, and to interview him too. We didn't tell you because we wanted it to look authentic."

Thomas just sat and smiled at his resourceful detectives.

After leaving the Colorado Springs Police Operations Center the Feds had returned to their local office to review the Harrington House Murder Book. It wasn't what they had wanted, now pared down to the basic essentials, but they had signed and accepted it nonetheless. Tomorrow they'd start at the beginning, interview the Williams guy and look over the crime scene, despite having pictures of everything and the written investigation report clearing Williams prepared by Detectives Cane and Jones. Locals, you never could rely on locals, both Special Agents thought.

At 8 AM the following morning the dark blue government issued 4 door sedan, pulled up to the front gate of Harrington House and the driver chose to disregard the intercom and simply blew his horn several times waking up the neighbors. When no one responded he blew the horn again. In a quiet neighborhood one block from the famed Broadmoor Hotel, the blowing of a horn was considered unbelievable, and it brought many of the neighbors to their front porches or windows to see what was going on. They all saw Ta walk down to the gate, insert a key and pass through locking it behind himself. The two agents saw the size of the man and his fierce look and wondered if they had the correct house.

"We're Special Agents from the FBI, investigating the Harrington House Case. We want to tour the crime scene and interview a guy named Williams."

As the neighbors just watched and listened Ta just grunted, slightly bowed and pushed a number on his cell phone. Brent immediately answered.

"Do you have an appointment?" Ta asked.

"We don't need one," said Parr. "Either open the gate or we'll be back with a warrant."

Ta repeated the statement, smiled his most evil smile at the two agents and pointed to a sign he'd attached to the gate yesterday. It read: "NO GUNS ALLOWED ON THE PREMISES."

"Please leave your weapons in your vehicle, park it at the curb away from the gate and I will escort you inside," he smiled.

Parr considered getting out of the car and putting handcuffs on the big Jap, but he wondered if he'd cooperate? At a stalemate, and unwilling to disarm, he asked the Jap to get Williams. Ta said something into his cell phone, closed it and returned to the gate just as Brent, Stewart and another man whose vehicle was parked in the garage, slowly walked down from that direction.

"What do you want?" asked Brent trying not to smile.

"Access to the crime scene and an interview," said Parr without identifying himself or his partner.

"And you are?" Brent asked.

"FBI Special Agents Parr and Kimes," he said through the bars of the gate. "Now enough of this stalling. Open the gate and cooperate or we'll be back with a warrant," Parr smirked.

"No you won't," smiled Brent as he nodded to Ta and the big gate swung open.

"I'm Brent Williams, an attorney and this is my personal representative from the law firm of Sheffield, Andrews, Preston & Blatt in Denver, Mr. Stewart Andrews. I'm certain that you've heard of them. I operate a satellite office here at Harrington House in conjunction with them, therefore if you wish to seek a warrant to search a legal law practice, feel free to do so. Also, this is Chief Judge T.F. Onnan of the local District Court, the man who most likely would have to sign your warrant or who could override one from outside the community. Now as far as an interview, if you can read, then check out the Murder Book. And as for a tour, unless you're invited by me, look at the crime scene pictures. Anything else?" Brent smiled.

"Ta, please escort these two clowns back to their car and see that they leave the area," said Brent turning and walking back to the garage with his two friends. Ta pushed the two angry agents towards their car and when Kimes objected, Ta touched a nerve in his shoulder, picked him up as he collapsed, as if he weighed nothing, and gently set him in the passenger seat. He grunted, turned and walked away.

Captain Art Thomas and Detectives Cane and Jones were parked across the street in a neighbor's driveway watching the show. They laughed as Ta took out the agent and then picked him up and effortlessly carried him to the car and placed him inside. They all knew that he was strong, but never guessed that he was that strong.

"That guy looked like he weighed at least 200 pounds," laughed Jones. "Ta laid him out like nothing and never even flinched when he picked him up. He's one scary dude," said Jones hoping that Ta never had occasion to get upset with him.

"Yeah," said Thomas with a smile. "That was some show," but he still had some questions about Ta's background and Brent acting as Ta's lawyer, wouldn't let him ask any of them.

"Thanks for coming, Judge," said Brent as he held the car door open.

"They'll probably be back, you realize that, don't you?"

"Unfortunately you're absolutely right. As I counted them, this morning there are 27 deaths in three states, all tied into this and the idiot Feds are more interested in fighting turf wars, than in solving the crimes. I find that very difficult to accept, but then some things never seem to change. I had big hopes that the creation of the Department of Homeland Security would straighten out all of this, but so far I can't see that it has. Judge, I want to cooperate, because it was my wife and friends that were killed in my own house. Since I used to be a detective with an above average closing record, this is just eating at me. Now I live behind an iron fence, have security systems surrounding me and I carry a gun again. This is in my own country and my own back yard. It just doesn't seem right to me, but the Feds don't care." Brent paused for a moment then smiled.

"Sorry gentlemen," he said glancing at both Judge Onnan and Stewart Andrews. "I guess that sometimes I find it impossible to shut up, especially when so much is wrong and so much needs to be done."

That night when Judge Onnan got home, his wife Judy and he sat eating their dinner in the family's large kitchen.

"So what did you think of the house?" she asked rather anxiously.

"The place is huge, and he makes no bones about having inherited it. Seems like a really nice guy. I understand that he's a pretty good lawyer too, even makes house calls when necessary."

"Well I really like his wife Michi. She's fun to be with. Talk about having no big ego and just wanting to help out. And as far as Harrington House goes, to her it's just a big house that her parents take care of. I mean this girl is what 28 or 29 and she's really down to earth. I'd like to invite them over some night, if that's ok with you dear?" He just nodded as he ate. Later that night after she had gone up to bed, he called a friend that was the head of a local political party, and they talked for nearly an hour.

A week later, Brent had gone to the courthouse to drop off some papers for a case scheduled later this month. Judge Onnan would be the presiding Judge and he'd asked Stewart to accompany him. First off, Stew was bored and needed something to do, and secondarily, if the Feds appeared, he wanted Stew close by, because by now he was really upset and might take on both of them with his fists, as silly as that sounded. However, the Judge's bailiff had spotted him coming in and he quietly asked him to join the Judge in his chambers. As he walked in with Stew right behind him, another man stood up, introduce himself as Bill Lofgren the head of the local Republican Party. As Brent was about to back out of the room, Judge Onnan held up both arms in surrender and asked if he would please hear them out. Bottom line was that the Party had lost the last election for District Attorney by a landslide and were eagerly searching for a qualified candidate to run against the incumbent. Brent had thanked them profusely for even considering him, but in all honesty the job didn't pay well enough for him to give up what he had going, besides he had some contractual agreements with Sheffield, Andrews, Preston & Blatt that he couldn't walk away from.

"Above all else gentlemen, I need a real paying job and unfortunately that's not it." But he sincerely thanked them, shook hands all around and returned to the courtroom only to see Phillip Paulson waving at him.

"Phil, good to see you. You have one up before Judge Onnan this morning?" he asked.

"Yes I do Brent, but I'm out of my league here. This big corporation my client is suing has a whole legal staff, and its six of them against only me."

"How about if Stew and I sit in as second chairs?"

"You'd do that?" he asked.

"Might be fun," said Brent reaching down and grabbing a brief, then handling it to Stew.

As the Judge entered his courtroom and the bailiff called the case, Paulson stood up and addressed the Judge asking him to allow Mr. Brent Williams and Mr. Stewart Andrews of the law firm of Sheffield, Andrews, Preston & Blatt, to sit second chairs in the case about to begin. Judge Onnan smiled and quickly agreed.

The morning session was filled with legalese and sparring between the two opposing sides. When Judge Onnan broke for lunch, he was surprised to see all of the attorneys gathered in the hallway working out a solution. He fully expected that by the time he returned and his courtroom was back in session, an agreement would be presented to him. Of course he'd dismiss the jurors and accept it. If asked by his wife at dinner tonight or any of his colleagues, he'd have to admit that he had really enjoyed this morning's session. It was obvious to everyone in the courtroom that Stewart Andrews knew what he was doing and was the seasoned expert. He handled the opposing attorney's, the jurors, the witnesses and even the Judge himself with tact, diplomacy and ease. You immediately liked him and wanted to believe whatever he said. But Brent Williams had performed extremely well too, far beyond his years of experience and seemed to be taking his clues from Andrews' performance. The two of them made a great team despite the inexperience of the attorney of record, Phillip Paulson. Without them, the trial would only have lasted an hour or less.

*

"I got a call yesterday from Judy Onnan," said Michi, as if Brent should immediately recognize the name.

"Who?" he asked looking across the kitchen table at Ta, who just shrugged his shoulders and kept his face buried in the sports section of the

180

newspaper.

"She's Judge Onnan's wife. We're on a committee together at the Fine Arts Center. She's been really nice to me. I'm the youngest one and they're a bit cliquish. But it's been lots of fun. I invited her to have lunch with me tomorrow in case you're interested."

"Where are you going?" he asked, concerned more about her safety than anything else, despite the fact that she now had a gun permit and a weapon that she could handle.

"I made a reservation at the Hotel's Tavern Room. Want to join us?" she asked, hoping that he would, but knowing that he wouldn't.

"Where's June?" he replied referring to Stewart Andrew's wife who always seemed to be somewhere close by Michi.

"She's driving up to Denver with Stew. Hank Preston called and asked him to come up. Must be something important, because he rarely calls.

"Can I bring Ta?" Brent asked and the big man suddenly came alive shaking his head "No!"

"You mean Mr. Grouchy?" she laughed, looking over at him.

Brent just looked over at Ta who closed his eyes.

"Daddy scratched his new truck yesterday and you'd have thought that he killed someone or that the world had ended. You men and your toys are something else. I mean here's a tiny little, maybe a quarter inch rub mark and he goes ballistic. I kept telling him that it was a truck, and that's what happens to trucks."

"Can we fix it?" asked Brent looking over at Ta.

"Already have," he replied. "That's the first new vehicle I've ever had, and something like that really upsets me, especially when it was my own fault."

"Where was it?"

"In the bed," Ta answered.

"No bed liner?"

"No, it didn't come with one."

"Better call the dealership and get one tomorrow," Brent said.

"You two are both nuts," said Christy joining in the discussion.

"What about lunch Brent?   Are you coming?" Michi asked.

"Can't Honey, have to meet with a client. But you girls have a good time," he said hoping that his weak excuse worked.   But he would call the Hotel's Security and ask them to keep an eye on Michi.   Then he thought to himself that every red-blooded male in the room would be doing the same thing.

It was later that morning when he'd caught up with Ta next to one of the flowerbeds he was preparing for spring planting. Despite his size, he handled the plants as if they were as fragile as eggs. They sat down in the warm sun and Brent handed Ta a white Styrofoam cup of fancy coffee.

"Where'd you get this?" Ta asked looking at the foamy concoction.

"Your daughter bought a new coffee machine. Makes all kinds of lattes. I'm still looking for the old coffee pot," he laughed.

"Aaah." he replied, shaking his head.

"Ta, I've been trying to sort through these killings and I have to admit that I'm confused. We have all of these dead people in so many locations, and I'm having trouble tying them together. Thought that maybe you had a better handle on it than I did," said Brent.

"In my opinion," said Ta, "someone wanted to send a message to Uncle Taniaka. They couldn't get anywhere near him, so they took out what they considered the next best thing, someone he cared for, Tani. The four others were, what did you call them, collateral damage. When Taniaka heard about it, he wanted revenge, but from who? He must have had an idea and he probably checked you out too. So he sent his men to Tani's employer's to find out who she modeled for believing that there might be a connection. I think that the street punks that he sent got carried away and killed the three employers. But they did get a list of the shows that she had modeled in. They didn't know what they were looking for, but they couldn't go back empty handed so again they got carried away and tossed the first designer off the roof. That is something that they would do. The next two in Italy and France were the same thing; they wanted information that the victims didn't have. Now I'm guessing that Taniaka also had other people researching this. They would pay or do anything to get the information that he demanded. I think that the Yakuza in New York were killed because they belonged to the wrong group or refused to cooperate. Maybe Taniaka's people questioned them, then couldn't afford to turn them loose. He is very powerful in Japan and in California. Even for the Yakuza, nine deaths will attract attention, and they don't want that. They prefer to stay in the shadows in the US. In Japan many still think of them as the protectors of the little people like the samurai warriors were. It's a cultural thing that most Americans don't understand."

"What about Carlos and his friend?" Brent asked.

"Carlos was after you. I think that the Yakuza that killed Tani left one of the two killers behind to clean up if necessary. Carlos was a loudmouth and stupid. It wouldn't have been that difficult to learn that he hated you. All you'd have to do was buy him a drink and agree with him and you'd be a trusted friend. If they'd been able to get inside, and Carlos survived, then the killer would have taken him out as they left."

"Is there any way to determine if the dead Yakuza belonged to your Uncle?" Brent asked.

"The tattoos might tell you, but you'd have to know what to look for. Only someone that was raised as a Yakuza would know and he wouldn't tell anyone. It's all part of the culture and their beliefs."

"Would you know?" Brent asked.

"Maybe, but it would be a sign of betrayal to my Uncle. Then he might come after me, and possibly Christy. But it really wouldn't tell you anything either."

"Do you suppose that Tani could have been killed because she either did something or refused to do something?"

"I've wondered about that too," said Ta. "She told Michi that she had some money hidden away and a friend down in the islands, but I never heard exactly which island or her friend's name. And by now I would think that Taniaka would know who her friends were. He had people watching over her when she modeled so he had to know who she modeled for and partied with."

"I'm just missing something here," said Brent.

"It is confusing, but we don't have any

control over how or when it will play out," smiled Ta.

Chapter 19

Michi was the first to hear the beeping sound, but thought that it was something in her dreams. When it continued she woke up, but it didn't go away. Just a steady soft "beep, beep, beep" coming from somewhere in the house. Sound carried in the stillness of the night and Brent never slept with a closed bedroom door. She sat up in bed trying not to wake Brent, and the sound continued. When she glanced at the clock on the nightstand, she couldn't see it. In fact as she looked around the room she couldn't see the nightlight in the bathroom either. She grabbed her robe, slid out of bed and walked to the door using the little light from the full moon that seeped between the closed curtains. The safety light in the hall wasn't on and she quickly walked back into the bedroom and awakened Brent.

"Honey, something's wrong. All of the lights are out," she said as he awoke with a start.

He reached over to the nightstand on his side of the bed, opened the drawer and removed his gun as he swung his legs out of the bed. He threw on some clothes, tucked the gun in his waistband and whispered in her ear.

"Where's your gun?"

"In my purse on the dresser," she whispered back.

On their way out the door she grabbed it. As they crept down the stairs the beep, beep, beep became louder and more irritating. But Brent saw

186

that the rest of the house was pitch black and they quietly made their way over to the security room and stepped inside. The electrical power had gone off and the backup batteries kept the security system operational and the main monitor blinked the message "Power Interruption, Please Reset" over and over. He quickly reset the alarm, then turned it completely off. Paranoid after what had happened in the past; Brent removed a double barrel shotgun and an ammunition bandolier and handed it to Michi. He grabbed an AK and a canvas case of four 30 round clips and slung both over his shoulder. Another AK for Christy and another shotgun for Ta and they quietly backed out of the room feeling their way down the hall to the servants quarters. Michi quietly knocked on the door and seconds later Ta opened it. In the eerie darkness, he was almost invisible.

"Ta, the electricity's off and I don't know why?" Brent said. Ta disappeared for a minute and returned fully dressed with Christy behind him. Brent passed out the guns and they found the staircase down to the garage and felt their way down the stairs emerging in the cavernous garage. Ta looked out the window and grunted.

"Streetlights are out and so is the neighbor's porch light," he said as he quietly unlocked the door and slipped outside into the night. Like a giant cat, he moved into the trees and shrubbery and circled the property checking for any signs of entry using only the moonlight. He returned minutes later, entered the garage and locked the door behind him. By now Brent had found a flashlight and they filed into the house and to the kitchen where Christy placed a pot of coffee on the gas-fired stove. Brent had found his cell phone and called the emergency number for the Colorado Springs Utilities who confirmed that there was a power outage in the area. By now Christy and Michi had found candles and placed them around the main floor.

"Utilities said that they had a problem and were working on it," Brent said to the others. But almost at the same moment they heard a muffled explosion, like maybe a small propane tank on a gas grill had exploded off in the distance. Ta disappeared and Brent called 911. The operator took the information, thanked Brent for calling about the same time that the sounds of fire engines could be heard off in the distance. Fearing that something might have happened at the Hotel just to the southwest, Brent rushed outside only to find Ta staring off in the darkness to the east. It wasn't the sound of a single fire engine, but several and by now the sky started to turn bright with flames and smoke about two blocks east of Harrington House.

"You go," said Ta handing Brent the remote for the gate and taking the AK and the extra clips from his shoulder. "They see me in the night and they might shoot first," he laughed. Brent tucked the semiautomatic pistol in the back of his waistband, covered it with his shirt and pushed the button. As he walked down the street the first of the fire engines had arrived and the firemen were connecting their hoses to the hydrants. He joined the group of neighbors across the street watching the house burn down. A half hour later, after watching more fire engines arrive and the firemen struggling to contain the flames, he returned home and told the others. The electricity was still off. As the others returned to bed, Ta sat alert and watching.

The electric service hadn't been restored until noon of the following day. Brent and Michi walked down to the still smoldering fire to see what it looked like and were surprised to see that nothing was left but the foundation, ashes and melted metal. A single fire engine supported four men who continued to probe and extinguish any still burning areas. The one thing that Brent immediately noticed but didn't mention to Michi was that the house had sat on a corner lot and if he remembered correctly after passing by it so many times, it was a two-story home facing east.

In addition to the firemen, a man wearing a jacket with "Fire Investigator" written across the back was carefully inspecting the foundation and occasionally bending down and retrieving something. Brent wondered if it was an arson case, but didn't say anything. They walked back to the house and he looked for Ta, but found that he was taking a nap after being up all night. At lunch, he was still asleep.

Brent was sitting in his office thinking about last night. It was hard for him to believe that Gus had never considered losing electricity. She had the house and grounds covered for nearly everything, but a backup generator. He began researching them on the Internet, then went through the telephone book and called several of the closest and bigger electrical contractors asking for price quotes. Normally they'd insist on making a personal inspection however since Brent knew that the house had 400 AMP, 3 phase service, something normally reserved for large commercial applications, and where the underground entry point and service panels were, they readily supplied approximate figures. Before he committed himself, he'd have to do a little work with his pencil and paper. These things weren't cheap and he'd have to decide exactly what lines needed power and which ones he could live without. Freezers, refrigerators, water heaters, furnaces and alarms systems came first. He was in the process of making a secondary list when the telephone rang.

"I'm sitting down at the gate," said Art Thomas. "Push the button and put on the coffee pot."

"What's this?" Art said looking at the cup that Brent had just handed him. It was filled with some foamy off color white substance.

"Michi's new latte machine," he shrugged and began sipping his. "Ta's still looking for the old coffee pot. Come to think of it so am I."

"Ok, let's get through the business stuff first. Last night just after midnight, somebody took a few shots at the power sub station over on 21st Street. Must have used a silenced weapon, because no one heard the shots. Now the shooters seemed to know exactly what to shoot at to disable the place. So it went belly-up and every alarm in this residential section went to backup or battery power. But the streetlights, the stoplights and all normal electrical stuff suddenly went off the air. Two blocks east of Harrington House, sitting on a corner lot and positioned about the same, was a two-story house with a garage. Now this place couldn't compare to Harrington House in any way, but it had the same identical street address. Detectives Carol and O'Mally caught it and as of a little while ago it was reassigned to Cane and Jones. We believe that the juice was turned off by someone intent on burning down Harrington House and everyone in it and that they just got the streets confused. The fire investigator has already labeled it as arson. Fortunately the place was insured and the owners were on vacation. But they did have a fancy alarm system and whenever they weren't there, a timer was set to turn the lights off and on in many of the rooms. And they did have a bunch of those spotlights that come with motion detectors. You know the kind where you walk by them and the light suddenly turns on for 3 or 4 minutes, but without any electricity nothing was working."

"So you think that they were after me again, and just picked the wrong street by accident?" asked Brent.

"Good assumption my friend," smiled Thomas. "They had the right numerical address, but were on the wrong street. Kind of scary huh?"

"Ta and I have been going over this from day one and we can't figure it out either. But since this was the third attempt, I just have to believe that whoever's behind it was looking for me in the first attempt and not Tani. But I can't figure out who? Sure I've worked a lot of cases when I was with the CSPD, but not one individual or family with a real score to settle comes to mind."

"Well Cane is pulling all of your old cases and making a list of names. Maybe it's a mute point, but we have to start somewhere. Meanwhile you need to keep your eyes and ears open because this isn't over."

"Fortunately I have a lot to do right here, so I'll be on the grounds for the next few days," said Brent.

"Maybe its time to hire a bodyguard or some security service, to sit out front. I'll check around and see if any of the uniforms are looking for an off duty job, say for a month or so."

"That's going to cost a bundle," said Brent with a frown.

"Maybe so, but it sure beats dying," laughed

Thomas as he finished off his latte and left, closing the front door behind him. Christy buzzed him out.

*

"Brent, its Art Thomas," said the voice on the phone. Four days had passed and the electricians were nearly done with the backup generator now sitting on a concrete pad in the back of the house. Camouflaged in a soundproof metal housing, it really didn't look as bad as he had imagined it would. The transfer unit would automatically sense any drop in voltage and start the natural gas fed generator. While the unit was fairly large, Ta had already been searching through the nearby nursery looking for something to hide it. A uniform cop in a police car was now parked just outside the front gate at the curb and Brent could see the dollar signs flashing by in his head. The old Tennessee Ernie Ford song "16 Tons" and the line, "another day older and deeper in debt," kept running through his mind.

"Morning Art," Brent replied. "Any good news, for a change?"

"Have the Feds ever contacted you after that first encounter that you told me about?"

"Nope, haven't heard a word. I fully expected them to return and toss their weight around, but so far nothing's happened."

"Well I just got a call from the Special Agent-In-Charge of the Denver office asking me the same question. Wanted to know exactly what had happened down here, so I walked him through it step-by-step. He especially wanted to know about all of the documentation and the murder book and who had it. I said that I had signed receipts and that his agents had taken it with them. The guy paused for several moments, and then when I questioned him further, he said that the agents had done the same thing in New York. They stormed in, took over the case and removed all of the documents. Apparently when they left here, they flew out to California, specifically LA, and did the same thing. However now all of the documents and murder books have disappeared and so have the two agents."

"Wow, that's a scenario that I wouldn't have pictured," said Brent. "So everything is gone and so are they." Brent chuckled to himself.

"To tell you the truth Art, I'm still hung up on why someone would want to kill me. The newspapers keep reporting how the FBI seems to lose everything these days so the loss of two of their more arrogant agents doesn't even raise my eyebrows. Right about now, I'd vote for the kidnappers. Those two were way over the line and even Judge Onnan agreed. Hell he was standing there listening to them spout off."

"So how are you and the Judge getting along these days?" laughed Art.

"He's a nice guy and his wife and Michi are pretty tight. Lately when she's not here, she's over at the Onnan's. Stewart's wife June usually tags along. Sort of like the three musketeers. But they all seem to enjoy each other's company so who am I to comment on it?"

"Still want you to run for office?" Thomas asked.

"Every time that we meet, he mentions it. But realistically I haven't been practicing law that long and I've tried to stay away from any criminal cases. I prefer to leave that to the experts, but the Judge feels that I could surround myself with experts. I actually sat down and figured out my fixed expenses and my income. Now the income part is really flexible with some months good and others not so good. Over a year it evens out, but in-between the bills still have to be paid. That job pays less than half of what I now make and there isn't any way that I'd survive financially. I guess the job does have a certain amount of prestige, and it would be good for a guy's ego and resume, but after it was over I'd be standing in line over at the Marion House waiting for a free meal with the rest of the down and outers."

"Just thought that I'd ask. But if you do stumble across any wandering FBI Special Agents, please tell them to call home, just like ET," laughed Thomas who had no admiration for the Feds either.

"Say Art, you play golf don't you?" Brent asked.

"Yep, I play at the game, but I'm not very good. Why?"

"Because I belong to the Broadmoor Golf Club, but I've never played golf before. If I made you a deal to pick up the check, would you give me some pointers?"

"Be happy to and my first suggestion is to buy a set of golf clubs," Thomas laughed. "It's easier to play if you have them."

"Smart ass," mumbled Brent. "It's my understanding that Frank Harrington enjoyed golf and played whenever he had the time. Gus willed me their membership and Allen Sheffield described Frank's golf clubs in great detail. Apparently Allen was an excellent golfer too. He and Diane played whenever the weather was nice. So while I've never been there, my guess is that Frank's old clubs are probably stashed in his locker at the Club. Gus mentioned the membership, but never the clubs. Since she was so strict about what anyone brought into her house and since I can't find them here, my guess is that he never brought them home."

"You have a locker number?"

"Yeah, it's marked on the key ring that I found in her safe. Locker 64, as a matter of fact. And since it's so nice out today, you interested?"

"Sounds good to me and at least I'll know where you're at. I'll stop over in a bit. Already have my clubs and shoes in my trunk."

Ninety minutes later they were standing on the practice tee and Brent was wearing Frank Harrington's old golf shoes and swinging his custom-made golf clubs. Occasionally he'd even hit the little white ball, but most of the time it rolled off the tee of its own accord or perhaps it was the crosswinds. When they finished, Brent decided to take everything home and polish it because it had been sitting in the golf bag for several years and needed some tender loving care especially after Art had told him how much Frank's clubs had probably cost. They had stopped in the Golf Club Grille for a drink and rehashed the disappearance of the two FBI agents again. Finally Art looked at his watch, said he had to leave and both men walked out to their cars parked nearby. The afternoon had been very enjoyable and Brent couldn't wait to get home and tell Michi all about his new adventure, but he knew that he wasn't very good at it and doubted that he had the passion to become much better. Maybe he'd try tennis next picturing what Michi would look like in a short white tennis outfit.

A few days later Brent was sitting on the front steps waiting for FedEx to arrive when Ta walked up and sat down beside him.

"Well I finally finished?" he said with a sigh.

"You managed to hide the generator?" Brent asked.

"No, no, not the generator. Your golf clubs," he replied.

"You found a way to make them work better?" Brent joked.

"No, I cleaned and polished them. Michi told me about your golf game and when I washed the Lexus I found them in the trunk. They were in pretty bad shape and I had to use some special polishing paper to get rid of the tiny rust spots and steel wool to clean up the heads. Then I waxed them and now they look like new," he said proudly.

"Well thank you very much, but I found out the other day that I'm not much of a golfer."

"Maybe you should try to relax more, Brent. You already told me that Mr. Harrington was a golfer, and Mr. Sheffield and his girlfriend were golfers too. Maybe you were trying too hard. Oh, and I cleaned up the bag too, but it was an expensive one and the leather was very dry. I've tried to restore it but won't know whether it will work until it has a few days to set in."

"Well thanks, I appreciate it," said Brent just as FedEx pulled up and Ta walked down to open the gate.

Back in his office, Brent began to think about Ta's comment about Frank Harrington and Allen Sheffield being good golfers. He knew for a fact that Allen and Diane played golf as often as they could, yet when he'd searched for assets in closing out his estate, he had never found his golf clubs. In fact at that time with the death of Tani, he hadn't even thought about them. He'd gone through the leased condo here in the Springs, and the other one up in Denver, but other than a few personal possessions, there hadn't been anything related to golf. Yet the man had a passion for it. He reached for the phone and called the Broadmoor Golf Club Manager, identified himself and asked some questions.

"Would you know if Allen Sheffield ever belonged to the Club?" Brent asked.

"He most certainly did Mr. Williams. He and Mr. Harrington used to play together all of the time. If I recall correctly, it was Mr. Harrington that sponsored him for membership. In fact, I think that he still has a locker here. That may sound strange, but memberships and lockers are hard to come by and sometimes family members forget about it or show up years later wanting to claim it. So the policy is not to bother the bereaved for at least a year or more. That keeps everybody friendly and prevents any hard feelings."

"Well I'm his executor and I guess I better come on over and clean it out. Thanks for your help," said Brent sitting back in his chair and wondering if he had just stumbled on Allen's hidden assets. Two hours later he was back in his office accompanied by a set of very expensive golf clubs, an old golf bag and a sealed box. When he unzipped the hood of the bag, an envelope fell out. Brent picked it up, sat back in his chair and ripped it open.

"Dear Brent," it began.

"Trying not to sound like Gus, but not knowing how else to say it, if you're reading this letter then I'm six feet under. We did have an interesting time together didn't we? I thoroughly enjoyed every moment of it, just as Gus promised that I would. As you've probably assumed by now, we were a tad more than just good friends. She personally groomed and watched over both Frank and I, and I guess in a way she made us what we

became, i.e. successful. She suffered through my many marriages but for the life of me I just couldn't seem to get it right. I loved women and always had my eyes open looking for the next one. Maybe that was my problem right from the beginning."

"I never planned to write something like this, but I guess Gus' influence changed all of that. I wonder how I passed on and hope that it was with some dignity. Hopefully it was a beautiful blond about 20 years old and my poor old heart just exploded in joy. Or maybe my ex-wives all got together and decided to give me one last group freebie. Wouldn't that have been funny? I hope you remember my comment one day about hiding everything and not giving a single penny to any of them. However my death occurred, I decided long ago to name you as my executor and heir. While I was married four times, none of them ever produced any children and with no one related by blood worthy, I followed Gus's suggestion and left my few belongings to you. Oh in the beginning, I certainly had my reservations, but as time passed and you proved yourself again and again, I became quite fond of you. So my dear boy in my golf bag and the sealed box, you do hereby inherit all of my earthly possessions. God bless you and may you live a long and happy life.

Your friend and mentor, Allen.

PS: Financially you are now pretty well off. Please take my advice and ease up a bit and learn to enjoy life to its fullest, because it's far too short.

Brent read the short letter for the third time and laughed to himself. It sounded exactly like Allen, short and to the point. He looked through the golf bag and found that the clubs were duplicates of Frank Harrington's. Even the golf shoes were identical and he wondered if Gus had been responsible for that too. Then he opened the sealed box and found all of Allen Sheffield's wealth. Numbered bank accounts in the Bahamas and several other small island nations, bearer bonds, a bundle of cash in very large denominations, a few uncirculated gold coin proof sets, some raw diamonds, a large man's diamond ring and a key to a bank safety deposit box in Denver. Everything was quickly placed into Gus' safe upstairs except for the vault key. He, as executor of Allen's estate, would have to obtain a letter from the court to enable him to open it. That meant that he would have to fill out some papers and he fully expected that the four ex-wives would hear about it.

So two weeks later to the day, he appeared at the Bank with the necessary papers in hand and met with a senior vice president who invited him into a conference room next to the walk-in vault. Sitting in the room were four attractive women of various ages, all eagerly awaiting instant wealth from Allen Sheffield's estate. The box was brought in and when Brent opened it, he saw four envelopes inside. These were the large manila 8" x 12" size and on each envelope was written the name of an ex-wife. Brent somewhat surprised by it, just smiled and handed them out as the vice president watched. As they opened the envelopes the screaming began. Allen had rated his wives from best to worst and had left them $1,000 for the worst and $4,000 for the best. To add insult to injury he had included personalized colored ribbons like at a county fair livestock judging contest and had attached small naked pictures of the recipients to them. Knowing

Allen and his sense of humor, it took everything that Brent had to keep from laughing. As they argued between themselves, he stood up, excused himself and left the building. Wait until he told Stewart Andrews and everyone else about this one.

As Brent drove back to Colorado Springs he began thinking about Gus and everything that had happened since that fateful day when he'd been summoned by Allen Sheffield to the reading of Gus' last will and testament in Denver. He'd been a lonely cop, dedicated to his job, living like a hermit and now look at him. A huge house, a growing law practice, a beautiful wife and now Allen had made him a wealthy man. He had it made, all except that someone wanted him dead and he had no idea why!

Chapter 20

"Nice tan," said Phil Paulson sitting across the desk from Brent.

"Combination vacation and postponed honeymoon," Brent smiled thinking of the two weeks he'd just spent visiting the Caribbean Islands and watching Michi in her barely there bikini. He also thought about all of Allen Sheffield's numbered bank accounts and the millions that they held.

"I just wanted to thank you in person for all of the business that you've been sending my way. I took your advice, moved my office into my home and leased a new car. My wife even took me out shopping for some new clothes and now she wants me to change my hair style. I think that I might have unleashed a monster. She's even helping me when the kids are in school. Things are definitely looking up," said Paulson.

"How are your old partners taking it?" asked Brent.

"Overall, not too well. Said I was making a huge mistake when I moved out. But I've handled more clients in the past three months than I did in the two years with them. If the situation was reversed, I bet I'd be jealous too. I try to keep it lite whenever I see them, but it's hard since I'm working and they aren't."

"Well I asked you to stop by this morning because I wanted you to be one of the first to know, and I'd appreciated it if you kept it to yourself until I go public. I've been asked to run for the District Attorney's position. I seriously doubt that I'll win because the incumbent is well known and they always seem to have a big lead right from the start, but I'm going to give it a try. That means that I might be sending even more business your way."

"You've got it made here in private practice. Why would you ever even consider running for public office?" Phil asked.

"I know that it sounds stupid, but I've done very well since I left the police department and I'd just like to give something back to the community. I don't hate the DA, nothing like that, but I figure that if I challenge him, then he'll work all the harder once he's reelected and I can go back to my small practice feeling that I actually accomplished something even though I lost."

"Sorry, but I still don't see it," smiled Paulson.

"Have you met Bill Lofgren?" asked Brent.

"Obviously I've heard of him, but no, we've never met. He's the head of the Republican Party in El Paso County and we travel in different circles," smiled Paulson.

"Well don't be surprised if he contacts you for help. I know how these politicians work and once they rope me in, then they'll look around for people that I already know or do business with. You realize that it's all connected, from the politicians to the judges, to the police, the DA, the City officials and the County Commissioners. Everyone knows each other and the politicians sit in the background pulling the strings. Anyway, that's how I see it," laughed Brent.

"What happens if you win?" Paulson asked.

"There's a zero chance of that happening,"

laughed Brent. "I'm an unknown attorney, an ex-cop and live in the Broadmoor area. Guess that should get me about a hundred votes, wouldn't you say? But Judge Onnan asked me to at least give it a try. To me that means that they couldn't find anyone else willing to run and so I became the prime candidate because today is the cutoff for the ballot."

"This could cost you some bucks, I mean not only the expense of running, but the hit your practice will take. Can't be two places at the same time."

"That's true, but I think that it'll be fun," replied Brent, but what he didn't say and what Paulson didn't know, was that Brent had decided that if he was in the limelight, then whoever wanted to kill him might back off, because of the publicity and pressure his death would cause. For that alone, it would be worth his time and effort.

Eventually Paulson left and Stewart had walked in and dropped into a chair.

"You look bushed and its still morning. What's up?" asked Brent.

"I just finished 18 holes of golf in the hot sun," laughed Stewart. "You need to cut an old guy a little slack," he laughed.

"Well, I notified Bill Lofgren earlier and he's handling the particulars. Said that the party had a tight budget, but in the case of the DA's race, they would find whatever it took. Anything new up in Denver?"

"Growth! It's killing us," Stew laughed. "I talked to Hank earlier and he's adding more people to our staff. I actually don't know how many we now employ, but it's a lot. What's that saying about the big getting bigger? Anyway he's quietly positioning the firm for a merger or buyout. Allen originally set it up so that most of the top level players got to buy into the practice. But after his divorces he decided that the ex-wives wouldn't get any more and so he signed over his percentage to me and worked on a salary basis. Sidney sold his percentage to Hank when he retired, so now the two of us own about 61% of it. I haven't a clue how much its worth, but it has to be a bundle."

"So where are you banking these days Stew, because that's the place I want to go and ask for a loan," joked Brent.

"Same place Allen banked, down in the islands," Stew laughed getting up and heading towards the kitchen. He was the only one that really liked the new fancy coffee machine Michi had bought.

Brent thought about Stew's comment and smiled. Even without Michi in her bikini the trip to the islands had been worth it. At each bank, he withdrew $10,000 just to make certain that the accounts were actually there and that he had access to the funds. At each bank the transaction went flawlessly and at each bank he asked for the balance and committed it to memory. He could easily retire to a life of leisure thanks to Gus and Allen Sheffield.

*

The days until the election flew past at an alarming rate. Brent attended fundraisers, parties, made speeches and socialized with groups that he hadn't even know existed. Michi accompanied him everywhere, as did a bodyguard, usually an off duty cop. Occasionally Ta would travel with him, but just the sight of him scared off a lot of people. Besides, Ta was extremely busy maintaining the property, to the point that Brent had suggested that he consider hiring someone to help him. The Harrington House looked spectacular, better than ever before and its grounds abounded in colorful flowers and foliage, all thanks to Ta. A national gardening magazine had asked to photograph it and had been refused. Charities asked to hold their fundraising events there, and they too had been turned away. Ta struggled to keep up, working from sunup to sundown and also handling the maintenance and security. Christy had mentioned it to Michi and she in turn discussed it with Brent, but learned that he had already asked Ta to find some help.

Then midway through the summer months, just before the schools reopened, Brent drove home one evening and as he entered the garage, a strange man wearing a white long sleeve dress shirt, his collar buttoned at the neck and his sleeves unrolled, met him. The man, in his late twenties or early thirties, bowed to Brent, addressed him using some Japanese term, and looked over his shoulder at Ta standing nearby. Brent just nodded and walked inside. Ta issued an order and followed along behind him to the office.

"New help?" Brent asked with a smile.

"I need to explain this to you Brent. The man is from Japan and doesn't speak much English, but understands a lot of it. You can't pronounce his name, so just call him Joe. He's here legally, has a work permit and all of his papers are legitimate. He will be our new houseman and in his spare time he'll do whatever I tell him to do. I've set him up in one of the guest rooms outside of my apartment, although he'd willing sleep on the floor in the garage if I told him too. He wears that shirt because he is Yakuza and if you didn't notice part of his little finger on his right hand is missing. I told him to wear a glove whenever he was out in public or we had a guest. Basically, he was going to be killed because he screwed up an order from his kumicho. His options were to commit suicide or wait and be killed. I purchased him in your name, so you have become his Oyabun or father. He has pledged his life to you. Whatever you say, he will do without questioning it," Ta paused. "I hope that you're not mad?" said Ta.

"I can't even begin to understand the Japanese culture, Ta. How you can buy and sell people. How men commit themselves for life and would rather kill themselves than fail. It's all new and strange to me. I just want peace and happiness for my family, that's all. If you want this man working for you, then I'm not against it. I've already lost one of your daughters and four of my best friends to people I don't even know. I don't want to lose Michi or you and Christy. You're my family."

"I paid a reasonable price for him. He came highly recommended, and actually he's a distant cousin on my mother's side. His loyalty cannot be questioned. Now, he has a cousin that would like to join him here. I better explain a little more," Ta smiled. "In some Japanese mountain cultures, eunuchs are treasured. Young males with little hope for the future are neutered and trained to serve others. They are called eunuchs. Joe is a eunuch and so is his cousin. By tradition they have been trained as bodyguards and servants."

"Did Taniaka have anything to do with this?" asked Brent.

"Actually no, he didn't. I called a relative in Japan and began asking questions and two names popped up. I didn't have enough money in my account to cover both of them, so I just took Joe. If you want the other one too, I can arrange for that," said Ta with a smile.

"What do you think?" asked Brent.

"Well the off duty cop sitting at the end of the driveway is costing a bundle and I personally question whether or not he's effective. Sure he's visible, but how good is he? Trust me, the eunuchs are well trained and excellent warriors. Two of them would equal a dozen of your US gangsters. Under the circumstances, I think that we need them."

"Then lets do it," replied Brent. "And tell Michi how much we owe you and how much more you'll need. We'll have our own police force here at Harrington House," he smiled.

While Michi wasn't overjoyed with the hiring of Joe and Jim, Ta and Brent were. They helped Christy in the kitchen and in doing household duties, helped Ta outside on the grounds and accompanied Christy to the grocery store. Occasionally Ta would assign one of them to follow Michi as she shopped at the Broadmoor Hotel's small stores. Whenever they entertained, they acted as waiters and doormen. And on those rare occasions when Brent and Art Thomas met for a round of golf, Joe would drive the electric golf cart.

While Brent had never mention anything about the Harrington House's new employees, Thomas had accidentally seen the tattoos on Joe's right arm and just assumed that he was Yakuza. Maybe with all of the deaths surrounding Brent, he didn't blame him for taking what he considered to be extreme measures to protect his family. But as he thought about it, he just assumed that the connection was through Ta. But he'd seen the man working shirtless around the grounds and there weren't any tattoos. So was it someone else that Ta was closer to than they had originally believed?

While Brent and Michi attended to their political duties, they had to admit that they actually were enjoying themselves socializing with both the elite and the working masses. Neither had any expectations of winning and so it was all one big party to them. But for party boss Bill Lofgren, having the attractive young couple on his side meant a lot, regardless of whether Brent was really qualified, or they won or lost. Newspaper and television reporters covered their every move and comment and surprisingly to Lofgren, neither of them had said or done anything stupid so far. Brent always came across as a nice friendly, but smart guy, and Michi melted the hearts of the male voters without saying a word. But when she did speak, it wasn't the normal gibberish expected of politicians or their wives, but intelligent comments that reached the common man or woman.

As expected, Phil Paulson had been recruited to help Brent's campaign and several jobs had suddenly materialized from party members. He thought that it was nice for a change to be a part of a successful group of businessmen, rather than his old demoralized partners sitting around complaining about the economy.

As time passed the second helper suddenly appeared at Harrington House and Brent immediately noticed a change in Ta. While he was still working, he was also managing his two helpers. And whenever Brent and Michi went out to a political rally during the evening, he was dressed and waiting for them. He'd drive the big Lexus, and act as a chauffeur and bodyguard as his two eunuchs watched over the house and grounds. Brent always had the feeling that if Joe or Jim caught you on the grounds during their absence, your life had ended and your body would never be found.

Since Brent never had any expectations of winning the election, his defeat meant very little to him. The vote had gone 49% for the incumbent and 47% for Brent with 4% lost in space as he referred to it. The closeness of the results had party boss Bill Lofgren riding on a high note, because he'd expected far less than that. The celebration parties that night seemed happier with the losers than the winners and as Brent and Michi circulated around the decorated hall, Ta wasn't far behind.

It was a week later when Brent had been sitting in his office and Stewart Andrews rushed in and sat down, a look of concern on his face.

"Judy and I have to go up to Denver, Hank Preston had a stroke late last night. He's in the hospital and still alive but someone has to take over the firm in his absence, and I'm the only one that's left."

"What about Sidney Blatt?" Brent asked.

"He's in an assisted living home. Developed dementia shortly after retiring and his wife couldn't handle him at home any more."

"Can I help?" he asked.

"You want to run the firm? Just say the word and you'll get my vote. Personally I think that you'd be nuts to do it, but it's your choice."

"I guess you're right. I'm cutting back as Allen suggested. Running a law firm as big as that one would really be time consuming."

"Smart man," said Stewart as he got up and left.

While Brent was deep in thought wondering how he could help out his friend, he heard the telephone ringing and thinking that Stew had forgotten something or maybe on considering his offer to help, had thought of something he needed. He answered it and heard Art Thomas' voice.

"Have you heard what happened?" he said almost out of breath.

"You mean Hank Preston?"

"No, not Hank Preston, I mean our new District Attorney. He was shot late last night at some kind of a pep rally of his supporters. The guy just walks in covered with old campaign stickers, a sign and a hat and walks up to the podium where the DA is in the process of giving another "thank you" to his supporters. He pulls out a gun, shoots him three times point blank and disappears out the back door. No one remembered seeing him come in and he didn't leave any forwarding address either. Slick and clean as a whistle. Carol and O'Malley caught it and they have absolutely nothing to go on. Talk about the perfect hit. I bet one of the TV networks will pick this one up and make a movie out of it. I heard that Crime Stoppers hasn't received any creditable calls on it either. I talked to Carol a few minutes ago and he's ready to stamp it unsolved. Nothing on the street, no snitches, it's like the shooter suddenly became invisible."

"Is he dead?" Brent asked.

"That's the strange part. He was wearing a vest at the time. Told Carol that he always wore one when he went out, but I think that's a bunch of crap. So now we're all sitting here wondering exactly what's going on over at the DA's office that makes him wear a vest?" said Thomas.

"So am I a suspect?" laughed Brent.

"Not that I know of, and I assume that your family and staff were tucked in their warm beds while this was happening," replied Thomas.

"I'm not sure about the others, but the house alarm was on and Michi and I were naked under the sheets."

"You really didn't need to tell me that, did you?"

"Eat your heart out copper," laughed Brent.

"Ok, so what happened to Hank Preston? He's the guy that runs Sheffield, Andrews, Preston and Blatt up in Denver, isn't he? The same guys that are trying hard to make you rich so that I can stick you with the luncheon check and not feel guilty about it."

"Same guy. Apparently had a stroke last night. Stewart's on his way up there as we speak. Sounded to me like he'll be taking over."

"He's not happy?" asked Thomas.

"Not a bit and neither is his wife, I imagine. They have over a hundred attorney's working out of that practice and it has to be a zoo at times. He offered it to me, but I turned it down and he thought that was a smart move. I'm cutting back a bit and enjoying life a little more. All at Allen Sheffield's suggestion of course."

"He talks to you from his grave?" laughed Thomas.

"Sometimes I think that he actually tries," chuckled Brent.

"You might want to ask him for some golfing tips," laughed Thomas before he hung up.

*

It was late that afternoon when Michi and Judy Onnan had decided to go out to dinner with their husbands that evening. Michi had suggested going over to the Hotel and that Tom, Judy's husband could meet them at Harrington House since it was on the way. The Judge had immediately agreed when his wife called him at work. She certainly had a way of manipulating him when she wanted something he chuckled to himself. After leaving the Courthouse he drove over there and up to the gate. My God it was a big impressive place," he thought.

"Its Judge Onnan," he said after pushing the button on the intercom outside of the Harrington House gate. Without a word, he heard the lock click and the gate began to swing open. He drove in and around the circle drive to the front door. An oriental man in a white coat opened his door, bowed slightly and motioned for him to follow. Tom Onnan looked around, noticed that the gate had closed and admired the grounds and the water fountain in the center of the circular drive. He was escorted into the huge two story foyer just as Michi ran down the stairs with her high heel shoes in her hand and Judy right behind her.

"Sorry Tom, Judy and I are running behind. Come on in and have a drink. Brent just got off the phone with Stew up in Denver. He'll be down in a minute," said Michi. "How about playing bartender?"

They followed her into the large formal living room, and she pointed out the professional well stocked bar towards one end as she dropped onto a couch and began to put her heels on. She certainly was a looker Tom thought as he walked over to the bar and began to take inventory. By the time Brent appeared, the drinks were made, but he chose a soft drink. From the looks of the bar, Tom thought that he was in a liquor store. He had everything that you could think of and yet the guy just had a soft drink. They socialized for a while and finally Brent said it was time to go and he and Michi led the way down the long hall and into the garage. Two oriental men with white long sleeve coats opened their doors and bowed, more so to Brent than the others. He just nodded as Ta had instructed him to do.

At the Hotel he was addressed by name by the valet, and several others and again by the man that met them at the elevator at the Penrose Room. Brent had asked for a table off to the side and the management had happily accommodated him. The band played, they all danced and ate, and enjoyed themselves. Finally Tom spoke up.

"Off the record, what did you think of the shooting?" he asked.

"A friend called and told me about it. I can't imagine what the DA was doing wearing a vest, can you?" he replied.

"His office isn't saying anything, even to me," replied Onnan with a smile.

"You know that they're not the most comfortable thing to walk around in. Since he was wearing one all evening, my guess is that he knew someone was after him and might show up at that party. So if he knew that a shooter was on the loose, why didn't he notify the local police or have his people guarding the door, or for that matter why didn't he have one of his own investigators pick the guy up?"

"Same question that Bill Lofgren and I have been asking. Bill hates the guy and keeps saying that he probably hired the shooter himself just to get the public's sympathy."

"Have you heard what he was shot with?"

"Just that it was a small caliber weapon. It was found out in the alley next to a garbage can. Like the shooter just dropped it as he ran by."

"Maybe he just ran around to the front door and walked in," Brent smiled. "What's that expression, hidden in plain view?"

Judge Onnan just smiled and nodded his head, but by then Brent had taken Michi out on the dance floor, said something to the band leader and began to dance. The Onnan's quickly joined them.

They danced until the band took a break and Tom had watched as Brent and Michi held each other so tightly. It was good to see someone actually in love in this day and age. Finally Brent signed the check, and they called it an evening. Everyone on the staff made certain that they personally thanked the Williams party for their business and Brent tipped each one accordingly as they left the Hotel and drove the one block to Harrington House. Once in the garage, Brent made them an offer.

"Look you've both been drinking and I personally don't want to see your name in the morning papers. So either spend the night with us or let Ta drive you home. The choice is yours and Judy immediately spoke up and said that they'd stay, surprising her husband.

The remainder of the evening was spent talking and shooting pool, girls verse the boys. Brent drank a beer as the others mixed drinks and ate snacks brought in by one of the white coated oriental men. Each time they would look at Brent and bow, backing out of the room as if he was some kind of a god. Tom wondered about that but let it go. They needed new life in the party more than they needed to see if their future candidate had some indentured servants.

Finally they said goodnight, Judy picked out a bedroom suite and the doors were closed. Ta made his usual nightly rounds, set the alarm system and went to bed. His two helpers did the same. In the morning Judge Onnan showered in the largest bathroom suite he had ever seen. It was large enough for a dozen people or more and Judy told him each of the six suites had the same thing. While the house looked big from the outside, it wasn't until you got inside that you realized just how large it was. Downstairs, they found Brent and Michi sitting in the kitchen having breakfast. Christy joined them, and then Ta and Joe walked in and sat down. Tom watched as Joe stared at his plate and never raised his eyes as if in a trance. As soon as he finished Ta excused him and the man disappeared down the hall.

"You'll have to excuse Joe and Jim," said Brent. "They're new hires and it takes a bit to get them used to our western customs. Ta found them in Japan and they are excellent workers and completely trustworthy.
And just for the record Tom, all of their papers are in order too." Brent laughed for a moment, but the interest had passed. The Onnan's left an hour later.

"See how enjoyable that was, Tom," said Judy.

"They're a nice couple," he replied, but after seeing the house he wondered about all of the people that had been killed there and if the two new oriental men were some kind of an internal security force? But then if it had been his family that was killed, he'd probably have mercenaries armed with rifles and dogs on the grounds 24/7.

*

It had been two weeks since Brent had last talked to Stewart Andrews, and he was beginning to get worried about him. He knew that he'd call if he needed help, but so far he hadn't. And when he asked Michi about it, she hadn't heard a word from

215

June either. In normal times he would have just driven up there, but now he was holding down the fort by himself and his dance card was full, at least for the moment. Suddenly, Stewart was standing in the doorway with a broad smile on his face.

"Come on in Stew, I hadn't heard from you and was getting worried," said Brent.

"It's all over my young friend. I sold the practice," he said with a smile.

"You're kidding?" said Phil, who'd stopped by to drop off some files and was sitting across from Brent.

"Nope, Brent didn't want it, and I'm too old to fool around with it. I made a few calls and one of my competitors had enough ready cash to swing the deal. However the new owners already have an office down here in the Springs, so all of that referral business is going to quickly dry up. We'll have to make it on our own from here on out," smiled Stew as if he cared.

"Good timing," said Brent. "I think that both of us were about to back away from it. Now you've solved our problem."

"Wait a minute here," interrupted Phil. "You're saying that you both were looking for a way to dump all of the referral business you got from Denver? I know guys including myself that would kill just to get a piece of that action. And you're just walking away from it?"

"Yup, that's what we're doing alright. Look Phil, sometime back both Stew and I decided to cut back a little. When this DA thing came up, the odds were 100 to 1 against me, that's why I went for it. It gave Michi and I a chance to meet a lot of people and to attend a lot of parties and social affairs. Because of that I was all for it. So when I lost, I was very happy. The more I thought about Stew, the more I believed that somehow he'd walk away from his practice up in Denver, simply because he really was enjoying his retirement. He could do whatever he wanted to, whenever he wanted to. While we were partners, he was mostly my mentor. I also knew that we both wanted out of the referral stuff. So I looked around and saw that financially it wouldn't bother either Stew or me, but that you'd take a hard hit, and that was right after you upgraded everything at my suggestion. To square things and not leave you hanging out there waiting for jobs that were no longer coming your way, I just decided to add you to our tiny law practice. Now our business cards will read Andrews, Williams & Paulson PC. I hope that's ok with you?" Brent smiled looking over at Stew.

"I don't know what to say," replied Paulson, "other than thanks."

"You're welcome, but you do realize that both of your partners are in the process of cutting back and so you'll be fairly busy."

"That's perfectly ok with me, but out of curiosity just how busy?" Phil asked.

"Oh, probably enough that you'll have to farm out some of it. You might even want to tease your old partners with it. Wouldn't that be a kick," and Paulson just sat smiling as he thought about it.

That night Christy prepared a big dinner for themselves and the Andrew's. After cleaning up Stew said that he was tired and was going home and Ta walked out and opened the gate for them. He watched as they drove up the street, around the corner and disappeared from view.

As he and Brent we closing up and setting the alarm, he told him that Joe had seen the same car pass by the house seven times today. Since Ta wasn't home and Joe couldn't read English, he had run in the house, grabbed the house camera and rushed to the opposite side of the property and hid in the bushes. As the car passed by his hiding place, he took pictures of the front, side and rear. When Ta returned, he had downloaded them onto the computer and printed them. Tonight while they slept, Jim would take the first watch and Joe the second.

Brent had grabbed a quick breakfast and was sitting talking to Jimmy Cane at the CSPD when Captain Art Thomas finally arrived, saw the look on his face and motioned him into his office closing the door behind him.

"I assume that something has happened?" Thomas asked as Brent handed him the series of pictures.

"Thomas picked up the phone and dialed, then read off the license plate number and smiled, before hanging up.

"Rental car, stolen off the lot night before last. I'll put it on the hot sheet, but there are a lot of them on it right now. Guess it's easier to carjack something or just steal it, than taking a cab or riding a bus."

"There appears to be two people in the front seat, but with the tinted windows, its hard to say and impossible to identify," said Brent.

"How'd you come across them?"

"Joe watched them drive by seven times in the same day. He was outside working on some landscaping project when he first noticed them. Poor guy can't read English so he used the camera instead."

"Why do I have the feeling that the perps in

the car were lucky that they didn't stop?" asked Thomas.

"I assume that you're referring to Ta and not to my two humble employees?" Brent chuckled.

"How does anyone of them, fit your question?"

"Well I don't believe that Ta was home at the time."

"I guess that he saved the Coroner a trip then?"

"When you get through ragging on me, what's new on the DA's shooting?" Brent asked with a smile having already talked to Jimmy Cane.

"Everyone asks me the same question, and I tell them that we weren't invited guests and that the DA's office is using their "No Comment," option. We have zip at this point. Small caliber .25 semi-automatic, untraceable and wiped clean, dropped just outside the scene. The description of the shooter fits more than half the guys in the room. We still have zip! To bad it wasn't fatal; then we might be able to solve it. In fact then maybe you'd be the DA?"

"Never was much chance of that happening Art, that's why I agreed to go along with Tom Onnan and Bill Lofgren in the first place. I'm looking to cut back, not join a zoo like the DA's Office. Just look at the number of people there and the projects that are covered. Noooo thanks," Brent smiled.

"If I hear that the car you're looking for is located, do you want me to pick them up or should I just call you and you could send out the local Yakuza to handle it," Art laughed.

"You noticed?" Brent smiled.

"Hard not to buddy. They hover over you, but they keep one eye scanning the area. I'd hate to be the guy that slapped you on the back as a gesture of goodwill. He'd probably lose an arm and wind up in a box."

"Between us, they were about to be killed and I bought them."

"Whoa there, I was just ribbing you. That's need to know stuff and I don't need to know it," laughed Thomas, but he knew that Brent wasn't joking either.

Chapter 21

As fall arrived, Ta had his men working feverishly preparing the flower gardens, trees and shrubbery for winter. On warm days both Joe and Jim could be seen touching up the big black wrought iron fence surrounding the property. On Ta's list of inside winter projects was redecorating the interior of the house, but until Michi chose her colors, nothing could begin.

Brent was now spending half days in his office and afternoons playing tennis with Michi, visiting friends or in wandering around the City with Stewart Andrews. Occasionally they'd take the wives up to Cripple Creek to gamble and have lunch, but none of the group appeared to be real gamblers. Mostly they enjoyed the ride up and back and the companionship. Most recently Brent had been helping Stewart find local investment opportunities and property to be developed. Since he'd sold the law firm, his pockets were bulging with money to invest and keeping it in a bank with their unbelievably low interest rates just wasn't an option.

Occasionally he'd have lunch with his old friends from his Police Department days and pick up the check. They'd discuss the latest happenings around town fully knowing that Brent would never pass it on. Once a week he and Captain Art Thomas would grab a lunch together, or maybe get together for dinner with their wives. Several times Brent had arranged for a round of golf with the wives, but he still sucked at the game. The vehicle that Joe had photographed had eventually been located down in Walsenburg, Colorado on a used car lot. During a title search with the State and a Carfax Report, conflicting information had brought it to the attention of the local police. However by that time any fingerprints or evidence was long gone.

Despite several attempts by Thomas to reach the Special Agent-In-Charge of the FBI's Denver Office, he hadn't been successful. The last that Thomas had heard, the two agents that had carted off the documentation and murder book on the Harrington House case had disappeared. A call to Captain Harry Grimes at the NYPD hadn't been informative either. The local case had gone to the Feds and that was it. While he wanted to call somebody out in California, he knew that the Feds wouldn't say a word. Calling the locals would be about as productive since he didn't have any contacts. Art Thomas found it difficult to believe that with the number of dead bodies loosely connected to the Harrington House case, that no one was actively working the case anymore. Then the shooting of an officer occurred on the west side of the City and all of Art's thoughts and efforts were refocused there.

The highlight of Brent's week had been discovering that the lease on his white Lexus was coming up. He'd been notified by the leasing company and had gone down to the local dealership to see what the latest models offered. While the new car was nice, it didn't match up to his expectations although if pushed, he probably couldn't have listed them either. Sometimes you saw something that turned you on and other times you didn't. So the following day he and Stewart had driven up to the

Mercedes dealer in Denver and Brent immediately saw something that he liked. That evening he drove it home, and the leasing company had agreed to pick up the Lexus at the dealership in the morning. Stewart was so impressed with the car that he intended to drive back up to Denver in the morning and buy a black model just like it.

Brent had thought about just buying out the lease on the Lexus and using it as a house car, but Michi liked the one she'd picked out and the only way to get Ta away from his fancy pickup would be to kill him. Besides neither Joe nor Jim could get a driver's license since neither spoke nor read any English.

Brent was working in his office when Christy softly knocked on the door. He motioned her in and pointed towards a chair. Then she noticed that he was on the telephone. Moments later he hung up.

"I forgot to tell you Brent, early yesterday you received a phone call from one of your brothers in Chicago. He told me that he'd seen a recent article about you running for DA in a magazine. Everyone back in Chicago was happy for your success and so much so that they'd decided to pay you a visit over the Thanksgiving Holidays. I hope that you don't get mad, but we've discussed your relationship with them before, so I identified myself as one of your caretakers. I said that it was my understanding that you'd be away in the islands over both the Thanksgiving and Christmas Holidays. I offered to check your schedule and return his call, but he refused. I told him that Mr. Williams did not accept overnight house guests and that if he'd like, I would be happy to call the Broadmoor Hotel and preregister he and his party. However I would need the exact date of arrival and departure and his credit card number. I also suggested that he could call and book the rooms himself and I gave him the 800 telephone number. He thanked me, well he almost thanked me. I think by then he was wondering what to say. Now not more than an hour later you received a call from the Hotel's accounting department wanting to know if you would accept the room and service charges for a party from Chicago over either Thanksgiving or Christmas. I told them that Mr. Williams would definitely not accept the charges. They said that's what they figured, but wanted to check with you before they refused to make the reservations. End of the story," she smiled.

"That was perfect Christy. You know when I dropped out of law school back in Chicago to follow the love of my life out here, they all just wrote me off. I'd talk to them every so often, but by then I had become the black sheep of the family. I tried to keep in touch with my folks but even that cooled off after a while. In all that time, when I really could have used someone to talk to, they weren't there. So now they read an article in some magazine and they want to come and visit at my expense. That's a joke, but be sure that you tell Ta about it. If they suddenly show up at the gate, it's his ballgame. I definitely don't want any of them here in my house."

"Are they really that bad? You make them sound like a bunch of gypsies," she joked.

"First off, they all have kids. Disciplining them isn't even a consideration to any of them so the kids run wild while the parents look the other way and party it up. My first wife couldn't stand them, and that was probably the only thing that we ever agreed on. Dad took an early retirement for health reasons. I have three sisters and two brothers. I can't remember what their jobs are anymore, but they all were quick to write me out of their lives. So I've come to accept it. Actually I did that some years ago. I don't mind talking to them on the phone, but none of them have called in maybe three or four years. I can't remember exactly, but that would be a close guess. You did exactly what I would have done had I been here. And seriously I like your idea about the island thing. Now that we have Joe and Jim, the four of us could fly down and stay for a week. What do you say?"

"The only way that you'd get Ta on a plane is to knock him out. He came here to bury Tani, but I doubt that he'll ever fly again. To him this is a piece of heaven and he wouldn't leave it. Besides in the Japanese culture, he can't leave his two workers alone either. I can't explain it but just don't include us, please. We're very happy here doing our thing."

"Ok, no pressure, just a suggestion."

"You and Michi could go, maybe even take Stewart and June with you?" Christy offered.

"Nope, if Ta doesn't go, then neither will I. Besides this year I want to get a big Christmas tree and have a train running around underneath it."

"You're kidding, aren't you?" she asked.

"Absolutely not. I know it sounds as if I've lost my mind, but as a kid we had to share everything. I never had a train of my own but this year I definitely will. You girls can handle the tree decorating and Ta and I will take care of the train."

"Baloney," Christy said. "We girls need Ta to put up the tree," she laughed.

"Tell you what," smiled Brent. "I'll hire the service that Gus used to decorate the house. That way you can just put the finishing touches on it." They both laughed, but as soon as she left his office

Brent called the landscaping and decorating company and added his name to their list.

Chapter 22

"Yo Jimmy, its Harry Grimes in New York. How you doing kid?"

"Harry, long time no hear. I'm doing good, how about you?"

"Same old crapola, if you want an honest answer," laughed Grimes. "Look kid, I got the feeling last time we talked that you guys were way out of the loop and that I better keep you clued in."

"That's a pretty fair assessment Harry," Cane laughed.

"Ok kid, listen up. I got a guy I know pretty well that works for the Fed's. Occasionally we'll meet for a drink and trade some information. It's all off the books kind of stuff. Like I'd never remember telling him anything if I got subpoenaed. Likewise with him. So last Friday night we're getting sloshed together and about midnight just as I'm thinking about calling a cab, he blurts out that the Feds just fished one of their own out of the Pacific Ocean just north of LA. Apparently the guy had been living with the fishes for some time, but his dental records identified him as someone named Trevor Kimes. That name ring a bell with you?"

"Yeah sure, that was one of the Feds that carted off our murder case and then disappeared. My Captain has been calling the FBI up in Denver trying to follow up, but they never return any of his calls. Even the local FBI guy just clams up."

"Well since there were two of them that hit

us and probably you too, I'm guessing that its just a matter of time before the second one turns up unless Shamoo got him," laughed Grimes. "Once the body was identified the Feds poured into the area, but couldn't find any of the case files either. Everything had just disappeared."

"I'll be damned," said Cane.

"Kid, we'll all probably be damned by the time this thing's over with. But I just wanted you to know what was happening."

"Thanks Harry, I'll pass it up the line and see what shakes out," said Cane.

"Remember that officially it didn't come from me, ok?"

"You got it buddy. Wish that I could reciprocate, but we have nothing to add to the murder book. Like all of the action suddenly moved on. Oh, except for one thing. Remember how all of the first murders occurred at a place called the Harrington House? Well not too long ago someone knocked out a neighborhood electrical sub station and in the dark burned down a house only two blocks away from it. It was a big two story on a corner and had the same numerical street address as the Harrington House. Coincidence? I doubt it. But it was definitely arson."

"Boy kid, this thing just won't go away. Any more bodies?"

"Nope, the homeowners were away."

"What about the original guy that survived because he wasn't home?" asked Grimes.

"Now that you mentioned it, something else happened. The guy that lives there pissed off some low rider and he came after him one night. Brought a friend too, some guy that was tied into the first murders."

"No kidding, you get anything from them?" Grimes asked.

"Nothing but ashes Harry, cause they mysteriously burned up in their car across the street from Harrington House. Our ME didn't have much left to work with."

"Boy it just keeps getting better and better out there."

"It seems like it, doesn't it?" laughed Cane before thanking Grimes for the call and hanging up. This thing was just like one of those paddle balls, where you kept knocking the ball away and the rubber string kept bringing it back. He looked up and saw Captain Thomas waving at him.

"I've got to update the brass on the Harrington House case this morning. Anything new?" he asked fully knowing that like every time he tossed out the question, everyone just shrugged. Only this time Cane nodded yes, and sat down in the office to tell him.

*

Art Thomas had invited Brent to have lunch with him although he fully intended to argue over the check and eventually stick Brent with it. They were sitting in the back of a restaurant in the Antler's Hotel finishing their coffee.

"You look like a man with something to say," said Brent.

"Yeah, I just don't know where to begin," replied Thomas.

"The Harrington House case?"

"Yep, one and the same. So this morning I had to update the Brass on our progress and just before I left my office, Jimmy Cane got a call from that Captain back at the NYPD. Apparently he and Jimmy have gotten pretty close. Now every week my report on that case has been zip, but this morning after talking to Jimmy he told me that the Feds lost both of their agents somewhere out in California and that all of the case files had disappeared too. In a way it was good news because for once I had something to say when asked. Now I'm waiting for the Deputy Chief to ask the magic question when he suddenly takes over the conversation like he's got some war secrets he doesn't want the terrorists to hear and he begins to quietly tell me about a call he got from the Feds. At this point I told him that I already knew about the missing agents and case files. His first question was who had told me and I just said a confidential informant and left it at that."

"Now he's dancing around trying to decide how to ask me if by chance I had any copies of what we had turned over to the Feds? I told him that I had a written and signed order from him, directing me to turn over every scrap of paper that we had and I also had a signed receipt from the Feds acknowledging that I had done so. Suddenly he's very quiet and I can see him thinking of ways to squirm out of this, so that he's not the one looking guilty. With nothing else on the docket I left."

"If the Feds lost two agents, I bet that they had the troops out looking for them long before the first body was found. I mean if they didn't report in on schedule, the alarms would go off. And it doesn't surprise me that the paperwork vanished with them. I mean that's what the perps were after in the first place. Now everything related to the case from New York, to here and out to California is gone. Kind of hard to solve a mystery if all of the evidence and records disappear." said Brent.

"Just between us, I know that a complete copy exists, or at least the part that went on here in the Springs. And I think that if Cane asked his buddy Grimes about it, he might be able to rustle up a few scraps of paper or some personal notebooks."

"But the bottom line is that no one wants to help the Feds," smiled Brent. "What about our new DA? Was he anyway involved?"

"We didn't have any suspects to charge, so I doubt that anyone at the CSPD even talked to him. And even if they had, so what because when the Feds swooped in they cleaned everyone out."

"Tani mention to her sister that she had put some money away, but after her death I could never find any trace of it. I mean even if you had an offshore account wouldn't you at least write down an account number or maybe an amount on a scrap of paper? I went through everything that she had and so did Michi, but we both came up with zip. I even looked for a key thinking that she might have a mailbox or storage unit that I didn't know about and found nothing. Still I keep feeling that somehow I missed something. Like it was hidden in plain sight. I mentioned it to Ta and he's begun going over the house with a fine tooth comb, but so far nothing."

"Won't that arouse the other's suspicions?"

"No, the house is scheduled to be repainted after the holidays and he's just taking measurements and nosing around."

"I've always thought that it was funny when the killers didn't toss the house," said Thomas. "They just got in, killed everyone and left. The perfect contract hit. Use silenced .22's, take your car to get away in and they're gone. It probably didn't take more than five minutes. And from the pictures you can see Allen's Rolex watch on his left wrist and his big diamond ring too. Boy, if I was the shooter, that really would have been tempting," said

Thomas.

"I don't think that Tani ever went downstairs into the basement, although I checked that too. And while she knew that Gus had a special safe room and knew how to open it, she didn't have the combination to the big safe."

"We're forgetting that she probably knew the house and grounds a lot better than you did. Hell, she'd been visiting the place since she'd been ten years old. Little girls always have special places to hide their diaries and favorite things," Thomas smiled.

"Art, I think that you just might have stumbled on something," Brent said reaching out to grab the check. It might be well worth the price of the lunch, if he and Michi could find something.

That night after dinner was cleaned up, Ta left to check out the grounds, Joe to wash the new Mercedes and Jim to the Shinto Shrine. Brent sat down on a couch in the formal living room with the high ceilings and fancy wooden trim and began to talk to Michi who was sitting on his lap.

"When you girls were young, did you ever have any secret hiding places in the house or outside on the grounds?" he asked.

"Sure, we always had them, but Mrs. Harrington usually found them and told Alice. But that just made us try harder the next time," she laughed. "Surprisingly Mrs. Harrington didn't make a big fuss over it either, like it was something that she had done when she was a girl. But she'd just turn over whatever she'd found to Alice and then we'd hear about it. Henry was so good natured that he'd leave the room whenever Alice scolded us for being naughty."

"How long did this go on?" Brent asked.

"It never stopped, now that you mentioned it. When you moved in and we visited for Christmas, we still had our hidey holes, although by now it was so commonplace that we rarely talked about them. In fact I forgot all about them," she smiled.

"Can you remember any of them? He asked.

"Sure. Come on and I'll show you," she said reaching out and taking his hand.

For the next hour they toured the grounds and inside the house as Michi pointed out a loose flagstone tile, an unused underground sprinkler control cabinet, a small hole under the front concrete stairs and so on. Each time she pointed out something, Brent would closely inspect it. Then they moved inside, and continued. Finally they entered the garage and by now, Brent was pretty discouraged at finding nothing. The search of the cavernous garage provided nothing either and they wound up back in the kitchen, drinking coffee.

It was just past 1:30 AM when Brent was suddenly awakened by Michi, who was vigorously shaking his arm.

"Wake up, I just thought of another hiding place," she whispered to him.

"Where?" he asked coming out of a deep sleep and not certain of what was happening.

"Right here in this room," she smiled, as she slipped out of the bed and disappeared.

Brent sat up and watched his naked wife crawl towards the wall and begin to feel the carpet along the baseboard with her hands. He tossed her a robe and immediately regretted it. But Michi ignored his comments and continued around the room patting and feeling the carpet.

"When we stayed in the guest rooms in the servant's wing, sometimes Tani would work the edge of the carpet out from under the baseboard and over that thing with nails in it that held it firm. She hid her stuff under the carpet and pushed it back." said Michi opening her robe and flashing Brent. "Alice could never find it although I think that eventually Henry knew but never said anything," she said, slipping out of her robe claiming that it was too warm. The sight of his naked wife with her backside in the air as she crawled and inspected, brought Brent out of the bed and beside her.

"You start over at the door and work your way towards me," said Michi pushing his arm to get his attention, not realizing that she had his full attention. Reluctantly Brent crawled to the door and began the search although he wanted to just sit and watch her. Michi began inspecting under her makeup table and suddenly hollered at Brent.

"I think that I found something?" she said digging at the carpet with her fingertips.

Between the two of them they managed to get the edge of the carpet out from under the baseboard and he gave it a final yank. Two large manila envelopes laid flat on the sub floor. Michi picked them up as Brent put the carpet back in place. Tomorrow he'd ask Ta to reattach it to the nail strips. They climbed back into the warm bed, and opened the first envelope. It had several bank books and statements, a New York driver's license, a US Passport, and a key to a bank safety deposit box. The second envelope held a handwritten account of Tani's last two years working as a model. It wasn't exactly a diary, but more a record of where she'd been, who she'd worked for and with, how much she'd made and anything that had happened to her along the way.

The first bankbook hadn't been issued by any

bank, but probably just purchased by Tani to record what she wire transferred to the offshore accounts. On the inside of the cover were a list of names and international telephone numbers. On the next page were some banks, their phone numbers and account numbers. The other bank book had account numbers on two accounts for a bank in New York City and their balances. All together the balances amounted to nearly 1.25 million dollars, more than enough to live comfortably in the islands. The picture on the driver's license nearly brought Brent to tears, as did the one on the passport and he quickly slid them back into the envelope. This is what he'd been searching for after her death. Who would ever have guessed that both she and Allen Sheffield would have hidden their wealth so effectively. He looked at the vault key saw a series of numbers stamped on it, but no bank name.

As Brent put everything back in the envelope, Michi was deeply engrossed in reading her sister's handwritten account of her life. So much so that Brent turned his bedside lamp off and fell asleep as Michi read on.

At breakfast the next morning, Michi looked at him.

"How much do you want to know about Tani's life before she met you?" she asked.

"I don't know how to answer that," he replied. "Was she involved in something?"

"Let me just say that she wasn't a nun. She was a top fashion model on the international circuit. She told me that she wanted to get out of the business, but while she was there, she lived the life. I have to read it again because there's a lot that I didn't understand last night."

"Ok, so I'll take envelope Number 1 and

pursue what's in it and you can handle the second one."

A broad smile crossed Michi's face and Brent nearly wilted. While he and Tani had bonded and he believed at the time that he really loved her, it was nothing like whatever he and Michi had. If that had been love, then he just didn't have a word to describe this.

Banking was so easy when you only had to call and enter your account number and sometimes a second code. Tani's offshore accounts had all been transferred and closed out within thirty minutes, moving the bulk of her wealth to Allen Sheffield's old accounts now owned by Brent. The bank accounts in New York would require a series of documents proving their marriage, her death and her last will and testament. And as her executor, additional documents would be needed. Brent felt that it was much easier to initially include everything that he could think of rather than to await a call from some mindless bureaucrat demanding some additional paperwork. His best guess was that it would probably take at least a week to ten days before he received a check by registered mail, which they'd most likely bill him for. So by shortly after noon, Brent's part in the agreement with Michi was nearly over, with the exception of the vault key.

Brent thought that his choices were few, either go to a bank and ask if they could help identify the key, or find an experienced locksmith. Uncertain after what Michi had said about Tani's past, he chose an old locksmith that he'd met while he worked for the CSPD. The man had taken one look at the key and the series of numbers, consulted a large master book, and within a few minutes identified the bank, which surprisingly wasn't in

New York City, but rather Chicago. He asked him to check it again and for the second time it came up the same. Brent thanked the man, handed him a large bill with a picture of a dead President on it and drove home.

He looked up the Bank's address and phone number on the Internet, and then placed a call to them. It took several minutes for the receptionist to route the call and eventually he'd gotten some Vice President and explained his problem. He had a deceased client, a vault key and was the client's executor and he wanted to know exactly what court documents he'd need to gain access to the box in the State of Illinois. They turned out to be the same as in Colorado and he made an appointment for a week from today, thanked him and hung up. He called the airline and inquired about the cost of three, first class round trip tickets and discovered that unless he went out past seven days, he'd have to pay top rate. Not entirely happy about flying even in first class, he called a charter airline at the Colorado Springs Airport. They would fly up to six people round trip to Chicago and back on the same day for not much more. He immediately hired them and asked if they could arrange for ground transportation from O'Hare to the bank and back. They readily agreed.

At dinner Michi never said a thing when Brent explained that he wanted her to join him on a trip to Chicago next week. He'd already talked to Ta who was very pleased that Brent had included Joe and that he wouldn't have to argue with him about it. In fact since there was plenty of room on the plane, he just might send Jim along too. The following day Brent gathered the documents for the Chicago Bank and was in his office explaining to Stewart that he'd be away for a day following up on the bank in

Chicago. Stewart, on his way up to the casinos in Cripple Creek with his wife, never batted an eye before leaving. Since neither Stew or June were gamblers, he guessed that they just wanted to go for a ride and have lunch together. Michi had left earlier to attend some fundraising luncheon with Judge Onnan's wife Judy.

Suddenly Ta appeared at the office door and quietly knocked before entering and sitting down.

"Problems?" Brent asked on seeing his face.

"Not really. What I could use right now is a small greenhouse."

"Ok with me," smiled Brent.

"No, it's a problem. See this house faces the east. I can't put it on the west side because it wouldn't get any sun especially during the winter months. Behind the garage to the north is too shady and to the south it wouldn't look right. Jim wants to raise some bonsai trees and I don't have a place to do it."

"What about the property next door?"

"Big house, completely landscaped lot, too much money," he grunted.

"Personally I like the idea of having a professional green house put up. Christy could grow some of her herbs. Maybe we could raise some flowers and whatever else you wanted. Couldn't we put it on the west side and add some kind of special growing lights? Or maybe make it hydroponics, where it grows 24/7? It wouldn't necessarily have to be attached to the house if it was insulated and heated."

"Good idea," said Ta obviously processing the information in his brain as he got up.

"Wait a minute Ta," Brent said and Ta sat back down.

"Is there anything that you or Christy need or want? Anything? Other than a greenhouse, is there anything missing here at Harrington House?" Brent asked.

"Well we could use some new mowing equipment and maybe an ATV with a box on the back."

"What about the Shrine? Is it large enough?"

"With three of us we have to schedule our time." Ta smiled and Brent could only imagine how the others could fit in there with the enormously sized Ta.

"Would you please consider adding a larger shrine to your greenhouse plans, and maybe attaching it to the back of the garage so no one would have to go outside to use it?" Brent asked.

Ta just smiled, nodded his head and said "aaaah,"

The days had flown by and several files had been given to their new junior partner Phil Paulson who was very happy to get them. His old partners upon hearing about his new relationship with Andrews and Williams, were besides themselves with jealousy. Paulson being the better man, just kept his head down and smiled. Ta was roughing out a scale model of his proposed expansion before presenting it to Brent for approval. Then they'd need an architect and a builder too. But today Brent and the others had left for the commercial charter side of the airport and he thought that he must have looked like the President of the US accompanied by his two so called aides. They opened the doors, scanned the rooms and checked everything out following Ta's orders, which had been carefully explained last night. Once on the plane they sat quietly in the back and watched.

Brent had leaned over and whispered in Michi's ear.

"Want to join the mile high club?" he laughed and she had elbowed him in the ribs.

Due to an overcast sky and extremely heavy air traffic at O'Hare, they had been rerouted to land at the old Midway Airport on the west side where a limo scrambled by the Charter Air Service met them. Both Joe and Jim checked out the car and patted down the driver, much to his dismay, but on accidentally seeing the tattoos on Jim's neck and wrist, the driver just shut up.

At the bank, everything went smoothly and Brent emptied the few contents into his attaché case without examining it, closed the long metal box, returned it to the VP and thanked him for his help. They returned to the limo and drove back to the airport. The city seemed so dirty and crowded as they looked out the windows at the passing scenery. About two blocks from the commercial terminal the limo suddenly stopped. A motorcycle cop walked up to the driver's window and explained that there was an accident up ahead and all traffic to the commercial air charter hangers was being detoured. For the moment, this was the closest the limo could get. The passengers overheard the conversation and decided to just get out and walk the last two or three blocks. Without any luggage other than Brent's attaché case, it wasn't any big deal. So the four passengers got out, Brent signed the driver's ticket and they listened as the man explained the shortest route to their waiting plane. As they walked between two buildings, Joe watched the driver slowly maneuvering the big car and leave the area. Jim led the parade, followed by Michi and Brent and Joe brought up the rear. Brent had the case in his right hand and Michi held onto his left arm. They were walking on a little used part of the commercial side, hidden from view by several hangers when their walk came to a halt. A man with a handgun, suddenly stood between them and their plane, which they could see parked just over a block away. Jim just hung his head low and let his arms drop to his side so as not to appear to be a threat. Brent saw a motion behind them and two more men with handguns approached them from the rear. One of them demanded the attaché case and walked closer to get it while pointing the gun at Michi's head. Now the gunmen were within an arm's length.

Suddenly the two Yakuza's in white jackets exploded attacking two of the gunmen as Brent extended his arm offering the case to the third one. Before the man could grab it with his left hand, Michi had attacked him, grabbing his gun, breaking his wrist and throwing him to the ground. Before he could react or roll to protect himself she had hit him once more and by the time Brent moved, the fight was over with. Joe motioned to Jim who began going through the pockets and removing wallets and cash. They motioned to Brent and dumped everything including the guns into his case. Michi grabbed Brent's arm and dragged him off towards the plane. Brent turned and watched, as the white clad tornados were tossing the last of the three men into a large nearby dumpster. Jim was the first to catch up and he carefully scanned the area as they continued to walk towards the plane. Half way there, Joe joined them and handed Brent something bloody wrapped in a hankie and part of a torn shirt. He didn't look nor did he ask as he placed it in his attaché case.

They were flying west at nearly 25,000 feet

when Brent looked at Michi.

"Let's have it dear. Where did you learn to fight like that?"

"I told you that when Tani and I were in school the other kids picked on us. We even invented our own language, which I told you about, and daddy also taught us to defend ourselves. We were two Eurasian girls pretty much on our own, in a neighborhood that didn't welcome us and we learned very fast. Daddy wanted to enter us in some competitions, but we wouldn't do it. We made a really good team, but after a while we couldn't find anyone willing to practice with us. That was right after Tani nearly killed some big arrogant football player that put his hand on her breast. It was really cool. After her first strike, he forgot all about her being a girl and went for the kill. I mean this freak was blind with rage, but she'd already broken his nose and blood was flowing down into his mouth. She only hit him three more times and actually it would have been easier to kill him, but she just wanted to really hurt him, especially in front of his friends."

"Where were you while the fight was going on?" Brent asked with a smile.

"Oh, I was busy holding off some of his team mates. It's really tough for those big macho guys to admit that a skinny little girl like me can whip their ass. When she finished with Mr. Macho, I was done too."

"So you never entered any competitions or got any, what do they call them, black belts?"

"Oh no, we would never be allowed to do that. We were fighting and defending ourselves, so we fought dirty and to win. We didn't pull any of our punches. Daddy taught us to end all battles as quickly as possible, and then walk away before the police arrived."

"You ever get caught?" he asked.

"Only once, towards the beginning. We were window shopping in LA, dressed like all of the other girls our age in miniskirts and halter tops. Maybe ours were too tight or too short, I can't remember, but some street guys jumped us. They tried to drag us into an alley. One of them had a big knife and kept yelling at Tani that he'd cut her real bad."

"So what happened?"

"Well some bystander called the police on his cell phone, but by the time they arrived, Tani had taken the knife and stabbed her attacker, before she took him out. We cleaned house on three more and the rest just ran off and got away. The police refused to believe that the two of us could beat up a street gang. Especially two girls in miniskirts that looked like us. But by the time that they arrived we had straightened out our clothing and were walking away. I think the story that they finally came up with was that we were with our boyfriends, who beat up the four gang bangers and then had run off chasing the rest of them down the alley. It was something like that. Anyway, when we got back home, we dumped the miniskirts and halter tops. As I told you, we were fast learners."

"And Ta taught you how to defend yourselves?"

"Yes, Mom told us that at one time in his youth, daddy was some kind of a champion in Japan, but he won't talk about it."

Brent sat back digesting what his wife had just revealed to him. There was a lot more to the Mishinko family than he would have guessed. Back at the airport, he a trained police officer, had been outflanked and protected by his own wife. As much as he hated to admit it, she had done a better job than he ever could have. Finally they landed at the Colorado Springs Municipal Airport.

*

"So what did you do then?" asked Stewart Andrews.

They were sitting in Brent's office discussing the events of yesterday. Stewart would have been the first to admit that he sometimes lived vicariously through his partners activities.

"Well Ta met us in the garage and questioned both Joe and Jim. I couldn't understand any of the conversation because it was all in Japanese. But they went at it for several minutes. Then Ta asked me for the rags in my attaché case and I set the case on the hood of the car and opened it. He carefully removed the rags, and he disappeared with both of his guys behind him, looking like they did something that displeased him and were about to get a beating."

"Hard to believe that Michi took out a guy holding a gun to her head," Stew said.

"You should have been there. If you blinked your eyes, you probably would have missed it. I mean my wife took this guy out as if he was nothing. There was never a doubt in her mind that she could do it and afterwards she grabbed my arm and we continued to walk towards the plane as if nothing had happened. Honestly, I've had guys point loaded guns at me before and my knees were knocking."

"Its still hard to picture. Hell, Michi can't weigh more than what, 120 pounds at most?"

"Trust me, she's a killer in a short dress," Brent laughed.

"So what did you do with the guns?"

"My intention was to give them to Art Thomas and see if he could get any fingerprints off of them, but that idea changed this morning."

"Why?"

"Because out of curiosity I pulled up a Chicago newspaper on the Internet. I wondered if any traffic accidents at Midway Airport had been reported. I mean somebody tipped them that we were on our way. Could have been at the bank, or the limo company or maybe someone's been following us from right here in the Springs."

"And you found what?" Stew asked.

"No report of an accident tying up traffic at Midway. But some street people searching for aluminum cans found three bodies in a dumpster at Midway."

"Whoa, think that they're the same ones?"

"Sort of. There weren't any wounds on them. Just a bunch of bruises and each had a broken neck."

"Yakuza?" asked Stew.

"That would be my guess and it would explain why Ta got so mad."

"I'm guessing that it wouldn't be too bright to ask Art to look for fingerprints on the guns, if the three guys are already dead and identified."

"Nope, it would only lead them back to us, or Joe and Jim. But I fully believe that they would have killed us once they got their hands on my attaché case. So I'm not shedding any tears, especially after everything that's happened around here."

"I fully agree with you," smiled Stewart. "Have you talked to Ta yet?"

"Nope, that's next. He's been avoiding me so far, but I'll catch up with him sooner or later."

"Where's Michi?" Stew asked.

"Believe it or not, she had a hairdresser's appointment at the Hotel, then a fundraising meeting and a luncheon to go to. In fact I think that your wife was going to join her later."

"Guess I won't have to worry about her safety, will I," he laughed.

"Ta sent Joe along with them, just in case. I sort of felt sorry about him being cooped up with the women all day, but I couldn't say anything."

Stewart laughed, stood up and walked down to the kitchen to raid the coffee pot as Ta walked in and sat down.

"I'm sorry Brent, they screwed up."

"Who?"

"Joe and Jim. They were there to protect you and not to advertise that they're Yakuza. The killings I can understand, but if they hadn't cut off the fingers, no one would know who was involved. They're both very sorry and afraid that you'll kill them. In their world in Japan, that's the way it's done."

"Hey they saved our butts, Ta. They, and your daughter. She took that gunman out as if it was absolutely nothing. He was unconscious on his back when Jim took over. If I hadn't been standing there, I think that she would have stomped him into the ground."

"She always did get a little carried away. Tani was good, but Michi was a born athlete with a gift. Together they were really a handful."

"Well please let up on Joe and Jim, because they were just doing their jobs. The finger bit is all in your domain, but the police already found the bodies."

"How?"

"Dumpster divers, looking for aluminum cans."

"Brent you have to understand that to a trained warrior, when you attack him it's a life or death battle. They only reacted with what they've been trained to do. If you don't take out your opponent when you have the chance, then they'll come back and get you at a later time."

"What I'm worried about Ta, is having it all traced back here to us. Ground transportation, chartered planes and bank appointments all leave a paper trail. It might very well end up with Joe and Jim having to take a vacation for a while, maybe even out of the country."

"That serious?" Ta asked.

"As an ex-cop, I look at it this way. Dead Yakuza in New York, then more dead Yakuza in California, the two Feds looking into it disappear and one's eventually found face down in the ocean, and now three white guys with obvious Yakuza connections dead in Chicago. And that doesn't include the Yakuza burned up in the car parked down the street or what happened here at Harrington House. I hope it all gets passed off as a territorial disagreement, but if it doesn't, at some point a sharp investigator will be on our doorstep."

"Was Tani involved?"

"I don't know Ta. I got an envelope out of her safety deposit box, but I just haven't been ready to open it yet. That may sound silly, but she meant a lot to me. I guess we all develop a mental image of a person, their morals and ideals, and who they are. We put them on a pedestal. Then reality sets in and we find out that they were just like everyone else and the image is destroyed forever. I'm not ready to find out if that's the case with Tani. I'm sorry,"

Brent said.

"I understand," mumbled Ta, as he stood up and left the office.

Brent opened his safe and looked at the three handguns taken from their attackers at Midway. He should have just left them at the scene, but at the time no one had died and he was thinking ahead to identifying them by their fingerprints. But after the article in the newspaper, everyone that could read knew exactly who they were. However no mention had been made about all three losing a finger. That was probably withheld by the police investigators. And who had hired them? They were white guys, not Japanese, and Brent began to wonder if the case had just taken on a new dimension?"

Chapter 23

"All of this stuff was delivered this morning," said Ta, as Brent stood in the open garage bay looking at it.

"Yeah, I ordered it last week, after we got back from Chicago," replied Brent as he smiled.

"And your intent was?" asked Ta.

"That bit in Chicago showed me that I needed to get more exercise. My reaction time is practically nil, so I got to thinking about what Gus had told me. According to her, Frank Harrington was a couch potato. Not only that, but so was his buddy Allen Sheffield. Gus was the one that got them started playing golf and she pushed it until they just gave up and actually began to enjoy it. It got both of them out of the house and moving, getting some fresh air and exercise. Then she realized that over the winter months they'd be back to being couch potatoes so she bought a couple of exercise machines and made a small gym in the basement. When Frank died it sat idle for a long time before she had Henry push it back in the corner and cover it. Allen was the one that told me all about it. So I went down and searched and it was still sitting there in the corner. My plan is for Joe and Jim to drag it out and clean it up. Then we can move it over towards Frank's old private pool room and set it up. The mats are for the floors and walls so that Michi doesn't kill me when she tosses me around," laughed Brent.

"I think that I'll need to give you some pointers first," smiled Ta. "My first one is not to challenger her. She can be brutal if she wants to. In the beginning I used to take both of them on at the same time, but as they learned and trained and got older, I cut that back to one at a time. She's quick as a cat and deadly. It finally got to the point that I was really working at keeping her in check."

"I asked her about being in a competition, but she said that didn't interest either one of them," said Brent. "Kind of surprised me."

"At that time neither one of them knew what a Yakuza was, but when they fought, they refused to hold back. Oh, with each other they pulled their punches, but with anyone else it was all out war, until I couldn't find anyone other than myself to practice with them. Occasionally Christy would get a call from the school because one of our girls had shown up with a black eye or a bad bruise. It took a lot of explaining before anyone believed us," Ta smiled remembering old times.

"Well that's the plan unless you have a better suggestion?"

"No, that sounds good to me too," he answered.

"How's the greenhouse coming?"

"I sketched out exactly what I wanted and where I want it, and Stewart found an architect, but so far it's been very slow. Something about having to go to the Planning Commission, then obtain a building variance and then a plans check at the Regional Building Department. I might have missed something, but you get the idea. If it's up by Spring, we'll be lucky."

"Any idea how I can get rid of the three guns from Chicago?"

"Cut them up in little pieces and spread them around the City in garbage cans. Or you could bury them up in the mountains? Or you could grind off the numbers and trade them in the next time the police offered an exchange program," Ta smiled.

"With my luck they'd use acid to bring the numbers back, or a big old bear would dig them up. So I guess I'll settle for option one," smiled Brent, removing the three handguns from his safe, dropping the clips and checking for a loaded round. He took out his hankie, wiped them down removing any fingerprints and stuck a pencil in each barrel. He handed them to Ta, one at a time before the big man quietly walked out of the office looking for Joe and Jim. Before it was over, the weapons would be disassembled, cut into small pieces and smashed repeatedly with a 15 pound sledge hammer. Nothing recognizable would remain.

It had been ten days since Brent had talked to Art Thomas and so when the call arrived inviting him to have lunch, he'd been most agreeable and suggested the Tavern Room at the Broadmoor Hotel or the Golf Club. Art chose the first option and said that he'd be bringing a guest. As Brent drove up and handed his car keys to the valet, he saw Art and another man waiting for him.

"Brent, meet Tony Martinez. He's an old friend of mine, actually a classmate back in DC."

"Classmate?" asked Brent.

"Yeah, in my younger days the CSPD sent me back there to take some special training offered by the Feds and Tony and I were roommates."

They walked over to the Tavern Room where the head waiter immediately recognized Mr. Williams and escorted him to his favorite table. This didn't go unnoticed by either of his two guests.

"Boy you're getting better at this rich guy stuff all the time," laughed Art nudging his friend Martinez.

"Well Michi spends so much time over here that I expect pretty soon they'll dedicate a room in my name," laughed Brent as they settled in and read the menus. Minutes later Brent raised his head and a waiter was suddenly standing next to him taking their orders.

"So what's the latest?" asked Thomas before the lunch arrived.

"Not that much, but I finally did locate Tani's safety deposit box. Found it in Chicago. Actually I found the key hidden in our bedroom and had a locksmith trace the numbers on it. Michi and I flew back there last week and opened it," he paused.

"And found what?" asked Art.

"Just a big envelope. But I haven't had the strength to open it."

"Was it sealed?"

"Come to think of it, yes it was and still is. Why?"

"When you get around to opening it, just make certain you have plenty of witnesses and that none of them are family."

"The Feds?"

"None other my friend. They sent in a new team just to see if we had anything lying around, by accident of course. Again I gave them a copy of my direct orders and the signed receipt, but they didn't seem too impressed. Jimmy called Harry Grimes at the NYPD to warn him, but they'd already been there the day before. No one knows or is saying any more about what went down in California," said Thomas.

"Doesn't surprise me a bit," replied Brent. "I

used to believe that even if they were ordered by the talking heads in Washington, to tell us something, they'd figure out a way to get around it. Come to think of it, if they don't have the file on the Harrington House, then how'd they wind up with you?"

"I asked the same question and one of them said that they were following up on some notes left on a day calendar."

"So they figured out that they should come here, but that was it?"

"Apparently so. Kind of gives me a fuzzy feeling at night knowing that the Feds are watching over us," laughed Thomas.

"What are your new helpers up to these days?" asked Thomas, and the little hairs on the back of Brent's neck began to tingle.

"Right now, they're building a gym down in the basement. Ta's had them finishing up outside and clearing some space for the new greenhouse. They finished up the drawings and hired an architect, but Ta thinks that we'll need a zoning variance before it's approved. In between, he has them redecorating the inside of the house. If I could find more just like them, I'd hire them. Bottom line is that it takes a lot of pressure off of Ta. He was killing himself trying to keep up and now he's become a part time manager. But I think that even Gus would admit that Harrington House has never looked better. And just wait until you see it decorated for the Holidays, it'll be spectacular, trust me," smiled Brent thinking that he had just skirted the original question very gracefully.

"Let me explain a little about Tony." he said looking at the man who'd remained silent since they'd been introduced. "He works for the

Department of Homeland Security," said Art. "Better yet, maybe it would be better if he told you the story."

"At the time that Art and I met, I was working at a medium size police department back East. Like him I took advantage of any training that came my way. When I had the opportunity to get into this terrorism business, I jumped at it and it wasn't too long before the Department of Homeland Security was formed and I got offered a job. In some ways it's no different than the rest of the Feds, and in other ways its much better because its new. About a year ago some nutcase back in Washington, did a profile search of names on the Homeland Security roster looking for Spanish sounding surnames and came across mine. My guess is that he probably figured that Antonio Martinez was another Mexican and so I wound up down on the US-Mexican border as a translator. Now, I was born and raised in Detroit to third generation Mexicans who spoke perfect English and no Spanish," laughed Tony. "I called and wrote letters telling my bosses that somebody had screwed up by sending me down there, but no one cared until recently. No one's saying anything officially but after a year in the southwest I suddenly got transferred back to Washington, DC."

"I was told that the Japanese Ambassador to the UN personally contacted our Ambassador and complained about the bad press all of the Yakuza deaths were causing. Unofficially, I heard that they were pretty good friends and I doubt that any complaints were officially made but regardless it made its way to our chain of command and the Director of Homeland Security called in the FBI to see what was going on. I guess when he heard about all of the deaths he nearly popped a vein. Bottom line is that the FBI will continue to do their thing, however in the meantime, I've been chosen to see what's actually happened and where it's going and report back to my Director. Now on the plus side," smiled Martinez, "this is a lot better than sweating like a pig down on the border, especially when you don't understand the language."

"Maybe you should have changed your name to something like, Martindale?" laughed Thomas.

"In looking back, old friend, maybe we both should have chosen different paths," Martinez joked.

"Tony decided to start here with us because that's where the whole thing actually began, here at Harrington House. I told him that you were an ex-cop and got yourself hurt on purpose so that you could retire on a disability," smiled Thomas.

"Yep, took me a long time to find the right drunk too," replied Brent.

"Look Brent, Art tells me that you're a straight arrow kind of guy so may I ask you to show me what happened and walk me through it?"

"No problem," Brent replied as he signed the check.

Ta heard the gate opening, walked to the window and watched as Brent drove up the driveway and into the garage. Another car that he recognized as Captain Thomas' pulled around the circular drive and up to the front door and was met by Joe and Jim. Both men bowed slightly as they opened the car doors. Ta walked up with Brent and was introduced as his father-in-law.

Tony Martinez extended his hand to Ta and when he turned to say something else, both Joe and Jim had disappeared. He glanced at his hand in comparison to Ta's and thought that it was only half as big. And Ta's was calloused as if he practiced martial arts on a regular basis. Brent took them through the front door with a running commentary and Ta walked down, made certain the gate was locked and returned to the garage, closing the overhead door to Brent's bay behind him.

An hour later they left the grounds and walked down the street as Art Thomas explained what the investigating detectives and forensic people had found in the burned out car. Shortly thereafter, Tony thanked Brent for his cooperation and the lunch, and they left.

"That Ta guy is huge," said the diminutive Martinez. "Have you checked out the size of his hands?" he asked.

"Not only is Ta Brent's father-in-law, he's also become his protector. When he was running for the DA spot, Ta was always within an arms length. Each time something connected to this case occurs, Ta or one of his two helpers act as bodyguards. One of them is always following Michi around. When they first arrived I tried to get the helpers fingerprints, like on a tool or a glass, but they never seem to touch anything in my presence. Like they knew how the game was played. However if anyone could ever justify having protection, then its Brent. Personally I don't care where they came from as long as they keep him and Michi safe. I've known Brent from his first day on the job, and they just don't come any better than him."

"How was he after he found the bodies?" Tony asked.

"I found him sitting on the curb outside the front gate in a state of shock. In fact he stayed at my place for a couple of days. Didn't have any where else to go. It wasn't a good picture in fact I made certain that either I or another officer was constantly with him. Then his in-laws, who he hadn't met, arrived and he went to pieces for a while. Now as he looks back he's beginning to blame himself, wondering if he wasn't the one that the killers were after?"

"What do you think?" asked Tony.

"Actually I've given it a lot of thought now that you mention it. I even had Cane and Jones dig through all of Brent's closed cases. Hold that thought for a moment," he said pulling the car over to the curb. "See that vacant corner over there. At one time a house stood there and it had the identical numerical street address of the Harrington House. Somebody torched it."

"Whoa, you mean recently?"

"Yep, not too long ago. We think that they were after Brent's house only got the streets mixed up. Nobody got hurt, but the neighborhood lost a beautiful old home. It was definitely arson, but no suspects. Actually we think that it's connected to a local electrical power sub-station being vandalized. Knocked it offline and the entire area went dark in the middle of the night."

"Man-o-man," said Tony. "This just gets more confusing, but my count here is six dead at this point, right?"

"No, actually it's seven. But then we heard that there were three or four more in New York and after that it gets cloudy. Then that Yakuza stuff got started and the numbers skyrocketed. And just recently Chicago joined in with three more unexplained deaths which somebody back there thinks may belong to us."

"I don't understand it," said Tony. "A cop gets a break and inherits a house from some rich old lady who insists that before he can get the title, he has to finish law school and everything goes downhill from there. What about her kids? Were they questioned?"

"Nope, a boy and a girl but no one ever saw them here nor could my guys find anyone that had. Brent told me that Gus had taken care of them financially and that neither liked the house. If she left it to them, they'd just sell it off for the cash. Funny part was that Brent had never been here either. I was with him on his first visit and it kind of overwhelmed both of us. I mean this guy was living like a hermit in a tiny one room apartment in an older section. He was a workaholic and his whole life was the police department. I had to order him to take time off, and even then when he came back, he'd work around the clock to catch up and pull his own weight."

"Did the old case files bring up any possibilities?" Tony asked.

"Not that we could see, but how would you ever really know?"

"What about the new wife, the victim's sister?"

"I personally checked and she was in California at the time. She's the splitting image of her older sister, but I'd stake my reputation on her not being involved."

"What about Ta?"

"He was in California too. Being Japanese, Ta's family in Japan was either close to or somehow connected to the Yakuza at one time. But he doesn't have any tattoos and he isn't missing any fingers either. Brent swears that Ta is very religious and isn't directly involved nor has he ever been a Yakuza. I wondered about his family back there and after some digging I found that he has an uncle that's connected, but Ta hasn't been in contact with him since he moved to the States and that was a long time ago. By trade he's a welder and his wife's a schoolteacher. On some of this stuff you just have to go with your gut feeling as to whether or not you believe it, but in this case I do."

"And the guys that burned up in the car?"

"The Mexican guy was definitely after Brent, no doubt about that one. But as for the other one, who knows? Speculation is that whoever pulled off the first killings left this guy behind to watch over things. How the two of them got connected is anyone's guess."

"So, who killed them?" smiled Martinez.

"Good point, but the people in Harrington House were all accounted for," said Thomas.

"Maybe he just has a guardian angel and doesn't know it?" replied Martinez as they drove back to the CSPD Operations Center.

"One last question Art," said Tony. "For a guy that you told me lived like a frugal hermit, he sure looked comfortable when he signed that check and everyone in the restaurant, hell even the Hotel seemed to know him. Does any of this strike you as odd?"

"It would if I hadn't been here to see it from the beginning. The woman that left him the house also insisted that he finish law school in order to inherit it and he did. What he didn't know was that she also arranged his future once he passed the bar exam. He literally fell into a lucrative legal practice. Brent's smart enough to see a good thing and he got right in step with the program. In a short time he was raking it in all because of the referrals that came with the practice. As far as the Broadmoor Hotel, I think that's the only place where he feels safe these days. They watch over him like the prodigal son and he willingly pays for it. During the campaign he and Michi were seen everywhere, but since then, I think that the Hotel is the only place they ever go."

"I just wondered Art. The way he signed the check, without even looking at the figures, I mean everyone that I knows adds them up first."

"Yeah, but everyone that you know doesn't have the bucks that Brent has either."

*

Tony Martinez spent the remainder of the day and the next one interviewing people that the Harrington House case had touched. His next stop would be New York City where the infamous NYPD Captain Harry Grimes would stonewall every effort he made and continually explain that he had already turned over all of his documentation to the Feds. In desperation he reverted to reading newspaper reports in the NYC Public Library. As he read, he copied down names and addresses that had been printed in the various stories. Then for the next week he tracked them down and interviewed them. Finally he left for Chicago, the third stop on his tour.

Typical of the spirit of no cooperation between any local police department and the Feds, all he learned was that three local hoods had been found in a dumpster at Midway Airport. All three had empty holsters, and the bodies showed signs of a severe beating, but no weapons had been found at the scene. The cause of death listed by the Medical Examiner on all three men was that each had died of a broken neck. No mention was made of the missing little finger. As far as Tony could determine, it was probably part of a territorial dispute between rival crime families and had nothing whatsoever to do with the Harrington House case.

Convinced that he'd find nothing else, he moved on to California, where the FBI had taken control of the case, including their missing agents, documentation and all of the dead Yakuza.

Chapter 24

It was a beautiful fall day. The sun had risen to a clear blue sky and the weatherman predicted that the temperature would be above average and very comfortable for the next few days. At Harrington House things were operating as normal. Christy had made breakfast, Ta was supervising his two helpers who today were repainting the interior of the large garage, Brent was hard at work in his office with Stewart, and Michi was on the telephone talking to Stewart's wife June. An early morning committee meeting had been canceled due to illness and both Michi and June wondered if the illness of their friend wasn't actually a hangover from the previous nights partying? The woman's reputation apparently preceded her. So the girls had agreed to meet later this morning at the Hotel and do some quality shopping, before having lunch in the Tavern Room. Brent had been invited to join them, as had Stewart, but both men had declined.

Later Michi would leave the house with Joe following closely behind her. She hated the fact that her father insisted that someone accompany her whenever she went out by herself. It reminded her of an old Chinese movie that she had seen where the servants walked exactly ten feet behind their masters, because despite her best efforts, Joe absolutely refused to walk next to her. She could only wonder what it would look like if Jim had been ordered to join them. But since the weather was beautiful she had decided to just walk the block or so up to the Hotel. Why take the car when you needed the exercise?

Brent answered the ringing phone only to hear Art Thomas' voice.

"You busy?" Art asked.

"Always have time for you if you're buying?" Brent joked.

"I'm a block away and Jimmy Cane and Matt Jones are with me. Ask Ta to open the gate," and the connection dropped off. Brent explained the call to Stew and while he cleared off his desk, Stew watched for the undercover car to approach and pushed the button on the remote control. The three men pulled up around the circular drive and parked, as the gate closed and locked behind them. Stew opened the door, said hello, and led them into Brent's large office.

"No donuts?" asked Brent as he pointed towards the chairs.

"Nope, no donuts, but if Christy has any of those big sticky buns, I'd take one and coffee," Art smiled. Brent dialed Christy's number and nodded.

"You're in luck this morning," said Brent, just as Michi walked in, sat on his lap and whispered in his ear that she was leaving and would be back later. The four men smiled as she kissed Brent and left.

"Boy this must really be important for all of you to come out here, or did you just want to get to see Michi again?"

"That too," laughed Thomas as he handed Brent an envelope.

He quickly scanned the contents, sat back and handed it to Stewart.

"I got it this morning. Figured that you

might want to see it and maybe tell Ta about it."

"So the South Pacific Rim Trade Conference will be held here at the Broadmoor Hotel & Events Center Complex in two weeks. And the countries attending will consist of Japan, Korea, Taiwan, the Philippines, Vietnam, Cambodia, Thailand, Laos and Malaysia. Your concern I assume, is that it might include some bad guys and having them staying only a block away, might place Harrington House in harms way?"

"I checked into it and the organization has grown from only three countries to ten during the past five years. Each country sends about a dozen delegates to represent them, and each delegate is supported by a staff. They look for a neutral place to meet and so far they've stayed in Honolulu, Seattle, LA, New York and Chicago. This year they chose Colorado Springs. Of course our State Department will probably pick up part of the bill and all of the security costs. I called a guy I know in Seattle and he said that they were legit, but really liked to party once the meetings ended. Maybe that's why they're not meeting in one of their own countries," said Art.

"After all that's happened around here and the Yakuza stuff, it has to make you wonder," added Jimmy.

"Maybe you should think about taking a vacation," said Matt.

"And maybe I should hire more troops, dig a moat and buy some hungry alligators?" smiled Brent.

"That might work too," laughed Thomas. "Seriously Brent, when we saw the letter asking for our support services, the first thing that we thought of was you. And so we're here this morning to put together a plan of action. Hopefully three weeks from now we'll all sit here and laugh about our paranoia, but until then we need to have a plan just in case. Now I've informally talked to some of our guys and checked the work schedule. As you know around this time of the year it gets really thin. But if we decide that we need them, I have half a dozen names."

"Out of curiosity, do you have a list of potential attendees?" Brent asked, "maybe something that we could run through the Federal System?"

"No we don't. I asked about it, but all I could get were the total numbers of representatives from each country. So what I'm asking today is that we all begin thinking about how to handle this."

"I think that we have to be realistic about this," replied Brent. "I'm not about to let the bad guys chase me out of my house or even out of the country while they party a block away from here."

The discussion went on for nearly an hour before the group broke up, but they hadn't come up with a solid plan before they left.

"So Stew, you've been pretty quiet. What's your read on this?" asked Brent.

"I believe that you need to discuss this with your father-in-law," smiled Stew as he stood up, grabbed his coffee cup and headed for the kitchen.

Later that afternoon, as Brent was about to close up his office, Ta knocked on the doorframe and waited for Brent to look up.

"Just the man that I'm looking for," joked Brent motioning him to come in and sit down. "Have you heard about the conference?"

"Actually I got a letter from a relative in Japan yesterday. She sends one twice a year just like clockwork. I didn't mention it to you because I wanted to think about it for a while." Ta removed an envelope from his pocket and set it on the corner of Brent's desk. It was written in Japanese, but addressed by the sender in English.

"And you're worried?" asked Brent seeing the expression on Quasimodo's face.

"Concerned, better describes it. I told you about my Uncle Taniaka and the Yakuza. My relative wanted to warn me that Taniaka and a guy named Sukara, who holds the same position in another family, are at war. Seems that Sukara took offense at something Taniaka did and since my uncle was so well protected, he looked around for someone related or close to him to take his frustrations out on and to send Taniaka a warning. This isn't unusual and probably the reason that the families stay so close together. Apparently Sukara's people did some research and came up with Tani. What he never expected was that my uncle would respond as he did. Once word of her death reached Taniaka, Sukara fled into the mountains and no one has seen or heard of him since. Taniaka is very powerful and he sent in the troops to square things. They are responsible for all of the deaths in New York, France, Italy and LA. In Japan there are many more, some of which have been found and most that haven't and probably never will be. Taniaka's kumicho (supreme boss) is very ill and expected to die soon and when he does, Taniaka will take over. Right now he's seeking revenge and no one in his family is strong enough to question him. I doubt that he'll stop until Sukara is found and his family eliminated. Taniaka is big time Yakuza and probably controls tens of thousands of followers."

"Wow," replied Brent. "Think that he'll come here?"

"I doubt it, but I wouldn't be surprised if he sends someone, especially if his kumicho dies. At that point, he'll no longer be able to leave Japan. You have to understand that a lot of people in the government secretly support the Yakuza. Some of it goes back to their upbringing. It's kind of like here in the States, with many people and many groups. So Sukara even if he's found and killed probably has many secret supporters that will try and carry on. Taniaka knows this and so he'll have his people kill as many as they can find, but some will always survive. Until he has Sukara's head on a pole, he won't stop. I'd bet that as we speak he has at least a thousand men searching the mountains. Sukara's men and relatives will try and hide him, but eventually he'll be found and unfortunately by then, many will die."

"Think that he had the FBI agents in California taken out?" asked Brent.

"I really don't know. If they got in his way he wouldn't hesitate but why waste the time. Their investigation wasn't going anywhere so why do something that would bring more focus on you?"

"So it's not over?" asked Brent.

"I don't think so and this conference thing is a big deal in Japan and the other countries. There are big write-ups in the daily newspapers, lots of TV coverage and interest. Having been born over there, and knowing my uncle as well as I once did, I can't believe that he wouldn't somehow have a hand in selecting some of the delegates. But we need to talk about Carlos Gonzales and the other guy," said Ta, "because Taniaka didn't have anything to do with them."

"Whoa, hold on there a moment Ta," said Brent, holding up his hand. "That's on a need to know basis and even as your attorney, I don't need to know any more about it than you do regarding what happened to Michi and I in Chicago."

"Ok," smiled Ta, pleased with his son-in-law's decision.

"What does worry me is who sent the Asian guy with Carlos, and the three guys that attacked us in Chicago and why? If this is all about a fight between Taniaka and Sukara, why would anyone be interested in what Tani had in her safety deposit box? As an ex-cop, I knew that as soon as I handed over my attaché case, they would kill us. There was absolutely no doubt in my mind."

"I think that the Asian guy was left behind by Sukara's people to keep an eye on things," said Ta. "Kind of like insurance, since you survived and just like the Yakuza, you would never give up seeking revenge. He probably heard about you and Carlos and decided on his own to help him because in doing so he'd eliminate the last part of the local puzzle and could go home."

"What about Chicago?" Brent asked.

"My guess is that one of Sukara's people escaped Taniaka's vengeance in New York City. Remember that I told you the Yakuza had formed many relationships with gangs in the States. Not all of them were Japanese. It wouldn't take much for the survivor to cut a deal. And like I said, they probably have many secret supporters, just as my uncle does."

"Maybe so, but I still wonder," said Brent. "Actually I worried about how that Chicago business would affect Michi. I mean here she was right in the middle of it. And I know that she saw your eunuch's tossing the bodies in the dumpster. But she never hesitated or missed a step, just as if it had never happened, like it never affected her."

"That's partly my fault," smiled Ta. "I'm the one that trained both of my daughters to protect themselves. I already told you that when Michi fights, she puts everything that she has into it. It's the way that I was trained as a youth and I just passed it along to her. To a Yakuza, if you are attacked then it's up to you to do what you have to survive. It's a matter of honor. If that means taking another's life, then so be it. Michi just reacted the way that I taught her to."

"I don't think that I'll ever understand all of this oriental stuff."

"In time you will, don't rush it," Ta paused. So you still haven't opened Tani's envelope?" Ta asked."

"No, like I said before, maybe I don't need to know what's in it either?"

"It's your call, but I just wanted you to know about my letter."

"Maybe you should burn it," smiled Brent.

*

A week and a half later, right on schedule, the delegates and their staffs began to arrive in Colorado Springs. Most would find rooms or suites at the exclusive resort hotel, however others would be scattered around the city, allowing them to move more freely and practically unnoticed.

Chapter 25

The South Pacific Rim Conference had been designed to allow for formal meetings on Monday, Wednesday and Friday. In between, committees and sub-committees would meet, but mostly the delegates would socialize and party. Saturday night, the organizers would host a large formal dinner, followed by professional entertainment. When it ended, the cash bar would open and the real reason for most delegates attending would begin. As usual, there were very few female delegates or staffers in attendance.

*

"Anything unusual so far?" asked Thomas, as he speared a grape out of Brent's fruit salad.

"Nope, not a thing," he replied, "and keep your hands off of my fruit," he said and then realizing what he'd said, he broke out in a big grin. They were having a late lunch in a restaurant on the east side of the city, along the growing commercial Power's Corridor.

"Did you ever open Tani's envelope?" Art asked.

Brent, with a mouth full of food, shook his head, "no."

"I've been concerned because it's been too quiet around here. You'd think that with nearly a thousand or more Orientals running around the city, that at least one of them would be interested in you," Art laughed.

"I've already got Michi, so eat your heart out," replied Brent.

"You know what I mean. Oh and I clued in Jimmy and Matt on that story you told me about two overseas groups fighting with one another. I told them that it was a fictitious story, but if they chose to believe it, that was up to them. They both understood what I meant. And I heard from my old friend Tony Martinez too. Captain Harry Grimes in New York just brushed him off, but Jimmy told me that Grimes just hates all of the Feds. You already know what he got from us and he said that LA was still ticked off about the way Parr and Kimes treated them so he got squat from them too. He said that the FBI provided nothing but a bunch of worthless paper and notes."

"Its good to see that the spirit of cooperation continues," laughed Brent as he reached over and swiped some of Art's butter for his roll.

"Well Tony said that he hardly expected much more. However he did his homework, mostly in the public libraries reading old newspaper stories and in interviews. He's come up with his own version of a war, which he attributes to two strong LA gangs with nationwide ties. What he told me is that everything fit fairly well together other than the deaths of the two FBI agents. While they were obviously arrogant assholes, Tony can't believe that either of the gangs would take them out. That brings a lot of attention and they're smart enough to realize that. So if the gangs didn't kill them, who did and why?"

"Look Art, after the way that they treated me, if you were going to take up a collection to hire a hit man, I would have definitely contributed."

"Yeah, I felt the same way," replied Art.

"Anything ever turn up on the DA shooting?" asked Brent.

"Now that you mentioned it, yes. Seems that our newly elected, highly regarded, totally trustworthy DA was cheating on his wife and her husband found out about it. We never got the case, other than that first night. The DA's office immediately stepped in and took over the investigation. Off the record, I heard a rumor that our beloved DA came up with a wad of cash to make it all go away. It's a wonderful world isn't it?" Art asked, shaking his head in disbelief.

"Maybe I should have tried harder to win the election," smiled Brent.

"No, maybe you should never have gotten involved with Bill Lofgren."

"Getting back to our conversation. If neither you nor I took out the Feds, then who did?"

"Maybe their own?" said Art.

"Could be. The way they were handling the investigation, I can see where their peers might take exception with it. What's Tony think?"

"He's stymied too. Actually, he wanted to pin it on you, but I told him he'd screw up my free lunches, so he backed off. But seriously he doesn't have a clue either."

Lunch ended with the toss of a coin to see who would pay, and Brent won the privilege.

*

As Brent pulled into the driveway of Harrington House, Ta was using the dolly to move six large boxes delivered by the UPS man from the curb to the garage. He carefully stacked them in front of his big pickup truck as the Mercedes pulled into the first bay and the overhead door came down. Ta looked at the boxes and then at Brent as he got out and walked over to join him.

"You order something?" Ta asked.

"Not that I know about. Maybe Michi got something?" he smiled.

"Nope, it's addressed to you. Says "Personal and Confidential" all over it. Seemed kind of heavy too, like they have a bunch of books inside," said Ta.

Brent stooped down for a closer look, but couldn't ascertain who the shipper was, but he saw that the shipping point was somewhere he didn't recognize in California. By now Ta had his knife out and was carefully cutting the tape on the first box and peering under the lid looking for trip wires. When he found none, he opened the lid and removed it. Inside were binders filled with white sheets and dividers. Ta removed one and handed it to Brent.

"Holy crap," said Brent who was nearly speechless. "Ta, these are the missing murder books on everything that's happened. This was the stuff that the two FBI guys got from the NYPD, the LAPD and the CSPD. I bet if you look through the rest you'll find every scrap of paper that they collected along with any evidence that they picked up along the way. Who the hell would send this to me and why?"

Ta opened the remaining five boxes and Brent was right, this was probably all of the missing documentation beginning with the Harrington House murders up to and including those of the Yakuza in California.

"Nice present," Ta chuckled.

"No it isn't," said Brent. "Having this stuff puts me and my family right in the middle of things. How could I ever explain it and who would believe me when I said that the UPS man brought it from an unknown admirer. Besides that, all of the cases involving your uncle that are now believed to be part of a gang war and closed, would be reopened. This would bring in the Feds again in a big way. I could get disbarred if they tossed their weight around. This stuff needs to go away as quickly as possible."

"Ok, let's ship it off to somebody else then," smiled Ta.

"I think that a big fire in the fireplace might work out better. Ask Joe to start one in the largest fireplace in Harrington House while you and I start sorting through this stuff. Now, let's make several piles. The first will have all of the meaningless stuff in it and Joe can begin burning it as we sort through it. Don't forget the boxes it came in too."

The remainder of the afternoon and long into the night was spent sorting and burning. Out of the first box Brent saved about a dozen papers to read later on and Ta saved even more and many crime scene pictures. As the volume grew, Joe handled the burning, Jim the carrying and Ta and Brent the sorting. When Christy suggested dinner, Brent asked for just a sandwich, which she and Michi quickly made and brought to them. When they finally finished, it was just after midnight and Brent had a stack of papers and photos nearly three inches thick to review and several other small items of evidence. He locked them in his office safe before going to bed. Ta dismissed his helpers, checked the grounds, turned on the alarm and went upstairs to join Christy in bed.

It was just after 5 AM when Brent heard the eerie sound of approaching sirens echoing off in the distance. He'd had a restless night and had been sleeping on and off for the past few hours. He reached over and nudged Michi and they sat up listening as the sirens got louder and closer, and then stopped. For a moment they wondered if the Hotel had a problem and the sirens had been turned off so that they wouldn't disturb the paying guests. Nervous, Brent jumped out of bed, yelled to Michi to get Ta and he quickly dressed, grabbing his gun and sliding it into his waistband behind his back. By the time he reached the door, Ta had already gone to the security room, turned off the alarm system and was right behind him, gun in one hand and a knife in the other. Together they stared out the large front office windows but with the thick landscaping around Harrington House, Brent could only see the flashing lights of the fire engines reflecting off the house and any shiny surfaces. He grabbed a coat and tossed another to Ta as he was instructing Joe and Jim to guard the house and women, then opened the front door and walked down to the locked gate. Ta had ditched the knife and gun and caught up, and unlocked it. By now several police cars had arrived and their flashing lights just added to the confusion. Ta locked the gate behind them and they turned to the right and began walking up the street in the direction of the Hotel. The police had already strung yellow crime scene tape from Brent's black wrought iron fence to a shade tree next to the street, down a hundred feet to another tree and back to his fence. As they approached he looked up to see what the uniforms were looking at and froze. A body was facedown and impaled on the spikes on the top of Brent's fancy iron fence, nearly eight feet off the ground. He identified himself to one of the uniformed officers, who didn't know Brent and was asked to wait around until the detectives arrived to take his statement. Brent shook his head knowing that the cop should have taken his name and asked him to make a statement and sign it right now.

However he had to cut the guy a little slack because the scene was chaotic as the firemen leaned ladders against the fence in order to reach the body. Fresh red blood flowed down the wrought iron and onto the ground. Somehow three of the heavy pointed one inch square iron bars had penetrated the body and once the firemen got close enough, they knew that the man was already dead. By now the detectives had arrived and they took one look and called for the Coroner. Later Brent would learn that the early morning newspaper delivery person had spotted it while making her rounds.

CSPD Detectives Carol and O'Malley had caught the case but when they saw that it was on the corner of Harrington House property, Carol had called Captain Art Thomas at home. He in turn had called Detectives Jimmy Cane and Matt Jones to take over the case. By the time that they arrived, Brent and Ta had returned to the house and dressed more warmly. Christy had brewed a large pot of coffee, courtesy of Ta finding the old coffee pot that Michi had tossed out and had sent Joe, dressed in a white coat and hat with Harrington House embroidered on it, out to offer it to the fire and policemen on the scene. Joe had glanced at the crime scene, but to him it really wasn't that spectacular.

By the time that the sun rose in the eastern sky, the Coroner, with the help of the firemen, had removed the body and transported it to the County morgue, much to the relief of the management of the nearby Hotel. Visible dead bodies were probably bad for business. By noon, Cane and Jones had viewed the body, read the statements of the first responders and the newspaper delivery girl and the people at Harrington House. The CSPD crime scene tech's had photographed the scene and removed anything that they thought would help to solve the case.

It wasn't until the following morning that Cane and Jones called Brent and asked to talk to him. He'd immediately agreed and as the two experienced detectives drove past the corner, they noticed that nothing remained of the crime scene. Someone had scrubbed the wrought iron fence and touched up any scrapings made by the firemen's equipment. Also, the blood soaked ground surrounding it had been scrapped up and replaced with fresh dirt. To a guest at the Hotel looking in this direction, everything seemed normal. To neighbors, if they hadn't seen it, they probably wouldn't have believed that it had happened.

Surprisingly, grumpy old Quasimodo welcomed the two detectives, locked the gate behind them and escorted them into Brent's office. Christy suddenly appeared and offered coffee or fancy coffee, your choice and her home made sticky buns favored by Brent. She carefully poured a cup of plain coffee and placed it on the corner of his desk next to a fresh warm bun.

Brent walked in, plopped into a side chair and sighed.

"You here to arrest me?" he joked. "Should I call Stewart?"

"Why do you ask that question?" said Cane.

"Because lately everything seems to happen at my house and involves me," he laughed breaking off a piece of the sticky bun.

"It does make you wonder what the hell is going on, doesn't it," said Jones.

"That's an understatement," replied Brent. "You've read our statements, but I've got to tell you when I woke up and heard those sirens, all I could think about was the house up the street burning down. Then when Ta and I walked over to the corner, we couldn't believe it. Here's a pretty good sized guy on top of my wrought iron fence with three of the rods poking through him. I mean I could see them coming out the other side. That takes a lot of force. I'm guessing he had to be maybe three feet or more in the air and then just dropped like some dead weight. So how would you do that without waking up the whole damn neighborhood?"

"According to the Medical Examiner, the guy was probably already dead when he was dropped on the fence. There was blood at the scene, but not enough, so we think that he might have been killed somewhere nearby and dragged over here."

"So some perp is now driving around with a bloody trunk or back seat?" asked Brent.

"Could be, but we haven't even identified the victim yet. We're on our way over to the Hotel to see if any of the Japanese delegates recognize him. We have two sets of pictures. One is from the waist up and the other is only the face. The body shot shows that this guy was partially covered with fancy looking tattoos. That immediately got us thinking about our previous discussions regarding the Japanese crime families," said Cane.

"That and the fact that the Conference is still going on and that Japan has a sizeable contingent attending," added Jones.

"Why me?" asked Brent. "And why Harrington House?"

"We have no idea," answered Cane. "Personally and off the record I think that this must go back to the original murders. But what's the point? I mean to toss a guy up on top of a tall fence takes strength and manpower. They, assuming that there's more than just one of them, had to know that we'd take it down before the Hotel's guests were up and moving around. Why bother?" said Cane.

"How can I help?" asked Brent.

"You can ask Ta to confirm that the deceased was Yakuza," smiled Jones.

Brent immediately dialed Ta's number and asked him to come to the office. Almost before he hung up, Ta was standing in the doorway.

"Ta, please look at these pictures and see if the dead guy was Yakuza," he said handing him the pictures and pointing towards a chair. Quasimodo quietly moved to the chair and sat down. He stared at the picture for only a few seconds, and then looked up at Brent.

"It's ok Ta. They just want to confirm what he was, not who he belonged to." Ta shook his large bald head and smiled.

"He was Yakuza," said Ta. "Maybe 30 years old, give or take a year. Maybe three or four levels higher than the street punks. His tattoos weren't complete yet, but the work was probably done in Tokyo. See the colors here," he said pointing to the corpse's arm. "Some of the ink has run together."

"Would you have any idea how the killers could get him up on the fence?" asked Cane impressed with Ta's answer.

"Maybe two large strong men? The man in the picture weighs what, 175 pounds. Two very strong men weighing about 250 to 300 pounds could easily toss him up there. His body weight as he came down would push the points of the fence through his body. My guess would be that someone is trying to send a message?"

"To who?" asked Brent, Cane and Jones all at the same time.

"I don't know, I'm not a detective," smiled Ta as he stood up and left the office.

"Well we better get over to the Hotel and get started," said Cane.

"Before you go, what about the press?" asked Brent.

"Well with the conference in session the State Department had the Feds and the local uniforms seal off the area. Basically they set up checkpoints on all of the access streets and roving security patrols. So keeping the press away wasn't any big deal. Actually by the time they realized that something had happened, it was all cleaned up. The State Department told us that they'd prepare a brief press release once the conference had ended. Unfortunately, to the guys manning the checkpoints they're all a bunch of Orientals and they can't tell one from another. So who comes and goes is sort of up in the air."

"Think any Japanese suddenly left the area?" asked Brent.

"Who knows for certain. There are over a thousand people attending including the delegates and their staffs. Then you have all of the translators, the public relations people and then our State Department and the spook guys providing in-house security. From what we've seen so far it's like a revolving door out there. But we have a list of names of locals that have been manning the checkpoints so when we're through up at the Hotel, we'll probably move on to them next," said Cane.

"Thanks for the coffee and rolls," said Jones as he and Cane left.

After Ta had buzzed them through the front gate and locked it, he returned to Brent's office and sat down.

"The dead guy was one of Sukara's men," he said. "I didn't tell them that because I wasn't sure how much they already knew. But my guess is that Taniaka was sending a message to the world to leave Harrington House and all of its occupants alone or you'll wind up the same way."

"Don't these people ever send cards, or faxes? Maybe even an email?" joked Brent as he opened his safe and took out the papers he'd set aside last night.

"Here, you can start looking over these with me," he said as he handed Ta a handful of papers.

"What am I looking for?" Ta asked.

"I really don't know, but I figured that if we both read all of them, maybe we'd come up with a better understanding of what's going on and why they took out Tani. I realize that you said it was to get even with Taniaka, but maybe there's more to it. When we're through please have Joe burn them."

By dinnertime that evening, Joe had burned the remaining papers taken from the Harrington House case files and had carefully placed all of the ashes in a secure metal ash bucket. Jim carefully washed the interior of the fireplace, and then ran a flexible chimney brush up to the top and back. He vacuumed everything that came down and then washed it for a second time. By the time he finished, the ornate fireplace cherished by its previous owner, would look as if it was brand new.

*

The night of the murder a tall thin Oriental man, about 40 years old, stood quietly in the shadows and watched. He'd dressed in an expensive black suit, topcoat and hat and positioned himself about midway between Harrington House and the beginning of the Hotel's grounds. Under other circumstances he'd remind you of a scholarly professor just out for an early morning walk. In his native country of Japan, he actually was a respected university professor. His orders had come directly from Taniaka, and he knew that he couldn't refuse. While his body wasn't covered with tattoos, he was as much a genuine Yakuza as was possible. Since he'd been chosen weeks ago to attend the conference, Taniaka's ailing boss had finally died and Taniaka had risen to the all powerful position as the head of the family. He owed everything in his life to Taniaka and only hoped that tonight's activities would please him. If so, the rewards would be many when he returned to Japan.

Detectives Cane and Jones had interviewed many of the conference attendees with the help of a series of translators and had moved on to the Hotel's staff, and the English speaking security people. So far, they had zip and continually wondered how they could ask a simple yes or no question and the translator would take so long to translate it. Yet the answer would be the reverse. However when they talked to one of the uniforms that had been on duty at the Lake Avenue checkpoint, the guy remembered seeing a limo pass through during the early morning hours, shortly before the fire engines had rolled. To the best of his recollection the car held a driver and three large passengers. He knew the men were large because he'd managed to poke his head in the driver's side window and look as the driver searched for his authorization pass. He'd gone off duty shortly thereafter so he didn't know if the limo and its passengers had ever returned.

The next stop was with the supervisor of the Colorado Springs Municipal Airport's control tower. From his time spent on active duty in the Air Force,

Jones knew that the air traffic controllers maintained a log of all flights in and out of the airport, regardless of whether they were military aircraft, commercial flights, chartered planes or privately owned aircraft. With the help of the supervisor, they searched the log and found a corporate Gulf Stream V jet, registered in Japan that had departed the airport shortly after the fire engines had arrived on the scene at Harrington House. While it all fit together, the case was over with and both men knew it.

Out of courtesy to Brent, who was a friend and had been so cooperative, Jimmy Cane decided to host an informal dinner party at his home. He invited his partner Matt, Captain Thomas, Brent and their wives. His feeling was that they could all easily explain socializing, but each meeting in Brent's office had to be explained and meeting for lunch exposed the foursome to outside focus. However in the privacy of his own home, he could take as long as he liked to explain the status of their investigation. Of particular interest was the call from Captain Harry Grimes of the NYPD relating his most recent information swap with his FBI friend. Apparently the Feds had decided to cut their losses and declared that the two special agents had been taking a break from the investigation and had rented a small pleasure boat. Their intent had been to view the coastline and that the boat had developed engine trouble and the pumps quit working. The boat sunk and they both drowned. As far as the location of the missing files went, no one had a clue but the Feds were closing out the inquiry, saying that they had found nothing to indicate it was any more than a territorial dispute. Off the record two seasoned Special Agents would be assigned to review anything new that turned up.

It had been several weeks since the last contact Captain Thomas had with Homeland Security Agent Tony Martinez, but even he didn't have any concrete evidence of what he surmised had happened. He definitely had his suspicions but no way to prove any of them. The PR release regarding the deaths of the first two Feds was a bunch of crap and he knew it. No way would the FBI ever back off from pursuing the deaths of any of its people. And he wondered what had happened to all of the case files? He found it difficult to believe that warring gangs wouldn't destroy them. Why would they ever even consider saving them? So now the only two Feds that had a clue were dead and everything that they had collected had vanished into thin air. Now he was only going through the motions of winding up his investigation because he expected that he'd soon be recalled to Washington, DC and reassigned. He only hoped that he wouldn't be shipped back down to the US-Mexican border.

Chapter 26

Detective Jimmy Cane was a larger than average man, standing nearly 6' 4" tall and weighing in at a solid 235 pounds. With dark curly hair which he wore in a short military style and a pleasant smile on his face it was easy to see why he intimidated the crooks and appealed to the victims. People, regardless of their prejudices and religions or backgrounds, just liked to talk to him, like he was some friendly old uncle. At 35 years of age, he definitely wasn't old, at least not physically, but in his ten years of working for the local police department, the last four in homicide, he'd seen more than his share of sorrow and brutality, enough to last him a lifetime.

He lived with his wife Cindy, five years older than him and until recently her son from a previous disastrous marriage. The son was now enrolled in the University of Northern Colorado on a rare science scholarship. The three of them were extremely close, including Jimmy and his adopted son who he encouraged and fathered as if he was his own child. To Jimmy, his son's origin really didn't matter. He had helped Cindy raise him and that was good enough for him.

Like a lot of others, when they'd gotten married they had very little in the way of assets. Jimmy lived in a small rented apartment and Cindy in a City funded housing unit. Neither of them had any really close friends at that time. She was escaping an abusive husband and trying to hide and that's what had brought the two of them together. He was one of the original responding officers to her 911 call and had arrested the husband for domestic violence. As was so common at that time, the Judge was more sympathetic to the husband than the wife and released him on personal recognizance. After a few drinks and some partying with his equally useless drinking buddies, he'd found her and his son and had beaten the hell out of her. This time neighbors made the 911 call and ironically Jimmy was assigned the call. For the second time the husband was arrested, but because he'd been drunk, he'd been taken to a detox facility. A month later, after two more 911 calls, the drunken husband had pulled out a gun and Jimmy, the responding officer, had killed him with one shot. Witnesses all substantiated Jimmy's explanation, but he knew that he'd goaded the man into making his move. Eventually cleared by the review board, he moved on with his life.

It had been two months later during a routine traffic stop that he'd met the woman again. This time she smiled and thanked him for his help and for the very first time he realized that she was attractive and now a widow. During all of their previous encounters she'd been beaten up, bandaged or scared to death, but now she was cleaned up and seemed to be getting her life back together. Way out of character for him, he'd made a quick decision and asked her to have dinner with him. Surprisingly for the very first time, he learned that she had a small son. After all of the times that he'd been at her apartment, he'd never seen the boy. She had explained that her husband hated the child, claimed that he wasn't the father and abused him too. So whenever she knew that he'd be out drinking and would probably return home drunk, she'd pay a sympathetic widowed neighbor to baby sit for the night.

After several dates, despite the odds, they seemed to bond as if they had known each other all of their lives. He was kind, gentle and caring both to her and her son, something that she had never experienced during her lifetime. A few months later they had quietly gotten married in a civil ceremony. Now she was a full time housewife and mother and she loved it.

Jimmy was somewhat of a closet carpenter and handyman. He'd purchased what the realtor had called a fixer-upper, but he knew was a nightmare. During his spare time he remodeled it and eight months later he managed to sell it. The profit from it allowed him to buy another similar condition home on the east side and again when he sold it he made a profit. This continued for several years until they felt financially secure enough to buy their first home that they would actually live in. By now her son was in grammar school and they carefully selected a home in a school district with above average schools. While there wasn't anything wrong with the home that they had, Jimmy constantly remodeled one room after another until the place was like brand new. Then he located a fixer upper in an area called Village Seven and he fell in love with it. Unfortunately it had been abandoned and repossessed by a local bank. The insides were a shambles but the neighborhood was good and so they easily sold one home and purchased another. However this house would require considerable remodeling and repair but as he had explained to Cindy, it gave him something to do in his spare time and when he finished it, their equity would be doubled.

By now he'd risen through the ranks and was about to take the test to become a police detective. However in his own neighborhood he found it difficult to handle the prejudice and racism that occasionally overwhelmed him since he was black and his wife and adopted child were both white. As a result most of his neighbors gave him a wide berth and rarely would any of them hang over a fence on a Saturday afternoon just to chew the fat. Sometimes he attributed it to him wearing a police uniform and carrying a gun, but then he'd smile to himself because he knew the real reason.

One of his best friends was a guy he'd met on the police department named Brent Williams. The guy was a good officer and race had never seemed to enter into any of their discussions. Jimmy had even invited him to dinner several times and they had gone up to Denver more than once to watch the Bronco's play football. Several times he had roped Brent into playing baby sitter for his growing stepson while he and Cindy spent a rare night out on the town or took in a show up in Denver. And once Brent had volunteered to watch the boy over a weekend after Cindy had won some contest and the prize was a free trip to Las Vegas. But Brent was brutally honest and when he'd been told about the latest home purchased he told Jimmy that he was nuts moving into a cracker neighborhood. He guessed that he'd been right.

The two story, four bedroom home sat on the corner facing north in an older established neighborhood. A once proud property showed all of the signs of abuse and neglect. When the black guy had moved in all anyone could believe was that they were seeing the beginnings of a crack house and prostitution. Property values would go straight to hell according to all of the rumors. But slowly and carefully as if guided by some almighty plan, the expected results never materialized and the corner house as it had come to be known, began to gain a renewed life. After several years it outshone many of its neighbors and Jimmy never stopped making improvements whether he could afford them or not.

The house next door, just to the west, or the second house down from the corner was owned by a wealthy older retired couple who spent most of their time traveling the world or living at their winter home in Sun City, Arizona. Rarely did any of the neighbors see them anymore. A landscape service took care of the exterior and an alarm company secured the interior. The third house down was exactly what Jimmy would have built if he had the time and money. Again it had four bedrooms, was a modified two story with high ceilings and large open spaces. He loved it and since the very first time he had passed by, he wished that he owned it. In the back of his head he always thought that if it ever came up on the market, he would be the first one in line to buy it. But over the last few years the large family that owned it had lost their pride of ownership. When the husband was laid off from his high tech job, all maintenance had ended. With four useless sons and a nagging wife, Jimmy didn't envy the guy.

Like the saying, all things come to he who waits, eventually the house came on the market and as he had promised, Jimmy was the first one in line to buy it. As usual Cindy just went along with her husband but after all of these years, she too knew that it would be another step up for them. So the corner home now in pristine condition was quickly sold and the big house two doors down purchased. He was elated and quickly began to strip it clean and begin to rebuild it. Fortunately their son was now accepted to the University on a scholarship and would miss most of the action. For Jimmy, life was good, his job secure, and he now had another house to remodel. The only drawback was that the house came with the ugliest dog that either Cindy or he had ever seen. It looked like a combination pit bull and Rottweiler but its exact heritage was somewhat of a mystery, even to their veterinarian.

The dog really hadn't belonged to the sellers, but one of the sons had found it several blocks away one night on his way home from drinking. At first he thought that he'd hit it with the family car, but on closer inspection he saw that it was just a frighten puppy and so thin that he could see all of its bones. He took it home and the garage became its doghouse. What it ate, since at that point things around the house were lean, no one knew but it somehow managed to gain weight and get its health back. However it wasn't a friendly poodle and the neighbors gave it a wide berth as they did with the humans that owned it. When they moved they somehow failed to remember to take the dog and Jimmy didn't have the heart to call the Humane Society and have it forcibly taken away. So the dog stayed and as he and his new owners became friendlier and they were no longer viewed by him as a threat, he moved into the warm house and became the sergeant at arms. On the down side, his previous owners had never given the animal a proper name, preferring to just call him "Dog." Despite Jimmy's best efforts to rename him, "Dog" was the only name that he'd answer to.

Dog's relationship with Cindy and her son had been excellent right from the start, but then since she was the only one that fed him, it was understandable. And her son was the one that walked him through the neighborhood and down to the park, so he was high up on Dog's approved list too. However, it took a while for Dog to accept Brent Williams, a virtual stranger no matter how often he visited the house. But Brent, who'd never owned a dog or been around them, had quickly learned Dog's favorite kind of dog cookie and he'd purchased several boxes which he stored in his old car. Each time that he visited, he'd bring in a handful. As for the neighbors, it didn't really matter since none of them socialized or talked to the Cane's anyway.

Jimmy's job with the CSPD was a love hate relationship. He loved the job, but hated what it entailed, dealing with the dead. But he looked at it as representing the deceased in their last earthly attempt at seeking justice. It was up to him to determine exactly why they had died and who or what had killed them. Natural deaths were bad enough especially if the body wasn't discovered for some time, but violent deaths were the worst, especially if small children were involved. And he'd had his share of those. Then the murders had occurred at Harrington House and through a strange set of circumstances, he and his partner Matt Jones had been assigned to the case. It was strange because normally the case would have gone to more senior and experienced detectives, especially with the deaths of five people. And it had all occurred in the home of an ex-police officer, a guy that Jimmy considered to be one of his best friends. But suddenly everyone but he and Jones were tied up elsewhere and his Captain had assigned the case to them.

As he'd told Cindy, it was probably on the second day of the investigation that he and Matt Jones came to the conclusion that the case would wind up being unsolvable, at least with what they'd uncovered so far. Shortly thereafter the Feds had swooped in and taken over, and despite his eagerness and desire to solve it, the Feds had taken a great weight and responsibility off of his shoulders. But it kept coming back to haunt them, and even more deaths had occurred.

After Brent had left the Police Department, they continued to keep in touch, but due to their differing schedules it was mostly by telephone now. But Jimmy knew that if he ever needed a real tried and proven friend, then Brent would be the one that he would call. On the other hand, he'd been there for Brent when he'd gone through his post divorce period and then again after his wife had been killed. And Brent had been the second officer to respond to the scene on the 911 call when Jimmy had shot and killed Cindy's ex-husband. He'd been the first to testify and attend the review board hearings and later he'd learned from Captain Art Thomas that Brent had fully supported his actions and followed up by saying that if Jimmy hadn't fired the fatal shot, then in seconds he would have.

With their son away at school, Dog had pretty much been confined to the fenced back yard. Occasionally when Jimmy got home early, he'd feel sorry for the cooped up dog and would change clothes and jog down to the park with him straining at the end of his long leash. Because of what Dog looked like, and the fact that the neighbors still hadn't accepted Jimmy, no one ever stopped to chat with him, or for that matter no one even waved when he ran by. Dog didn't seem to care and that was good enough for Jimmy too. Tonight as he ran he noticed that the corner house he'd once owned and remodeled was completely dark, except for the gaslight on the post outside of the front porch. He wondered if his neighbors were on vacation or out of town. The second house with the older couple that traveled, had a fancy alarm system that turned internal lights on and off at random, using a computer program. In the short time that he'd lived next door to them, he'd only seen them once and that was when they'd told him that they would be in Arizona for the winter. The third house was his and it was looking better with each passing day. The renovation was only affected by the availability of money, and since his son was attending college on a scholarship, Jimmy had figured that his out of pocket expenses would be few. Wrong, he had discovered with the first phone call for book money. So Jimmy's remodeling had slowed down considerably. When Brent had heard about it he wanted to help but knew that his friend would never accept any money. So he had collaborated with Cindy and they had added new boards to stacks of lumber in the basement and new tools to replace some of the old beat up ones. They knew that eventually he'd notice, but no one ever said anything.

When he and Dog had gotten home he'd told Cindy about the dark house on the corner and the contrast between it and the one next door lit up like a Christmas tree. Soon dinner was ready and their conversation moved on to a letter they'd received from their son today. Both of them were extremely proud of him. Around 10 PM Dog visited his favorite tree in the back yard and the Cane household retired for the night.

*

For the past week a silver SUV had driven through the neighborhood several times a day. With the dark tinted windows the neighbors couldn't see inside and they just assumed since the car was going so slowly, that someone further up the street had gotten a new vehicle. Tonight the car quietly pulled around the corner and parked beside the corner house away from the streetlight. Four people dressed in black emerged and moved through the trees and bushes to the front door. One of them either picked the lock or they had a set of master keys, because in minutes they were inside. Using small high intensity flashlights they went from room to room, but the entire house was empty, not only of residents but furniture too. Whoever owned it had quietly moved out. Frustrated, they quietly returned to the front door and out into the side yard. They looked towards the second house just as some lights turned off and others turned on. Then they saw the security company's signs in the front yard. The intruders circled through the shrubbery to the third house and quietly checked out the lock on the front door. It was one of the newer high security ones, specifically designed to prevent anyone from picking it. One of the people dressed in black, signaled the others and swung a sledge hammer and the door popped open but sounded like an explosion.

Upstairs in bed, Cindy and Jimmy had awakened with a start as they heard Dog growl and charge out the bedroom door. Jimmy had grabbed his service semiautomatic from the nightstand, removed the safety and followed behind. Halfway down the stairs in the dark he heard screaming as

294

Dog tore into one of the intruders, probably the home invaders that had been striking various homes around the City for the past few months. Then there was the sound of gunfire and Dog going down. He returned the fire, but took a round in the leg spinning him around and sliding down the stairs. He continued to search out targets and return fire from his fifteen round clip. He caught another one in the left shoulder just as he fired his last shot and collapsed to the tile floor. Cindy had found the old shotgun in the closet, and with trembling hands she had finally managed to load the five shells in it and moved to the top of the stairs. Seeing Jimmy down, she had emptied the gun in the general direction of the front hall as the invaders backed out of the door dragging their wounded with them. As she dialed 911, she heard the screech of tires as the bad guys pulled away. She ran down the stairs, saw Dog bleeding out on the light colored tile and Jimmy unconscious and bleeding. Then she smelled the smoke coming from the multiple light-switch next to the door and grabbed Jimmy's good arm and dragged him out the front door, across the porch and onto the lawn. She raced back and grabbed Dog by the collar just as the flames exploded from the wall and climbed towards the ceiling.

In what seemed like hours but was only four minutes, the first patrol car arrived on the scene and called for backup, a fire engine and an ambulance. At seven minutes and counting, as the uniform officer who'd recognized Jimmy performed first aide trying to stop the bleeding, the fire department and the paramedics arrived and took over. The fire was quickly put out but the internal smoke damage was extensive and the front foyer was destroyed. The remaining rooms were cleared and secured and the crime scene tape quickly strung up. By now Jimmy and Cindy were on their way to Penrose Community Hospital several blocks away and the CSPD brass had been notified of the attack on one of their detectives. Because it was Detective Cane, one of the uniforms had bundled Dog into the back of his patrol car and was rushing him under red lights and siren down to the all night Animal Emergency Clinic on south Academy Blvd and Airport Road.

*

Brent was awakened by the sound of the ringing bedside telephone. Only Ta, Christy, Stewart Andrews and Captain Art Thomas had the unlisted number and he immediately knew that something had happened. He wiped his eyes as Michi handed him the phone and whispered that it was Art.

"How bad is it?" asked Brent without even greeting his friend.

"Pretty bad. Somebody hit Jimmy's place a little while ago."

"Like he got shot?"

"Twice that I know of. Cindy's ok, but they took out Dog too. The place caught fire, but it was confined by the FD to the front hall. The rest of the place is smoked damaged. Jimmy's in the ER right now and they're working on him. One of the uniforms rushed Dog to the Emergency Clinic and I haven't heard any more about him. The Crime Scene guys have the home under a microscope. I just talked to Matt Jones and he's on his way to the house. He said that he couldn't do anything at the Hospital so he might as well start at the house. I got to go. See you later."

Brent told Michi and asked her to go get Ta while he dressed. In five minutes she returned with him and Christy, and while Brent filled them in, she dressed and got ready.

"Think that it has anything to do with us?" asked Ta.

"I don't know, but sure sounds strange. He's been connected to Harrington House right from the beginning and I don't hold much with coincidences. Michi and I are going to the Hospital, and I need you to hold down the fort."

"You can't go alone Brent. Either I go or you take Joe and Jim with you. What's it going to be?"

"Ok, you can come, but I don't want Christy alone right now so she goes too. Turn your guys loose to watch the house and grounds at all costs, no holds barred. Ok?"

*

The scene at Penrose Community Hospital was chaotic at best. An off duty plain clothes police detective had been shot twice during a home invasion and the call had quickly gone out for blood. Patrol cars began to fill the parking lot as the locals, the county and the state sent in officers to both guard and donate. Civilians needing medical care weren't turned away, but if you were high on drugs you might want to try another emergency room tonight. Ta maneuvered the big white Mercedes through the confusion to the front door and parked it in a no parking zone as Brent and Michi rushed out and inside. Ta and Christy were right behind them. From the look on Brent's face and Ta's, no one wanted to stop them. Then Art Thomas walked over, whispered something to Brent and ushered Michi and Christy over to the reception area where Cindy was still in a state of shock.

One of the uniforms, on seeing Ta, moved to

stop him and Brent quietly spoke up, said that he was his personal bodyguard and unless he wanted to die on the spot, now was not the time to become a cowboy. Most recognized Brent, and for those that didn't know him, Brent announced that he was Detective Cane's attorney. While Michi and her mother tended to Jimmy's wife, Brent and Ta learned what had happened or at least what the investigating detectives now on the scene had learned. Hours later the doctors announced that their patient had survived, but wouldn't be doing much for a while. He was being moved from the operating room to recovery and his wife could visit him.

"Think this has anything to do with your case?" asked Thomas once he'd gotten Brent aside.

"Art, I really have no idea. However I'm just not a big believer in coincidences. Have you been out to his house yet?"

"Yeah, I got the first tour with the CSI's. It's going to take some cleaning up and rebuilding. The front hall is gone and the smoke damage is pretty extensive. Jimmy isn't going to be pleased with the water damage either. I know that he had it well insured but once we release it, then the real fight with the insurance carrier begins."

"Not this time Art. Now he has a couple of bored attorney's representing him right from the get go. What the story on the dog?"

"The uniform that drove him to the Vet's thought that he was dead, but he apparently wasn't. Last that I heard they were working on him. Kept asking everyone what kind of a dog he was, but no one could tell them. You know?"

"Nope, I don't. Kind of looks like some kind of an unusual cross. I do know that he can be meaner than hell. Took a long time for him to accept me and then it was only if I brought him some big dog cookies."

"I guess we'll just have to wait and see on him."

"Since Jimmy's in recovery, I'm going to have Cindy come home with us tonight. I know that you'll have guys posted here, so put me in the loop if his condition changes. Ok?" asked Brent.

"Yeah sure. Don't expect that we'll know much until midday tomorrow. I'll give you a call after our update meeting," said Art.

As the sleek white Mercedes left the parking lot of Penrose Community Hospital, a uniform patrol car intercepted it and led the parade all of the way back to the gates at Harrington House. The officer waited until the big wrought iron gates closed and locked before he drove off. In their absence, Joe and Jim would have willingly sacrificed their lives to protect the house and grounds.

In the morning Jimmy had awakened and Captain Thomas had sent a patrol car to Harrington House to pick up Cindy. Michi, not wanting her to be alone, accompanied her. The others returned to their normal activities and Christy began explaining what had happened to June Andrews. Brent, Ta and Stew were rehashing everything in the office.

"We won't know anything until Art calls and his meeting isn't until later today. But Jimmy's house is a mess and I know how much he loved that place. When they release him I'm going to try and bring him here. He can't go home and doesn't have anywhere other than a hotel or motel to stay. Neither one of them has any relatives that I know of, except for the son and I'll call him this morning. Stew could you look into the insurance angle for him? Maybe if we let them know up front that he has a law firm representing him we can cut through some of the red tape?"

"Consider it done," said Stew who was bored and welcomed something to do.

"Maybe it's the Gods telling him to find another house," smiled Brent. "Because he's a light skinned black and she's white, the neighbors never accepted either of them. You finally find the house you love and it becomes like an island. And that's after you fix it up so that it equals or is better looking than all of the neighbors. Go figure."

As the morning passed on, the detectives and the crime scene people discovered the break in of the corner house. Speculation covered the board from a revenge thing to a random home invasion. However the four intruders had been very well armed, not the usual two guys with a shotgun. And until not too long ago, the Canes had lived in the corner house.

It was late that afternoon when Ta heard the sound of a car horn and looked outside towards the gate. Captain Art Thomas was parked in front of it in his personal car waiting. Ta pushed the button and met him at the front door.

"Afternoon Ta, I need to see Brent." Ta grunted something and ushered him into the office where Stew had just gotten off his cell phone as Brent talked on the house phone. Stew motioned him to a chair and waited for Brent to finish.

"You don't look happy my friend," said Brent.

"I'm not. We've posted guards on Jimmy's room and a uniform car in front of his house. The gun fight started the fire. Either a bullet or some shot hit the switch and it arched and started the fire so arson wasn't involved. Jimmy's doing as well as can be expected. He got hit in the right leg and the left shoulder. He'll be out for some time and maybe if he's smart he'll go for a medical disability. I sure wouldn't blame him. Now the feeling right now is that it wasn't a random home invasion, but a planned hit. Neighbors have reported seeing a strange SUV driving around the neighborhood for the past week. There are tire tracks left in the pavement around the corner that have been identified as coming from a late model Chevy Tahoe. Footprints next door tell us that there were four of them and from the casings on the floor of the foyer, they were well armed and didn't hesitate to fire. The lock on the front door of the corner house had been picked and that takes some talent and unique tools. Remember that not too long ago that house was owned and occupied by the Canes."

"So you think that the perps hit the first house, found it empty and just moved on?" asked Brent.

"We don't really know. Maybe they had several addresses and just started with the corner house. But the one in the middle is well lit up and protected. Any professional would know to leave it alone and move on. Maybe the third house wasn't on the list but since they'd already taken out the corner one, they'd do the third one just to keep from arousing suspicions. Like they were just interested in the loot, not the people. But Cindy said that Dog heard them come in and started the fight. By the time she found the shotgun in the back of the closet and loaded it, Jimmy was already down and they were starting up the stairs. She just opened up and kept pulling the trigger until she'd gone through five rounds of heavy buckshot. At that point the shooting was over with and in the dark they dragged out the wounded and got away. Hopefully they all suffered fatal wounds and we'll find them in a roadside ditch."

"I doubt it," spoke up Ta.

"Why?" asked Brent.

"Because this was well planned. They had the right address, just the wrong time. They carried lock picks and probably a sledge hammer. Kind of hard to have a sledge hammer handy, unless you had planned ahead. Besides Jimmy was the lead detective on the Harrington House case and has tried his best to stay on top of it." Ta smiled and Brent knew that he had more to say but that it could wait.

"That's why he has the guards?" smiled Thomas.

"Where's his car?" asked Stewart.

"The Department picked up the unmarked city car this morning and his is still parked in the garage. Why?" asked Art.

"We need to get the car over here, before they release him," said Brent. "He doesn't know it yet but he's moving in here until this thing shakes out."

"Well the insurance carrier is on board as of my last call. Their investigator has already been in contact with the CSPD and will visit the scene today. Jimmy can expect to get their first offer by the end of the week. I told them to make it a fair offer because I was bored and would welcome the chance to take it to court on a pro bono basis. They don't want to spend a ton of money going to court when the payout is probably less than 100 or 150K. I expect that their first offer will be acceptable."

"Ta, off the record," said Art, "do you think that this is somehow connected to the Harrington House case?"

"Yes, I do," he answered.

"Ok, if you think so then I'm going to push in that direction. It beats some of the other ideas that I've heard today and ties into an ongoing case," replied Thomas.

"Oh, when you walked in I was talking to the Vet treating Dog. Apparently he took a hard hit and lost a lot of blood. They would normally have just put him down, but because a cop had brought him in they thought that he was some kind of a police dog and went the extra mile. He got several blood transfusions from donor dogs, one of which was a big Great Dane and he's still breathing but not on his own. He's wired up like some high tech toy but only time will tell if he makes it. I didn't realize it but even the Vets have specialized practices. This guy does general practice and he called in several others that specialize in internal wounds and gunshots and something else that I can't remember. It took all four of them to handle the surgery. I've never been in the place, but it must be something special. I told him to send all of the bills to me."

"That's generous of you," smiled Art.

"No, that's what friends are for. You, Jimmy and Matt took care of me when Tani was killed and I'm just doing a small thing to return the favor."

*

Seven days later, Jimmy Cane was released from the hospital at the request of his health insurance carrier. It was right in the operations manual. One gunshot wound allowed you five days of care and two gave you an extra two, although the insurance carrier would have been happier if you'd been treated on an outpatient basis. Jimmy told every visitor the same identical story. His wife Cindy had come to visit him every day and had stayed from early morning to late evening. Either patrol cars would pick her up and bring her home or Ta would drive her in the big Mercedes. The house no longer had the yellow crime scene tape wrapped around it and a restoration company had removed most of the external damage before boarding it up and securing it. Inside had been cleaned but the charred front foyer still set the tone for any visitors. Brent had taken pictures of every wall and corner and had shown them to Jimmy, who just let out a sigh. Their son had been convinced by Brent to stay in school and not worry about his stepfather and mother. Reluctantly after talking to his parents, he'd agreed.

An abandoned, silver Chevy Tahoe had been found parked in the long term parking lot at the Colorado Springs Municipal Airport. The interior was covered with blood, which the forensics' lab had identified as to the type and DNA, but couldn't match it to anything in either the local or Federal databases. However four different DNA's were identified. From the amount of blood that had been found, there was much speculation as to whether two or three individuals had bled out. The vehicle had been towed to the police garage and the crime scene technicians had carefully gone over it but had been unsuccessful in finding any fingerprints in the interior. Only occasional smudges could be found on the exterior. The ownership would be traced back to an older couple in Boulder, Colorado, and the police report would indicated that the practically new SUV had been stolen from a shopping mall parking lot in Broomfield, Colorado nearly two weeks earlier.

Attempts to get anything from confidential informants and street people had been unsuccessful. And the local Crime Stoppers network hadn't received a single call in regards to the shootout. It was as if a giant blackout had descended upon the attack which for publicity purposes the police public relations representatives had chalked up to a simple home invasion gone bad.

Chapter 27

At Brent's insistence, both Jimmy and Cindy Cane hesitantly moved into Harrington House for his period of convalescence. He was confined to a wheelchair, but since the house had a large elevator operating between the basement and the second floor, once he got his bearings he could move around fairly well, but slowly. His biggest problem, after the pain, was boredom. He'd always been a very active individual and suddenly here he was confined to a wheelchair and operating with only one good leg and arm. Watching movies and television in his upstairs bedroom suite only interested him for a short time before he was down sitting in Brent's office looking for something to do.

"I'm going nuts buddy, isn't there something that I can do to earn my keep around here?" he asked Brent.

"Ok, my friend. For recreation we have not one but two pool tables on two floors, a complete recreation room with professional stand alone electronic games, a poker table, a huge TV with all of the latest gaming from Sony, IBM and others, a fully stocked bar and TV's everywhere along with a large library of both books and movies. Downstairs we have a fairly complete gym and many exercise machines. Christy has a professional kitchen and she awaits your requests and Ta is watching over you like a Godfather. What more do you want?" Brent joked.

"I'd like my house and life back the way it was, if you want the truth," Jimmy replied.

"I've been there, and maybe you want to think about that a bit. Stew got the insurance carrier to cough up enough dough to put your house back together and to allow you to purchase all new carpeting, drapes and clothing because of the smoke damage. Inside anything that smelled of smoke will get replaced. So as I see it, besides you whining about some tiny bullet holes in your arm and leg, you're coming out ahead," Brent laughed.

"Yeah sure," smiled Jimmy.

"But please consider getting another house. I know how difficult it was for me to move back in here, and you can't be much different. You'll always look at the front door and remember that night. It'll never leave your thoughts. You're fortunate, you actually can move on and probably make a buck on the sale. I didn't have that option. If I did, I'd be living somewhere else."

"Cindy's been mentioning the same thing to me. She said that she's thinking about getting a job so that she isn't home alone in the house for long periods of time. I got the message loud and clear. Oh, she'll do whatever I come up with, but I know how she feels."

"So now the time has arrived for my sales pitch. Sit back and listen up my friend, because I'm going to share some of my superb wisdom with you at no charge," Brent smiled as he sat back in his chair.

"Within the next 30 to 60 days you're going to have to decide whether you want to return to work for the CSPD or take a partial medical disability retirement. Should you return to working for Art Thomas, he will have no choice but to reassign you to anything that's not connected in any way to the Harrington House case. In fact he may be forced to transfer you out of homicide. Remember now that I've personally been through a lot of this. Ok, that's point number one. Number two is your house, and as I said you may want to dump it and buy another one for reasons we've already talked about."

"So the next question you probably have is what would you do if you took the money and ran? My law practice consists of Stewart, myself and Phil Paulson. It's officially named Andrews, Williams & Paulson PC. As you know Stew is retired and only helps out if he has nothing else to do or if I ask him to. But he's the senior partner and his name carries a lot of weigh in our legal system. I've been trying to step away and decrease my workload which is why I brought Phil on board. He's young, aggressive and hungry. Until I roped him into joining me he was starving. Now he has so much work that he's been forced to farm out some of it."

"What we've never had but always wanted was an in-house investigator just like the DA's office has. That brings me to you. You're very proficient at your profession, and I think that having you on board would be a real asset to my practice."

"You want me to work for you?" he said in amazement.

"Yep, that's about it. I've already discussed it with Stew. In fact it was originally his idea, so he's all in favor of it. And I know that Phil's spending too much time trying to be an investigator which he hasn't been trained for. It substantially decreases his billing hours, which costs everyone money. With you on board, he could go back to generating more billable hours. Now as I see it, we could be competitive with what the DA's Office pays and could cover some benefits too, but some of the benefits would have to come out of the year end bonus."

"You're serious, aren't you?" asked Cane.

"Yep old buddy. See it's this way. I already have Ta who's obviously Japanese. So if I had a big black guy too, then maybe I'd qualify for some low interest government grant money?"

"Yeah, sure. But you're really serious about this?" he asked.

"Look Jimmy, going back into the line of fire for the CSPD doing a different job, wouldn't be my choice, but it might be yours. I'm just trying to offer an alternative. I could really use your help, but whether you take my offer or not won't change anything between us. We've been friends for a long time and I wouldn't want to risk ruining that."

"I don't know what to say," replied Jimmy. "Wouldn't I need a license for that?"

"Stew told me that his old law firm had a dozen investigators on the staff. Each was trained and licensed as a "Private Investigator" or as they say in the comics, a PI. Each had a Concealed Weapons Carry Permit and they were always armed. Now he suggested just buying a car for you rather than fooling around with the mileage reimbursement thing and I agree. Insurance wise, you'd go on the same medical and life insurance policy that I have. It's a small group thing and everyone's on it including Stew's wife. He's 65 and covered by Medicare. If you decided to join us, then moving closer would be in your best interest and your new home would have to be large enough so that you could have an office in it. From the look on your face I know what you're thinking so just hold on a moment."

"When Stew sold the Denver practice he walked away with a lot of money because it was a cash sale. Those are really rare these days but he was just at the right place at the right time. We've been driving all over town looking for investments in raw land that we can develop, and buildings like warehouses, apartments, and small shopping centers. We even looked at a high tech company with existing management. He's already invested a bundle in a local bank and if you decided to join us and move, I can assure you that his bank would be happy to finance it. The nice thing about that is that all of the paperwork on the front end would be pretty much eliminated. And Michi wanted me to mention that you would probably need someone to answer your phones, run your office and all of that and that Cindy would be a perfect candidate."

"Boy, you've got everyone involved in this," he laughed.

"Well I don't expect an answer right now, but I just wanted to get my hat in the ring before you had to talk to Art and his people. Besides that, the sooner I can get you moving on this, the sooner I can get you into another house, hopefully close by and the sooner I can get that damn dog of yours out of my house," Brent laughed just as Dog trotted into the large foyer, heard voices and walked into Brent's office. With the patches of shaved hair all over his body he looked as if he gone through a war, which in a way he had. He licked Brent's outstretched hand and sat down beside Jimmy's wheelchair resting his big ugly head against his one good leg.

"He's quite a warrior," smiled Brent.

"Yep, he sort of surprised me too. He jumped in there right away. Reminded me of the saying, "show no fear." I figured that he was a goner. No way that he could survive. But he's healing up pretty good. Couple of months his hair will have grown back and he'll look as good as new."

"I hope that he looks better than he did," laughed Brent. "In fact I asked the Vet if he couldn't do something to make him look better while he had him knocked out."

"Funny how things sometimes work out. I mean you and I becoming good friends. Who would have thought it? And now I'm living in your house and eating your food. I guess there's a good story there if you're a writer. But I want to thank you again."

"For what? You'd do the same thing for me."

"Hell no 1 wouldn't. I'd tell you to keep your ugly dog away from my house and charge you by the night and meal," he laughed as he rolled out of the office and headed towards the kitchen.

Brent laughed as he watched the dog and his master leaving his office. He had invested a fortune in keeping that ugly brute alive and when it came time for him to leave the Vet's animal hospital he didn't know what to do with him. Christy, a dog lover insisted that it was only right to bring him to Harrington House but she had Ta install a number of low expandable gates to keep him somewhat confined. She fully expected that as he healed and could move better he'd either crash through the gates or jump them so that he could go exploring all of those fancy rooms and their expensive contents. Until then he'd hang around the kitchen mooching tidbits from her.

The surprise had been Jimmy's wife Cindy. She definitely wasn't a slacker and from the very first day had insisted on helping out with the cleaning and cooking. She washed floors alongside of Joe and Jim, cleaned rugs next to Ta and washed windows with Christy. Fortunately it was still cold outside otherwise she'd have been out helping Ta attend to the flower beds. Christy knew that she was just grateful for a place to stay and wanted to earn her keep so she just backed away and enjoyed the help.

The house had three laundry rooms complete with oversize front loading commercial washers and dryers, ironing boards, built in sorting tables and cabinets. One was down in the basement, a second was right next to the servant's quarters and the last and largest one was on the top floor at the end of the hall. Cindy had made a point of searching through all of the rooms each morning and handling the dirty laundry. Since Jimmy didn't have anything else to do, he'd slowly roll along behind her as she stacked everything in his lap.

Because of his injuries, Jimmy had numerous appointments with his primary care doctor, surgeons, therapists, and others and each time Ta would help him into the big Mercedes if it was available and drive him to his appointment. Sometimes Cindy would accompany him and other times it was Brent, Michi or Stewart. However he noticed that when he was with Ta, he was never asked to wait in the reception room and he thought that was funny. Brent's original description of his father-in-law as looking like Quasimodo was very accurate and no one ever wanted to stare at his nearly black piercing eyes. If his size didn't immediately get your attention, then his scowling face and bald head definitely would. Even people his own size or larger took one look and got out of his way. The more that

Jimmy thought about it, the more he wondered if the name Quasimodo even covered it?

With each passing day he healed just a tad more and by the end of the third week he'd managed after much trial and error, to finally master the dreaded crutches. Granted, he couldn't move very fast, but he could at least move. Several times he'd asked Ta to drive by his old house just to see what was happening and surprisingly, he had. A construction company arranged by Brent and Stewart were just finishing up the building stage. Next, the painters and carpet cleaning people would move in and finally the new furniture would arrive along with some of their new clothing. But each time he returned to his home, it looked less desirable than it had.

One afternoon he'd asked Ta if he'd go for a drive and Ta who'd come to like the tall black guy had readily agreed. They'd driven up and down streets in several nearby neighborhoods and Jimmy had copied down the names of realtors and addresses whenever he saw a home for sale in his price range. When he returned to Harrington House later on, he'd make some follow-up phone calls.

It was week six when Brent had called him into his office.

"Art called this morning and asked to set up a meeting with you. He said that he could come here, but if you didn't mind it would be better if you met him at his office at the Police Operations Center. I checked your schedule and set it up for 9 AM tomorrow. That ok with you?" asked Brent.

"Sure, no problem. And by the way, thanks for handling my house rebuilding. Cindy and I have driven by and it looks pretty good."

"My question is, do you want me to

313

accompany you as your attorney of record tomorrow morning or would you rather do it on your own?" Brent asked.

"You know, I've been thinking about this meeting for some time, and maybe I'll just have Cindy drive us over there if that's ok with you?"

"No problem here. But I'm available if you need me."

That night Brent had received a phone call from Phil Paulson asking for his help and had spent the next day in District Court. As a result it wasn't until the third day at breakfast that he met Jimmy and asked him about his meeting at the CSPD.

"It was really something Brent. They had Captain Thomas who didn't look very happy, a Deputy Chief, the Human Resources Manager, the Department's Medical Advisor, the Assistant City Manager, a City attorney and a representative from the Mayor's Office. I didn't even know who most of them were. Wouldn't you think that I'd at least have met the medical guy? I mean he had over a month to dial up and holler hello."

"I can see where this is going and why Art wasn't very happy," replied Brent thinking of how old Allen Sheffield had protected him. "I'm sorry Jimmy I should have insisted on attending with you."

"Hey, no problem buddy. Cause on my side of the table was myself, Stewart who'd called earlier and insisted on joining me after he'd talked to Art last night, Ta who insisted on standing behind my chair in his most threatening manor and grunting the word "assholes" in Japanese, my union or Police Protective Association Representative, a expert Doctor supplied by Stewart and a newspaper reporter."

"No kidding," smiled Brent.

"First off they had a big argument about having a member of the press present. They said that it wasn't allowed according to the CSPD manual and that really set Stew off. Later he told me that he was just doing that to improve his bargaining position. So finally he agreed to dump the reporter if they would dump the Mayor's rep. Now it settled down a bit, but Ta was still calling them assholes under his breath and it just broke me up because they had no idea what he was saying and neither would I if he hadn't told me beforehand."

"So what's the bottom line here?"

"The bottom line my friend is that you now have a full time investigator on your staff," Jimmy smiled.

"That's great, but did you get your disability?"

"Well they tried to stonewall Stewart and finally he just stood up and told them to go to hell that he'd see them in court and invite all of the press to attend. He said that he'd include a free lunch and football tickets to the first fifty to accept his invitation. Then he tied my shooting to the Harrington House case and said that it occurred in the line of duty and that he'd be suing not only for medical bill reimbursement, but compensation for the loss of my house, the money spent on lodging since then, mental anguish, oh hell he had a whole string of things that I can't remember. So finally the city attorney and Stew sat down and reached a compromise. I retire at the end of this month with a 40% medical disability. The City will cover all of my medical expenses including any deductibles. They will buy my house for the appraisal value or an average of three certified appraisers, one chosen by me, one by them and another picked from random. On top of that I'll get a lump sum payment of nearly a quarter million to make me go away."

"That sounds like a perfect deal," smiled Brent.

"Hell if I'd known that it would work out this way, I probably would have shot myself years ago," Jimmy laughed.

"Ta told me that he'd been curbside house hunting with you. Find anything?"

"As a matter of fact I have picked out three homes in my price range. One's brand new and the others are resales. Now that I'm getting around pretty well with my cane, Cindy and I are lining up the grand tours. Shouldn't be long before we're out of here and you're on your own again," Jimmy laughed.

"Hey, there's no problem here. You can stay as long as you'd like. Seriously, we've enjoyed your company so don't rush into anything. This house is so big that sometimes it feels like we're living in a barn."

*

Exactly four months from the morning of the shooting, the Cane family moved into their brand new home in a nice residential neighborhood just east of the resort hotel. For the first time since they'd been married Jimmy wouldn't be tearing apart and remodeling the house as they lived in it. As a part of the deal, the builder had agreed to convert one of the first floor front bedrooms into a large office. Sometimes in a slow market, one had to bend some rules in order to accommodate a buyer, especially one that was pre-qualified. Jimmy's building activities would be confined to designing and building a new dog house for Dog. However it was unlikely that he'd spend much time outside in the large fenced back yard.

During his time spent recovering as Brent's house guest, Jimmy had quietly pursued the idea of becoming a private investigator and had taken several Internet courses from reputable schools. He'd also applied for and gotten a weapons carry permit from the El Paso County Sheriff's Office. Filling out the necessary forms to become licensed with the State hadn't been any big deal either. With Stewart's help, they'd set up the ownership of the new house as being a Limited Liability Company in order to keep Jimmy's name off the title. Insurance, utilities, phones and taxes were all billed to the LLC. Michi, June Andrews, and Judy Onnan had pitched in to help Cindy pick out her colors and furniture and Jimmy did his best to distance himself from that adventure.

Their only son had returned from school several times during the period that the Canes' were living at Harrington House. He obviously was impressed with the place and especially Michi. Around her, he acted like a love sick puppy, which wasn't that unusual since most males acted the same way. But he really liked the new house and especially the neighborhood that had welcomed all of them so warmly. He also liked to borrow Jimmy's new car, a silver Chrysler 300 that he'd leased at Stew's suggestion. Otherwise he drove his older Honda back and forth to school up in Greeley.

Dog had captivated everyone's hearts with his recovery from deaths door. His confined quarters hadn't lasted long and he had quickly gained access to the entire house. According to Ta, never once had he had an accident, nor had he destroyed any of the expensive furniture. But Dog was smart enough to know that something was happening that would affect his future, but he didn't know exactly what until the final day. Brent doubted that there was a dry eye in the house, when Dog had been loaded into the new Chrysler and driven away.

Chapter 28

Art Thomas and Brent were having a very late lunch at the Broadmoor Hotel, in one of their restaurants that neither one had been in before.

"Boy I hope that you're paying for this one," he laughed after scanning the dollar column on the menu.

"Cheapskate," smiled Brent. "Invite me out to lunch and then stick me with the bill."

"I never expected this place. Actually I didn't even know it existed," Art replied.

"To tell you the truth, after you called this morning I called to make reservations and everything that I mentioned seemed to be booked so their representative suggested that we try this place. Guess I never realized that they have a dozen or more places to eat. Maybe we should ask for a list and start at the top?"

The waiter appeared as soon as Brent looked up from his menu and seeing Art's confusion, he just went ahead and ordered for both of them.

"So what's going on?" Brent asked.

"Remember that blood that our techs found in that abandoned SUV out at the airport? You remember that we suspected that it was tied in with Jimmy's shooting? And we did manage to tie it to the blood samples at the crime scene."

"Sure, but it didn't get any hits when you ran them against the local and Federal databases."

"Exactly, now there's some controversy

about whether or not a DNA sample can be used to identify a general race. Like the Swedes, or Germans, or the Irish, that sort of thing. Until recently most scientists agreed that it was impossible, that there wasn't any way to specifically identify a tribe of origin. However during the past month a Swiss research firm announced that they had a breakthrough. I don't know the particulars and even if I knew them I doubt that I'd be able to explain it. But on a hunch I contacted Interpol and asked for their help. Basically I explained that it was all connected to maybe 40 or 50 deaths around the world and most likely it all began here in Colorado Springs."

"Wow, kind of a stretch isn't it?"

"Whatever I told them seemed to work and I air expressed the four sample DNA's to them and they asked the Swiss firm for help. Bottom line is that yesterday I got a call from my Interpol contact and he told me that the four samples all had enough genetic information for their testing or comparisons and that our four guys were most likely all oriental. They had all kinds of qualifications and exceptions, but the results showed that Japanese was well within the realm of possibilities"

"Here we go again Art. We're back to the Yakuza angle. But why would they be even remotely interested in Jimmy?"

"Probably because he was the lead detective on the Harrington House case and everything anyway connected to it thereafter. His name is all over the reports and files. So is Matt Jones and I'm not certain what to do about that one either."

"How's he holding up? Losing a partner sometimes gets pretty personal."

"He took Jimmy's retirement pretty hard.

Said that he figured they'd be partners until they got their twenty in and retired together. I think what the talking heads at the department and the city tried to do to Jimmy really soured him and a lot of other guys. I mean why stick your neck out to protect the general public because if you're injured in any way there just might not be anyone pulling for you. Without Stewart, Jimmy would have been railroaded, no doubt."

"You know, I could never figure that one out. Why act like the injured party was trying to put one over on the city. I mean the guy got shot and we all knew it. Right from the start it was obvious that he had nothing to do with it. Why did he suddenly become the enemy?"

"I don't know but as soon as I got that feeling I called Stew at home. At the time I didn't think that you'd be able to help because they probably figured that you were as bad as he was. But Stew handled it perfectly. You should have heard the screaming after he and Jimmy left the meeting. The City's attorney just wanted to quietly settle it out of court, but the others must have had some bad information because they were screaming and fighting like cats and dogs."

"Well at least it worked out well for Jimmy," replied Brent.

"Yeah, I talked to him yesterday and I can't remember ever hearing him so happy. He loves his new house which really is a beauty, the friendly neighborhood and especially his job. Now he works from home, Cindy helps and it sounds as if the weight of the world has been removed from his shoulders."

"I think that he'll do well as a investigator for us. He always was aggressive and curious. His size is big enough to intimidate a lot of people which in that job is a definite plus. Even Phil's excited especially since he's the first to admit that he was a mediocre investigator. Did you know that Phil lives only four blocks from Jimmy?"

"No I didn't. Kind of a contrast though," smiled Art.

"Sure is. Phil looks every inch the lawyer, and there's no doubt that Jimmy's the big tough ex-cop."

"Well I wanted to keep you in the loop and also ask you to get Ta's opinion especially after what happened during that Pacific Rim Conference."

"Honestly Art, I'm beginning to think that Ta doesn't know anything more than we do. Oh, he can explain a lot of what's happened from the Japanese angle, but so far we haven't been able to get on top of it."

"Well ask him anyway, ok?"

*

The next two months passed by uneventfully. Brent worked primarily from his home office handling bigger cases and wealthier clients. Stewart assisted him whenever he asked, but really looked forward to spring and golfing, perhaps even a bit of fly fishing which he'd never done before. Phil Paulson due to an overload, continued to farm out cases and occasionally he'd even pass one on to one of his old partners just for kicks. Everyone was pleased with the way Jimmy Cane had worked out handling the investigation side. And Jimmy was now kiddingly calling himself the "Dick Tracy of the Harrington House Gang".

Ta was beginning to prepare the flower beds and was raising seedlings in the new greenhouse which was nearly completed. Joe and Jim had nearly completed painting the interior of the big house and looked forward to getting back to helping Ta. For the rest of the Harrington House Gang, it was business as usual.

Chapter 29

"Good morning Christy," said Brent as he entered the kitchen.

"Morning Brent," she replied not looking up from the stove.

"Have you seen Ta this morning? I need to ask him something."

"He's not here Brent. He left last night and told me to give you this letter. I don't know what it says, but it took him a long time to write it," she replied.

Brent looked at her extended hand with the letter and then at her eyes which were filled with tears. He took the letter and returned to his office, closed the door and sat down behind his desk, then he noticed that the envelope was sealed. He ripped it open and began to read it.

"Brent:" it began.

"I'm very sorry that we didn't have time to discuss this, but I only got the phone call late yesterday. I'll be gone for a while, exactly how long, I don't know yet. But let me start at the beginning. I left Japan because I had killed three very important people. They had attacked my family, and had to be dealt with Yakuza style. I knew that it wouldn't end there so to protect those remaining family members I left the country and went to California using a new name and identification papers supplied by my uncle. I

became Ta Mishinko. That was many years ago. I assume that your friend Art Thomas ran a background check on me and that it came up with nothing prior to thirty years ago when I went to work in LA. In my absence my uncle's position in the family continued to rise until just recently he became the head of the family. Sukara is the blood son of one of the men that I killed. He and my uncle have been at odds since his father's death, however he wasn't powerful enough to attack him until just recently. I told you that one of my distant relatives had written me a letter and part of it described my uncle and how he was now at war with Sukara and had chased him into the mountains. My uncle's men finally found and captured him and took him before our family. Sukara demanded that his accuser face him and somehow he managed to get close enough to stab Taniaka, before my uncle's guards beheaded him."

"Taniaka was my mentor and guardian and had trained me to follow in his footsteps. When I was forced to leave it devastated both of us. However he has now asked for my help and I cannot refuse his request. I don't know how badly he was injured, but I assume for him to ask such a thing, it must be serious. I know that you won't understand all of this so just chalk it up to the Japanese culture and the Yakuza tradition. His Number 2 man sent a plane for me as soon as I spoke with him and it will pick me up at the Colorado Spring's Airport. For security reasons and also to keep Interpol and the Japanese National Police unaware of my presence, our route back to Tokyo will not be direct."

"I have instructed Joe and Jim to obey your every command and while they still can't speak much English, they do understand most of it.

Actually they've done very well since they've been with us and while I'm in Japan I hope to get their death sentences removed. They know this and also that when I do return, I had better find you, Michi and Christy safe and sound, or they will die. They know who my uncle is and they know who I am too."

"In my absence please keep them busy and protect yourselves at all times. Now, for the most difficult part. I need to ask you to explain all of this to Michi and Christy. Please tell them what they need to know to understand. I know this is difficult, but I was unable to find the right words last night. You are good with words and I know that you will find a way."

"May your God bless and protect you,"
Signed, *"The enemy of your enemies, Ta."*

Brent read the letter several more times. He wondered if Ta would ever return or would he be captured by the police, or killed by his or his uncle's enemies. Had all of the attacks on Harrington House, been because his uncle's enemies had discovered his hiding place. But they had nearly thirty years while he lived in California to find him? And the attacks had begun before he'd arrived. He attempted unsuccessfully to rationalize how this all came together, but couldn't figure it out. It was hard enough discovering that his father-in-law was some kind of a Yakuza killer hunted by the Japanese police and Interpol. And what about the latest attack on the Cane's? How did they fit into this? Jimmy was just a cop doing his job. Had he made some telephone calls that pulled up a red flag? He sat back in his chair for a long time thinking about it. Wondering how you could get an expensive long range jet aircraft into the US and out again without being detected. Or maybe they had some cover story or had paid off the right people. He took out a map, found Japan and wondered where it would land? Same problems there as here, he thought. After about an hour of organizing his thoughts, he developed a plan, called Michi on her cell phone and asked her to find Christy and meet him in the kitchen. This was going to be a tough case to sell.

*

The sleek Gulfstream V aircraft had barely come to a stop at the Colorado Springs Municipal Airport shortly after 3 AM when Ta boarded it. The tall thin well-dressed professor that met him, bowed deeply, and welcomed him aboard. Ta just slightly nodded his head. He was one of Taniaka's trusted advisors and during the flight back to Japan, he alone would update Ta on what had happened and his uncle's condition. Ta was a man to be feared by one and all. He was Taniaka's nephew, he was well trained as a Yakuza and he had already killed many enemies. His reputation was that of a fearless warrior, one to be avoided at all costs. Even his own people refused to meet his stare, afraid that he'd lash out and kill them on the spot.

Ta's flight would cover nearly 10,000 miles and several stops, both to pick up additional passengers and refuel. By the time that they reached their final destination, he would be fully briefed and surrounded by heavily armed and trusted Yakuza bodyguards. For him to return to his home country was exceptionally dangerous. Not only would his uncle's enemies be eager to kill him, but the government agencies would consider his capture or death to be something like the second coming in the Western world.

*

Each morning after breakfast, Brent would search numerous English speaking Internet sites in Japan looking for any news of Ta or recent Yakuza activity. Occasionally he'd check the US State Department web sites looking for travel warnings in the Far East. So far after two weeks of searching he hadn't seen anything of interest. Inquiries regarding Ta's absence from Phil Paulson, Jimmy Cane or Art Thomas were answered with the story that he'd been asked for help by one of his distant relatives living in southern California, and had taken a short vacation to accommodate them since they were elderly. Brent offered nothing more, but any astute observer could easily see from the looks on Michi and Christy's faces that something was drastically wrong. Only Stewart Andrews knew the truth and since he was Brent's personal attorney, he couldn't pass it on to anyone including his wife.

Around Harrington House, everything operated the same, but different in a way. Brent was now carefully watching over the security system and Joe and Jim had split the day into two overlapping shifts. While one slept, one watched. In between they caught up on their normal duties. However shortly after Ta had left, the Colorado Front Range had been hit by a tremendous spring snowstorm and had been buried under nearly three feet of snow. Very little was moving around the City and just as soon as the main streets were passable, a second wave inundated them for the second time within ten days tearing down power lines and shutting off electricity. Since Brent had installed the large natural gas fed backup generator shortly after moving in, it automatically cut in and no more than a flicker of light was observed. However, the neighborhood looked strange with everything blacked out except the Hotel, Harrington House and two other privately owned homes.

The storms had raged for nearly 48 hours and just when the flakes quit falling, the strong northerly winds picked up creating a blizzard and whiteout conditions. By this time the Andrew's had walked to Harrington House and literally moved in. Even with Brent's conservation of electricity and only using what was absolutely necessary, the facility was well lit and warm. Since the kitchen had several large commercial freezers and refrigerators and two huge pantries, everyone would continue to eat well. And as long as telephone service was available, life within Harrington House would operate fairly close to normal.

With everyone's attention drawn to the snowstorms and the wind, the pursuit of information on the absent Ta had dropped considerably. Then from one extreme, that of cold and ice, the prevailing winds had shifted, the sun came out and the tremendous piles of ice and snow left by snowplows and graders slowly began to melt creating new problems of slush and flooding. Storm sewers throughout the city became plugged, catch basins filled beyond capacity, streams overflowed their banks and flooding prevailed. At night streets became skating rinks with dangerous black ice. While the overall crime rate dropped dramatically, the number of domestic violence complaints rose according to how long people were confined to their homes and apartments.

Time is fleeting as the saying goes and at Harrington House it was no different. It was now three months since Ta had left in the middle of the night and since then Brent hadn't heard from him, nor had anyone else. He continued to closely follow the English versions of several Japanese newspapers and web sites and had expanded well beyond Tokyo. Recently it was taking him longer and longer to complete his morning searches. But he knew from what Ta had told him before he left, that the likelihood of a westerner being able to find anything of value would be slim to none. If the authorities didn't cover it up, then the crime families would. Notoriety, just didn't improve either of their positions and many high ranking government employees were either quietly sympathetic or connected by blood or marriage to the Yakuza. But Brent would continue to search each morning in the hope of finding only a small mention of crime family activity.

The law firm of Andrews, Williams & Paulson PC continued to grow, despite two of the partners best efforts to cut back on their participation. The addition of a full time in-house investigator had been a brilliant and financially sound move. And surprisingly the fact that Brent had recently run for the office of District Attorney and had increased his public exposure to the community resulted in a continuous stream of inquiries. Phil Paulson was beginning to think of himself as a clearing house as he sorted through the requests, picked out the easiest and most profitable and farmed out the remainder.

As soon as the weather permitted Stewart and his wife had pretty much abandoned the practice in favor of the golf links. While he was always just a phone call away and willing to help, he and June were trying their best to play every golf course in Colorado, a considerable feat.

Chapter 30

The specially outfitted, sleek white Gulfstream V/550 jet flew about 200 feet above the whitecaps over the Sea of Japan, then climbed to 40,000 feet and passed over the northern island of Hokkiado. Its ultimate destination after passing close to Alaska and over the Canadian border was Colorado Springs, Colorado.

Takeshi Miike, also known as Ta Mishinko, sat quietly and alone in the big private jet, with a drink in one hand thinking about the past six months of his life. In trying to do the manly thing, the Yakuza way of handling honor, his uncle Taniaka had allowed his sworn enemy to get too close to him and as a result had nearly died. However the old man, as Ta thought of him, had refused to enter a hospital for treatment, lest one of his underlings might move in and attempt to take over in his absence. Ta doubted that it would have happened, the way the Japanese crime family was set up, but then you never really knew. Taniaka's number one man had accessed the situation and unofficially contacted Ta for help. He knew that if he continued to be treated in his own home, Taniaka would probably die. And if that happened the family would be prone to attack by their enemies, especially any survivors that Sukara had left. So he'd taken it upon himself to make the call.

Upon seeing the condition of his uncle, Ta had immediately stepped in and taken charge. If he hadn't been Taniaka's nephew and raised as a Yakuza, he would have been killed right on the spot. However Ta's reputation before he left Japan was well known and even now many years later, just the look of him frightened most family members. So Taniaka was quickly taken to a nearby hospital where under guard, he was treated by professional doctors, some of which were Yakuza or even Yakuza sympathizers. In his absence, Ta announced to the hierarchy that he would be in charge. His first orders were to find any remaining relatives of Sukara, men, women or children and to abduct and kill them. His next order was that if the bodies were found or any witnesses appeared later on, then the abductors would die a similar death. Ta knew that in the Japanese Yakuza culture if you left only one blood relative alive, they would undoubtedly come back later and try to eliminate you. Better to handle it up front and get it over with.

All Yakuza families profited from illegal activities and Ta made certain that anyone even suspected of taking a share without his permission would be skinned alive and left to die in the streets of Tokyo. No one doubted his order, mostly because of his previous reputation. Despite his age, none of the younger family members or the street gangs wanted to challenge him.

Taniaka finally submitted to the wishes of his team of doctors and eventually survived his near death experience. The professor and other trusted members kept him advised of Ta's activities, some of which even surprised him due to their brutality. But by the end of the second week, Ta had already made his mark on the family. And by the time Taniaka was finally discharged from the hospital, all of Sukara's blood line, were dead and buried.

However his sympathizers would always be lurking in the shadows wanting revenge, but not willing to give up their lives for it.

There had been some minor problems with the Japanese National Police, but Taniaka's people acting on Ta's orders had managed to solve them peacefully. Ta doubted that any gaijins or foreigners would ever understand the Japanese culture and the relationships between the police and the organized crime groups. Hell, some groups even had brick and mortar storefronts with signs advertising who they were hung out in front. And in many crowded neighborhoods the residents were more likely to complain about a problem to the local Yakuza, than they were to the local police at their koban (small neighborhood police building). It wasn't like the Yakuza were hard to find with their full body tattoos, distinguishing haircuts and sometimes strange clothing.

But the Japanese government had survived side-by-side with the crime families for as long as anyone could remember. Departing from tradition, more and more Yakuza were adapting a more western style wearing more modern clothing and using firearms, which are prohibited in Japan. Now the various groups continue to jockey for power and prestige. Their influence on major businesses and sporting activities is usually from a financial standpoint and as long as they receive their cut, everything works as it should. Because of their history as a legitimate feudal organization and their close connection to the political and economic system they have become somewhat a part of the Japanese culture. However that doesn't eliminate nor justify their occasional outbreaks of extreme violence.

Ta looked around the empty plane and smiled to himself. It was owned by a large Japanese conglomerate that ultimately was controlled by his uncle. He couldn't guess at what it had cost, nor how much this trip alone would run. But it was equipped with every gadget and avionics accessory available. He assumed that hidden somewhere in the plane were weapons, but he really didn't want to know exactly where they were.

When he'd left Japan as a youth years ago he accepted the fact that he'd never be able to return. But time has a way of changing everything and he was no longer a hunted man, one wanted by the National Police. Maybe Taniaka had managed to fix that, but he wouldn't say. But the old man actually had tears in his eyes when Ta told him that he had to leave. He knew that his visit was only a temporary thing and that Ta had only taken the risk and entered the country to protect him, to avenge a wrong and to heal a long overdue wound. But as he had done his best to explain, he had hoped for more, and why wouldn't he? He had riches and power beyond belief to offer Ta, his only nephew, but it required a different way of life, one going back a thousand years.

Ta had done his very best to thank him for his kindness and during his visit had spent many hours discussing the death of Tani, and all of the others. He had to walk a thin line because he didn't want to show any sign of being disrespectful, yet he wanted answers to some questions, many of which might be embarrassing to the old man. Eventually he'd gotten the whole story or at least one side of it because everyone on the other side was now dead. It amazed Ta, how some things just had a way of going awry. Like before it ever happened, you could already see it going wrong.

He dosed off, awoke sometime later, and walked forward to talk to the pilots. This flight was 100% legitimate and at the Colorado Springs Airport they'd be met by the US Customs Agent, but Ta only traveled with the clothes on his back and had nothing to declare. However his passport was made out in someone else's, almost impossible to translate and pronounce, Japanese name.

The flight had been timed to arrive in the Springs at mid-morning, and once he cleared through Customs which actually took less than three minutes, he called a cab and waited. It struck him as funny because in Japan all he had to do was snap his fingers and a car or whatever else he wanted was there and waiting. Guns, drugs, young women and any perversion that could be imagined were only a finger snap away. Now here he was standing at the curb waiting for some well used cab and a driver who could have cared less who Ta was. But this was home and he was happily married, and so was his daughter. He didn't have to worry about them being heavily guarded as they would have been in Japan, or his headstrong daughter Michi doing something that might be contrary to the wishes of the family and having to pay a price for it.

He was pleased since he'd always felt guilty about leaving his uncle and coming to America. In the beginning as a young man, one who had been respected and feared in Japan, it had been most difficult because he couldn't do anything that would draw attention to himself. He was forced to stay out of the limelight and away from any involvement with the local gangs and the police. It hadn't been an easy or pleasant time in his life, but then he'd met Christy and had fallen head over heels in love. Talk about a clash of cultures, she being a white Irish Catholic woman and he, well he was just a Yakuza. But despite the odds they had managed to work out their differences and have two beautiful daughters.

The cab finally arrived at the commercial air charter service hanger and Ta gave the driver the address. As they drove away he could smell the heavy cigarette smoke of the previous occupant and again he had to smile because in Japan, he first off wouldn't be taking a cab, and secondly if forced to, he'd have a group of people scrubbing the hell out of the car before he got into it. Now he'd just have to remember to wash his hands once he got home. Six months was a long time to be away, especially from the people you loved and respected. He only hoped that he'd be forgiven for his absence, but it had been unavoidable. Now Taniaka was healed and back to running the family as he wished. However Ta had made some suggestions and attributed them to the changing times. His uncle fully understood, and Ta actually believed that he'd implement them.

During their long conversations, Ta had revealed a lot about himself and his family. His uncle had quietly listened and much to Ta's amazement he'd committed every word to his memory. He told the story of Harrington House, his son-in-law, the death of Tani, his own marriage and the life history of Michi, his wild child. Taniaka thought that she must have been a handful to raise and that she must have put her parents through hell. Ta couldn't say enough about Brent, the ex-cop and how he had tamed Michi, or at least kept her in check. He even told the story of Joe and Jim, his two eunuchs and why he had purchased them. Upon hearing the story, Taniaka had immediately removed the death sentence, since they were soldiers protecting his nephew and his family in America. Ta had thanked him and made the comment that he wished he had another one since they had worked out so well.

The cab drove up to the big black wrought iron gate at Harrington House and stopped at the curb. Ta paid the driver who had been somewhat intimidated by his passenger's size and looks. But he tipped the man rather generously, grunted a heavily accented "thank you," and pushed the button on the access remote.

Inside the house, it was Joe's turn to handle any callers and he looked out the window, recognized Ta and ran down the hall and across the foyer to push the button to open the gate. Ta heard it click and lock behind him as he entered the front door. To his amazement, both Joe and Jim were lined up to greet him with broad smiles across their faces. Their excited conversation, all in Japanese took nearly ten minutes before they'd let Ta enter any further. But Ta had learned that his wife and daughter were grocery shopping and that they'd roped Brent into driving the car and watching over them. As Joe calculated, they had been gone for nearly an hour and wouldn't be back for at least two more.

Ta had gone up to his apartment, showered, shaved and dressed in his normal comfortable clothes. He hung the outrageously expensive custom made clothing provided by his uncle's personal tailor in the closet. His five-month old Rolex watch and the two large diamond rings were placed in the dresser next to his socks and underwear as if they meant nothing to him. He walked down to the kitchen and turned up the coffee pot. He smiled, thankful that Michi hadn't tossed it in the garbage again during his absence. But he opened the morning newspaper, poured a cup of coffee and began his normal morning routine as if he had never been away. With Joe and Jim now running things, he relaxed for the first time in six months. It had certainly been interesting if nothing else. Here he was alone and could relax and be himself, but over there he was surrounded by aides and bodyguards and sometimes found it difficult to breath. There he was always on the alert, watching and waiting, ready to instantly react to protect himself, his uncle and the family. He knew that many had died as a result of either him personally, or at his direct orders. He also knew that he'd have to spend a lot of time in his shrine trying to appease his God.

Tomorrow he'd FedEx the borrowed passport back to Taniaka with a short note thanking him for its use. If anyone investigated, Ta had no connection to the landing of the fancy Gulfstream plane at the Colorado Springs Municipal Airport, nor to the lone passenger that had cleared Customs. Ironically the video camera system at the commercial hanger had been down for repair when Ta passed through. Also, thanks to Taniaka, Ta had receipts for a rental car and the accumulated mileage to support his explanation of driving from Colorado Springs to LA and back along with all of the gas receipts. If questioned, the Customs Agent wouldn't be able to remember the lone passenger since he'd been so busy at the time.

*

Two weeks had passed since Ta's return and during that time he'd managed to make peace with his wife, daughter and son-in-law. With the exception of Brent who was also his personal attorney, no one knew the real story of what had

338

transpired in Japan and Brent was certain that he didn't know all of the details and didn't want to. Stewart, Phil and Jimmy Cane all welcomed him back and hoped that his trip had been successful and Ta had just grunted something, his usual response before moving on.

With summer, the new greenhouse was filled with seedlings and Joe and Jim were planting and caring for the numerous flowerbeds from sunup to sundown. The lawns were mowed nearly every other day and the bushes and trees trimmed to perfection. Brent had noticed how beautiful the place looked and every so often he'd look up to the heavens and wink at Gus, who he knew was watching. Even the neighbors had noticed and one of them had even called the local newspaper to boast how beautiful Harrington House looked, like something in a travel magazine. That resulted in an inquisitive reporter driving by to check it out and being refused entrance to the estate after he pushed the button at the front gate. Then Quasimodo had appeared and refused his request for an interview with the property owner. That meant that the reporter would return to the El Paso Assessor's Office where he'd look up the ownership on the tax records. Unfortunately he'd learn very little other than the owner didn't want his name known. A search through the newspaper's archives resulted in the name of Brent Williams, an attorney who at one time had run for the office of District Attorney. A phone call to a contact at the telephone company produced an unlisted number which he immediately called and left a message on the answering machine. When he didn't hear back, he called and left a second message, then a third and a fourth.

Investigative reporter John Wye was

checking his morning email when he'd been summoned to his publisher's office on the top floor. Besides the day he'd been hired, he hadn't been there again and so as he walked up the stairs he began to wonder if he'd stepped on someone's toes and was being fired, or if he was being promoted. He knocked on the door, entered the office and was invited in. A very distinguished looking well dressed older man was sitting on the couch, with a cup of coffee in his hand. His publisher was seated behind his desk explaining something, doing most of the talking with his hands. John wonder if he'd be able to even talk if someone duct taped them, but he entered and took a seat.

"John, let me introduce you to Stewart Andrews, he's Brent Williams personal attorney. Stewart recently merged his large Denver law practice and semi retired down here in the Springs."

John reached over to shake Stewart's hand and nodded his head.

"Now as I understand it, you've been making numerous inquiries regarding Mr. Williams, who also is a successful attorney and an ex-cop. Mr. Williams has had a lot of sorrow in his life and wishes to be left alone. On his behalf Stewart has obtained several court documents including a restraining order signed by Chief Judge Onnan directing you to stay out of his life, to not go anywhere near him, his family, his home, his employees or known clients. In view of this, I am directing you to end any further inquiries regarding Mr. Williams. If you choose to disregard my request and that of this newspaper, then you'll be on your own in the future, should Mr. Andrews choose to pursue it. Are we clear on this?"

"I guess so," answered Wye. "But wouldn't

it have been easier to just call me on the phone and refuse my request? Why all of the big guns?" he asked.

"Because you're a reporter, and probably a pretty good one and honestly, we, speaking for my client and I, just don't want to be bothered. He was nearly killed by a drunken driver, chose to retire, got married and had his wife, housekeepers and my old partner and his wife all murdered in his house. Since then it's just been a string of other misfortunes. Now it appears to be quieting down and we'd like to keep it that way."

"But the guy ran for public office, that's not a quiet non-intrusive thing."

"It was a favor to the party. They needed a name and picked Brent. Everyone knew he was never a threat and you know beating an incumbent is nearly impossible. But it gave him a rare chance to get out and socialize. In his eyes it was a win-win situation right from the start."

"We are clear on this, aren't we?" asked the publisher.

"Yeah, sure," answered Wye getting up and walking out of the office while he grumbled to himself.

Back at his desk, he gathered up everything relating to Brent Williams and placed it in an attaché case. Later he'd take it out to his car. This was getting interesting and he wasn't about to just walk away from it.

Chapter 31

"Ta, there's a semi truck parked at the end of the drive," said Brent, before hanging up the phone in his office.

Ta folded his cell phone, walked around the building and looked towards the front gate. A big yellow semi tractor and trailer was parked in the middle of the street and the driver was in the process of opening the trailer's overhead rear door. Because of the size and number of pallets, he'd have to use his pallet jack to move boxes to the edge. Ta hollered for Joe and Jim and as they walked to the truck, Brent was watching from his office window and pushed the button to open the gate. Ta told Joe to get the dolly from the garage, as he walked down to the trailer.

He read the bill of lading, didn't really understand it and called Brent on his cell phone.

"It's something from Japan," said Brent after looking though the papers. "Maybe something from your uncle?"

It took all four of them to unload the boxes and haul them into the first open garage space. Lined up, they were as long as Ta's truck and half as wide. Stacked up, they were nearly five feet high. Brent smiled, slapped Ta on the back and returned inside to lock the gate and go back to work. But all of the commotion brought Michi and Christy to the garage to help Ta. He and his eunuchs began to open the boxes and to carefully lay out their contents on the concrete floor. Finally the parts of the puzzle came together. During his uncle's convalescence, he and Ta had discussed many things and when the conversation had run out of subjects, Ta had described his old shrine in the back of the garage in great detail and had walked his uncle through what he planned to do in the building attached to the new greenhouse when he returned. As he looked back, they had spent many hours going over every detail and Taniaka had remembered all of it. According to a letter within one of the boxes, Taniaka had hired a skilled temple craftsman to build a shrine to his specifications, then to disassemble it and ship it to Ta. This was the ultimate Shinto Shrine.

"So does it fit?" asked Brent. Ta was in the process of updating him and they were sitting in Brent's office.

"As near as I can see, it's a perfect fit. However Taniaka has offered to send the craftsman over here if it doesn't. I'd probably have to keep him here so that he wouldn't be killed for screwing up when he returned home," Ta laughed but he knew he was right.

"How soon will it be ready?" asked Brent.

"This is a first class setup. I'd bet there isn't another one like it in the States. I can't even guess at what it cost but you'd better up our insurance coverage a bit. I'm guessing maybe a week until it's reassembled and finished. But then we'll need to take the original one apart. No sense having two in the same house. Maybe I'll pack it up and ask that guy who helped you to see if he has any use for it, otherwise I'll send most of it back to Japan."

"Well whatever you decide to do, count me in," smiled Brent.

"I know," replied Ta getting up and walking

out.

*

Five days had passed, the shrine was well under way and both Ta and the eunuchs were exceptionally pleased with the way it was turning out. He guessed that the craftsman had begun around the clock work on it shortly after his uncle had been released from the hospital. Or perhaps it had been in progress for some time and Taniaka had just taken over as he was prone to do if he saw something that he liked. Either way, Ta now had it and he wasn't about to turn loose of it. The hand polished rare woods felt like glass and no expense had been spared. He was extremely happy! Then his cell phone rang, startling him.

"Ta, some guy from US Customs out at the airport is on the house line. Says he has something for us. You expecting anything?" asked Brent.

"No, nothing for me. What is it?" Ta replied.

"He won't say, other than to ask that one of us come out right away."

"Ok," muttered Ta as he issued some orders to his two men and began to get into his truck. Brent rushed out and joined him.

"Suppose Taniaka sent you something else?" smiled Brent.

"I can't image what that could be," replied Ta as he maneuvered the big truck towards the airport on the east side of the city.

Brent recognized the police guard at the door and asked if he could page the Custom's agent. They were directed to an office on the lower level and the cop personally escorted them as a favor to an old comrade in arms. As they entered the office, it was obvious that the Customs guy was frustrated and really didn't know exactly what to do. Sitting on

344

chairs against the wall with their heads down, were two bald Japanese men, probably somewhere in their early to mid thirties. Tattoo's peaked out at their wrists and neckline although they did their best to cover them up. Both had identification papers attached to a heavy string around their necks and one had an envelope attached to his front breast pocket. Ta walked over, uttered something and the two men suddenly came alive and sat up straight and the one with the envelope pointed to it. Ta carefully removed it and opened the letter. He read it and burst out laughing, an emotion that he rarely used, then handed it to Brent who took one look and handed it back. Ta immediately apologized since it was in Japanese.

"Sorry," smiled Ta. "Loosely translated, it's from my uncle. One night after some sake, he asked me if there was anything that I needed. This was long after Tani was killed and we had some other problems and I guess I must have said that another helper or two wouldn't hurt. So he found two more and sent them to us. It's taken all of this time to get the right papers, both to get them out of Japan and legally into this country. He guarantees that they are both legitimate and trustworthy. There's something about them being somewhat related to Joe and Jim, but I'm not certain about that. At least they all came from the same part of Japan. And in answer to the question you're about to ask, they are identical to our guys. Both are highly trained martial artists and were highly prized for their abilities. At one time they both fought professionally for a friend of my uncle's. Fortunately while they were in route, no one attempted to manhandle them," laughed Ta as he handed the Custom's forms to Brent, who signed them.

They were driving east on Lake Avenue on their way home when Brent asked:

"What are we going to do with them?"

"Good question," laughed Ta. "I can't really send them back. Over there it would be thought that they had failed and they'd either be killed or wish that they were. I'm kind of stuck in the middle. We have two guestrooms next to our apartment and I'm thinking that we could either divide them in half so that each would have his own room or we could double bunk them. That would take care of the housing problem. Work wise I think that at least during the warm months we could use them, and I 'm assuming since Taniaka sent them that they are very skilled at being protectors or bodyguards, just like Joe and Jim. But neither speaks any English and apparently they don't understand much of it either."

"Hear me out on this," smiled Brent. "As long as they'll get a death sentence if we return them, how about taking the house office which you never use and the two guest rooms and gut the place. Then we could rebuild them into four smaller bedrooms, and each could share a bath or for that matter we could even make four baths if the space works out. I'm assuming that they're eunuchs too?"

"Definitely," answered Ta. "And I like your idea. In Japan they're not treated very nicely, because of what they are and what they do. Most likely they've been staying in some unheated barn or outbuilding in some small village. Both are Yakuza warriors, but of the old school. You don't see many of them anymore in Japan. They are raised to be defenders, and in order to remove their natural desires, they are castrated. Taniaka has put the fear of God in them and they fully believe that you're the leader of the family and that I'm your right hand man. They will do whatever I tell them too without questioning it."

"So my friend," smiled Brent. "Exactly how are we going to break this to Christy and Michi? On second thought, maybe its better if you handle that since both of them were so happy when you returned. I'll handle Stewart, Phil and Jimmy. Guess I better include Art Thomas in that too. Actually this is really funny Ta. Here we were under attack, and then we began to build our own army. Maybe you just had to have been there from the beginning?" laughed Brent. In the back seat of the big truck, the two men sat quietly looking at the floor. They had been warned by Taniaka, a man they knew and feared, that Ta was his nephew and that his spoken word was the same as if it had come from Taniaka himself. Neither knew what to expect.

The following morning as Brent walked into his office with Michi, Ta was reading the morning newspaper and waiting for them. Instantly a man appeared in a white uniform with Harrington House embroidered on the left breast pocket, placed coffee and a plate of sticky buns on the table, said something, bowed deeply and backed out of the room.

"Well that certainly seems to be going well," laughed Michi.

"We had a long meeting in our apartment last night. As of this morning we have at least 8 mouths to feed at every meal, and sometimes more. I learned that one of the new guys likes to cook so he's now a part of the kitchen staff. He'll help Christy to cook and clean up. He'll also go shopping with her or at least help make out shopping lists. It should be interesting since he speaks no

English and she no Japanese. But at least when she's out shopping, someone will be with her for protection."

"Who's protecting who?" laughed Brent.

"Good question," smiled Ta moving right along. "I measured the rooms upstairs and your idea to make four smaller bedrooms is a good one. I know that Henry loved his small office, but I rarely use it. But then when Henry was alive, times around here were different. So this morning, Joe is finishing some work in the shrine, Jim will be outside mowing and trimming and the new guy will begin demolition. I'll call a contractor, actually the guy that put up the greenhouse and let him handle the rebuilding. Meanwhile our guys will move their living quarters down to the basement. I explained that it was only a temporary thing, that they weren't being punished. Oh, and we're going to need more identical furniture and some uniforms and clothing for them too. Michi, maybe you can handle that. Get their measurements or have someone come to the house."

"An estate this large always needs to have something done to it in order to keep it looking like new. And with the new greenhouse, there's always work to do. Christy wants flowers and so we're going to begin raising them. Between the maintenance work around here, the greenhouse, cooking and cleaning and protecting, I think that this is going to work out very well."

"Good," answered Brent.

"One more thing," said Ta. "Yesterday I got my latest bank statement and there's a deposit of $9,950. I called on it and the bank's bookkeeping department transferred me to the wire department. They said it was from some large bank in Japan that has worldwide branches. Is that legal?" asked Ta handing the sheet to Brent.

"Let me look into it this morning. I'm assuming this is from your uncle?" he said.

"Most likely," answered Ta. "Again, if I try and return it then the war starts all over again. That would be construed as being disrespectful with a capitol "D". Once he makes up his mind it's nearly impossible to change it, although if I explained that it was illegal, he'd probably send his plane over here with a suitcase full of cash instead."

"Do you think that this will happen again?" asked Brent.

"I don't know. I never would have guessed that he'd do it now. But he does have mood swings. I saw that first hand. So let him send the money if it keeps him happy and we can use it to buy food or whatever else we need."

"We're not exactly broke Ta. I have all of Allen's money and some from Tani too. And as I take stock of things, we all have new cars, live in a beautiful mansion, have anything that we want, so my bottom line is that we're darn lucky people. In fact today I plan on squandering some of it," Brent laughed.

"Lunch at the Hotel with Art?" asked Michi.

"Exactly my dear and maybe I'll even pop for some rich desert. Eat your heart out," he laughed but he wondered how a Yakuza warrior would ever learn how to be a cook and exactly what would he toss in the meat pot?

*

"Damn," smiled Art Thomas, "another new restaurant. What's the count now, six that we've eaten in?"

"Who cares Art? I haven't noticed you

complaining about the food or service yet."

"That's because they fall all over you and I'm just an add on," he laughed.

"Hell the way you eat, the Chef's probably have your phone number on their speed dial," smiled Brent as he buttered another hand made roll.

"All kidding aside, this is certainly the way to live if you can afford it. But I'm just a poor humble public servant kissing someone's butt in order to get a free lunch," he laughed.

"You mean that I have to pay for this. I thought that it was your turn?"

"Sorry, the Credit Union was closed when I drove by. Hell I'd probably have to take out a loan just to cover the gratuities."

"Actually you only get what you are willing to pay for and since this is a business meeting I'll probably write it off."

"Now I feel better. So how come we aren't playing golf anymore?" asked Art.

"Probably because I stink at it? However if you're willing to go with me and keep your smart ass comments to a bare minimum, I guess I could be persuaded. You name the day and time and I'll arrange it."

"Are you going to let Joe drive the cart again? Because he thought that he was in downtown Tokyo at rush hour the last time. Scared the hell out of me. Figured that I'd have to shoot him to get the damn cart stopped."

"That was sort of exciting, but Ta taught me how to say the word "stop" in Japanese so now we can at least get his attention. Oh, he also taught me how to say "or die" too. Maybe that will help."

"Are you working hard these days?" Art asked.

"Nope, not if I can help it. Stew's on call, and I do the accepting or rejecting and Phil does the grunt work or at least some of it. Jimmy's handling the investigations for all of us and on any cases we farm out, and I hardly see him anymore," said Brent.

"I talked to his old partner Matt Jones last night and I guess Jimmy's very happy. His kid is doing very well in school and talking about going on to graduate school, his wife is working and helping in the office and Jimmy's out on the street where he's the happiest. He told Matt that if this workload keeps increasing that he's going to talk to you about adding another guy. That true, that it's growing?" Art asked.

"I can see it expanding. Times have changed and before we waste any time talking to a liar, it's easier to have Jimmy check them out first. Phil used to try and do both the preliminary checks and the case work, but he was spinning his wheels and wasting time. Jimmy knows how to get the job done and fast. Honestly if he wanted Matt to join us I'd go along with it. First off I really liked both of these guys. Second I always believed that they were good detectives and trustworthy types. So sure, I'd be willing to add him to the payroll."

"Heard that you had an interesting time with Customs out at the airport," said Art.

"It wasn't interesting, it was hilarious. You should have been there. Here's this Custom's Agent and two oriental guys who don't speak nor understand any English. Both Ta and I were holding our sides. Everyone's talking and no one knows what the other is saying, but Ta. So now we've increased our staff by two."

"Where'd they come from?" asked Art.

"Hell I don't know," laughed Brent. "We

sure didn't expect them. Suddenly I got the call from the Customs guy and we drove out there. Ta didn't know who they were either. He'd gone back to California to help some distant family member and the next thing he knew, two guys from rural Japan were knocking on our door. Come on Art laugh, because it really was funny."

"So what are you going to do with them?"

"I honestly don't know, but I pray that no more show up because we're running out of room. Funny how things work out, but Christy's already taken one of them in the kitchen. Apparently the guy knows something about cooking and now he belongs to her. At least when she goes shopping I won't have to worry about her."

"Are they like the first two?"

"Too soon to tell, but my guess is that they probably can handle themselves pretty well. Anyway Ta has a demolition crew tearing apart some rooms in order to expand our sleeping arrangements."

"So they're permanent party?"

"It's a big house, always needs something done to it. But Ta thinks that if we send them back, that they'll probably be killed. I checked all of their papers very carefully and they are definitely legitimate, both here and in Japan. But as I thought about it there are now eight of us and that's too many for Christy to handle on a regular basis. So now both she and Ta have some helpers. I'm good with that. How long it will last is my question? But they clean and cook and keep up the grounds. And when they repainted the inside of the house last winter, they did an outstanding job. Bottom line is that I'm very happy."

"Hear anything new on the Harrington House

case?" Art asked knowing that Brent would probably hear from the Feds before he did.

"Close it Art. It's over and done with at this point. Nothing more will come from the Feds, and I doubt that anymore killings will happen."

"You speaking from actual knowledge or just opinion."

"Just my opinion. The bodies are buried, the case files are gone and we haven't had any new murders attributed to that case in some time, so it's my opinion that whatever it was is over and done with."

"I wonder about that," sighed Art finishing off his desert and reaching across the table to steal a sample of Brent's.

*

"Brent, its Jimmy," said the voice on the phone. "You got something that you want to tell me?" he laughed. It was two weeks after the luncheon with Art Thomas and three days after their last golf outing. As usual Brent had been badly beaten.

"Like what Jimmy?" he asked.

"Like my wife just called me on the cell phone. It seems like our yard has been invaded by the Chinese. They're out there cutting the grass, trimming the bushes and making the place beautiful. Her car's parked in the drive and one of them is actually washing it. She panicked and locked the doors but Dog is just sitting in the window and watching. Strange since he always barks."

"Is Ta's big white pickup parked at the curb?"

"Yup, there's a white truck out there," he answered. "Not sure if it's Ta's or not?"

"Then it must have been a slow day and he

decided to have his helpers do some yard work for you. By the way, they're not Chinese but Japanese. Oh and before you go busting in there, they're all martial arts experts. Got any problems with the neighbors that need resolving?" Brent laughed.

"I didn't before your guys arrived. I can just imagine the conversation over the fence tonight," he chuckled.

"Well don't be surprised if you get a call from Phil, because once Ta gets started he'll include everyone. Since I have you on the phone, we need to talk in person. How about coming for dinner tomorrow night?"

"Can I bring a date?" Jimmy kidded.

"Only if it's your wife, otherwise I'll be attending a funeral and looking for a new investigator at the same time," Brent replied.

"I'll tell her, and thanks for the lawn service, hope that it doesn't ruin my reputation in the neighborhood. I mean these people might start to believe that I've become a gardener or something."

The following evening, dinner was served in the formal dining room. Brent had invited the Thomas's, the Andrew's, the Jones's, the Canes, the Onnan's and the Paulson's. For the very first time since he became the owner of Harrington House, every place at the large table would be filled. Ta's helpers would assist Christy and then sit at the far end of the table, something unheard of in Japan, and eat dinner like human beings. As expected Michi was the perfect hostess and afterwards as the men in white cleaned up, everyone else moved into the formal living room and the recreation room. A game of pool began, someone turned on the huge wall mounted television and music played in the background as Brent offered after dinner drinks to everyone. Finally he was able to get Jimmy alone.

"So do you think its time to hire another investigator?" Brent asked.

"Definitely wouldn't hurt. I've run the numbers and I'm convinced," Jimmy replied.

"Matt?"

"My choice for sure," he smiled.

"How close is he to his twenty years?" Brent asked.

"He's nearly there, but it doesn't matter anymore. The City changed the retirement program and pushed it up to 25 years. He'll get something at 20, but nothing like he expected. We talk all of the time and he's definitely not a happy camper. Art tried to keep him in homicide after I left, but someone above him pulled him out and assigned him to another department. Then they assigned a new partner who really sucks. Art's been trying to get him back or have him reassigned, but so far nothing he's done has worked out. My guess is that if you made him an offer, he'd jump at it."

"What about his wife? Would she be good with it too?"

"She and my wife are pretty tight and its my understanding that she's been encouraging him to send out some resumes," he smiled.

"I'll talk to him tonight," said Brent as he patted Jimmy on the arm and walked away looking for Matt.

*

"You're serious about this?" asked Matt Jones.

"Definitely," replied Brent glancing at Stewart and then back at Matt. "But you need to understand that Jimmy is our lead investigator and that you'd be working for him and both of you, for us. He gets to sign off on everything before it reaches me. Then I either accept or reject the case based on what's in the report. We're kind of informal around here, so a lot of times Jimmy will just call me and tell me to toss it because the clients trouble."

"I just can't believe this is happening. I'm so fed up with the Department that I've been putting together a resume. Mary's been helping me but neither of us has ever prepared one before, so we're checking self help books out of the Public Library. Realistically, most smaller departments can't afford me what with all of the budget cuts going around. Even the Sheriff's Department has been cutting back, so Mary and I were guessing that we'd probably have to relocate. Now this comes along," he said shaking his head in amazement..

"Jimmy can fill you in on the particulars, like insurance, licensing, pay scale, hours and the rest of your questions. I don't know where you live but being close to Harrington House has its advantages. And you'll need a nice car and new clothes, and a better weapon. Again Jimmy can answer all of your questions and we'll make you the same offer regarding a new house as we made him. Just pick it out and the bank Stewart has invested in will handle the financing. However this is a big decision and you'll definitely want to talk it over with your wife before you commit yourself," Brent smiled.

"Can I borrow your office?" Matt asked and when Brent agreed he quickly walked away looking for Mary. Twenty minutes later he cornered Jimmy. Brent was at the pool table when Matt walked over and asked to shake his hand. The deal had been made!

On such a pleasant evening, some of the

couples moved outside on the huge patio and began to stroll around the grounds. Ta had the place looking like some kind of a fancy botanical garden and Judge Onnan doubted that a single blade of grass was out of place. As they passed by the new greenhouse the latest blooming flowers were basking in the artificial light provided by special growing bulbs. To Onnan it looked just like he pictured a rainbow should. And the four Japanese men, dressed in their white uniforms, placed strategically around the property, stood awaiting any requests or more than willing to protect the guests.

The party finally broke up and the last to leave was Art and Sally Thomas. Brent stopped them at the door and motioned Art aside.

"I owe you a lunch," he smiled.

"He went for it?" asked Thomas.

"Definitely. But if we get any more CSPD retirees over here I'm going to apply to the City for funding," Brent laughed.

Chapter 32

Taniaka, the fearless Yakuza warrior, knelt alone in his Shinto Shrine, asking for forgiveness. He had made a big error in judgment, and wanted to do something to rectify it, but didn't know what to do. Not only that, but he, born and raised in an oriental culture didn't have anyone to ask either. He slowly unfolded the letter from his nephew, and with tears running down his cheeks, he read it again and again.

After years of abandonment, Ta had come to his aid without being asked once that he knew Taniaka was injured. He'd moved in and had taken over the family by force, being extremely brutal in his dealings with the enemy. It had been the right thing to do and exactly what Taniaka would have done if the situation was reversed. For six months he'd ruled with an iron hand and never once had he asked for anything. Countless hours had been spent catering to Taniaka and in explaining Ta's life in America. Taniaka remembered every single word having committed each to memory. Now a simple thing like sending him a shrine had resulted in a letter, not only from Ta thanking him, but from his wife and daughter too, and he had never even met them.

Taniaka knew that he wasn't getting any younger, although he now felt better than he had in a long time. But Ta's wife had thanked him, then patiently tried to explain how different their cultures

358

were and that some acts frowned on in Japan, were actually necessary in America. She apologized for not being more knowledgeable about the Japanese way, but wanted him to know how thankful she was for sending Ta back to her and how she hoped that Taniaka's life would prosper. Then she explained a lot about their lives, their friendships, their hobbies, their jobs and many other things. Towards the end, Michi, a young woman he had never met, added another page about her life, her marriage, her husband, and how she too thanked him for allowing Ta to return to her and how she would pray for Taniaka's health and future. The letter was nearly 10 pages long.

"Taniaka wasn't comfortable with sentiment like this. In his world he made all of the decisions, based on facts or yen. People lived and died on his one word or nod. Now here was his nephew's family offering thanks for his kindness when it was he who should be thanking them. It was he who owed them a debt of gratitude for allowing his nephew to come and help him. For the first time in his life he wished that he could just sit in a room with them and talk, get to know them better than he had by reading their thank you letter. He remembered Ta's written words in the beginning, that they had asked to add something of their own to the letter and that he hoped that it was pleasant because he hadn't been allowed to read it.

In Japan, Taniaka was powerful and wealthy beyond belief. The mere mention of his name brought fear into the hearts of men, and made his enemies flee. He was an old Yakuza, a fearsome warrior and everyone knew it, including his family, the government and his enemies. He controlled many companies, some that were well known in the

United States and his dark side controlled many illegal operations such as importing drugs and guns. Prostitution, extortion, and anything else that was illegal poured money into the family's coffers. Now here he was, thousands of miles away from the only person on the face of the earth that he fully trusted and he didn't know how to begin repaying his indebtedness.

Ta, his only nephew, despite his remarkable abilities and instincts, had chosen to live a quiet life in America. He'd chosen an occupation that he enjoyed and when that career choice had unexpectedly ended, he and his wife had chosen to replace Ta's only sister and her husband after their untimely death. So many times the name Brent Williams had come up that Taniaka felt like he actually knew the man. He'd suffered many deaths of those he loved only to come back to successfully running the family. Ta not only liked him, but admired and in a way worshiped him. They had spoken for hours about the man and his history. If Ta believed in him, then that was good enough for Taniaka too.

*

"Nice suit," commented Stew as he walked into Brent's office and sat down.

"You realize that my old ones were custom made, don't you?" he laughed. "It was actually Allen's idea. Perception, he kept telling me over and over. If you look successful, then people will believe it and flock to you."

"I think that he was right," said Stew. "You do realize that Gus was behind all of us. She dressed Frank Harrington and that in turn made his best friend Allen Sheffield look like a poor cousin. Then she took on his redo and he in turn made all of us up in Denver look like hillbillies. In the end she had all of us looking like kings, but you know, she was right and it did work."

"Well this suit came from Japan. Don't ask me how, but it's a perfect fit and I have a dozen more upstairs in the closet. In fact I have shirts, ties, socks, shoes and underwear to match. I'm sort of like a clothes horse these days," he laughed.

"Well you do look good, especially for a starving lawyer," Stew said.

"Starving, boy isn't that a joke. Did you hear the latest?"

"Just a part of it. Michi was explaining it to June and I just happened to be passing by. What's the real story?"

"I don't have a clue, but suddenly we're getting a lot of stuff from Japan. I mean the Custom's Agent out at the airport and another up in Denver are on a first name basis with us. Ta got his shrine which you already know about. Then Christy received a bunch of diamond jewelry which really blew her mind especially since when she immediately sent Ta's uncle a thank you note, he sent her a prepaid gift card for the shops at the Broadmoor Hotel. The way she shops, it could be years before she zeros out the card. Then Michi got a huge shipment of clothing from one of Japan's top designers. Everything was in her size and favorite colors. Her thank you note was followed by a truckload of the latest Japanese sewing and embroidery machines in all sizes and makes. If you remember before we got married she was a clothing designer. Now both Ta and I have more custom made clothing than we'll ever wear. And finally, just yesterday I was notified that the local Lexus dealer was holding four new cars in my name. Out of curiosity and maybe some sarcasm I asked him what models, and he answered that the purchase order that he had, said whatever models and colors that I wanted, but they had to have every available option that Lexus offered."

"I thought that you liked your Mercedes?" smiled Stew.

"I do," answered Brent. "But I think that if I refused them, the dealer would have a stroke and old Taniaka might send his Yakuza after me," he laughed.

"So what do you intend to do with them? Hold a raffle?"

"I talked to Ta and as usual with Taniaka, sending them back or refusing them isn't an option. And, he specifically stated that he has no intention of giving up his big truck. You and I both are very happy with our Mercedes so we're out. Michi and Christy have vehicles that they're happy with, so I'm back at square one. Just maybe I can get the girls to upgrade but I'm not sure. Any ideas?"

"Certainly, now that you asked. Get the biggest and most expensive one they offer and make it into a fancy Saturday night car. Gus had one for special occasions. Then get two of their biggest and best four- wheel drives and give them to Michi and Christy in exchange for theirs. Now at this point you'll have one more new one to go and the two old ones from the girls, which by the way are nearly new and in perfect shape. So moving right along, give the girl's cars, with no strings attached to Jimmy and Matt's wives. They're already paid for and you wrote them off last year, but I think that it would be a very nice gesture. As I've heard the story, neither of them currently have cars so it will definitely be appreciated. And as far as the last one goes, pick a middle of the line sporty looking one and assign it to Phil. You can't just give it to him because then your name wouldn't be on the title and I'm certain that somewhere along the line good old Taniaka will see it."

"What about Phil's current car? It's almost new."

"Have him turn it over to his wife, or give it to Art, that would really blow his mind. Any idea what kind it is?" he asked.

"I'm sure he told me but I can't remember," replied Brent.

"Better yet, since Art's been in this from the beginning, and business has been good, lets get Phil to just give his wife the car and let's buy Art a brand new one. I'll split it with you. We can do it through the business and keep it on our books, but he gets to keep and drive it."

"Too risky, if the IRS stumbles on it, we're dead in the water, but I like your thinking. So how about if we just lease one, for say two years and give it to him?"

"Excellent, any idea of what kind?"

"Maybe a big SUV? He's a big guy in case you haven't noticed."

"I have it Brent! Either a big Range Rover or a large Hummer H3."

"Let's make it a red one so it really stands out," laughed Brent.

"You make the call and let me know what my share is," said Stew as he left for the kitchen and a fresh cup of coffee.

Three days later Brent had arranged for a round of golf with Art. Since Stew was involved, he invited both he and his wife to join them. At the first tee, which surprisingly wasn't busy today, Brent and Stew got into a discussion and they decided to divide up into two teams and play 18 holes. As expected it was Stew and June, two really good golfers, verse Brent and Art. It began at $10 a hole, and by the third hole had escaladed to $500 per. Art, who wasn't a bad golfer, wasn't holding up to the pressure and began flubbing his shots. Brent on the other hand was consistently lousy and as the holes passed by and the dollars rose, Art was becoming worse and worse until he and Brent were playing the same. At the 12th hole, Brent got into an argument with Stew and the stakes were raised to $1,000 per hole. Art was on the verge of having a heart attack and by the 16th hole he just gave up and walked off the course. At this point Brent was beating him.

They caught up with Art back at the Clubhouse, and as Stew added up the results and the dollars, Art sat quietly listening. With all of the bets and side bets the final figure came up to nearly 40K and Brent suggested double or nothing. June refused his offer, but said that she would make a counter offer. They would flip a coin. If it came up tails, then Brent and Art would owe the Andrew's the money. If it came up heads, then she'd fork over her new Hummer which was leased for two years. Brent glanced at Art, who was almost in a state of shock and agreed. He removed a dollar size coin from his pocket and tossed it to Stew, who flipped it in the air and let it land on the table. Art's eyes bugged out as he saw that it had landed heads up. He let out a huge sigh as June tossed the car keys to Brent and he immediately handed them to Art with the excuse that he had to use the restroom right away. As he left, June decided to powder her nose and she disappeared. Then the telephone at the bar rang and Stewart was paged.

It was nearly fifteen minutes before Art realized that he was all alone and that the others weren't coming back. He tried to pay the bill only to learn that Brent had already taken care of it. Wondering what was going on, he walked out the door to the parking lot just in time to see his old car being hauled off on the back of a flatbed tow truck. In a reserved space right next to the entrance door sat a beautiful new red Hummer H3 and Art hesitated for a moment, looked around and not seeing anyone, he walked over, inserted the key and slid inside. Words couldn't describe the feeling that passed through his mind sitting in the expensive vehicle.

"Back at Harrington House, the connivers were on the speakerphone talking to the Golf Club Manager who was looking out the window and describing everything in great detail. Minutes later they heard the buzzer for the front gate, which Joe answered in person. Since he was in on the joke too, all he would say once Art pulled up to the front door was, "aaah, nice car."

"Ok, what's this all about?" asked Art Thomas as he settled into a overstuffed chair across from Brent. Stew and June were on the couch.

"Well Stew and I just got to feeling sorry for our poor humble public servant and decided to do something nice for him." He paused for several moments. "Actually Art, we're doing some car shuffling around here and you were the only one that came out on the short end. So Stew suggested that we just lease a car for you for two years since we couldn't actually just buy it outright and hand it over. We felt that approach might attract too much attention with the CSPD."

"I love it," he said. "Don't care what anyone

else thinks!"

"Well since you always ride me whenever we play golf, it gave me the opportunity to get even, but you got the consolation prize anyway."

"The lease is in your name," added Stew, "and the payments, insurance and taxes have been prepaid for the two year period. We just hope that the color is ok and that you'll enjoy it."

"No doubt about that," said Art as he got up, thanked everyone and shook hands, then practically ran out to the new vehicle and drove away.

"One question," said Stew.

"Sure," replied Brent.

"You mentioned earlier that Michi got an armload of sewing and embroidery machines from Japan. How many and what's she intend to do with them?" he asked.

"The last that I heard she was setting them up in the basement and couldn't wait to play with all of them. Since she used to be a clothing designer she apparently knows how to use them. I counted the large boxes and there were fifteen of them. If she enjoys working with them, I'm going to suggest that she move all of them into one of the upstairs bedroom suites. I think that would be more convenient. Why do you ask?"

"Because I split a seam on my jacket and hated to waste half a day taking it to a tailor. Think that I could convince her to fix it?"

"I don't know Stew, her rates are pretty high as I hear it. Maybe we could just staple it together or use super glue," Brent laughed.

*

Several weeks had passed and the residents of Harrington House were all busy with their occupations. For Brent business was good, and Phil

Paulson was in the process of trying to convince him to bring another lawyer on staff. He'd picked out a well educated, aggressive young man, somewhat in his own image. Since the business was there and he was already farming out a good deal of it, he figured that it was just a matter of time before Brent agreed.

The car giveaway had overwhelmed both Jimmy Cane and Matt Jones, two really large guys. With their wives ecstatic with the gifts, both men felt that they had to repay the favor by working harder and Brent was doing his best to convince them to slow down, that life was too short. But Matt's wife Mary, had asked for some decorating help with her new home only a block away from the Canes, and Michi, June Andrews, and Cindy Cane had immediately responded. Judge Onnan's wife Judy had later joined them since no one had been around to shop with.

Michi, continued to insist that Brent exercise more and use the small gym down in the basement. In her spare time she had one of the upstairs bedroom suites cleared out and all of her new sewing and embroidery machines brought up. Designing clothing was just something that she had enjoyed doing as a business and now as a hobby.

The demolition of the small office and bedrooms outside of Ta's apartment had gone well due primarily to the four eager Japanese helpers. Something that would normally take weeks once the permits were obtained, took only days. Ta and the contractor that he'd hired were very impressed. But as the project came together Ta could see that his helpers needed something more to occupy their spare time. In Japan no one would have cared, but here in America, he just didn't feel right treating them like indentured servants or slaves. So after a discussion with Brent and Stew, they had agreed to make some renovations to the basement which extended under the entire house. The far south end held all of the unused antique furniture left over from Gus. The far north end held Frank's old pool room, a large laundry room, food storage/pantry, and the gym.

In the new scheme of things the antique storage area was walled off but accessible through large double doors. The gym was fully enclosed and the equipment upgraded and mirrors added to the walls. The pool room was expanded, new flooring added and the walls painted. The other rooms received new lighting, painting and protected white plastic walls and a new recreation room was added with a huge wall mounted television and several game machines. When the helpers weren't busy, they could watch Japanese movies, play games, just kick back and relax, play cards, whatever they wanted. Ta was pleased with the way it turned out and his helpers were very grateful.

Christy originally somewhat apprehensive about having the four eunuchs in the house quickly adapted. One helped her in the kitchen and seemed to have a knack for picking up on what she wanted done and in remembering it. A second insisted on cleaning and vacuuming, something that took her most of the day was completed in record time. Jim adopted the vehicles checking their fluids and tire pressure every day and washing them at least once a day. And Joe became Ta's assistant, but preferred to work with his hands in the greenhouse or on the grounds outside. He was in charge of making certain that fresh flowers were grown and distributed throughout the house. While Ta enjoyed working and keeping up the grounds and house, he didn't have to work as hard as he once had and enjoyed every moment of it.

Overall, life at Harrington House had taken a turn for the best after a long period of tragedy. And Brent was taking advantage of all the amenities at the Hotel on a more frequent basis, especially whenever Michi could join him. Whenever she entered a room, all eyes were immediately focused on her. And with all of the new stylish clothing she'd received from Japan, and after she modified it to her own designs, she looked outstanding. Without Brent and surrounded by her girlfriends, she could browse and shop at the Hotel's unique shops by the hour under the ever watchful eyes of the Hotel's security people. Since more often than not, she'd find something that she liked; she and her entourage were always treated like royalty.

Ta really wasn't that surprised when his monthly bank statements continued to show a deposit from a wire transfer in the amount of $9,950. From what Brent had found out and Stewart had confirmed there wasn't anything illegal about it, just unusual. But for the first few months Ta insisted on spending most of it in outfitting his helpers and purchasing even more equipment to maintain the house and grounds. If good old John Deere made it, then Ta wanted at least one of whatever it was and maybe more. When Ta's pickup truck got its second scratch while unloading some machinery at the Cane's, the following day several large boxes of machines were delivered so that he wouldn't have to transport anything other than his helpers again. Matt Jones received the same treatment as did Phil Paulson. Finding room to store it was the biggest problem since now all of the garages were filled with vehicles, so Ta purchased three fairly large Tuff Sheds and had them delivered to the respective back yards.

Brent had been asked to place Harrington House on the local garden tour but had turned down the offer. He could just see Ta's helpers chasing the tour guests around the property and if one of them happened to drop a Kleenex or a cigarette butt on the ground, they could be killed.

Chapter 33

It was Saturday and Brent's birthday, something he really didn't care about, but Michi did and she insisted on throwing a party. Art Thomas, tipped off by Michi, had called and invited him to play a round of golf at the Broadmoor at his expense. Brent had accepted, but he knew that Art wasn't a member and couldn't sign or pay for anything, but still it was a nice gesture and far better than playing on a public course.

Michi's schedule for today was to pick up the birthday cake and some other pastries at the new German bakery downtown on Kiowa Street, then stop at the dry cleaners off South Nevada, followed by the liquor store, Walgreen's and then return home. Ta had insisted that Jim and a new guy accompany her since Joe was already scheduled to go with Brent and drive the golf cart and he was running out of things for the two new guys to do. Michi rarely argued with her father since he was so stubborn and if she didn't cheerfully accept the two men, she might wind up with Ta instead. Driving the big new white Lexus SUV, she left the mansion heading east on Lake Avenue, turned north on Nevada and drove into the downtown area. She passed by Kiowa an eastbound one-way street, circled around and finally turned east off Cascade. The bakery was on the south side of the street midway down and luckily she found an empty diagonal parking space directly in front and pulled in.

For a Saturday morning, the area seemed fairly busy. As Jim patiently waited and the new guy sat quietly in the back seat, Michi fished around in her purse looking for parking meter money, found her change purse and inserted the coins. She looked in the front window of the bakery admiring what was on display and thinking that maybe she should increase her order. She kept forgetting that now there were eight mouths to feed on a regular basis and usually more since everyone liked Christy's cooking. They walked in, took a numbered ticket and as Jim stood silently off to one side Michi waited her turn. When it finally came, she gave the clerk her name and someone in the back overhearing it, began to bring out her special order birthday cake and the remainder of her order. But now she was adding to it. Finally she paid and nodded towards Jim who rushed over to carry as much as he could handle without crushing it. She insisted on carrying the cake. The bakery owner opened the door while thanking her and as he looked up the street he saw a gang of youths moving east on Kiowa in his direction, not an unusual event these days.

Monument Valley Park is located about two blocks to the west and just north of Kiowa Street. It follows Fountain Creek along the east side of Interstate-25 for a long distance. Runners, joggers, dog walkers, hikers and sports oriented people are found along the paths. Unfortunately in this day and age, the openness of the big park also attracts the homeless and gangs of youths with nothing better to do. Where the paths end at Kiowa Street, a soup kitchen on the north side of the street also attracts large numbers of homeless and down and outers just looking for a free meal. Unfortunately they begin to move into the area long before the doors are open and float throughout the neighborhood panhandling and killing time. Also Acacia Park a notorious hangout for druggies, is located one block to the north and a tad east. It's just across the street from one of the City's oldest high schools. A north and south alley dissects the block about fifty feet east of the building housing the bakery and other small businesses. Between all of these factions, groups of homeless constantly panhandling for loose change and the youths always looking for some excitement, sometimes it gets very interesting.

Michi had push the button on her remote entry keychain and the rear hatch popped opened. She and Jim carefully placed all of the fragile baked goods on the rear floor and as he stood back, his eyes constantly darting around, she slowly closed the lid, nodded to him and pushed a second button on the keychain. The hairs on his neck began to rise as he watched one group of troublemakers quickly approaching on the sidewalk and a second group exiting the alley across the street and heading in their general direction. He began to open the passenger side door and was immediately surrounded by the gang demanding money.

Michi reached for her door handle and one of the other gang members grabbed her from behind in a bear hug. Another reached out for her car keys, as another one called her a bitch and grabbed her small purse. The bakery owner seeing what was happening ran for the phone and called "911" for help. An unarmed parking enforcement officer (meter maid) was parked across the street and the unarmed female officer was in the process of writing a parking ticket, when she heard a cry and looked up. A full grown man had just been thrown through the plate glass front door of the bakery.

Jim had backed off, smiled and closed the front passenger door as he muttered something in Japanese. The new guy slipped out of the back door and joined him. Then he partially bowed as the first youth tried to kick him and the battle began. Unfortunately for the attackers, they weren't aware that they were now engaged in a no holds barred street fight with two highly trained Yakuza warriors.

Michi, well trained in the martial arts, had pushed back and when the largest youth standing directly in front of her had reached out to grab her by the throat, she kicked him with both feet so powerfully that he flew backwards and through the window of the bakery's front door. The heavy broken glass dropped down in jagged pieces severely cutting him. Then she stomped down on the instep of the one holding her, broke his instep and swirled around taking out two more with her swinging kick. As Ta had taught her, both hands and feet were weapons and she went to work on her attackers and carjackers.

"By now, Jim and new guy had taken out those close to them and had chased down several others. They dragged them back to the wide sidewalk and began breaking fingers, wrists and arms. On Jim's second pass he broke all of their noses. Michi was still in the process of cleaning up.

By the time the meter maid called it in, the police already up the street at the soup kitchen handling a small disturbance, had gotten the call. Ironically they and a westbound patrol car arrived about the same time, only to find Jim standing quietly leaning against the side of the Lexus and the new guy sitting quietly in the back seat, as Michi finished off her final attacker. She had kicked him in the face hard enough to break both his jaw and nose with one blow. Then she stood quietly, looked around and began to straighten out her clothing and pick up her purse, furious that she had broken the heel on her new shoes.

With so many lying on the ground, some bleeding and moaning, and others unconscious, it was difficult for the cops to believe that this slim young woman and the short oriental man had reeked such havoc. But Michi was quickly going through their pockets removing any cash, wallets and weapons. The bakery owner, tired of having his customers hassled by the street youths and homeless, followed behind her. The cops were dumbfounded as she handed them a bunch of razor sharp knives and three handguns. The cash she handed to the bakery owner while apologizing for his smashed front door.

The cops called for backup and ambulances, as Michi walked up hardly out of breath and demanded that they arrest the attackers and that she wanted to sign the complaints right now or she'd have her husband sue them and the whole damn city. What began as a simple assault call was turning into a mess, and the fun had just begun.

Further up the street a college student who was interning at a local television station was in the process of filming a documentary. The news business must have been slow today, because he had convinced the station manager to let him use the brand new remote transmission unit. The truck had a driver, a technician, a cameraman and normally a reporter, but today the intern was filling the last position. It was parked nearly a block east of the bakery when something had attracted his attention and he had shouted at the cameraman and pointed west. The entire event had been filmed and the station manager on duty this morning had chosen to break into the normal boring cartoon programming with a live onsite broadcast. Fortunately Jim was on the opposite side of the vehicle and what he did was blocked from view. But the watching public saw this slim young woman fighting for her life against a gang of carjackers and for lack of another description, rapists.

Now the cops were on the defensive, but the merchants along both sides of the street and their morning customers poured out of the businesses rallying to Michi's support. This wouldn't have happened, they shouted if the police did their job and patrolled the streets as they were paid to do. Lock up the transients, chase the homeless out of town and jail the crooks and gangs!

At the Broadmoor Golf Course, Brent was in the middle of screwing up another putt when Art's cell phone rang. It seemed to him that he'd never get the hang of this sport no matter how hard he tried. He wondered if it was just because he didn't care or if the God's had directed it. But suddenly he was being hustled off the green and towards the golf cart.

"Michi's had a bit of a problem downtown. She's ok, but her adoring public is gathering and about to lynch the two responding cops," Art laughed. By now Joe was sitting in the backseat of the Hummer, and Art had placed a flashing light on the dash and was speeding east on Lake Avenue towards the Interstate. At the Bijou exit he'd get off and swing over to Kiowa Street. Brent just sat quietly and prayed that Art wouldn't drive the big Hummer over the top of some sports car along the way. But Art, after leaving the Interstate, saw all of the stalled traffic pulled up on the sidewalk and crept east.

"Damn, will you look at all of the people," exclaimed Art.

"Must be three or four hundred," answered Brent, as they got out of the Hummer, locked the doors and pushed through the crowd.

By now more cops had arrived and they barricaded the street, attempting to do some crowd control. Other television stations hearing of the story had sent their mobile transmission units and they were parked in the alleys. And the police dispatcher had sent in Air One, the city's police helicopter, which continually circled high in the air but made a racket.

Art followed by Brent and Joe quickly passed thorough the police lines and finally he saw that Michi, the shy Eurasian girl was having a ball rallying the troops and being interviewed. Every so often she'd turn and wave at the crowd and the roar shook the windows on the nearby businesses. From what Art had told him along the way, this part of the city had become a problem area, with the homeless, the gangs, the drug dealers and the muggers. Something was always going down. Then suddenly this morning a slim young woman and her helper had taken all of them to task. Thirteen injured had been hauled off to Memorial Hospital, along with police escorts and Michi had instantly become the local hero. Then one of the reporters recognized her, as the wife of Brent Williams, the lawyer who'd run for District Attorney.

As more police began to arrive on the scene, Art stepped in to organized their defenses hoping that whoever was actually on duty this morning would hurry up and get here. By then Brent had finally reached Michi and she rushed into his arms and whispered into his ear.

"Isn't this fun?" she smiled. But since the attack some time ago back in Chicago, she and Ta had been teaching Brent how to defend himself and they both were pleased with his progress. If he had been with her, there may not have been 13 injured. But then he was always armed.

"Aren't you Brent Williams, the attorney?" asked one of the television reporters as she pushed a microphone towards him.

"Yes, I am and this is my wife Michi," Brent smiled one of his best smiles ever recorded on film Michi later told her Mother. "Most importantly she and her helper are ok, and the bad guys are in custody. I just hope that in the interest of the community, that the District Attorney and the activist judges enforce the laws that we have on the books regarding assaults, carjacking and armed robbery. Seems like they spend more time in defending the criminals than in protecting decent citizens like ourselves. So folks, the next time an election is held, please think long and hard before you select someone. And always remember that the police are here to help you, but if we continually cut back their budgets, they're spread much too thin. Response times right now are approaching 12 minutes in the city. So when the bad guy is stealing your car or breaking in your front door, what do you do? Tell him to take a time out."

The crowd had quieted down trying to listen to Brent, and now they began to holler and shout in answer to his brief comments. Seeing that Michi had gotten their attention and he was holding it mainly because she was standing beside him, he continued on.

"So again those of you that can hear me, the next time that you vote think about the person you're voting for. Will he or she properly fund the police and fire departments that we depend on? Or will they whine and cry about money and hand out more budget cuts. Will they enforce the law like Judge Onnan does, or will they plea bargain every charge down to practically nothing? And I personally would rather have someone out there protecting me than handing out our hard earned tax money for all of the crap that our City Council now supports. I'm sorry folks, when it hits home as close as this has, then I think that I'm entitle to speak my piece. God bless you all and please remember this day and this event and my words the next time that you vote." Brent ended and both he and Michi waved towards the television cameras and the crowd cheering in the street. Jim and Joe crowded into the back of the Lexus with the new guy as Brent swung behind the wheel and drove through the crowd and the barricade on his way to the Police Operations Center on South Nevada. When they arrived, both Jimmy Cane and Matt Jones were already there and waiting.

"Wow that was some speech you made Brent. You running for office?" Jimmy laughed as Joe opened the front door and they walked inside. A round of applause rang out much to Brent's surprise as he announced to the Sergeant that they were there to make out the reports and to sign complaints. Everyone watched the three oriental men dressed in white coats with the name "Harrington House" on the breast pocket, as they positioned themselves next to the William's. But as usual, Michi was the center of attraction, and thirty minutes later when they walked out, every male watched and envied Brent.

*

"Quite a speech," said Stewart as he sat down on the office couch and put his feet up on the new ottoman.

"For a spur of the moment thing, it really didn't come out too bad did it?" Brent smiled.

"If I didn't know any better, my guess would be that you're about to run for some public office," sighed Stew.

"Nope, not me, but I just got ticked off and unloaded. Bill Lofgren called me a little while ago and he's on cloud nine. Even Tom Onnan called to thank me for my kind words regarding him. And our new Chief of Police even called to personally thank me. He also wanted to remind me that while they would charge all thirteen of the bad guys with everything that they could think of, exactly what and how much would be prosecuted wasn't up to them, but the DA. He fully expected all of them to bond out tomorrow morning at their arraignment."

"Think that they'll drop it?" asked Stew.

"I hope so because otherwise Ta will be digging some deep holes in the yard," Brent laughed but both men knew how upset Ta had been when he'd heard about it. His only surviving daughter under attack by lowlifes wasn't acceptable and required an immediate response.

The remainder of the day passed slowly. Michi's birthday for Brent had gone off without a hitch once the conversation had gotten passed the assault earlier in the day. But maybe next year she's just hold it over at the Hotel and invite more guests. Sunday had been fairly quiet, and she and Brent had joined Ta and the others working out in the gardens. The strong rays of the sun had felt exceptionally good and their suntans definitely needed some immediate help. A few phone calls had interrupted

Brent but for the most part it had been a fun day. Monday had been back to normal and Brent had patiently explained to both she and Ta how the criminal system worked and how he fully expected to see all the attackers bond out at their arraignment. Michi wanted to go down to the courtroom and to kick their asses again, and her comment had broken Brent up. His laughter irritated her and soon she was back upstairs working on some clothing designs.

Art Thomas had called to tell him that Brent had been right and that all thirteen perps had been turned loose to their waiting tearful families. While it was difficult to justify how a six foot three inch hoodlum weighing well over two hundred pounds could rationalize an attack on a thin 120 pound woman, they all tried their best to blame it all on a misunderstanding because Michi was part Japanese. Stewart had gone to court to get a signed court order to obtain a certified copy of all of the television stations videos covering the attack, as a "just in case its needed" sort of thing. Ta asked his helpers to be alert for intruders and had named the two new men Ying and Yang because he couldn't think of anything else.

*

The man named John Wye slowly approached the gate at Harrington House still wondering why Brent Williams had called him and why he'd responded. The call had gone directly to his boss and he in turn had transferred it to John but only after staying on the line and cautioning Wye that all of the restraining orders were still in effect, but that Mr. Williams wished to suspend them for 24 hours and meet with him. To Wye it was one hell of a strange request, but with nothing better to occupy his time, he'd agreed. But it was now too late to change his mind because some big Japanese guy that kind of reminded Wye of a movie character named Quasimodo was walking down the drive towards the gate. He opened it, walked up to the driver's side window and asked for identification. A quick glance at Wyes' driver's license gained him entrance and instructions of where to go and park. As he glanced in his rear view mirror, the big guy was locking the gate, and then returning towards the garage. Suddenly a knock on his window startled him and when he looked up a oriental man in a white uniform was beckoning him to get out and follow him. He did so and found a second man behind him. A third opened the big front doors and motioned for him to come in without saying a word. He followed the man into an elaborate large office and was met by the really big black ex-cop named Jimmy Cane who he knew. Matt Jones who Wye also knew of, but hadn't met stood up and introduced himself. He was as big if not bigger than Cane and suddenly Wye felt like a midget, or more politically correct as a small tree in a redwood forest. Matt asked politely if Wye was armed, somewhat surprising him, but he wasn't. Then a very friendly and attractive woman walked in said that she was Christy and placed a huge silver platter of fresh sticky buns and coffee cups on a table. She was followed by yet another oriental man with a large pot of coffee. As quickly as she had arrived she disappeared and Brent Williams in the flesh walked in and surprisingly dropped into a side chair facing Wye.

"Thank you for coming John, I know that my call was unexpected and I appreciate you placing aside our differences for this meeting. Would you like some coffee and rolls? They're my favorite. If you want a fancy latte we've got that too thanks to my wife," Brent smiled and the two large men just grunted as if there was a lengthy story behind the coffee.

"I'll try some," replied Wye.

"If you'll excuse me for just a moment," said Brent turning to Cane.

"I'm good with it if you are Jimmy. But take Matt with you, ok?"

Cane had smiled, finished off his bun, washed it down with the remainder of his coffee and both he and Jones got up, excused themselves and left.

"I didn't see their cars in the driveway," questioned Wye.

"They carpooled this morning. Matt lives about a block away from Jimmy. Jimmy's car is in our garage being washed. He never has the time and Ta's helpers do. But just in case you hadn't heard both retired from the cop shop and joined my legal practice."

"So now they both work for you? And no, I hadn't heard about that," said Wye. "Cops joining ex-cops."

"One of the smartest moves I've ever made. Before Jimmy joined us I had lawyers trying to be investigators and they weren't doing very well. Billable hours were way down. In fact Jimmy worked out so well that when Matt decided to leave, I jumped at the chance to hire him too. In their defense, neither approached me. But they have street smarts and common sense and they're both doing great. And now the attorneys can go back to being lawyers again. But that's not why I asked to meet with you John."

"I was hoping that you'd get around to that," answered Wye rather sarcastically.

"I've always felt bad about what came out of our last meeting. That definitely wasn't my style, but at the time I'd had enough prying eyes looking at my family. With the deaths, the near misses, even a house burning down, I'd just had enough. Anyway I'm certain that you've heard all about the attack on my wife last Saturday. Maybe I was a bit worked up at the time because as I look back at the tapes, I sounded as if I was about to run for office, which I'm not. But every television station has called asking for an interview and I just figured that I'd screwed you out of one story and that maybe if I offered you this one, it might square things a bit."

"So you want me to interview you?" asked a surprised Wye.

"Well as I told Stew at the time, you're probably a good reporter and in my book I owe you one. My only requirement is that I get a final review and edit before it goes to press. You can say anything that you want to about me and I really don't care. But as far as the rest of the family particularly my wife, then I do care. So what do you say?" Brent asked.

"And this interview would cover exactly what?" asked Wye.

"Whatever you want, but my guess is that you'd sell more newspapers if you included Saturday's activities up front. Everyone wants to know how a skinny little girl can kick the butt of some fairly big guy twice her size and weight, especially when he was armed with a knife."

"I sort of wondered about that myself," smiled Wye for the first time.

"No big thing John. She and her sister were two pretty Eurasian girls growing up in a bad part of LA. Their father couldn't watch them all of the time and so he taught them to defend themselves. And we have a gym downstairs, actually we just built it, where we all practice martial arts although it's really not any formal kind, just street fighting. Keeps my weigh down and my blood flowing." Brent smiled. "After everything that's happened to us, it just seemed like it wouldn't hurt to learn how to protect ourselves. Sure I have a gun permit, but so what. Hard to shoot a gun in a grocery store or a bank and not hit an innocent victim. And honestly while Michi had to drag me down there for a while, I actually do feel better since I've been exercising."

"Can I go back to your first wife?" Wye asked as sort of a test question.

"Sure if you wish?" replied Brent. "She and Michi were the nieces of my housekeepers. I met them that first Christmas when they came to visit. I guess it was a regular thing that began when they were ten years old. Actually they both knew more about the house than I did. But at the time I was in hock up to my neck, had just passed the bar and owed a lot more than I had to the Credit Union for my law school loan."

"I heard that you inherited this place," said Wye gesturing around the room.

"You heard right. I only met the owner once in person. Talked to her maybe a dozen times or more over the years. I thought that I was being sued at the time, but it was only the reading of the will."

"While it's interesting, it doesn't sound like any big time story that the wires would pick up," smiled Wye.

"Didn't to me either at the time. I was broke just like everyone else, only I was living in a big expensive house that I couldn't even sell off for 20 years according to the will."

"Who else are you talking to? I mean reporter wise." asked Wye.

"Nearly every reporter and talking head in the city has called. But I really don't think that I'm that interesting. So Stew and I got to talking about it and we decided to contact just you. If you think that there's a story there, good. If not that's ok with me too. And as a part of this you'd have to share anything you wrote with all of the others, but not until your story was printed."

"So I'd kind of be the lead guy on this?"

"For lack of a better term, yup, you'd be the guy."

"Where would you suggest that I begin?" Wye asked.

"Heck John, I don't really know. While the original owners were a tad bit different, in my opinion they surely weren't newsworthy. And neither was I until the murders occurred. But that's old news by now and actually, who cares about it other than me? But Michi really cut loose on Saturday morning and if you'd been there you'd understand. My guess is that the whole neighborhood was on edge with all of the panhandling and the gangs and when she was attacked, well it all surfaced. I got there a bit late, but even then I wondered if the crowd wasn't going to lynch the perps."

"So you don't think that she was at fault?" he asked.

"Let's see, they hauled off 13 of the perps to the hospital and the baker said that a number of others ran off. So it's hard for me to accept that a 120 pound woman in high heels would attack a gang of between fifteen and twenty guys. Hell I'm an ex-cop and armed and I wouldn't even consider that.

Would you?"

"No, actually I guess that I wouldn't. And yes, I've heard a lot of stories about what goes on in that neighborhood. Out of curiosity, do you think that she'll ever go back to that bakery again?"

"Lets ask her," said Brent as he punched some numbers in his cell phone. Minutes later she walked in and sat down. Brent did the introductions. The conversation lasted less than ten minutes, before she excused herself and left.

"She sort of sounded as if she enjoyed herself," smiled Wye.

"I think that I'd be happy too if I survived an attack like that. But you heard her say that she'd definitely be back there next Saturday. Because I work out of the house, we sometimes have a lot of people here. No one ever goes away hungry and at times Christy who you met earlier and who is Michi's mother can't keep up. Oh she now has a helper, but when people drop in you aren't always prepared. So Michi has made a deal with that new bakery to pick up the slack. They make some special stuff according to Christy's recipes and we pick it up. Some of it is frozen for later baking and some is ready to eat. If you haven't tried the place, you really should because it's good."

"Sounds like you have a houseful?"

"To me this place is huge. But like any older home it needs constant attention to keep it looking first class. Now the woman that left it to me sort of became a recluse towards the end. Normally she had a staff of four, but at the end it was only two. For special events, parties or unscheduled maintenance she would bring in outside contractors. Well I rarely entertain, but I needed to replace the older couple that came with the house and were killed. About

387

that time Michi's folks were looking for a change of lifestyle and I offered them the position. But like I said, it's an old house and needs constant attention. When I had the opportunity to hire two helpers for Ta, I jumped at the chance. And I'm sure you've heard the story about the other two arriving at the airport unannounced. If you haven't, then talk to the cop that was on duty that morning or the Customs Agent out there. So now I had four helpers, and none of them spoke any English. But my father-in-law saved the day because at least he can talk to them. I guess it's kind of like the league of nations around here," laughed Brent. "However, everyone works and we all get along."

"This is beginning to sound more like a book than a one shot article," laughed Wye.

"Its just life as the cards have been dealt," replied Brent. "I'm just an ex-cop pretending to be a plain old lawyer doing his thing under the watchful eye of Stewart. Fortunately we're doing well enough to hire two other lawyers and two investigators to assist us. Harrington House is very demanding and it takes a number of people to keep it operating and looking like new. I guess I don't even see a part of a book chapter there."

"I heard your speech on Saturday and I guess I'm finding it hard to believe that you're not planning on running for office again," Wye said.

"Guess I sort of unloaded. Judge Onnan and Bill Lofgren sort of cornered me on that DA thing. I only agreed to run because they didn't have any other name to pencil in. Also both of them promised me that I would lose. Let there be no doubt that I had no intention of accepting that office. First off, it would be a big salary cut and I just couldn't afford it. And secondly, I don't want to be tied down to a job like that. I'm looking to relax and enjoy life a little more, not work myself to death for the crazy legal system we now have. However on the up side of that, it did give Michi and I the chance to socialize with a lot of really nice people that we probably wouldn't have had the opportunity to meet. So overall it worked out in my favor. Actually Stew's been kidding me that I sounded like a politician too. Trust me, it wasn't intended. But both the cops and fire people keep having their budgets trimmed back and that just isn't right. Society is becoming more violent every day and we need to protect ourselves with a better police force and more fire engines."

"Still sounds like a campaign speech," laughed Wye.

"I guess it actually does, now that you mentioned it. But hear me loud and clear, it is not."

"So if I accept your offer, just how much time and access will I have to you and your family?"

"Whatever you need John. I have no idea how to answer that."

"Where would you want me to begin?"

"John, you're the reporter, and I'm not. So it would be your call. Come as often as you wish, and stay as long as you want. We're not nearly as interesting as you think we might be and except for living in Harrington House, we're pretty dull people. Now my suggestion, and that's all it is would be to return back to your editor and publisher and discuss it with him and his staff. Either way I'll ask Stew to get the restraining orders removed and to call and make peace with your people. I at least owe you that much."

"Ok, I'll start there."

*

The week passed very quietly, and John Wye had accepted Brent's offer after conversing with his boss and had been invited to dinner on Sunday. He'd been told by Michi that he could bring a date or his wife if he had one and he'd settled for a girlfriend and fellow worker. But the friendly group moved out to the large patio and Jimmy Cane proceeded to take over cooking on the big gas grill. He was assisted by Ta, two men in white and his old partner Matt Jones. Tom Onnan was elected bartender and Art Thomas became the waiter, delivering drinks to everyone. The evening passed all too quickly and Brent was pleased with how much fun his guests had been. Around 1 AM, shortly before the party was about to break up, Art received a call on his cell phone, and sat down as he asked the caller to repeat what he'd heard for a second time. His face showed concern when he looked up and those around him noticed it.

"That was my counterpart that's on duty tonight. There's been an accident on Interstate 25, just south of Fountain. An SUV with seven guys in it coming north from Pueblo ran off the road and rolled. Doesn't look like there were many survivors. He just wanted to give me the heads up. Anyway, its time to go home," he said as he stood up and looked around for his wife Sally. Within the next twenty minutes everyone would leave, and Harrington House would be locked down for the night.

Chapter 34

"Brent, its Tom Onnan, do you have a minute to talk?"

"Certainly Tom, business or pleasure," Brent joked.

"I guess this would come under the business part," he laughed. "I just talked to one of my associates. He told me that the DA had personally called him first thing this morning regarding that fatal vehicle accident on south I-25 last Sunday night. The police identified the northbound SUV that rolled, as being stolen in Colorado Springs sometime on Saturday."

"Yeah, that was the call that Art Thomas got before the party broke up," replied Brent.

"Well it seems that someone that was southbound reported to the State Patrol that they saw a red pickup truck run the SUV off the road. At that point the highway is fairly well separated and crossovers are limited. They figured that someone would report it and they kept on going. Apparently no one in the southbound car had a cell phone. Now here comes part two. A State Trooper found a red pickup on fire just south of DIA (Denver International Airport) about two hours after the SUV was found in the ditch. By the time the local fire department could respond, it was a burned out shell."

"So you think that it was a hit, that someone intentionally forced the SUV off the road?" asked Brent.

"Hold on for a minute because there's more to it. Now comes part three. The seven guys in the SUV were all in on the assault on Michi, and only two of them survived the accident. They were flown by helicopter to Memorial Hospital here in the Springs. As of right now their condition is critical."

"Tom if you remember we were all partying together about that time."

"No, no, I'm not saying that she did it, I'm just repeating what I heard. In fact she spent a good deal of the night with my wife and me. But it is strange and I wonder how the news people will treat it and the reaction from the perp's families. My guess is that they'll blame it all on the rich white guy that lives in the Broadmoor area. Anyway I just wanted to give you a heads up."

Brent sat in his office, feet up on his desk as he munched on a fresh roll. It certainly was strange. He dialed Ta's cell phone and asked him to stop by the office. About the same time Ta arrived sometime later, Art Thomas called. Ta dropped onto a chair with a mug of strong coffee in his hand and waited. It was several minutes before Brent hung up and looked at him.

"Seven of Michi's attackers were run off the road Sunday night. Five died at the scene and two are in the hospital," said Brent. "The guy or guys that did it dumped the truck up in Aurora not far from DIA and torched it. Now three more of the gang that are out on bond have disappeared off the face of the earth. That too happened sometime Sunday night. Any ideas?"

"Heck it wasn't me," laughed Ta not unhappy with the thought that ten of the thirteen gang bangers were out of the picture. "Any bets on the remaining three?"

"Not from me. But apparently the families of the missing or dead are asking the DA to look into it and pointing at me."

"Hey, all of us were here, including the Judge. Shouldn't take him long to figure that out."

"Onnan intended to call him, but it sure looks suspicious."

The conversation was interrupted by the phone on Brent's desk.

"It's John Wye, Brent. Have you heard?" he asked.

"About ten minutes ago, John. I bet that you never guessed that you'd become my alibi," Brent laughed. "But seriously, any idea of what's going on?"

"No, and actually I was hoping that you knew more than I do."

"Well they hauled off thirteen attackers and booked all of them into the County Jail. Then they all bonded out. Seven were in the stolen SUV when it crashed, five died at the scene and two are in the hospital, and three more have disappeared. That's about all I know, except that the families have complained to the DA that I did it."

"Did you?" asked Wye.

"John, you were here with us when it supposedly went down, so to answer your question, no I wasn't any part of it, although I'd have to admit that I'm not going to mourn their loss. And if the DA happens to call, I'll tell him the same thing, or my lawyer will. And just think about it for a moment, why would I want to draw anymore attention to myself?"

"Yeah, that was my answer too, but sometimes you just have to ask the question and clear the air."

"Do you have any contacts out on the street? Anything better than what Art Thomas has?" Brent asked.

"Maybe, I'll just have to ask around, but this sounds a lot like a professional get even operation."

"Who's getting even, not us!" answered Brent.

"Maybe someone that likes you," replied Wye.

"Trust me John, I don't know anyone that likes me that much. Michi, well everyone likes her including you and your date. But me, I'm just a gigolo. Art did mention that it might be connected to some turf war between gangs. Sounded pretty far out to me, but then these days you never know. Keep in touch," said Brent as he hung up.

"Taniaka?" asked Brent and Ta just shook his head.

"Could be. Actually it probably is. Look how many died when Tani was killed. Now he thinks that he owes me and that extends to my family too. So any attack on one of us is believed to be an attack on him. Remember Michi didn't even know that he existed until I left to help him. And then she sent him a handwritten thank you note for those sewing machines. In his culture, she's family and if you attack her, then you attack him. If I was one of the survivors, I'd think about taking a long vacation real soon," smiled Ta.

"Looking back, I don't think that it would matter because at some point his people would find you regardless of where you were hiding," replied Brent.

"I've watched that video tape several times, and somehow I'm finding it very difficult to have any compassion for those guys. I am very proud of

Michi and Jim and Ying, because they pulled all of their punches. It would have been much easier to just strike one blow and instantly kill the attacker than to try and incapacitate him," said Ta.

"So despite the number of attackers, she and the others weren't in any danger?" Brent asked.

"If she'd been scared, then the body count would have been high. I never taught her to take any prisoners, that was her idea. Killing them would have embarrassed you. Jim and Ying just took their lead from her."

"Well I expect that I had better call Stew and bring him up to date since the way this is going I fully expect that the DA will be calling on me," smiled Brent.

"That could be fatal from what I've seen," laughed Ta.

"With my luck he'd probably die from a lightening bolt along the way and then Bill Lofgren would push to have me fill out his term in office," said Brent but he wondered if push came to shove if Taniaka would actually go after him?

*

"John, its Brent. I'm one guy short for a poker game at my house tonight and I wondered if you might be interested. Art had to work, Ta doesn't play cards, Phil has a meeting with a client, Jimmy and Matt have to go out with their wives and so I thought of you. Any interest?"

"Sure if it's a low stakes game," he quickly answered.

"Actually we don't play for money, just for fun. Money always leaves hard feelings, so we decided when we began playing that it would be fun only. That and the fact that none of us are very good at it either. But once in a while we get together and just relax. In by 7 PM and home by 11 PM. We're a really wild bunch," Brent laughed.

Wye arrived right on time and found that tonight's players were Brent, Stewart, Judge Onnan and himself. Each got a box of chips and the game began. Christy brought in the snacks, Ta the drinks and the four men sat around a beautiful antique poker table in the game room, playing cards as if they knew what they were doing. Wye watched and wondered if anyone was cheating, but then he realized that the others were just having fun, so why cheat. You were either lucky or you weren't and tonight he wasn't. At ten minutes to eleven, the game broke up and shortly passed 11 PM he was home in bed.

"I tried to get you last night," said his boss as Wye walked in the next morning and sat down at his desk.

"I was playing cards and one of the rules was that no cell phones were allowed. Sorry, guess I forgot to turn it back on," Wye replied.

"Well it was a busy night, that's for certain. Someone blew up the DA's car right in his driveway, a police officer was wounded in a drive by shooting, and one of the two gang guys in the hospital died."

"Wow that was a busy night. Any connection between them?"

"The guy in the hospital didn't die of natural causes. Someone cut his throat."

"Who's on the story?"

"You are as of right now," he said turning and walking back to the elevator.

Wye grabbed his camera, recorder and IPod, and raced for the parking lot. Once inside his car, he thought for a long moment, then called Brent on his cell phone. It rang twice before Brent picked it up.

"A news flash from the front lines," joked Wye. "One of the perps in the hospital had his throat cut sometime last night. I'm on my way there right now. You might want to call Art Thomas and see what he's got. Oh, and the DA's car was bombed last night too. Just thought that you might want to know," said Wye as he hung up and narrowly missed a fire hydrant as he turned east onto Pikes Peak Avenue.

Ta was still sitting in Brent's office discussing the attack on Michi when Wye had called. Brent filled him in on the latest events.

"I can't believe that Taniaka would still have his people hanging around here," said Brent. "My read on the torched truck up in Aurora was that they did it on their way back to the airport. Get in and get out. Going after the DA, well to me that just seems like some kind of a warning, but the hospital bit just looks too risky. If the killer had been cornered, he'd have taken out too many to just write off."

"I agree," replied Ta, "but I told you that sometimes my uncle isn't rational. When he gets mad no one ever knows what he'll do, not even me."

Brent had called Thomas, got his voice mail and left a brief message to call him back at his convenience, no rush. Michi wanted to go shopping for something at one of the Hotel's boutiques and under the circumstances Ta had insisted on sending both Joe and Jim with her. Stewart had been briefed by Brent and decided to drive over to the courthouse and talk to Judge Onnan off the record. Maybe later he'd stop by the DA's office. Phil Paulson was in the process of finalizing his recommendations of who he wanted Brent to hire to assist him. Both Jimmy and Matt were out working the streets in regards to the attack on Michi and then the others.

The following day they met with Brent in his office.

"I'm telling you, we canvassed the whole town, talked to every lowlife we found and came up empty. No one has a clue about what's going on, except for the drive by shooting. The cop driving the patrol car was seen fooling around with some woman at a nightclub last Saturday. No one will testify to it but the word on the street is that she was married to some gang banger and he just wanted to send a message to leave his woman alone," said Jimmy.

"And over at the hospital no one saw anything. For some strange reason the surveillance cameras were not functioning. The guards had called tech support for help and had spread the word. They even called in some off duty guys for better coverage. The head nurse on duty didn't see anything unusual until she made her rounds. Oh, as usual they were operating short handed. Normally there are two on duty at that station, but one was downstairs having a baby and they couldn't find a replacement on short notice. Now I'm assuming that the head nurse had a lot to do and that maybe she even had to use the bathroom once or twice," said Matt.

"No cops around?" Brent asked.

"Sure, but they were down in the Emergency Room. According to the cop that I talked to, it was the usual zoo scene down there. The place was packed with impatient people. I pulled duty over there once or twice so I know what he means." Jimmy sat back for a moment to remember the bad old days when he was in uniform. Put the big black guy in the uniform right up front by the door.

"There isn't one word on the street about the rollover accident. And no one has a clue about who torched the truck up in Aurora, but that doesn't surprise me because it's so far away from here. As for some kind of a turf war, mum's the word. You know the feeling that if you open your mouth, you may lose your tongue," smiled Matt.

Stew spoke up. "I talked to Tom Onnan and he heard that a hand grenade was most likely what blew up the DA's car. With all of the military installations around here, and the troops going back and forth, he didn't seem to think that finding a grenade would be that difficult. And I stopped by the DA's office but they didn't seem too friendly or want to talk to me."

"Is it just me," asked Brent, "or does it seem like the whole damn town is suddenly going nuts right now?"

Shortly thereafter, the meeting moved into the kitchen because Christy had just finished baking several old fashion apple pies and as soon as they cooled, she promised to break out the vanilla ice cream. The men were content to just sit around and wait.

"Hi Art, about time you called," joked Brent after answering his cell phone which was more difficult to monitor and trace. "I was beginning to think that you were on vacation."

"Hi my butt," Art replied. "Have you killed or blown up anyone today?"

"Gosh, let me think for a moment," Brent paused, "nope, not that I can remember."

"Well it's been busy around the cop shop," said Art.

"Yeah, I heard that one of the uniforms put the moves on a dolly and her boyfriend didn't like it."

"Yep that was one of them, but I'm kind of surprised that you already know about it. You didn't supply the gun or anything like that did you?"

"Nope, Jimmy and Matt were out poking around. So who's on the suspect list for road rage, the bomb and the hospital stuff?"

"Well your name came up several times, but I told the brass that you didn't drive well enough to run anybody off the road and that you hate hospitals. That left the bomb, but I figured that you wouldn't know where to get one."

"Hey are you forgetting that you gave me one of those? Wonder which flowerbed Ta hid it under? I'll have to ask him. Any chance that you want it back?"

"Not yet, but I'll think about it. Seriously, the DA's people moved right in and took over that car business. We don't have a clue where it's headed, but after that shooting shortly after he was elected we have our doubts about it being an outsider. Since he's always considered himself to be somewhat of a ladies man, I'm not going to waste any time worrying about it. But the hospital thing is something else."

"Sounded strange to me too," said Brent.

"So how did you hear about that one?" Art asked.

"Got a call from the reporter John Wye," replied Brent. "And Jimmy and Matt heard about it too."

"Damn, you have better sources than I do," he laughed.

"It just seemed strange that the one time the surveillance cameras are out of service, a nurse suddenly has a baby leaving, her shift is understaffed and the perp gets hit. Wonder why they didn't take out the other one too?"

"Because he was already dead, but we hadn't released that info," replied Art.

"Sure doesn't sound like any gang bangers that I've ever heard of. That took some planning and up front information."

"You're probably right, but between us this kind of resembles the killings at Harrington House and we still don't have a clue about who was behind that one." Brent didn't say anything for a moment.

"Any time open for a round of golf?" he asked, trying to change the conversation.

"Not for a couple of days. The Chief has everyone pulling double duty trying to get to the bottom of this. He even suggested putting a 24 hour police guard on Michi since in his mind it all started with her. But at the rate we're going, no ones going to be left to complain. Can you picture that, Michi walking around with Ta's helpers protecting her and then the cops. I think that she'd probably take out all of them in frustration. I mean that girl can definitely take care of herself."

"You haven't heard the latest, but you will soon. After the attack was shown on TV, all the wives including yours, got together and asked Michi to give them some instructions in self defense. Since we have the new gym downstairs, they've agreed to meet here twice a week. Knowing how she fights, you might want to start bringing home some flowers every so often," laughed Brent.

After promising to talk again later in the week, the conversation had ended. Brent sat thinking about Michi's attackers. According to bystanders there had to be at least twenty or more after the two groups had merged at the alley.

Thirteen had been taken out and of those seven, were now dead and three more had disappeared without a trace and were assumed to be dead. Now the families were all pointing fingers and accusing anyone that they could think of and hiding the last three survivors. He wondered if another gang had moved in and taken over the first gang's turf yet? But mostly he wondered what to do about Ta's uncle? While he wasn't positive, he did think that he might be behind it. It was back to, if you attack my family, then you have attacked me and we're at war. He though about all of those that had died following Tani's death, including the totally innocent and even the Feds. Taniaka wasn't afraid of any of them whether they were in the US or Japan. He was ultimately responsible for the deaths of Sukara's entire crime family, including men, women and children. The more that he thought about it the more he believed that it was just a matter of time until the three gang bangers that were being hidden by their families, were found dead. Taniaka wouldn't let anyone who attacked Michi remain alive.

The next 48 hours passed by with a lot of rhetoric being exchanged between the press, the DA and the deceased's families. The word on the street was that the three surviving perps had jumped bond and relocated to the west coast. The dead had been buried without much fanfare and their families mourned, but no longer pointed their fingers at Brent, out of fear that they'd be next. Acting on a tip from Crime Stoppers most likely called in by the woman in question, the police had arrested the man responsible for shooting at the police car. And the explosion of the DA's car was now being explained as being a leaky gasoline tank dripping on a hot exhaust pipe. However, the DA had quietly convened a Grand Jury, and was seeking an indictment against Brent Williams for activities going all of the way back to the original murders at Harrington House.

Chapter 35

Three months had passed, summer had come to an end as fall began in all of its colorful splendor. With above average temperatures, the weatherman was predicting a very warm winter with occasional showers. He didn't specify whether the occasional showers would be in the form of rain or snow, or whether they would amount to flooding or blizzards. However in Colorado, even the natives knew that the weathermen talked out of both sides of their mouths and few, mostly newcomers actually believed them.

At Harrington House, Ta had the gardens and flowerbeds ready regardless of how the precipitation arrived and his helpers were scurrying around performing final outside maintenance before the weather turned. Brent had promised Christy a brand new kitchen and when it finally became too cold to work outside, Ta and his helpers would begin remodeling the huge professional kitchen.

Brent continued to work out of his home office with the guidance of Stewart Andrews and assisted by Phil Paulson, a new part time attorney named Harold Louden, and investigators Jimmy Cane and Matt Jones. Business was so good that he and Stew were discussing adding another full time attorney to assist Phil.

As good as things appeared on the surface, trouble wasn't that far off in the form of the DA pursuing a Grand Jury indictment for the Harrington House murders against Brent who he hated and was thoroughly convinced was as guilty as sin. Despite suggestions by Chief Judge Onnan that he consider taking another look at the evidence, he completely ignored him. Then his party chairman attempted to reason with him and was told rather rudely to mind his own damn business. Several of his Assistant DA's threatened to resign, and he told them get out before he fired them. His attitude and arrogance wasn't anything new, but his determination to ruin Brent by any means necessary was beyond belief. To Brent's credit, both Jimmy and Matt were keeping him abreast of what was going on in the Grand Jury room, although neither would admit as to exactly how they knew.

Brent and Stew had spent many hours discussing how to respond if the indictment was ever returned. It was all bogus, but it could totally ruin his reputation even if the charges were later dropped. He remembered Allen and his constant lecturing about perception. If the public saw you driving a big car and believed you were wealthy, then you were. If someone charged you with a crime, then you were probably guilty, even if the charges went away.

Newspaper reporter John Wye had completed his interviews and investigation and had written what Brent considered to be an outstanding story about him, his family and Harrington House. Since Brent had the right to edit it before publishing, John was surprised when the typewritten story had been returned to him without a single change. However after months of work, his publisher had chosen to sit on it until the rumored Grand Jury reached a verdict. Unfortunately only the DA could present anything to the panel and the accused was unable to attend and defend himself, so the presentations were really one sided.

Brent had discussed worst case scenarios

with both Ta and Stew. If everything went to hell, was it worth fighting it, or should he just disappear to an island and ignore it? While it would be nearly impossible for him to take that approach, he absolutely refused to let the ramblings of a paid misguided public servant hurt his wife or family. And while the DA would be spending public funds to attack him, Brent would be spending his own money to defend himself. He was in a quandary, but he'd do anything to keep Michi out of it.

*

"Morning Art," said Brent as he picked up the house phone.

"How'd you know that it was me?" asked Art Thomas.

"Cause you're the only one that calls me this early," Brent laughed.

"Well sit back and listen to the latest because once again, you're not going to believe it."

"Ok," laughed Brent, "go ahead, I'm buckled into my chair."

"So yesterday UPS delivered three boxes to the DA's office. Each one is about a foot or a foot and one half square and they're all marked "Personal & Confidential." These days they run all of the mail through some fancy machine looking for bomb and chemical substances and the mail clerk did exactly that. However because of the way it was addressed, she decided not to open them. Actually I think that she was afraid that if she did, she'd get fired. Or maybe she thought that they were full of some porno magazines, who knows, but she carried them up and stacked them on the DA's desk."

"Would have been nice if they were filled with drugs," laughed Brent.

"Stay with me here," replied Art. "So the

jerk finally arrives, sees the boxes, checks to make certain that they've gone through the bomb machine, and opens them with the help of his secretary. Inside each box is a human head in a plastic bag. Well the secretary passes out and he starts screaming like a banshee."

"Let me guess here, the heads belong to the remaining three guys that attacked Michi?"

"Exactly. They were shipped from some UPS Store in LA where the rumors on the street said they had gone. Now we both know that no one will remember who the shipper was. Trying to backtrack on them is a total waste of time. And my guess is that by now, the bodies are probably feeding the fishes out in the ocean."

"How'd they ID them?" asked Brent.

"When they were arrested and booked, we got photos. At the hospital, according to their latest policy which hasn't been made public yet, they took DNA samples. The DA insisted that both be used to identify them although the pictures would have been good enough. He's spread the word amongst the victim's families and his staff that you are part of a international smuggling operation and that he's dedicated his life to bringing you down. So my guess is that the next stop for the heads will be the Grand Jury."

"Boy, this guy must really hate me," said Brent.

"Actually I think that he hates everyone. He's the most insecure guy I've ever met. Thinks that everyone is after him and maybe they are the way he chases the skirts. Anyway, I thought that you might want to know. Talk to you later," and Art hung up.

Brent immediately called John Wye to fill

him in and then Stewart. Eventually Ta came in and sat down and he related the telephone call.

"This guy is just nuts," said Ta very calmly and without any emotion. Maybe I should mention it to one of my helpers," he smiled.

"I've got to agree that he's crazy. Art told me yesterday that he had gotten a call from Tony Martinez the Homeland Security friend of his and the DA had contacted him directly asking for help. He told him to go away. I guess he tried the FBI and got the same suggestion."

"You realize that he is definitely a nutcase, don't you?" asked Ta and Brent nodded his head in agreement.

"If he can't bring you down with the Grand Jury, he could show up on your doorstep with a gun in hand," said Ta and Brent knew that he was right.

Brent worried about it for the remainder of the week, wondering what to do and how to do it. He didn't want Michi anywhere around if it came down to him taking out the DA by force. Despite every scenario he thought of, he knew of no other way to stop the guy.

*

It had been at Ta's suggestion that Brent and Michi attend a social event at the Colorado Springs Fine Arts Center. They hadn't been out in public in a long time and he'd convinced Christy to mention it. She had, and now they were seated with the Onnan's and the Lofgren's in plain sight of hundreds of others, drinking, eating and thoroughly enjoying themselves. Ta who was playing chauffer this evening was outside watching over the new fancy Saturday night car that Taniaka had paid for. It had every option that Lexus offered in the top of the line model and Ta enjoyed driving it. It wasn't as good as his prized truck, but it wasn't bad. It was well after midnight when he dropped off the Onnan's and returned to Harrington House. As usual when the others went to bed, he'd check the grounds and then set the alarm system to "armed." In the morning, he reversed the procedure.

The next morning, after making love to his beautiful wife, and showering together, Brent and Michi put on their big white terrycloth robes and went down for breakfast. Christy as usual had prepared a feast and they took their fill, eventually returning upstairs to their bedroom and getting dressed. When Brent walked down to his office, Michi entered her sewing and design domain and went to work. She was actually selling some of her designs to manufacturers in New York. Brent sat thinking about last night with a cup of coffee in his hand. Boy, he had enjoyed going out for a change. Then the desk phone rang.

"I'm outside, push the button," he heard Art's voice say. He reached for the remote and opened the gate. Ying let him in the front door and Art made a beeline for the powder room, and then into the office.

"Thought my bladder was going to explode," he laughed.

"You're out and around early this morning," said Brent.

"Its mid morning and I've been in meetings since 5:30," Art replied with a look of disgust.

"So what's up?"

"How was the Fine Arts event last night?" Art asked with a smile.

"We haven't been out together in a long time and it was great."

"Lots of witnesses?"

"Hundreds!   Why has the DA found something else to accuse me of?" asked Brent not really wanting to hear an answer.

"Ok, good.   Actually I don't know where to begin.   Here goes.   Last night about 1 AM, the CSPD received a 911 call from a woman.   She's a well known young prostitute and lives in a motel room down on south Nevada.   She claimed a customer just beat her up, took her drugs, and that she needed medical help and fast.   So the neighborhood being what it is, the uniforms were nearby and they got there in time to see a big luxury car driving away.   They got the plate number and put out a call, just about the time the paramedics arrived. Now this woman was covered with blood and looked like she had really been assaulted and it took some time for them to get her calmed down and stabilized and on her way to Memorial Hospital.   Meanwhile another patrol car further north on Nevada spotted the car, but the guy refused to stop.   The uniform called it in to dispatch and he was told that according to the assault victim's description, the guy was a regular and drugs were definitely involved.   Now there's two cars in pursuit up Nevada.   I guess the guy breezed through the college campus doing over 100 miles per hour.   Lucky at that hour it was pretty deserted and he didn't hit anyone, but by now a third patrol car has joined the parade.   By now the plates have been run and it turns out to be our own DA in his brand new car.   Remember the other one was blown up in his driveway.   So lets add it up, buying drugs, sexual assault on a woman, evading the cops, speeding, running red lights, oh and along the way he sideswiped several cars and I'm certain there is something else that I probably forgot.   So he gets as far up as Fillmore Street and a big moving truck sees him coming and all of the flashing lights behind him, so the driver pulls the brake, jumps out and runs for cover leaving the semi idling in the middle of the intersection and blocking everything. With nowhere to go, the DA slides into the trailer and bounces off into a light pole. Then like a miracle, he jumps out and starts to take off, but now he has a gun in his hand. They chased him for a couple of blocks before he turned and raised the gun at the officers and they had no choice but to shoot him."

"Back up a minute here, where was his bodyguard?"

"According to his bodyguard, he got a call on his personal cell phone, just after midnight. His kids were sleeping and his wife had gone up about 10:30, so she was probably sleeping too. But the DA told the bodyguard that he'd handle it alone. The guy protested, but by that time the DA was backing his new car out of the driveway."

"So how is he?" Brent asked figuring that he had most likely been taken to a nearby hospital.

"Dead as a doornail about now. Actually the Coroner has him. Now we get to the good part. The drugs were injected into his system with a needle, but no needles were found at the motel by the Crime Scene technicians. That in itself was considered strange in that part of town. He had a pocketful of drugs that he'd stolen off the prostitute, but he was high as a kite on something else and so far we don't have a clue what it was. Maybe the toxicology tests will turn up something, but I just have a feeling that it won't. Oh, the car had some mechanical problems too. Touch the gas pedal and it runs wide open. Hit the brakes and it goes to the floorboard and barely slows it down. And the gun is the funniest part. It was super glued to his hand and was untraceable.

When he raised his arm, maybe to give up, he pointed the gun at the cops."

"Art, to be honest, it couldn't have happened to a nicer guy. In his case I just have no sympathy. So what happens now?"

"The number two man in that office has been told by the Court to take over until further notice. The guy is about as big an ass as his boss, but he's already decided to notify the Grand Jury members that they're dismissed, and he tossed all of the proceedings against you. Actually Tom Onnan ordered him to shred every bit of it and he's in the process of complying as we speak."

"What happened to the prostitute?"

"Funny that you should ask. The Emergency Room was a mob scene with sick and injured patients and their relatives stacked everywhere. According to the uniform at the door, they had run out of rooms and had people on stretchers lining the hallways. No one knows exactly what happened to her, other than when one of the nurses went to check on her, she wasn't there. She figured that with the confusion someone else had moved her into a treatment room or had taken her up to x-ray. Either way she was gone, and they didn't know that she was missing until later that day when the investigating detectives showed up."

"So she checked herself out of the hospital?" asked Brent.

"Probably never really checked in," replied Art. "Remember, she came in by ambulance under red lights and siren, so somebody had to sign for her. But then she just got caught up in the madhouse. In their defense that ER is always crowded and it doesn't take much to turn it into a circus. I've been down there when you had to wait in line just to get in the door."

"Yeah, I can remember pulling extra duty down there a few times," smiled Brent. "So where did she go, back to the motel?"

"It took a little digging, but she apparently caught a ride up to DIA and left on the first direct flight out for Cancun, Mexico. From there the speculation is that she caught a regional flight to Belize. Seems that they don't have an extradition treaty with the US. The funny part is how well timed this was. She reached DIA with only an hour to spare and her prepaid ticket was waiting at the counter. Kind of rules out any spur of the moment thing," Art laughed. "Oh, did I mention that she was oriental? Our records don't get any more specific other than that, but I'm guessing that she was probably Japanese."

"Sounds like he was set up, but I really don't know what to say at this point," smiled Brent.

"One more thing my friend, early yesterday an executive jet with foreign registry landed at the Springs Airport. According to the Customs Agent in charge out there, the two well dressed distinguished looking Japanese passengers carried no baggage and indicated that their destination was a meeting at the Broadmoor Hotel. A limo met them as soon as their passports were stamped and they headed off in that general direction. My investigating detectives followed up only because of the Asian connection and the Broadmoor has no record of either of them or any prearranged meeting. So for twenty-four hours they were on their own in the City and we can't find any limo company that has a record of transporting them either. And just to make it more interesting, the executive jet flew out of the airport on an emergency medical flight before the Customs guy went to work the next morning. According to their flight plan they were on their way to pick up a transplant liver in Houston. There's no record of the two Japanese passengers reboarding the plane. The company that owns the plane was contacted, and they belong to some worldwide air transportation group that helps whenever a heart or liver or some other organ needs to be transported to a recipient in another city or country, and their plane is available. They said it wasn't that unusual to fly out on a moments notice because they never knew when a donor would be found or which member of the voluntary air transport group would be available or the closest."

"What's the story from the wife?" asked Brent.

"Sort of funny in a way. Back before the election, she somehow convinced him to take out an insurance policy with her and the kids as joint beneficiaries. So once the insurance carrier ruled out suicide, which by the way they weren't very happy about, they will have to pay out just over a million bucks. Other than that she was asleep at the time with the bodyguard as a witness. And nearly everyone in town knew that he was a man of many affairs. So my personal observation is that she wasn't too sad to see him go. She's asked the Coroner to send the body over to the crematorium when he's finished with him and to send her the ashes. And my guess is that the "For Sale" sign will show up in the front yard in a day or so. Rumor has it that she and the kids are moving back to Iowa to be closer to her family, but I think that she just wants to put some distance between herself and Colorado Springs."

"Now tell me about the car," smiled Brent.

"Damn thing is what, a week old at the most? Our technicians contacted the manufacturer and they flew in several factory engineers the next day. Ironically the car was a top of the line Japanese model, but it was made here in the US, somewhere down south. Their conclusion was that the fuel injection module somehow malfunctioned and that affected the acceleration if I remember correctly. And again something in the computer, probably related to the first problem affected the brakes. However they were able to produce solid evidence that when the car left the factory, it was operating perfectly. So my question is did one of the two passengers from the jet have the knowledge to toss a monkey wrench in the works? I mean for a car that works perfect to suddenly go bad makes me kind of wonder. But right now it's been totaled out by the insurance carrier. It tangled with that moving truck and the light pole and definitely lost. What interests me even more is how did he ever survive the crash?"

"Where did the superglue come from?" asked Brent.

"Good question. Off the record, somebody really didn't like him. They knew about his dalliance with the prostitute and had her call and set him up. My guess is that when he arrived they overpowered him, injected some narcotic directly into a vein and turned him loose in a rigged car with the weapon glued to his hand. He must have been delirious about then and when they pointed him north on Nevada, he took off. But he couldn't stop and the car kept going faster and faster. I'm surprised that he didn't run into somebody long before he got to Fillmore Street. But whoever set him up knew that if he managed to stop the car and got out he'd look like a crazy person, and he'd probably try to surrender to the cops. So as he raised his arm, the weapon came into view and the officers on the scene had no choice but to take him out. I guess they tried to Taser him, but being high on drugs it didn't affect him. We've decided to leave the part about the super glue out of our official report, but it is in the working papers."

"Well like I said, I still have no sympathy for the guy. He was out to nail me for something and I still can't figure out why."

"Maybe you hung a parking ticket on him when you worked traffic," laughed Art.

"Actually Stew and I have gone back to when I arrived here in the Springs and we've walked through it very carefully. Neither of us could come up with anything other than maybe Harrington House, and he was jealous."

"Well that's it as of the moment and under the circumstances I do believe that you owe me a lunch."

Chapter 36

Brent had just finished bringing Ta up to date on how the DA had met his maker. They were sitting in Brent's office, munching on fresh hot sticky buns and drinking coffee from their favorite old coffee pot, rescued from the trash after Michi had once again tossed it.

"Got to thinking last night," mumbled Ta. "Did you ever open that envelope that you found in Tani's safety deposit box? Last time you mentioned it you said that you just weren't ready to see whatever was in it."

"Actually I guess I forgot about it, so the answer is no, I haven't opened it."

"Maybe we should do it now," he smiled.

Brent agreed that it might be the right time to wipe the slate clean so he left the office and went upstairs to retrieve it from Gus' safe in the hidden safety room. In minutes he returned and handed it to Ta as he sat back into his chair.

"You open it," Brent said.

Ta removed his knife and carefully slit the large 9" x 12" manila envelope across the top, just under the flap. He glanced inside, let out a sigh and emptied the contents on the desktop.

"Are those stamps?" asked Brent.

"Yes they definitely are stamps, but extremely expensive and rare ones. Please don't touch them without wearing gloves. Maybe I had better explain," sighed Ta sitting back and shaking his head in disbelief.

"Until I returned to Japan to help my uncle, I didn't know that in my absence and maybe before I originally left, that he'd become a stamp collector. With time on his hands and nothing to do, he apparently began to seriously collect them. Exactly when it went from being a hobby to an obsession, I have no idea. But my uncle only collected the rarest stamps in the world. I had some hints while I replaced him, but it wasn't until he'd survived and returned home that he told me about them as if they were his children. What you're looking at on your desk is something called the "Penny Black." It's extremely rare and I bet those are worth a few million dollars, and maybe more," said Ta.

"Stamps," muttered Brent. "You think that all of this was a argument between two stamp collectors? That so many died just because of some mailing stamps?"

"While he was explaining his collection he did mention something about these particular stamps. I didn't catch on at the time because I knew nothing about collecting stamps or this particular one. If I remember correctly this was the world's first official adhesive postage stamp. It came from the United Kingdom which at that time consisted of Great Britain and Ireland around 1840. There's a long story about how it came to be and the man who designed it. Uncle told me that there was some question whether it really was the first adhesive stamp or not because apparently at least the idea had been publicized earlier in Austria, Sweden and Greece. But he said that the project was well under way since 1837 or before. It has a profile of Queen Victoria on it. The word "POSTAGE" appears on the top and the words "ONE PENNY" are across the bottom. Now prior to this you would take your mail to a postal station and pay for exactly what it weighed. Now you could buy these stamps in advance, sort of a prepaid system. Oh, and if you look closely you'll see a star like design in the upper corners."

"What are the letters in the bottom corners?" asked Brent as he looked closely.

"These were apparently printed in sheets and those letters identified their position on the sheet. At the time they didn't perforate the individual stamps and the user had to cut each stamp from the sheet in order to use it. Ironically it was only used for one year before it was changed. At the time they used a red ink on the cancellation stamp and you couldn't see it on the black background. So in 1840 they switched to the "PENNY RED" and issued new cancellation stamps with black ink, which was more effective and more difficult to remove. If I remember correctly, my uncle said that it took eleven different printing plates to make the stamps and that the original presses were on display at the British Library in London. My guess is that these stamps we're looking at are extremely rare and priceless."

"Stamps," said Brent. "It was all about some stamps?"

"From what I know about my uncle and his obsession with collecting them, I wonder if he hadn't contacted Tani and she was either buying them in his name or somehow acquiring them as she traveled around the world and sending them on to him. You remember that Christy and I sort of lost touch with her when she moved to New York. And we know that he had some of his people keeping an eye on her over the years from what Michi had told us. How they met, if they ever did is a big question, but somehow she got involved. Maybe it was her idea or maybe it was his, but I think that she was fronting for him. These sheets in the perfect condition that they're in probably cost a million dollars apiece, maybe more. So we're looking at what, maybe five million bucks worth of stamps lying here on the desk? Tani didn't have that kind of money, it had to come from Taniaka."

"Do you think that Sukara was a collector too?"

"He could have been, but his beef with my uncle went way beyond that. However it could have been the catalyst that got everything rolling. Maybe they were both after the same thing and when Taniaka got it, Sukara took offense. I don't think that it would be very hard to find out who was doing the footwork for him. Maybe he didn't even realize that they were related, just that she was the enemy because she had helped him, his sworn enemy. So he sent in the troops to even the score, and when Taniaka heard about it, that his blood relative had been killed by Sukara's men, he went ballistic. However his rage had two directions. One was to eliminate the enemy and avenge the killings, and the second was to find his stamps. So his people backtracked through her life looking for leads. He couldn't expect them to remain silent once his people had questioned them, so he just gave the order to eliminate them. And Sukara's troops, all of the dead Yakuza found in New York and in California, were just part of the elimination of the enemy. My guess is that many more than that quietly disappeared in Japan and will never be found."

"Well that doesn't answer all of my questions, but it certainly is a start. But why would

Tani not send these on to your uncle?"

"This is just a guess, but I doubt that she ever intended to hold out on him. She met you, fell in love, saw you as a way out of her old lifestyle and then you were nearly killed and she probably forgot about them. This wasn't anything new to her Brent, from what I saw of my uncle's collection, she had probably been doing this for many years. So it wasn't any big thing. She'd arrange for the purchase, handle the paperwork for the wire transfer and take possession. Now how she got them to Japan is another question, but remember, she traveled around the world. Maybe she had just made this purchase and stored them in the Chicago bank until she returned after Christmas. Remember she was going to pass through Chicago on her way to New York and then overseas after the holidays. It would have been easy just to arrange for a short layover and pick them up. She was trained in the martial arts so carrying it with her probably wasn't any big thing. But then she met you and then you had the accident. I think that her priorities suddenly changed and she pushed that to the back of her mind. If she had lived, I'm certain that she would have eventually remembered the stamps and sent them on, but she didn't."

"So what's your game plan now?" said Brent as he bent over to more closely examine the fortune that laid before him.

"I'll make a short cell phone call to a number that I have in Hawaii. Taniaka will send a courier on one of his planes as quickly as possible. These stamps have too much blood on their existence and I'd like to get them out of Harrington House as quickly as possible."

Finis

www.ingramcontent.com/pod-product-compliance
Lightning Source LLC
Chambersburg PA
CBHW030030030726
47500CB00001B/33